UNTIL THE SHADOWS CLAIM HER

AMBER THOMA

For permissions, inquiries, or to follow the author's descent into further madness:

AuthorAmberThoma.com

Instagram & TikTok:

@Author_Amber_Thoma

Discord:

https://discord.gg/YpkMsKWbXM

TO THE DARK ROMANCE GIRLIES

The ones who see a red flag and think,
but what if he's obsessed with me?
The ones who hear, "run," and stay put
just to see what happens next.
The ones who fear nothing except a
soft, boring love.

This book is for you. For the bratty
survivors, the ones who would bite their
captor just to see what he'd do. The
ones who don't just want to be
chased—they want to be hunted,
cornered, ruined.

If you've ever whispered 'yes' when you
should have screamed 'no,'
if you've ever wanted the villain to win,
if you believe a knife against your throat
should come with a marriage proposal—

Then welcome home, darling. You're
exactly where you belong.

CONTENT WARNING

We're going to play a game. You can run. You can hide. But ready or not—here they come.

This book explores the darkest corners of power, obsession, and control, where fear and desire blur, and survival is never guaranteed. Within these pages, you'll find psychological manipulation, non-con and dub-con elements (scenes involving questionable consent, restraint, and forced submission themes), captivity, stalking, and violent intimidation.

The air is thick with ghosts and shifting walls, haunted whispers and an unreliable grip on reality. There are knives pressed to throats, hands that take without asking, blindfolds that steal sight, and shadows that do not let go. Trauma lingers in the form of past captivity, starvation, and physical discipline, while the present holds a relentless game of submission, fear-based arousal, and pleasure woven with punishment.

The sexual content is explicit, and she has multiple partners—at once.

If you seek comfort, turn back now. But if you dare to step forward—know that once you enter, there is no way out.

For a full list of triggers please visit authoramberthoma.com

DISCLAIMER

Please remember that this is a work of fiction. I do not recommend attempting any of the stunts performed by professionals (by professionals I mean my very fictional characters and experienced sex workers). I'm 99% certain that some of these acts would require at least a drs visit afterward. Thots and pears to the lady bits, and with that—read on if you dare.

If your name is **Lisa Thoma**, read this.
Mother, I have warned you to the best of my ability.
If you choose to read this book, I will not be accepting full-name text messages filled with pearl-clutching and scandalized gasps.
So, to spare us both, I have made you this handy chart.
Should you encounter a scene that is… a bit more educational than you were prepared for, simply refer to the chart and skip ahead before further "enlightenment" occurs.
Otherwise, enjoy (or pretend you didn't read it).
You have been warned.

Chapter 9- 🔥

Chapter 12- 🔥🔥

Chapter 14- 🔥🔥🔥🔥

Chapter 18- 🔥🔥🔥🔥

Chapter 20- 🔥🔥🔥

Chapter 23- 🔥🔥🔥

Chapter 25- 🔥🔥🔥

Chapter 26- 🔥🔥🔥🔥🔥

Chapter 32- 🔥🔥🔥🔥🔥

PLAYLIST

Also by Amber Thoma

Realms of Lore: Fae

Dark Fantasy Romance (A little less unhinged.)

Prince of Darkness

Heirs of Darkness

Queen of Light

Shadows of Light

Court of Whispers

Lilith sloan

Hybrids of the Kathir

Ultra Dark SciFi Romance (A little more unhinged.)

Their Hybrid to Take

Hunted by the Hybrid

Until the Shadows Claim Her

The Fate of Her Series

Amber Thoma

1

The rain is a living thing—violent, merciless—pummeling the windshield in relentless sheets, twisting the forest beyond into an anamorphic nightmare of grays and drowning greens. The wipers thrash across the glass, their frantic rhythm a losing battle against the storm. Each glimpse of the road lasts less than a second—distorted flashes of slick pavement and dense trees before the rain swallows them whole again.

If I blink, I'll miss it.

I lean forward, gripping the wheel like a lifeline, my knuckles aching. My eyes strain to follow the road as it snakes through the endless stretch of forest. It's the kind of storm that demands silence—the music turned down, breath held—like listening harder might make me see better.

The windshield keeps fogging up. My pulse is a live wire, stretched so thin I swear I can hear it fraying—one wrong move, one second too late, and I'll be gone. Erased like I was never here at all. The road could swallow me whole, and it'd be days before anyone found me.

No one would notice.

At least, not anyone worthwhile.

To make matters worse, I haven't seen another car for hours—not since my cell signal died. Which, of course, means my GPS cut out too, leaving me to navigate blind. Truly ideal conditions for a leisurely drive. Relaxing, even. I force my stiff fingers to unclench, prying them free one at a time. Wiping my slick palms against my jeans, I exhale slowly, forcing myself to breathe.

Of course, all of this isn't enough—because why would it be? My traitorous phone sits unassuming in the cup holder, its battery draining with each passing minute. I pick it up. Again. Like I have every few minutes since I lost signal. The screen glows back at me, showcasing the photo I took of the New York City skyline last night. I've never seen anything like it. Not even after passing through a few big cities on my way north.

I don't want to look, but my eyes flick to the corner of the screen anyway. 7%. I cringe. I risk taking one hand off the wheel, wiggling the power cord plugged into the dash—again. Unplug, replug. Nothing. I even switch ends, hoping for some kind of miracle. No matter what I try, that stupid lightning bolt never appears. Still nothing. Just my phone slowly dying, minute by minute.

"This is fine," I mutter, dropping the useless phone back into the cup holder. "Totally fine. Perfect, really." I sigh, shaking off as much of my growing anxiety as I can. It could be worse—so much worse. I know that better than anyone.

The words have become a mantra, one I've repeated a

thousand times since I left in the dead of night. No matter how bad things get, I know—intimately—that nothing is worse than where I've been.

Being lost on a backroad in the middle of a storm, somewhere in Vermont? It's nothing compared to the prison I just escaped. At least here, the walls are trees instead of stone.

My mother risked everything to get me out of there. She gave me a chance at a real life. I refuse to waste it complaining about a little rain and a dead battery.

The memories press in, creeping along the edges of my mind—dark, suffocating, waiting. They always do when my thoughts drift too far into the past. I take a breath. Shove them back down.

I made it out.

I survived.

And I'll survive this, too.

Just as my determination locks into place, the car begins to rattle—mocking every positive thought I just had. At first, the noise is faint, barely audible over the rain.

Maybe it's nothing.

Maybe the road just changed texture.

Then, a low, rhythmic clunk reverberates through the car —deep, unsettling, like the whole thing is coming apart beneath me. Dread spreads through my limbs like ice. I press my foot on the gas, as if I can outrun whatever's happening. A violent shudder runs through the frame, rattling so hard it drowns out the rain. The engine sputters, choking on itself before letting out a guttural, gasping wheeze—like a last breath before collapse.

"Come on," I whisper, begging the Toyota Corolla to be as

indestructible as its reputation. My knuckles whiten around the wheel. "Come on! Please! Not now."

The dashboard erupts in angry red symbols. The car gives one final, violent lurch—then dies, rolling to a pathetic stop at the side of the road. Silence settles in, heavy and absolute, broken only by the relentless drumming of rain on the roof and the useless swish of the windshield wipers.

Not that it does me any good.

I sit there for a long moment.

Then another.

Staring blankly at the steering wheel, at the glowing symbols behind it. My throat tightens, heat pricking behind my eyes. I swallow hard, forcing it back. Crying won't help. It never does. If anything, it makes everything worse.

I give myself a few seconds to wallow in the absolute horror of my situation. Then, with a deep breath, I shove it all away. Pack it up. Lock it down. Stuff it into the same faraway place where the worst of my past is already buried.

With a sharp exhale, I know there's only one thing to do. Reaching into the back seat, I rummage through the bag my mother meticulously packed, fingers brushing past neatly folded clothes until I find a jacket. Even though I left in the height of summer, I'm glad she thought ahead. It's new—just like everything else she packed. A quiet reminder that the past doesn't belong in the future—my future.

Staring out at the rain, I know any attempt to stay dry is pointless. An umbrella wouldn't stand a chance in this storm —not that I have one to test the theory. But the jacket is better than nothing.

"There's no time like the present, Celest." I throw my long, dark hair into a tight ponytail, hoping to keep it out of my face while I hype myself up.

Draping the too-large jacket over my head, and wrapping it around myself, I'm pleased to see it covers more than expected. I grab my small crossbody purse from the passenger seat, rummaging through it quickly. My fingers brush against the familiar shape of my charger—the one that works, just not in this car. It doesn't have the USB end I need for the outlet. Because, apparently, we have to have a different cord for everything.

Honestly, why do they do that? I sigh, shaking my head. At the very least, having a full battery might make me feel better.

Maybe.

I check to make sure the envelope—the one holding every detail of my new life—is still safely tucked inside, alongside my toothbrush and toothpaste. Satisfied, I slide my phone into the last bit of space left. With only the bare essentials packed, I pull the strap over my head and zip the bag safely under my jacket.

I glance out at the storm again, and—to my dismay, but not my surprise—the rain hasn't let up. Not even a little. No, of course not. Why would anything go even infinitesimally easier for me? My stomach sinks at the thought of stepping into the downpour. But I don't have a choice. It's not like I can stay here.

Wherever here is.

I force myself to open the door. Cold rain lashes against me instantly, soaking my legs in seconds. I wince and shove the jacket further over my head, a useless barrier against the storm. Slamming the door shut behind me, I brace myself and start moving.

The rain is shockingly cold, soaking through the fabric within seconds—completely undoing all of my previous efforts. Loose strands of hair plaster to my face, and rivulets of water streak down my skin, blurring my vision as I start walking. My teeth chatter. I wipe at my eyes, pointlessly, only to do it again seconds later.

I take one last look at the silver car, unsure what to do next. I know nothing about cars, and I've never had to deal with something like this before. I've driven more in the last few days than the rest of my life combined. I'm not stupid—I know there are places that fix cars. What I don't know is how much it costs. Or, more importantly, how I'm even supposed to get my car there in the first place. I take a deep breath. I'll figure it out.

The rest I can deal with later.

One minute at a time.

The road stretches ahead, twisting and vanishing into the storm's darkness. The downpour is unyielding, drumming against my skin, and each step is punctuated by a miserable squelch as my shoes fill with water. The oversized jacket clings to me like a soggy second skin, heavy with rain and utterly useless—offering neither warmth nor protection, only dragging me down with every step. I cross my arms, pressing my purse tightly against my chest, feeling its solid shape through the soaked fabric.

I have no idea how long I've been walking. My car disappeared behind me ages ago, lost in the downpour. The world around me is empty, unwelcoming—just rain, wind, and the endless stretch of road. I force myself to focus. One foot in front of the other.

I've survived worse than this.

I can survive this, too.

"I'm not going back," I murmur to myself.

"I'm not going back!" This time, I shout it—a raw, desperate declaration that vanishes into the storm. There's no one to hear me, no one to answer, but it doesn't matter. The words settle deep in my chest, anchoring me, fortifying me. They're a steady rhythm in my mind, until they feel real. Until I believe them.

The rain beats down, heavy and unforgiving, but I don't fight it. I let it soak through my clothes, my skin, washing away the past like ink running off a page.

Life can throw whatever it wants at me. Every storm, every hardship, every impossible road—I'll take them all. Because no matter how brutal it gets, it's still better than going back.

Not now.

Not ever.

I take another step. Then another. I don't know where this road leads, but as long as it isn't back to him?

That's all that matters.

2

The rain has finally abated, morphing into a gentle mist. I'm soaked to the bone, the weight of my clothes dragging me down, each step more laborious after hours of walking.

Is there anything worse than soaked jeans? The wet denim chafes between my thighs with every step, and it's agonizing.

At least I'm no longer freezing—a silver lining, I suppose.

Instead, I feel that strange, clammy sensation—chilled on the outside, burning from exertion on the inside.

The road has been nothing but a trail of endless hills, and I'd be fine if I never had to climb another in my life.

The overcast sky, heavy with clouds threatening another downpour, has slowly darkened as the hours pass. I worry that if I don't find a sign of humanity soon, I'll be walking in complete darkness. With the cloud coverage, not even the glow of the moon will light my way, and I really don't want to find out what roams these woods at night.

There's a break in the trees ahead, but I don't dare get my

hopes up. Without making the conscious decision to do so, my pace quickens. I don't know what I'll do if it turns out to be nothing.

Oh God, what if it's a service road?

"Please be a driveway. Please, please, please, I need this to be a driveway," I pant out under my breath.

I'm almost afraid to look when there's only a few steps to go, but when I do, relief nearly brings me to tears.

It's a driveway.

Not far ahead, an ornate, Gothic-style iron gate bars the way.

It's massive, impossible to climb with its menacing sharp points decorating the entire top. I guess that's the point, but my initial relief is already draining away.

That is, until I notice it's unlocked. I push, expecting the gate to swing open, but it doesn't budge—not even a fraction of an inch. I'm not proud of it, but I stomp my foot and let out a frustrated growl. Okay, I might've stomped my foot a few times, but I've earned the right to act like a child for a moment.

Besides, Father isn't here to see.

No one is.

I put my back against the gate, pushing with my entire weight, and finally, I feel it give way, sort of. The hinges squeal, the sound echoing into the distance.

I begin to worry that whoever lives here hasn't opened this ridiculous gate in far too long, making it a strong possibility no one will be at whatever awaits me at the top of this driveway.

It doesn't matter. Worrying about possibilities is pointless when things could go a myriad of different ways.

I push against the gate again, and this time it moves the slightest bit easier. A few more pushes, and I force it open just enough to squeeze through.

After several minutes of climbing the winding driveway, I feel my annoyance growing. Why would anyone want such an impossibly long driveway? The way it slithers through the trees makes it feel like it's far longer than it has any business being. Doesn't Vermont get a bunch of snow in the winter? I can only imagine how treacherous it would be to navigate this nonsense.

It's embarrassing how loud I'm breathing by the time I see the trees thin and begin to crest the top of the driveway. I'm two minutes away from gasping for each breath. To be fair, I have been walking for hours—soaking wet, no less.

With each step, the house reveals itself a little more, starting from the top points of the spires, until a full image finally materializes. Perhaps "house" isn't the correct word. The gate at the bottom of the driveway should have been a clue, that a gigantic gothic manor waited at the top. Set against dense woods and an ever-darkening, cloud-strewn sky, it looks even more imposing.

The heaviness of the stone walls and pointed archways are balanced by the delicate spires and stained glass windows. The place is massive, with too many chimneys to count. I can't imagine how difficult it must be to keep all those fires burning.

My eyes take their time as they drift across the roofline and snag on a hunched shape. I gasp, terrified of finding out whatever animal that might be. It's unnaturally still. Fear keeps me from looking away—until I squint and look closer.

A nervous giggle bubbles out of me the moment I realize

what it is, and my reaction to a silly stone gargoyle feels rather ridiculous. I don't think I've ever seen one in person. They're not the kind of thing you'd find on the sprawling antebellum manors back home.

The grounds are a strange blend—half-overgrown, as if nature's taking back what's not cared for, but carefully manicured patches suggest someone still tends to it, or once did. It doesn't give any clue to whether I'll find help here or not.

The flowerbeds, however, have been left to their own devices, wild and overgrown. An entire section of one wall is being consumed by ivy. Every so often, I catch a glimpse of what looks like a massive stained glass window, peeking through the gaps in the aggressive greenery.

The house feels... off, like it's holding its breath. Something's not right, but I can't put my finger on it. It's unsettling, like the beginning of one of those movies I wasn't allowed to watch. The ones where some deranged killer slaughters unsuspecting teenagers in increasingly graphic ways.

While I've never seen an entire horror movie from start to finish, when no one was around to catch me, I'd sneak bits and pieces on the TV. I saw enough to roll my eyes at their stupidity. Why would anyone enter a building that clearly screams, "enter and die," in the first place?

Now that I find myself standing before the dark wooden front door with no other options in sight, I think I just might understand.

Once I gain enough courage, I lift my fist to knock, and the door swings open after the first rap against it. I stand frozen, my hand still raised, for longer than I'd like to admit.

"Well, if that isn't foreboding..." I murmur, taking a deep

breath and stepping across the threshold. "Hello? Is anyone here?"

When several moments pass in silence, I take another step inside—then scream as the door slams shut behind me.

Get it together, Celest. It's probably just the wind that's starting to pick back up in preparation for another storm. That's got to be it. I keep trying to convince myself as I unwrap my jacket and tie the soaked fabric around my waist.

The entryway is vast and circular, with twin staircases curving up either side of the room, leading to—well, I'm not honestly sure, I'm assuming it's the second floor. The walls, covered in dark wood paneling and carved with pointed arches that mimic the ones outside, are on the verge of oppressive.

The intricate design continues throughout the room, reaching up to the impossibly high ceiling. The largest chandelier I've ever seen hangs at the center, its dull light casting eerie shadows. That must mean the power is still on, and that's got to be a good sign, right?

"Hello!" I call out again, just in case. The heavy silence is my only response—again. There's a little voice in the back of my head warning me to run and never look back. Against my better judgment, I ignore it, having nowhere else to go.

A hallway between the staircases is filled with shadows, hinting at an even darker interior. My fingers trail across the round table in the center of the space as I make the stupid decision to go toward the creepy hallway.

There's a large arrangement of fresh flowers in the center of the table—further proof that someone is here, has recently been here, or will be returning soon. Never mind the fact the flowers are black roses, which feels a little too on the nose if I'm being honest.

I try not to dwell on what kind of person chooses black roses in the middle of summer and call out again.

"Hello!" I'm not surprised when there's no response, and continue my way down the hallway of doom, deeper into the manor.

The darkness in the hallway is all-encompassing, making it impossible to see. I keep my hand on the wall, letting my fingers drag lightly across the grooves of the paneling.

I nearly jump out of my skin when a door slams somewhere in the manor.

My heart pounds against my sternum as I call out to whoever it was, "Hello?" Still, I get no response.

"Is someone there?" The hairs on the back of my neck prickle, and I get the uncanny feeling that I'm being watched. I shake my head after a panicked glance around, convincing myself that if I can't see, neither can anyone else.

I'm having to convince myself a little too often for my liking. Not that I'm feeling too positive about any of this.

My hand reaches the end of the wall, and the sound of my steps echoing makes whatever room I've stepped into feel cavernous.

I haven't risked checking the battery on my phone, but the glow of the screen will at least light up the room long enough to get a quick look around—if it turns on at all.

Unzipping my ruined purse, I breathe a sigh of relief that the rain was unable to soak through to the documents inside, and pull out my phone.

It's shocking when my phone lights up, and I smile, only for my heart to sink at the sight of the dreaded 1% across the empty battery icon. I try not to waste it and look around with the few seconds I have left before my screen goes dark again.

This must be the Great Hall. A few hallways branch off—wait, what was that? I swear I see a large shadow move in my peripheral, but just as I swing the faint glow of my phone toward it, the screen goes dark again. My breath comes in stuttered bursts, drowning out all sound.

Am I imagining it, or do I hear footsteps ghosting across the floor? I point my phone in the direction I saw the moving shadow, for a split second, my screen lights up again, just as it flickers and dies. That single flash makes me jump back, scream, nearly dropping my phone in the process.

The shadow moved. I'm positive. It was standing just a few feet in front of me.

"I-Is someone there?" My voice shakes. "Please... I n-need help." I hold my breath and listen, but not a single sound is made. Maybe I didn't see what I thought I did. Maybe my nerves are fried, making me imagine things.

I take cautious step after cautious step toward where I remember seeing one of the hallways. If I can just find a room with an outlet, everything will be all right. I know I have no signal and can't call for help, however, the thought of having a fully charged phone offers me a modicum of comfort and safety.

Ridiculous, I know.

I feel the entrance to the hallway and take a few steps down it, before I hear something heavy being dragged across the floor behind me. When I take a few steps back toward the Great Hall, I'm met with a wall—the opening is gone.

I run my hands along the edges, feeling two sharp corners where the wall has shifted. How is that even possible?

"Oh, God, what is this place?" My voice sounds like it's on the verge of hysterics. "Don't freak out. Don't freak out. Don't freak out." I force myself to take a deep breath, turn back, and continue down the hallway.

My fingers trace the wall, searching for a doorway. When I feel the wall give way to an opening, I think I might have found one, only to turn down another hallway. This time I pretend not to hear the sounds of the house shifting behind me and keep moving forward.

I squint, spotting a faint glow beneath a door at the end of the hall. Maybe my eyes are playing tricks on me—it wouldn't be the strangest thing to happen tonight. Still, the fact I can see anything at all is enough to make me get to the door as fast as possible.

"H-hello! Is anyone here?" I knock on the door with the faint glow beneath it, my voice steadier this time. "My car broke down a ways down the road, and I could really use some help." Silence greets me, thick and oppressive, broken only by the crackle of fire beyond the door.

I fumble for the knob, twist it, and push the door open—only to find the room empty.

The fire's glow is the only light, casting warmth across the room from a massive hearth that dominates one wall. Above it, the marble mantle stretches in a single, smooth piece, following the curve of the pointed arch beneath it. Its elegance stands out against the dimness around it.

For a few minutes, I stand in front of the fire, letting the heat seep into my chilled skin, trying to dry my clothes. I untie my jacket, draping it over a chair near the flames, then set my purse down beside it after pulling out my charger. My mind keeps skirting the strange things I've noticed, pushing them aside, unwilling to let them surface.

With a quick glance around the room, I notice there are no lamps or anything else that requires electricity. I convince myself—once again—that it doesn't mean there aren't any outlets. I'll just have to start in the corner and inspect every inch of each wall. It's not unusual for old homes to hide plugs in the strangest places.

I search the back of the built-in shelves that take up one whole wall last. It's tedious, but I remember watching on one of those historical home makeover shows, where they put a sideways plug in the back of the old built-ins.

Strange objects clutter the shelves, each more unusual than the last. Some are faded, others ornate, and a few down-right bizarre. I pick them up one by one, my fingers tracing their shapes, trying to make sense of them. There's a tarnished brass key with smooth, worn edges, a small porcelain figure of something unidentifiable, and a cracked glass vial with a dried flower inside. I can't help but wonder who collected such an eclectic mix.

Only a few shelves remain, and I still haven't found an outlet—but I refuse to give up. There's got to be at least a single plug somewhere in this ridiculously huge home.

Without warning, the exhaustion that's been building seems impossible to ignore.

Once I finish the obviously pointless task of checking these last few shelves, I'll let myself curl up in one of the chairs by the fire. Maybe by the time I wake up, this will have all been a dream, or at least I'll find whoever lives here and ask them to help me.

A glint catches my eye, pulling me from thoughts of a fire-side nap.

I pick up the hand-held mirror, its tarnished surface obscures the face staring back at me, but it still reminds me of the one back home—the one tied to memories better left in the past. This one only shows shadows, and I'm unsure which one I am now.

I stare at the old mirror, but my mind drifts. It flickers between the one I left behind and the reflection in my hands, pulling a memory to the surface—a memory I wish I could forget.

One of many.

3

The high, vaulted ceilings of the Sacred Hall make me feel smaller than I am. Fear already makes me jittery, but the shadows flickering across the walls, showing images of Josiah's teachings, make everything scarier.

I force myself to stand tall and not fidget.

Father said I've been blessed with a great honor tonight, but he warned me not to disappoint him like I always do. I never quite understand how I manage to fail him. Every time I think I've done it right, he finds something wrong. What if I mess up tonight too? What if he hates me more than he already does? I try to steady my shaking hands, but it's hard to calm them down.

He told me, just before we arrived at the Sacred Hall, that in my ten years of life I've never managed to do anything right, and tonight was my opportunity to make up for it. I promised him I would do a good job and not fail him.

I don't think he believes me.

In the center of the room stands the altar, draped in simple white linen. Josiah Wainwright stands to one side, while my father, Charles Abernathy, stands a few steps behind him. The flames atop the tall candles dance, and their light reflects off the ceremonial knife resting beside a small wooden box on the altar. I hadn't noticed the sharp blade until just this moment. Suddenly, fear crawls up my throat and gets stuck, making it hard to swallow.

Father hadn't mentioned anything about a knife, but then again, he didn't tell me much about the Ritual of Purity either. He just passed me this gilded hand mirror and told me not to lose it. Then promised me that if I broke it before the ceremony, I would have to answer for it when we got back home.

That was never a good thing.

My parents got me a new dress for the ritual. It's the best part of this whole thing. It's white and shiny. Mother said it's satin, but I just like how smooth it feels. Pearls are stitched into spirals on top, and lace sleeves fall just past my elbows.

It makes me feel like a princess, but my favorite part of the entire outfit is the matching white satin gloves, trimmed in lace. I love them so much. I wish I could wear them all the time.

Mother made a big fuss getting me ready. She even curled my hair, pulling some of it back with a large white bow. All the white makes my nearly black hair look even darker.

I couldn't wait to see all the other girls and their pretty dresses, but the moment we arrived, my excitement melted away.

I'm the only one not wearing a plain linen smock with a single braid down the back. The way the other girls are looking at me makes my cheeks burn, and my stomach feel funny. I don't understand why none of them got to wear pretty dresses for the ritual.

"Mother," I whisper, "I don't think I was supposed to wear this." She looks down and smiles at my wide-eyed expression.

"Oh, my sweet Tina. Do not fret, Josiah sent this dress himself," she says. "Now go on and take your place with the other girls." She turns away from me and goes to take her seat. It's the same place she always sits on the first wooden bench next to the same place I always sit. I take a deep breath and join the rest of the girls.

Usually, I'm sad that we aren't allowed to speak to each other, but tonight, their eyes make me grateful for the silence.

My family is held in high regard within the Covenant. Father says it's a symbol of our wealth and status. It doesn't seem fair to me. Why should any of us be above another?

I'm relieved when Josiah starts speaking. All the unfriendly eyes shift to him. I glance at Father in panic—can he tell I'm not listening? I'm trying, but I'm too scared of messing up to focus on what Josiah's saying.

He tells us that the ritual marks our transition into "spiritual responsibility," binding us permanently to the covenant and Josiah's teachings. There's a lot more about beauty, sin, and submission that I don't really understand. What does "spiritual responsibility" even mean?

"True beauty is found not in the face, but in obedience. Vanity is the seed of corruption, and today, we cleanse the most susceptible among us of its taint." Josiah looks at me and nods. I guess that means it's time for me to play my role —whatever that may be.

"The mirror is a symbol of earthly vanity, a sin that must

be renounced as proof of your dedication to the Covenant and loyalty to me." I don't get it. Vanity... is looking at yourself wrong? Isn't it okay to want to look nice? What if I fail this test? I glance at Father again, but he's not looking at me.

As Josiah talks, I step forward, my Mary Janes clicking on the stone floor. I feel everyone's eyes on me as I stand next to Josiah at the altar. I glance at Father; he's watching with a stern look, silently demanding perfection.

Mother sits with her hands clasped tightly in her lap. She wears one of her pretend smiles—she says she saves her real ones for me—but when her eyes meet mine, I feel a little less afraid. I clutch the mirror tightly, my small fingers trembling with the effort, begging myself not to drop it under the crushing weight of expectations.

If I drop it, Father will be disappointed. He'll think I'm careless. I should hold it perfectly, like he wants. Maybe then he'll finally say he's proud of me, just once. Or at least not hate me for making another mistake.

Josiah smiles at me, and it makes my skin feel strange. "Do you know why you hold the mirror?" I shake my head, too scared to speak.

He takes the mirror from me, before turning to look at the congregation and says, "This mirror reflects what the world sees—outward beauty, a fleeting and hollow thing. But we are not of the world. We are of the Light. To truly reflect God's will, we must shatter the illusion of earthly vanity."

Josiah sets the mirror on the altar and picks up the ceremonial knife. "This blade represents the Light and the strength it grants us to battle sin in its name." He lifts the blade high, holding it for a breath before slamming the tip into the center of the mirror with such force that I jump.

I'm lucky my gasp can't be heard over the sound of glass shattering and echoing through the hall.

Father wouldn't like that.

Josiah carefully gathers each shard of broken glass, placing them one by one into the wooden box on the altar. Once full, he closes the box and places it into my small, white-gloved hands.

"This is a reminder, Tina. Beauty is not something you see —it is something you become through obedience and purity." His words are quiet, meant only for me.

As soon as he dismisses me, I turn and walk to my mother, clutching the box of shattered glass just as tightly as I had the mirror. I take my seat beside her, and Father takes his seat on my other side. I hadn't noticed his quiet footsteps behind me. I should feel safe being sandwiched between both of my parents, but I can't help but wish I were sitting on the other side of my mother. The second the thought enters my mind, I'm filled with guilt. I must remember Josiah's teachings and honor thy father.

Tiny pricks sting my hands. I look down to find small shards of glass scattered across the box, glinting in the dim light. My white gloves are speckled with little drops of blood. I have to fight to keep my tears from falling. Not just from the pain, but for my lovely little gloves that I know I'll never get to wear again.

I really loved them.

My father leans down and whispers into my ear, "You did good tonight, Tina. Keep it up, and never forget the lessons of the ritual." My heart sings with his words, and swells with pride. I can't remember ever hearing him say anything like that before. I sit a little straighter, though I'm not sure I fully got the ritual's meaning. Perhaps if I hadn't been as concerned with making a mistake, I'd have a better understanding.

I look at my blood-speckled gloves and try not to flinch as I clutch the box. Maybe if I'm perfect, Father will tell me he loves me. I'll keep trying. I'll get better with practice.

A couple of hours later, while brushing my hair and getting ready for bed, my mother comes in. I smile, but it slowly drops when I see the tears in her eyes.

"Momma, what's wrong?" She says nothing as she grabs the wooden box off my dresser—I'd left it there not knowing what to do with it—and approaches me.

"Tina, I'm sure tonight's message was difficult to understand, but someday you will. I want you to remember this moment when you do," she says softly, handing me a silver hand mirror. While this one isn't gilded or ornate, it's elegant in its simplicity.

"I don't understand," I whisper.

"I know, my love, just remember this mirror—and know they don't get to take everything from you. Now, hide this well, and when you need to remember my words, look into it and say, 'They can't take everything from me.' Can you do that for me?" I nod, tucking the mirror deep into my drawer beneath my sweaters.

I climb into bed, and she tucks me in before kissing me on my forehead. "You are your own person, Celestina, and you are worthy of love. Never forget that." It's not often that my mother uses my full name, but tonight, with that tone, her words feel even more important.

"I won't," I whisper. She smiles, gently brushing my hair

away from my face. She nods, and gets up to leave, giving my feet a little squeeze, like she does every night.

Once she leaves, closing the door behind her, I lie in bed, trying to fall asleep. I run through the ritual in my mind, paying close attention to the words I managed to remember. I then replay the conversation with my mother, coming to a conclusion as sleep pulls me under.

While not everything made sense, I'm pretty sure the broken glass from the mirror was meant to represent me, and my mother refused to let me see myself as broken. I think I understand.

They can't break me unless I let them.

4

The past refuses to release its grip, threatening to drown me. My chest tightens as flickering shadows close in. I shake my head, trying to banish both the memory and the man it conjures. I don't want to think about *him*, and I definitely don't want to recall the way he'd stared at me with hunger, as though I were an offering instead of a person. I guess that's not too far off from the truth.

"You shouldn't be here," a deep voice snaps, slicing through the fog and yanking me back to the present. I spin around, and the mirror crashes to the ground, shattering on impact. My brain is slow to comprehend as I scramble backward, colliding with the wall. Finally, a blood-curdling scream rips across my vocals.

A man stands in the doorway, wearing a black mask with neon-red "X" eyes and a jagged grin. He's tall, the black hoodie he wears strains from the width of his shoulders. He prowls toward me—slow, methodical, like a predator—and I feel every inch the prey.

"What—" My voice cracks, and I instinctively step back, only to slam into the wall again. "P-please. I— I just needed —" I've never been very good at standing up to intimidating men. Faced with a masked man and the memory of Josiah fresh in my mind, I'm surprised I can speak at all.

"To steal from us?" His voice is low and cold, causing chill bumps to erupt all over my body. He stops a few steps in front of me, and I swear I can feel his gaze burning into me through the mask. "Who sent you?"

"N-n-no one!" I stammer, my breaths coming in gasps as black edges into my vision. "I swear, I...please d-don't hurt—" The words get stuck in my throat as his hand shoots out to grab my arm.

Finally, my brain wakes up, and I bolt for the doorway. Too late, I think about my bag—still sitting on the chair next to the fireplace. Everything I need for my new life is in there, and a sob wrenches out of me. It hasn't even been a week, and I've already ruined everything my mother risked for me.

My footsteps echo as I race down the hall, my heart pounding against my ribs. I don't know where I'm going. I just need to keep moving. The walls keep changing, but I can't stop. All I know is that I have to get out of this place. I don't know what I'll do without my purse and everything inside it, but that's a problem for later—assuming I survive tonight.

A wall shifts, revealing a new opening. I would've missed it if not for a sudden lightning strike nearby, illuminating everything for a brief moment. I look back, searching for the red glow of the man's mask, before disappearing around the corner. There's nothing there—only darkness.

Relief is short-lived, barely registering before I collide with something hard... and warm. I reach out, grasping for anything before I fall flat on my rear. My fingers fist black fabric as momentum pulls me into his chest. For a moment, I let my forehead rest against him, closing my eyes as I take a few shaky breaths—more half sobs than anything.

I can tell he's leaner, and slightly taller than the man in the red mask. Slowly, I look up and whimper at the sight of the black mask with a neon orange Jack-o-lantern face with a too-large smile. I cling to him for balance, my trembling breaths warming the air between us.

"Well, well," he rumbles, his voice low and menacing, vibrating in a way that makes my bones ache. His head tilts slightly—a mocking gesture laced with cold curiosity. "What do we have here? Is the thief lost?"

Glowing orange triangles stare down at me in place of eyes, the cruel, almost Cheshire-like grin perfectly matching his tone.

My throat closes, any words I might have said lodged behind the lump of fear choking me. I stumble back a step, my heart hammering wildly against my ribs as I try to put distance between us. I don't see him reach for me before my arms are in his grasp, preventing me from stepping away. His grip is firm, on the cusp of painful.

"You're trembling," he observes, clearly amused. "Scared?"

"Please," I gasp, shaking my head while my mind claws through the fog of fear, desperate for a way out.

"You should be," he whispers, leaning in until his mask is inches from my face. "But don't worry, little thief. We'll take good care of you." His laugh is dark and twisted, shooting icy fear down my spine.

I release a choked cry while trying to wrench my arm free.

"No. P-please. I'm not a thief. I—my car broke down. I just need—"

"Convenient story," he interrupts, tilting his head to the other side, assessing me. "But I don't buy it."

He releases my arm suddenly, causing me to stumble backward into the wall. Before my sluggish mind can tell my body to move, he crowds me, placing a hand on either side of my head. The position forces me to crane my neck to meet his hidden gaze.

I hold my panicked breath as he leans in to whisper in my ear, "You better run, little thief." The mixture of his words and proximity sends a shuddering jolt of heat through me, something I'm unable to name, yet feels amplified by my fear—insanity, I'm sure.

"Well, that's unexpected," he says as the fingers of one hand trace the curve of my jaw, both his words and actions confusing me. "I'll admit, the hunt excites me just as much as it does you."

I blink, snapping out of the spell he's had me under before slipping under his arm and running again. His laughter follows behind me, the dark sound as warm as it is terrifying.

"What is wrong with me?" I mutter soundlessly to myself, struggling to readjust to the darkness. The absence of the orange glow is both a blessing and a curse. My fear is so acute that my mind must be trying to compartmentalize some of it into other feelings—ones I've never felt before.

I feel my breath turn ragged as exhaustion threatens to overcome fear and adrenaline begins to fade. An open doorway appears around the next turn I take, illuminated by a streak of lightning. The following rumble of thunder is loud enough to rattle the windows and make me yelp before I bolt through the doorway into the unknown.

I have no idea where I am within the shifting manor; I haven't even come across the Great Hall again. The moon provides just enough light through the large windows for me to look around. It's not a decision I make—more of a natural instinct—when I start toward the shelves of books lining the entire room of the massive library.

"What are you doing, Celest? You don't have time to admire the absurdly wonderful room, and you definitely don't have time to breathe it in," I mumble to myself.

I can't help it. Is there anything better than the scent of books? With great reluctance, I pull my eyes away from the shelves and scan desperately for a way out or a place to hide. If the stitch in my chest pinching my lungs is any indication, I could really use a moment to catch my breath.

"Lost, little thief?" A new voice cuts through the tension-filled air.

I whip around, the dizzying movement blurring my vision before I focus on another man leaning casually against the far shelves, his arms crossed. Shrouded in the same dark attire, his hood shadows his face, but the glow of his mask is impossible to miss. Its electric-blue lines form sharp, angular shapes that carve out a pair of hollow, sinister eyes.

"I asked you a question," he says, his voice deep and unhurried, with an undercurrent of something dangerous. "What are you doing here?" That heady feeling returns, taking root in my abdomen.

I stumble back, pressing myself against the nearest shelf. My chest heaves, though I don't think it has much to do with exertion. Something stirs inside me, waking—something that terrifies me to acknowledge. It feels too much like excitement, and that thought alone steals the breath from my lungs.

"I just... I didn't know anyone was here," I manage to say through the tremor in my voice.

"And that makes it okay to walk into someone else's home?" The eerie glow from his mask reflects off the polished floors as I watch him push off the bookshelf and prowl toward me. His movements remind me of a cat stalking its prey—slow and deliberate, while savoring my fear.

I take a step back with every step he takes toward me. "I-it was open... I—I didn't mean to..." I stammer, my voice cracking. "I was just—"

"Just what?" he interrupts. "Admiring the décor? Stealing something that doesn't belong to you?"

"N-no." I hold up my hands in what I hope looks like surrender. "I wasn't stealing. I swear."

His laugh is low and humorless, vibrating with condescension. "Funny, that's exactly what a thief would say."

I glance around, desperate for an exit. The library doors behind him are the only way out. I weigh the odds of getting to them without him intercepting me. They aren't great.

He steps closer, dragging his hand along the shelves. I back away, but his movement is slow, deliberate. "You're shaking like a leaf in the wind," he observes, his tone laced with mockery. "Tell me, is it out of fear... or guilt?"

"Neither," I snap, surprising even myself with the defiance in my voice—never mind the fact I'm terrified. Panic threatens to consume me, as I try to hold my ground, and somehow time feels like it's moving faster and slower at once. "I'm not a thief."

"Brave words," he replies, never pausing his unhurried steps toward me. "But bravery doesn't mean much when you're caught."

"Please," I beg, shaking my head. He's only a few steps away, and I know I need to make my move. "I'll leave. I didn't mean—"

"Oh, we'll let you leave," he says, his voice dropping before he continues, "just not anytime soon."

I don't wait around to hear what exactly he means by that and run past him. My shoulder brushes against his, and he doesn't try to reach out to grab me or slow me down. It's like he knows he doesn't have to—like he knows I'm not getting away.

"Wrong move, little thief," his voice calls after me, before he tsks me, as if he were scolding a child.

I sprint down the corridor, dimly lit by the blue glow of his mask, while my breath comes in halting gasps. The sound of his footfalls following at a leisurely pace speaks more to his confidence than my chances of escape.

I cry out in relief when I realize I know where I am. With the constant flashes of lightning, the Great Hall becomes easier to navigate. Just as I see a red and orange glow out of the corner of my eye, I find the hall that leads to the rounded entryway.

Trying and failing to keep my thoughts on escaping this situation before dwelling on my next problem, I kick myself for leaving my purse behind. The relief I feel when my hand clamps around the brass handle of the front door and pulls it open is tempered by the knowledge there's nowhere for me to go.

Well, nowhere I'm willing to go at least.

The cold rain pelts me from all directions, drenching me the moment I burst through the heavy front door of the manor. The sound of it slamming shut behind me can barely be heard over the deafening storm. It's far worse than what I walked through earlier. Howling winds rip through the surrounding trees, as I sprint down the winding driveway, begging God that I don't slip on the slick pavement with each frantic step.

I glance back, just once—and wish I hadn't. Three dark figures emerge in the doorway, illuminated by both the glow of their masks and the dim light of the entryway. As one, they move, their voices cutting through the storm as they chase after me.

"Hurry, before she gets too far," one of them barks out the sharp command.

"Why run?" another calls, his manic laughter unsettling, and I just know it's Orange Mask. I love that he's having so much fun at my expense—how wonderful for him. "We just want to talk."

Yeah, right.

I'm one hundred percent certain they don't just "want to talk." The thought is so absurd I nearly laugh myself. Instead, the sound I make is more of a whimper than anything. Panic surges through my veins, and I change direction, running toward the woods flanking the driveway. My breaths come in short, ragged bursts as I plunge into the trees.

The woods are dense and dark, making it next to impossible to see more than a couple of feet ahead of me. Branches claw at my face and arms as I shove my way through the undergrowth. The weight of my drenched jeans tightens around my legs and slows me down, but I don't stop. I can't. The rain barely muffles the sounds of their footsteps—steady and deliberate.

I dart around a cluster of trees and scan desperately for a path forward. Rounding the trunk of a massive oak that seems to appear out of nowhere in the dark, I skid to a halt.

Orange Mask leans casually against the tree, as if he's been waiting for hours. His silhouette towers over mine, the dark fabric of his hoodie plastered to his chest by the rain. Even in the dark, I can make out the lean shape of him.

"Going somewhere?" he asks. His tone is playful, but the knife he tosses in the air and catches repeatedly—without looking, mind you—says otherwise.

My heart jumps into my throat as I wheeze out, "Please."

He tilts his head to the side—something I'm beginning to notice he does often—and I have a feeling if he weren't wearing a mask, his grin would mirror it.

Without thinking, I take a couple of small steps back, grab onto a fallen branch, and swing it at him with all of my strength. The wet wood cracks against his arm, causing him to flinch. The grip on his blade falters for just a moment. I don't waste the opportunity to dart past him and curse my feet for slipping in the mud as I run.

"You're only making this harder for yourself!" he calls after me, his voice still carrying that insufferable mocking edge.

My lungs burn and feel as if they are near bursting as I push myself harder, my legs trembling from the effort. The forest floor is slick and treacherous; every step threatens to send me sprawling. I don't dare look back again and risk losing my footing.

The sound of one of them is too close—branches snapping, heavy breaths cutting through the storm. How I can hear anything over my own labored breathing is beyond me.

Just ahead, I spot a narrow path that's barely visible through the trees. I veer toward it, hoping it will lead me somewhere—anywhere—that can offer me safety. As if to dash all of my hopes, just as I reach the path, another figure emerges from the shadows.

The man in the electric-blue mask.

His broad shoulders block the narrow space as he steps into my path. His movements are slow and deliberate, as though he doesn't see me as a threat.

Honestly, though, why would he?

"Enough," he says, his voice both calm and firm. "You're going to get yourself hurt."

I stumble to a stop, my chest heaving as I try to catch my breath. "Stay away from me!" My voice is shrill as I huff out the words in a near staccato, each one interrupted by a heavy inhale. I think of my mother's courage and stand a little taller.

I will not break.

He takes a step forward, raising his hands in a mock gesture of surrender. "You're lost. Let's talk—"

"No!" I cut him off, backing away before turning sharply to my right. I would have to be crazy to trust him. I don't look to see if he follows—I already know he is.

My legs scream, and I worry they might give out at any minute as I push my body further than I ever have before. My soaked shoes squelch with every step, and I can barely see through the rain. I didn't think it was possible, but it's gotten even darker. The trees blur together as I run blindly. Their voices grow fainter behind me; however, I don't—not for one second—think I've lost them.

I climb a slight incline, and my foot catches on an exposed root, sending me stumbling forward. I just barely catch myself on a low-hanging branch, my fingers digging into the wet bark as I struggle to stay upright. I refuse to be taken out by a tree root.

"You're persistent," a new voice says, startling me—seems to be the theme this evening. I whip my eyes around and come face-to-face with the man in the neon-red mask standing a few feet away.

I can't, for the life of me, figure out how they move so quickly. They can't be human. That's the only explanation. Everything about this night has me second-guessing reality as I thought I knew it.

His stance is casual, but his eyes are sharp. His dark clothing clings to him, equally soaked as I am, but there's an air of ease about him that sends a chill down my spine.

"Not human," I say with what little breath I have.

"Persistent," he repeats, "But not very careful."

I don't respond. I can't; my lungs won't let me. Instead, I spin on my heel, panic surging, and I bolt down the hill. Just as my foot slips in the mud, I have the presence of mind to admit that was a bad move. This time, there's no saving myself as I tumble forward. My body rolls down the steep incline while rocks and roots scrape against my skin.

This is it. This is how I die.

Pain explodes against my temple as my head hits something hard—a tree or a rock; I can't be sure. The world spins violently, and my vision darkens as I try to push myself up.

The last thing I hear before everything goes black is Red Mask clicking his tongue in disapproval.

"Now you've gone and hurt yourself," he mutters, his voice distant and low. He sighs, then picks me up and throws me over his shoulder. "Should've been more careful."

5

My head is *pounding*.

It's the first thought I have as I groan softly. The ache building behind my eyes makes it hard to think. I shift, testing out my ability to move, and my fingers brush against something smooth and soft—too soft. Flashes of running through rain-soaked woods flit across my tender mind. My eyes snap open, and I jerk up too fast, making the room spin.

This isn't my bed, and I'm not sure if I'd rather wake up back home or here—the unknown. I hope this is better, but after being chased through the manor and woods, I'm not so sure.

The room is large—almost overwhelmingly so—with dark wood walls and heavy curtains that block out most of the light. It smells faintly of cedar and something floral, but nothing about it feels familiar. My heart—which I'm surprised is still functional—thuds in my chest as I scan the space. I shiver from the slight chill in the air and rub my bare arms to warm up.

Wait. Bare arms?

My breath hitches when I look down at myself. I'm not wearing my T-shirt and jeans. In fact, I don't own, nor have I ever worn, anything like this. Somehow, I'm dressed in a pale-peach, silky negligee. The thin material is nearly transparent while thin straps barely cling to my shoulders. The fabric feels wrong against my skin—too intimate and far too revealing.

Where are my clothes? A brief scan around turns up nothing. They aren't draped across the back of a chair, or even in a pile on the floor. They're just...gone.

They changed me.

They stripped me naked and put this wisp of fabric on me. They didn't even give me undergarments. My stomach churns as realization crashes over me. They did this all while I was unconscious. There's no way for me to know if they did more than change me.

The air feels thick and heavy as I try to fill my lungs. Swinging my legs over the side of the bed, I hug my arms tightly across my chest, attempting to cover as much of my body as the thin fabric allows. Warmth is a lost cause, which is made even more obvious when my feet touch the cold floor. It's just shocking enough to ground me and push past the wave of nausea threatening to rise.

I tell myself to stay calm, take a few deep breaths, and put my tasks in order. First, I'll need to find something else to wear. There's bound to be something in one of these drawers. Then I'll find a way out of here. All I have to do is keep my panic in check, take it one task at a time, and everything will be fine.

If only I actually believed that.

I try a dresser on the far wall first, pulling open the top drawer with shaking hands. Empty. I try the second, then the third. They're all the same—barren, desolate, and completely useless to me. Just like this stupid thing I'm wearing. A sharp, panicked laugh escapes me as I shove the last drawer shut.

"Of course," I mutter. My voice is rough, and my mouth feels like I swallowed a handful of sand. "Why would it be that easy?" I close my eyes and try to get my breathing back under control, reminding myself that everything is going to be all right.

It's got to be.

There's really no other option.

I turn the knob of one of the three doors in the room and yank it open, revealing a bathroom with a huge clawfoot tub. Under any other circumstances, I'd be thrilled to have access to something so luxurious.

I have no idea what could possibly be making it hard to admire my surroundings. Nope. Not a single clue.

I was already parched, but now, with the thought of water, I can feel the way my tongue sticks to the roof of my mouth. I go to the sink and turn the handle. The water is clear, and I put my mouth under the flow.

The first few mouthfuls I swish around and spit out before drinking until I'm full. Which might've been a mistake, now that I can feel it sloshing around inside my empty stomach. I haven't had a real meal in a couple of days. I guess water will have to do for now.

I splash my face with cold water and then open every drawer and cabinet in the ensuite, just in case there's something I can use. I find towels in one of the cabinets, but nothing else. By the time I've made it back to the sink to check the vanity, the only other things I find are some random shampoo and body wash. Both look to be a decade old—at least.

I pull open the top drawer next to the sink and find a toothbrush and toothpaste—*my* toothbrush and toothpaste, to be exact. Which means they have my purse—and the metaphorical keys to my new life.

I can't leave without it.

I need to survive, and I need to find where they're keeping my things. I have no idea what they want with me, but they didn't kill me—so maybe they won't. No matter what happens, I have to stay smart.

After brushing my teeth—a few times—I leave the room and go back to try the second door. It doesn't open. I assume that must be the exit, which means I'm trapped in here. Trying not to freak out, I distract myself by searching behind door number three. I sound like one of those daytime game show hosts Father loves so much.

The door creaks open to reveal...nothing. No clothes, no shoes—not even a stray piece of fabric. It's an empty closet; there's not even a lone hanger to be found. I run my hands through my hair, wincing when I touch the tender wound that I somehow forgot about, and I try to steady my breathing. The task feels impossible, and I'm having a very hard time continuing to convince myself everything will be okay.

Defeated, I stand in the center of the large room and feel sorry for myself. I might as well, right? It's not like there's anything else I can do. It's obvious that I'll have to wait till the deranged masked men—if they can even be called men—decide to let me out of here.

They didn't hurt me. They could've, but they didn't.

Maybe they just want to chase me again. That wouldn't be so bad, and no, I'm not examining why that's my first thought. It doesn't matter anyway. I'm sure the... unusual feelings I had were a one-off.

There's no way they're human; their speed alone is unnatural. I bet that's got something to do with it

God, what's wrong with me?

With a long-suffering sigh, I grab the comforter from the bed and wrap it around myself, the thick fabric heavy and warm against my chilled skin. It doesn't help much, but it's better than nothing, and it brings me a bit of relief. My eyes dart to the closet, its door slightly ajar—the darkness inside a welcome reprieve from the vast openness of the room.

When I was little, I sometimes hid in my closet when I was scared. There's something about being less exposed that gives me the illusion of safety.

I shuffle toward it, almost in a daze. My bare feet are silent against the polished floor. Inside, the air is cool and a touch stale, the faint scent of cedar lingering here too. I sink to the floor, curling into the corner and pulling the comforter tightly around me.

I bury my face in the fabric, my breaths shallow and uneven. My chest tightens, and my hands won't stop shaking. With each beat of my heart, the throbbing in my head intensifies, growing into a skull-splitting beast. The darkness presses in, and it's getting harder to convince myself everything will be okay.

They changed me.

They saw me.

They touched me.

What else did they do to me?

The question is a constant loop in my mind, growing louder with each pass.

My father's voice cuts through the panic—sharp and condemning. "This is what happens to women who stray. The men outside the Covenant will strip you of your dignity. They'll ruin you."

Even worse—Josiah's cruel, sinister voice follows. "You belong to me. No one else will ever want you."

The pain makes my thoughts feel disjointed, out of control. Memories flash behind my closed eyes, no matter how hard I try to will them away.

The rituals.

The sermons.

Josiah's hand lingering on my shoulder, sliding down my body when no one was looking. My father's impossible standards, crushing me under their weight. Their voices echo in my head, relentless and maddening, smothering my thoughts

Were they right?

Am I naïve for thinking I could escape them?

Have I only traded one prison for another?

How could I be so stupid?

My mother put herself on the line for nothing. She should've expected me to fail, like I always do.

I grip the edges of the comforter, my knuckles white as I struggle to focus on my breathing.

In, out.

Everything's okay.

In, out.

I'm okay.

In, out.

Am I though?

In, out.

I don't know where I am. I don't know who—or what—they are. I have no clothes, no belongings, and no way out.

In... in... in—

I can't breathe.

Panic claws at me, dragging me under. My chest tightens, compressed, as if something is pressing down on me. My limbs tremble, the storm inside crashing over me, while exhaustion seeps into my bones. Everything feels unbearably heavy. My mind moves sluggishly, pain flooding in like a tide.

I don't want to sleep. I don't want to let my guard down. But my eyelids grow heavier with every passing second. Panic gives way to a bone-deep weariness I can't fight.

The comforter is warm—its soft weight lulling me into a false sense of security.

As I drift off, my last thought is a desperate, quiet prayer: Please, let me wake up somewhere else. Somewhere safe.

THERE'S NO COMFORT IN SITTING ON THE HARD wooden benches in the Covenant's Sacred Hall. I'm surrounded by the other girls my age, but none of us are really friends. Personal connections outside of family are forbidden for us.

It makes me sad when I see the boys my age playing games together. I don't understand why we're not allowed to, but it's not something I'd ever say out loud.

Father wouldn't like that.

Sometimes, when I see Hope, we wave and smile at each

other—but only when no one's looking. She's eleven, like me, and the only other girl who dares make eye contact. It's our little game.

It might not be as exciting as the boys, with their balls they kick around the field, but there's something thrilling about having a secret. I think she might even be my friend.

The hall falls silent, and I sit up straight, ankles crossed, hands folded neatly in my lap. My attention is fixed on Josiah —nothing else. I know better than to get distracted. The last time I didn't pay attention when he spoke, my father let Josiah take a belt to me.

I try not to shift in my seat as Josiah's stare lingers longer than feels right. It's like he's waiting for me to slip up. Finally, his eyes move to the rest of the room, and he starts speaking.

"You, daughters of the Light, are the purest among us. You carry the Covenant's future within you, and it's your sacred duty to remain untouched by the world and its corruption." He paces slowly, making deliberate eye contact with each of us, pausing again on me. I wish he wouldn't. It makes my hands sweaty and my tummy hurt.

"The world outside this sanctuary is a dark and sinful place. It's filled with men who would seek to destroy your most precious possession—your purity. They will not stop at simply harming your body—no—they will devour your soul."

How do you eat a soul?

What does it look like?

I blink and force my mind to stop wandering—just in time. Father steps forward to stand next to Josiah, looking directly at me as he begins to speak.

"You must understand—the men beyond these walls are worse than beasts—they're demons. They will charm you with sweet lies, promises of freedom, addictive pleasure, and unconditional love. But—hear me when I say—they're hearts are poisoned by sin, and their intentions are nothing but pure evil." He gestures toward the rows of us girls, his eyes cold—as always—but there's something else in them tonight. Something scary, as he looks at all of us—as if we're... we're disgusting.

When his eyes meet mine again, I do my best not to flinch. "Do you know what happens to girls who leave the Light? To those who believe the whispers of these wicked men?" His question was meant for all of us, but I feel like it was meant for only me when he continues to hold my gaze. Josiah steps back, breaking the stare as he places a hand on my father's shoulder, as if it pains them to tell us these truths.

"There was once a girl. She had been blessed as a daughter of the Light. But she thought she knew better than the plan God shared with me. She left the Covenant." Murmurs ripple through the room, and Josiah raises his hands, a gesture that silences the crowd. "I know, I know. This girl was led astray, thinking the world outside would offer her the freedom she desired."

He pauses, allowing the disapproval of the crowd to rise before he continues.

"What do you think she found? Men. Demons who promised her everything—but took it all instead." Josiah's voice softens, almost as if sharing a secret, forcing the room to lean in, hanging on his every word.

"They didn't kill her. No, that would've been far too merciful for these beastly men. They each stole pieces of her soul, piece by piece, leaving her a hollow, broken shell of the girl she once was. We never stopped looking for her; a shepherd does not stop searching for their lost lambs. When we found her, she begged for God's forgiveness, but it was too late. Her purity was gone forever, deemed worthless by the Light."

Josiah and my father each take a moment, as if mourning the girl he spoke of. I risk a glance at the other girls and see the same terror reflected that I feel. But in the next instant, the fear of having my soul stolen and losing my purity forever is taken over by something else—curiosity.

How do you steal someone's soul?

Father steps forward, taking the time to sneer at each of us. "Purity is the most valuable gift you've been blessed with," he says, as though we've already lost our souls. "Once it's taken, you cannot get it back. Not unless God himself demands it to be so. And once it is gone, so are you. You no longer have a place within the Light."

Father's eyes find me once again, and they seem to burn into me. "Remember, it is not just your body that's at stake. These men will strip you of your very essence, leaving you unworthy of God's love—of any love."

I've never given my father a reason to doubt me. I think it's because I'm a girl. He tells me all the time that girls are weak-minded and born of sin. That's why we have to spend our whole lives trying to be worthy of godly men and work hard to get to heaven.

I know he wishes Mother would've given him a son instead of me. I know a boy wouldn't need so much minding. I know I always disappoint him. It always makes my eyes sting, and I have to fight not to let the tears fall.

I can't let myself cry.

Father wouldn't like that.

6

Voices filter through my sleeping mind—low, deep, and far too close. For a single blissful moment, I don't remember where I am. Then I feel the hard floor beneath me, the comforter tangled around my legs, and it all comes rushing back.

The manor.

The negligee.

The closet.

The voices grow closer, and I squeeze my eyes shut—hoping that if I can't see them, they can't see me. If I weren't so afraid of making a sound or drawing attention to myself, I'd pull the comforter over my head and disappear beneath it.

But there's no hiding.

They've found me.

"Well, this is new," one of them says, his tone light, tinged with amusement—Orange Mask. I get the feeling he thinks everything is a joke, even chasing women through the woods

49

at night in the middle of a storm. "I don't think we've ever had a guest hide in the closet before."

I hope he has a bruise where I hit him with the branch.

A big one.

"We've never had a guest," the voice says, sounding incredibly bored.

"Quiet," another one snaps—cold and calculated. I think it's Red Mask. Making the bored one Blue Mask. "She's waking up."

Logically, I know there are only so many places to hide in this room. They were bound to find me. Yet their presence still makes my heart pound against my chest, as if it's trying to run away from them too, even though I'd been expecting them.

At least the pain in my head has dwindled to a dull ache.

I'm reluctant to let them know I'm awake. The lights from their masks spill through my closed lids, a riot of colors bleeding into my vision. When I finally work up the courage to open my eyes, three masked figures loom over me.

They're much closer than I expected—too close. The neon glow is blinding as they hover in the small space, and I struggle to sit up. The comforter slips from my shoulders, and I clutch it tightly, pulling it up to my chin as though it's armor.

"Easy," Orange Mask says, holding up his hands in mock surrender. His tone is almost playful, but the little hairs on my body stand on end, telling me this is anything but a joke. It makes my stomach twist. "We're not going to hurt you."

"Speak for yourself," the one in the electric-blue mask mutters, his tone slightly less bored. He's broader than the others, his dark blue hoodie stretched to its limit when he crosses his arms. I'm not sure I've ever seen arms that thick before. It occurs to me how easily he could break me, and I shudder at the thought.

"Enough," Red Mask says, his tone curt and commanding. The other two seem to defer to him. Orange Mask chuckles as he leans against the wall, his attention fixated on the stupid knife he's tossing again. "What were you doing in our house last night?"

My throat feels dry, and I swallow hard, wishing I could get a drink as I try to find my voice. "I—I didn't mean to intrude. My car broke down. I was just looking for help."

It's what I tried to tell them last night—or however long it's been. With storms rolling in and out, the sky thick with dark clouds, keeping track of time feels impossible. For some reason, their presence feels a fraction less terrifying—which is beyond stupid of me.

"So instead of knocking, you decided to invite yourself in and... make yourself comfortable?" The annoyingly playful one asks, his attention fully on me. He gestures to the comforter wrapped around me. "Nice touch, by the way. Fashionable—*homeless chic.*"

"I did knock!" I snap, hating that he's able to laugh at my situation. The rush of anger makes my head feel a little too light—I should probably eat soon—and the words tumble out before I can stop them. "The door swung open, and I called out, several times. No one answered. I didn't know anyone was here."

Blue Mask scoffs, "And that gave you permission to wander around like you owned the place?" I don't understand why they are so certain that I have nefarious intentions.

I clutch the comforter tighter, anger raging within despite

the fear that still grips me. "I've already told you, I wasn't trying to steal anything. I just needed somewhere to charge my phone. I don't even know where I am." A frustrated sob born of my mixed emotions escapes. I—faltering, I look at their feet and pull the comforter tighter, the fire within me snuffed out in an instant. My next words come out in a whisper: "There was nowhere else to go, and I didn't know what else to do."

Orange Mask chuckles as he pushes off the wall, clearly finding my despondency entertaining. He stretches, and I see a sliver of tanned skin above his belt, before he looks at the other three—disregarding me entirely. "Well, that was one hell of a chase she led us on. She's got guts; I'll give her that."

Where's a tree branch when you need one?

Red Mask mutters, "She's got something." His focus hasn't wavered from me for a moment, as if he's searching for cracks in my story. I stare right back, willing him to see the truth in my words.

His imposing frame towers over me as he leans in, offering a hand to help me stand. "Get up."

"What?" My voice wavers, my legs trembling as I clutch the comforter around me with one hand, placing the other in his. His grip is warm and surprisingly gentle as he pulls me to my feet. I don't realize he's still holding my hand until I feel his callused fingers brush mine as he slowly releases me.

"You're not staying in here." His tone leaves no room for argument. The softness he showed me a moment ago is already forgotten. "You want help? You'll get it. But it will be on our terms." He turns and exits the closet, leaving the door wide open behind him.

Orange Mask steps aside, offering a mocking little bow as

I edge past him with the comforter trailing behind me like a pathetic royal mantle. "After you, thief."

I glare at him but say nothing, holding tightly to the ridiculous comforter as I step into the dimly lit room. My pulse races, my mind spinning with multiple possibilities of what 'their terms' could possibly mean. Josiah's warnings about evil men and what they will do to me outside of the Covenant play on repeat.

Will they devour my soul?

Their expressions are a mix of amusement and something far more dangerous—something dark that feels both thrilling and terrifying, sending a shiver racing down my spine. I can't help but think that my soul is, indeed, on the menu.

"We've decided," Red Mask says, his voice laced with steel, snapping me out of my spiraling thoughts. His arms cross, and he tilts his head, looking down at me with a gaze that feels like it's cutting right through me. "You're going to play a game."

My stomach twists, and while I've always wanted to play a game, something tells me this isn't the kind I've always thought of. Yet, I can't deny my excitement at finally having the opportunity. "A game?"

"Yes," the one with the electric-blue mask says. "It's called hide and seek. You've played before, haven't you?" His tone suggests that it's a common game, possibly one for children, and his question is meant to be rhetorical. But something tells me we won't be playing by the same rules.

I swallow hard, glancing between the three. Anticipation rolls off of them in thick waves, and I'm certain that doesn't bode well for me. "No. How do you play?" I ask, my voice barely above a whisper. Oddly, I'm more afraid of their ridicule at my ignorance than the game itself.

They share a look between them, impossible for me to decipher with their masks, but somehow they understand each other. "It's simple," Orange Mask says, stepping forward, his voice low and taunting. "You get five minutes to hide. Anywhere in the manor. After that, one of us will hunt you. Fun, right?"

Red Mask cuts in, his voice colder, more deliberate. "You'll hide from each of us, one at a time."

"And when all three of us find you," Blue Mask says—just as I was starting to think their game didn't sound so bad—his voice dropping, "we get to do whatever we want with you."

My breath catches painfully in my throat while my heart pounds so loud I can barely hear my own thoughts. "And if at least one of you doesn't find me?" I ask, my voice trembling. It's been my experience that when a man says he can do whatever he wants to a woman, it never ends well for her.

Orange Mask shrugs like it's the simplest thing in the world. "Then you win. And we leave you alone. Simple as that."

I don't believe him for a single second.

"The game ends at dawn," Red Mask says as he steps closer. I instinctively take a step back, clutching the comforter, which at this point is more an extension of myself than a blanket. "If you manage to stay hidden from at least one of us until then, you're free to go."

"But when you don't," Orange Mask chimes in, a definite smirk in his voice. "Well, let's just say it'll be a long night for you." The way his voice drops, deep and possessive, is something I'm all too familiar with. However, where Josiah's voice makes my skin crawl, his makes my stomach do strange flips while heat floods my body.

I shake my head, panic—and that dark thing waking within me—rises in my chest. "You can't be serious."

"Oh, princess, we're more than serious," the blue one says, leaning in so his masked face is inches from mine. "But you can make it easier on yourself when the time comes by cooperating. The more you fight us, the harder it'll be for you. Though, I can't say we won't enjoy it."

My knees go weak, and I fear they might give out at any moment. Josiah used to say similar things to me, but it doesn't inspire the same dread when they come from this man. I force myself to stand taller, even as my heart races. "And if I refuse?"

"You won't." The one with the red mask opens the door to the hallway. I notice he doesn't actually answer my question, but I have no idea what it means.

This isn't a choice.

Or is it?

I'm so confused.

What would they do if I refused?

"Tick-tock, time's wasting," the orange one says, pulling a sleek watch from his pocket and tapping its face. "Five minutes. I'd probably start running if I were you."

I nod once, stiffly, and turn on shaky legs, taking off down the hallway. My bare feet slap against the cold, wooden floors as I race through the corridor, clutching the comforter tightly. The heavy fabric drags behind me, cumbersome, but I can't bring myself to let it go.

Not yet, at least.

Maybe not ever.

Five minutes.

Don't panic.

Five minutes.

Oh, God—

Lightning blinds me with its sudden brightness, and I cover my mouth to stifle a scream as thunder shakes the manor.

Why is it always storming?

The sound of walls shifting spurs me to sprint for the room that just appeared. It looks like a butler's pantry, with an entire wall of lower cabinets and upper shelves. I think I might fit in one of the cabinets. Without wasting another second, I find an empty one and climb inside.

A scream tears from me as the floor of the cabinet suddenly drops out, sending me tumbling into darkness. I slide down a chute and crash into the bottom of a massive grandfather clock. Somehow, I manage to hold onto my now filthy comforter. I scramble to my feet, brushing myself off, before taking in the room I've landed in. The furniture is draped in white sheets, and the air is thick with dust, smelling stale and musty.

The beat of my pulse echoes like a ticking clock. I should be afraid—I am afraid—but there's a strange thrill beneath the fear, a pulse of excitement that I can't quite shake. The thrill of the game mixes with my dread, creating a strange, addictive sensation. A hidden darkness stirs within me, wanting to know what happens when they find me, but I push it back to the secret corner of my mind before I can think further on it.

"Sixty seconds!" one of them calls. I don't even question

how their voice carries through the halls, all the way to whatever abandoned part of the manor I've fallen into.

A crazed giggle slips out as my panic surges, but I push it down and quickly scan the ghostly room again. I peer under the sheets, searching for something I can hide beneath. After what feels like minutes, though it could only have been seconds, I find a desk with just enough space to tuck into. I press myself into the corner, making sure every part of me is hidden, then hold my breath.

Save for the faint creak of floorboards in the distance, the manor falls silent—no clicking or heavy dragging sounds from the shifting walls—as if it's fallen asleep, offering no resistance to its masters. My pulse thunders in my ears as I strain to listen, every sound amplified by the suffocating stillness. It always amazes me how loud silence can be.

A voice echoes from somewhere in the house, smooth and taunting. "Ready or not, little thief... here we come."

The hunt's begun.

7

The room is silent, save for my shallow breathing and the faint creak of the manor settling around me. The air smells of mothballs and stale wood, untouched for years. My legs are cramping, and my rear aches from sitting on the cold floor for so long.

Maybe they've forgotten this room exists.

That hope fades a few moments later when slow, deliberate footsteps echo from the hallway just outside, as if my very thought summoned one of them.

"Come out, come out, wherever you are," a voice taunts, amusement dripping from every sing-song word. It's deep and smooth, sending shivers down my spine.

I squeeze my eyes shut, willing myself to be smaller, quieter—invisible. I hope he passes by, yet that darkness within is curious to see what happens when I'm caught.

The door creaks open. I can't see it from where I am, but I know one of them is here with me. His footsteps are measured and confident, as if he already knows exactly where I am, savoring the moments before he strikes.

"I know you're in here." His voice is softer now, coaxing. "There's no hiding from me, little thief."

I don't move.

I don't breathe.

I don't make a sound.

I can see the faint blue glow through the thin fabric of the sheet hiding me, growing brighter with each step he takes. I bite my lip, forcing back a whimper, as he starts pulling the sheets off the furniture.

One.

By.

One.

The blue glow settles directly in front of me, and I know I've been found. I hold my breath as the sheet shielding me is yanked away in one swift motion—exposing me. He tilts his head, studying me like a predator sizing up its prey.

"Well, well," he drawls, squatting down with ease, completely unbothered. I stare at him with wide, terrified eyes. "Gotcha."

I press myself further into the nook. The desk traps me on three sides, leaving the only escape directly where he crouches. My breath hitches as his hand—warm and calloused—brushes the hair from my face with an almost delicate touch.

"Didn't make it very difficult for me, did you?" he taunts, his voice a cruel caress. "You'll have to do better for the next one."

I flinch as his fingers trail down to my chin, tilting my face so I'm forced to look at where his eyes should be. His head tilts again, as if considering something, before he abruptly stands—towering over me once more.

"I'll give you a head start," he says, stepping back and sweeping his hand toward the door. "Go on, little thief. Your next hunter's waiting for you."

The comforter tangles my legs as I try to climb to my feet, the bulky material difficult to maneuver. Still, I'm unwilling to part with it. He shakes his head, chuckling as I wrap it around myself once again. I dart past him with a glare and don't look back.

Like the flip of a switch, the manor comes alive the moment I step into the hallway.

I run.

After sitting for so long, it's almost painful to move this fast, but I push through the stiffness.

"Five minutes!" he calls as I turn down a connected corridor, the low light from the wall sconces casting long shadows.

I stifle a scream as the floor beneath me shifts, making it feel like the entire hallway is turning. A door opens once the movement stops, but I don't trust it for a second. I turn and run in the opposite direction, but then a wall slides into place, closing in on me at a frightening rate, quickly shortening the hall.

"Oh, God." The prayer escapes in a whimper.

I stumble backward, tripping over the comforter as I try to run.

When I reach the doorway, I don't hesitate—I rush right through it. Turning just in time to see the wall stop mere feet from crashing into the other end of the hall. I suppose it's a relief to know I wouldn't have been crushed.

The room is filled with various musical instruments. My

blood runs cold as notes play from the harp—by itself. It stops abruptly, and the same song continues seamlessly on the piano—also by itself.

I'm not familiar with the song, but it's hauntingly beautiful. Honestly, I wouldn't be surprised if this place were haunted. I might be more concerned about being in a room with a ghost if I weren't being hunted.

A framed painting of a landscape takes up an entire wall —something about it feels off. Upon closer inspection, I notice hinges along one side. I pull it open, revealing another door behind it. I don't want to think about the reasons this door was hidden, but with no other option, I turn the knob and step through.

This house makes no sense. Why would a bedroom door be hidden behind a giant landscape in the music room? Then again, with how this place constantly shifts, it might not always be here.

"One minute, little thief!" one of them yells. It sounds like he's yelling from the other side of the manor—but who knows, the manor enjoys playing tricks on me. With no more time to waste, I slide under the bed and prepare to wait.

The cold floor presses against my cheek as I fight to stay quiet. The bedroom is silent, the manor no longer shifting, and the dust under the bed tickles my nose. Every nerve in my body is taut, my fingers digging into the floor as I fight to keep myself from trembling.

It's been a long night—more like a week—and my body is begging for sleep. My eyelids grow heavier with each passing second, and I drift in a half-conscious haze. Just as sleep threatens to pull me under, I hear it—a faint creak of a turning doorknob.

My eyes snap open, adrenaline rushing through me. The sound of his footsteps fills the room, light and springy—as if he's enjoying himself. He probably is. I don't need to see the faint orange glow on the floor to know who's hunting me now.

Then he starts to whistle, and I wish for that tree branch again. It makes me so angry! He treats all of this like it's some big joke. He wouldn't be laughing if he'd lived the same life I did.

The whistling stops, and his footsteps pause at the edge of the bed. I freeze, barely allowing myself to breathe. He bends slightly, the orange glow getting brighter.

Don't move.

Don't breathe.

Don't do anything.

After a long moment, he straightens, and a flicker of hope flares in my chest as he starts whistling again. The sound of his footsteps retreating sends a wave of relief crashing over me. I almost let out a deep sigh—

Hands wrap around my ankles.

I scream.

He drags me out from under the bed, my nails scraping uselessly against the floor—my comforter lost somewhere beneath me. Panic consumes me as I scream and thrash, but his grip doesn't waver.

Effortlessly, he hauls me up, pulling me flush against his body. His arm wraps around my middle, pinning my arms to my sides, while the cool edge of a blade presses against my throat.

I freeze.

The glowing mask hovers inches from the side of my face

as he leans in, his mouth brushing close to my ear. His voice is low—a teasing drawl that does nothing to hide the danger lurking beneath.

"Did you really think you could hide from me, little thief? Silly girl, you can never hide from me."

I'm quaking, every instinct screams at me to fight—to run—but his grip is ironclad.

"P-please," I whisper, my voice trembling. "Just let me go."

"Oh, I'll let you go," he says, dragging the tip of his blade down the side of my face without breaking skin. "But only because the game's just begun. It'd be a shame to end it too soon."

The blade travels further, skimming the column of my throat, down the center of my sternum, forcing me to take shallow breaths.

"Do you feel that? The way your heart's pounding? That's fear, little thief. It suits you."

Against my efforts, my body betrays me. Heat pools low in my stomach, and my breath hitches—fear has nothing to do with it this time. His voice, his touch, the... knife—it's all too much. Shame floods my cheeks as I try to fight the confusing rush of emotions.

His grip tightens, his tone dripping with amusement. "Oh, what's this? Is your cunt soaked for me, little thief? Naughty, naughty."

My face burns hotter. I've never heard anyone speak like that before, and tears sting my eyes. I can't tell if it's from fear or shame—or something else entirely.

"N-no, I'm not—"

"Liar," he purrs, his voice smooth as silk, sending shivers down my spine. "But that's all right. We'll have plenty of time to play later. You've got one last chance to run before you're ours—you like the sound of that, don't you?"

Without warning, he releases me, and I stumble forward, nearly falling to my knees. My legs feel like jelly, and I press a trembling hand to my throat where the knife had been. I turn to look at him, but he's already stepping back into the shadows, the glow of his mask the last thing to fade.

"Run, little thief," he calls over his shoulder, his voice echoing like a terrifying melody. "Run while you still can."

I crawl back under the bed, grab the comforter, and bolt through the hidden door he used—my mind tangled in confusion and terror. For a moment, I almost begged for something —I'm not even sure what—but it wasn't to let me go.

What's wrong with me?

Racing down the hallway, I skid to a stop and backtrack after passing a narrow staircase. With a hand on the banister and a foot on the first step, I look up, and pause.

Nothing in this place can be trusted, and falling down—or even through—the stairs is not something I'm eager to do. The sound of walls sliding shakes me from my indecision, particularly as the staircase is about to be closed in.

Deciding to risk it, I test each step carefully before placing my full weight down. It's a slow process, made even slower by my exhaustion.

How much longer until dawn?

Wait.

I never heard the start of my five minutes. It's probably taken at least that long just to get past the ridiculous number of stairs. Either Orange Mask gave me a serious head start, or I'm not getting a warning at all.

I imagine it's the latter.

It's not until I reach the top of the stairs that I realize how quiet everything is. The manor has gone back to sleep, which can only mean one thing: Red Mask is hunting me. The creak of the floor when I take my next step is far too loud. I freeze, straining to hear any sound of movement.

I don't let myself feel relief when there's no sign of a glowing red mask anywhere. The moment I let my guard down, he'll appear out of thin air. I don't know how they always seem to know where I am, but there's something unnatural about them.

Walking on my toes, I make little to no sound as I glide down the hallway. Most of the doors up here are closed, and I refuse to open any of them. With my luck, the door would squeak, announcing my presence to the entire manor. No, I'll wait until I come across an open door to hide behind.

There's a stretch of wall with the smallest windows I've ever seen, spaced evenly apart. When I look out, I'm almost certain the sky is beginning to lighten. At least, I hope it is, and I'm not just imagining it.

This "game" and this house have made my sense of direction impossible to trust. I'm surprised to see how far up I am and start to wonder if this floor is just below the attic. That would be a good place to hide.

Just past the little windows and their meager light, the hallway grows nearly pitch black. I feel my way along the wall and find what seems like a door casing, but when I reach for the door, there's only fabric. Must be curtains or something. My heart races, threatening to beat right through my chest, as I feel the fabric shift in a steady rise and fall, warmth radiating from it.

It's not curtains.

It's not something.

It's someone.

My hand trembles as I feel my way, already knowing what I'm about to find. The second my fingertips brush a fabric-covered face, the neon red lights flare to life. I yelp and scramble to retreat, only to crash into something hard just before I'm washed in an electric-blue glow. Using the force of the collision, I stumble backward and dive toward the nearest door.

Before my fingers can reach the brass knob, the door jerks open, and Orange Mask steps into the doorway. When I turn, I realize I'm trapped. The only possible escape is the small windows on the opposite side of the hall. It feels like some cruel twist of fate that our final confrontation happens just as the sky teeters on the edge of a cloud-heavy dawn.

The relief of almost making it to dawn shatters the moment Red Mask grabs my wrists and slams them above my head. I gasp as he presses me against the cold wall. His glowing eyes are all I can see—twin red X's burning into me. My breath comes in short, panicked bursts as I struggle against him, but his strength is unyielding.

He doesn't even budge.

"Would you look at that," he murmurs, his voice a low, mocking drawl. "You lost the game, thief."

"No! Look!" I shout, squirming in his grip. "Dawn is almost here! I won!"

"If only almost counted," Blue Mask adds as he steps closer. "You know the rules."

My comforter—the only thing that's kept me from feeling completely exposed all night—slips from my shoulders during the struggle. I barely notice before Red Mask releases my wrists and, in one swift movement, pulls a sack over my head. My world plunges into darkness.

I cry out, clawing at the rough fabric, but his hand clamps over mine, stopping me.

"Ah, ah," he says, as if admonishing a child. "Not yet. You don't get to see anything until I say so."

His hands shift, grabbing me around my waist and lifting me as if I weigh nothing. I scream, kicking out wildly, but he tosses me over his shoulder with infuriating ease. My body bounces against his as he starts walking, every step rough and unceremonious, as I beat my fists on his back.

"Careful," Orange Mask says somewhere nearby, his usual mirth missing from his tone for once. "She might bruise."

"Lucky for her, there's no time to do what I really want," Red Mask growls. I feel his words rumble through his chest. "But don't worry, thief. We'll be back to play at dusk."

A sharp smack lands on my bare bottom.

I freeze, the realization hitting me like a wave—I'm completely exposed in this position. I'm suddenly thankful I can't see them. My throat tightens, a wave of heat flooding through me even as fear prickles my skin.

Their voices surround me as they discuss—in vivid detail —the things they wish they had time for, using language more vile than I've ever heard. Each word tightens around me, a growing tension that I'm afraid to experience when it finally breaks.

A chill settles in the air the further we go. Wherever we're headed, the dampness seeps into the atmosphere, dragging up memories I'd rather not revisit.

I panic.

And thrash against his hold again.

"No, please... Don't leave me here. I—I'll be good, I promise," I sob, the memories bleeding into the present, making it impossible to tell where one ends and the other begins.

"There's a way out of this room—if you can figure it out," a voice says.

Was that Blue Mask or Josiah?

I'm jostled roughly before my bare legs connect with a flat, hard surface. My hands instinctively reach for the sack, desperate to yank it off. Before I can, a firm hand grips my wrist.

"Not yet," Red Mask warns, his tone sharp. "Not until we're gone."

"Please... Please, not here," I beg. "Not here."

I freeze.

My heart pounds.

I hear fabric shifting.

Oh God, he's here.

Any second, a bruising grip will seize me, and I'll try my hardest to float away. What I don't expect is something warm and soft draping over me. My breath catches when I hear Orange Mask chuckle. The sound is light and doesn't belong in my memories, but it calms me, makes the panic ease.

"Don't worry," he says, his amusement back in his tone. "I remembered your emotional-support comforter."

I'm too stunned to react as their footsteps fade. The sound of a door—or something heavy—sliding shut fills the space. I call out a few times, my voice cracking, but only silence answers me. Once I realize they're gone, I rip the sack off my head, its rough fabric catching on my hair. My chest heaves as I look around.

The room is dimly lit by a single candle burning on the

floor. Shadows stretch across the stone walls, broken only by the soft folds of the comforter wrapped around me. I scan the place again, my stomach sinking with each pass.

No windows.

No doors.

No way out.

My emotions war within me as my past clashes with my present. Panic, fear, and dread swirl together, but beneath it all, something darker and more unsettling simmers. My body trembles—not from the cold, but from their words, which still echo in my mind, and their touches, which have burned into my skin.

I tighten the comforter around myself and take a shaky breath, forcing my focus. They said there's a way out. I just have to be clever enough to find it—but right now, I can't fight the exhaustion overwhelming both my body and mind.

I need to be ready.

Whatever game this is, it's not over.

It's only just begun.

8

The stone beneath me is cold—the kind of cold that stabs like little needles into your bones. The comforter wrapped around my body should help, and maybe it would if there were any body heat to trap. Instead, it absorbs the cold moisture surrounding me. The air, thick with the earthy scent of stone, presses against my skin like layers of damp dirt—inescapable, suffocating.

I know this smell.

I know this feeling.

I squeeze my eyes shut, gripping the edges of the comforter so tightly that my frozen knuckles ache. A sharp pain in my stomach makes me curl into myself—hunger, my constant companion, twisting inside me. I blink against the haze clouding my vision, but it does nothing to clear the fog of confusion in my brain.

I've never understood the definition of silence. It's meant to be the complete lack of sound, but in my experience, it's louder than most. It's the hum of electronics, the anticipation between the ticks of a clock, the ominous creaking of a house.

Silence is an old friend of mine—though never a kind one. The cruelest thing about it is how it encourages dread to mount, swiftly growing and impossible to control. It builds in the echo of footsteps above, the groan of an opening door, the measured thud of footfalls on each step before he—

Fear wraps around my chest in a vice-like embrace, tightening with each shallow breath. Confusion pulls me between past and present, blurring the line between reality and delusion. I can't tell what's real—am I sixteen in the cellar, or twenty-five in the manor? Panic claws at my throat, ready for Josiah's cold, menacing voice to rip through the silence.

No.

That's not now.

I'm not there.

I squeeze my eyes shut, tossing my head in a futile attempt to shake off the past. It doesn't help. I can hear them—footsteps, slow and unhurried, creaking above me. Fear consumes me, my heart slamming against my ribs, my pulse a roaring thing in my ears.

The ceiling is made of stone.

It's impossible to hear footsteps.

There's no door or stairs.

He can't be here.

Yet, I hear footsteps.

I hear a door groan as it opens.

I hear the thud of each step.

The sounds send a chill down my spine. Even if he's not here, he's still able to terrorize me. It's a sickening reminder that Josiah's still out there. By now, he must be looking for me.

He'll ever stop.

A wave of dizziness washes over me—the lack of food fraying my mind at the edges. I'm no stranger to hunger. Josiah delighted in using it as a punishment. I think it was the effects hunger had on me that he appreciated the most.

I'd lose time, days blurring as everything bled together. I'd be too weak to fight, too confused to understand what was happening to me.

I refuse to let that happen again.

I grit my teeth and force myself upright. My legs tremble beneath me. The room spins as I adjust the comforter, steadying myself before carefully bending to pick up the candle.

Come on, Celest, focus on the here and now.

I can't let my mind sink back into memories that are already too close to the surface. I take a deep breath and look around, firmly planting myself in the present. The candlelight barely cuts through the darkness as I press one hand to the curved walls, dragging my fingers along the rough, uneven surface.

They said there's a way out—I just have to find it.

Pressing the candle closer to the wall, my eyes catch on something ahead—a small irregular section I almost missed.

My breath shudders as I move closer. I choose one of the small stones and press against it. It shifts beneath my fingertips, giving way ever so slightly.

I press a few at random and yelp when the room shifts—not just the wall, but the entire space around me. My stomach lurches, and I stumble back. The heavy grinding of stone reverberates through the room, followed by a soft click that echoes in the stillness.

That did… something.

I try another random combination, but this time, when the room jerks to a stop, there's no click. It reminds me of a giant combination lock. I chew on my lip, thinking.

If that's the case, then…

I repeat the first pattern, then experiment with another. The room spins again. Another click. My frozen fingers tremble as I repeat the process, trying different combinations until—

Click.

The wall shifts, a section of stone sliding away, revealing a dark opening beyond. I don't hesitate. Gripping the candle and comforter tighter, I step through.

The stone hallway ends at a set of wooden stairs. With each step, the air grows warmer. I reach the top and turn the knob, stepping into a room bathed in the muted glow of the sun. Even with the heavy cloud coverage, I blink several times, adjusting to the light.

I blow out the candle, unsure of what to do with it. Ultimately, I set it down on the first flat surface I find, then move to bask in the weak warmth of a sunbeam, letting it thaw me. As much as I'd love to stay here and follow the shifting light across the dark hardwood floors, hunger gnaws at me. I give myself a few more minutes before forcing myself to move.

Even with the manor quietly sleeping, it remains a chaotic maze. I've circled this place more times than I can count before finally emerging onto the second-floor balcony of the foyer, where twin staircases curve down to the front door.

As I descend the stairs slowly, I debate whether the door

will open. It seems silly to leave the front door unlocked if they want to keep me here. Maybe they didn't think I'd crack the puzzle of that ridiculous room. Who designs a room as one giant combination lock, anyway?

Then again, anything seems possible here.

I reach out with a shaking hand and grab the knob, turning it—it opens. The air outside is warm, and for once, it's not raining. That little voice in the back of my head screams at me to run. But there's another, darker voice telling me to stay—that I don't want to leave.

My stomach growls again, and I try to push the hunger aside, focusing on thinking logically while letting the warm air wash over me. If I left right now, I'm almost certain I'd die. I'm already starving, and all I have to my name is a slip of fabric and a dirty comforter.

I shut the door, telling myself I can't leave until I find my purse and some food. This has nothing to do with the dark desires the masked men have stirred inside me.

Absolutely nothing.

No, I'm just being rational.

I head toward the same hallway I took when I first arrived at the manor. There's no point in trying to remember where I've been or where each corridor leads—not with how this place constantly shifts.

In the light of day, the manor feels less sinister—beautiful even. The Great Hall opens up to a sweeping staircase, its two elegant spirals leading up to a second-floor balcony adorned with intricate wrought-iron railings. Towering arches frame the space, their ornate carvings drawing attention to the dazzling chandelier overhead.

It's twice the size of the one in the foyer.

Beneath the grand staircase, two arched hallways are tucked into shadow, while two others—one on each side— lead to the unknown. It's fewer than I expected, but then again, I only had a quick look around with the glow of my phone. I choose one at random, hoping it leads to the kitchen. Preferably sooner rather than later—I don't know how much longer I can keep going before I collapse.

I wonder what I'll find when I finally raid the pantry and fridge. At this point, I'll take anything, but fresh fruit sounds like heaven. The thought of an apple makes my mouth water. Maybe, if I'm lucky, I'll even find some candy bars.

Growing up, candy was forbidden. Josiah always said it was another temptation for women—one that men could never fall victim to. Sometimes, the boys were cruel. They'd eat their chocolate bars in front of us, savoring every bite, knowing we couldn't have any. I think they enjoyed taunting us more than the candy itself.

Since leaving, I've tried every kind of candy I can get my hands on. So far, Snickers are my favorite. I also really like the Sour Children. Sour kids? Something like that.

God, I'm so hungry.

By the time I finally find the kitchen—after what feels like an eternity—it's anticlimactic. The space is massive, with gleaming countertops and an old-fashioned stove straight out of a 1950s movie set. Unfortunately, that's where the allure ends.

The fridge hums faintly as I open it, revealing next to nothing—just a jug of milk, a mostly-empty bottle of hot sauce, and a single piece of slimy lettuce. Honestly, I'm afraid to even open the milk and that piece of lettuce is more likely to make me ill than anything.

The pantry isn't much better. A box of stale crackers, a dented can of soup, and a half-eaten jar of peanut butter— that's it. With a sigh, I grab the crackers and peanut butter, dragging them to the counter. Candy bars and apples remain nothing but a wish.

The cabinets are just as empty—no plates, no cutlery—but I'm too hungry to care. I twist the lid off the jar and scoop out a glob with a cracker, stuffing it into my mouth.

Nothing about it is satisfying, and it barely does anything to quiet the hunger gnawing at my stomach. At least it's something. I remind myself to be careful, eating small bites to avoid making myself sick.

One thing is for certain, this kitchen has not been used in a long time. Do they even eat? Of course they do, everyone has to eat.

The question is, *what* do they eat?

I have no desire to contemplate the possibilities. I'm still not convinced they're human.

At least not entirely.

Oh, God. What if they're keeping me alive just to eat me later? I quickly shove that thought aside. There's no point in dwelling on it. Besides, I've got enough to worry about right now.

I lean against the counter while I chew, while my mind continues to drift to the events of the past two nights. There seems to be a fine line between terror and thrill which I've somehow managed to find. I'm not certain which side I'll end up on, but either way, they've found the darkness inside me. I've kept it locked in a cage my whole life, but all it took was two nights with them to unleash it.

I should hate them for it—and I'm trying to. I really am. But I'm finding it difficult.

There's anger, that much I know, but there's also something else—something I can't quite name. It pulls at the darkness within me, tangled and buried deep beneath the surface, but impossible to ignore. I should be focused on surviving, on finding a way out of this place, yet my mind keeps circling back to them.

The sound of their voices, low and taunting, echoing in the dark. The thrill I felt as their footsteps grew near. How they seemed to appear out of nothing. The way my heart raced when the neon glow of their masks came into view. There's something excitingly sinful about it all—exactly what I've been warned against my whole life.

Maybe I'm just tired.

I press my palm against the countertop, trying to ground myself, but it doesn't help. Every time I close my eyes, I see them—their silhouettes in the dim light, the glow of their masks. Their words coil around me, igniting something I don't understand.

What's wrong with me?

I should be terrified—which I am, of course—but this fear is different. It's nothing like the fear I used to feel when Josiah called me to his home for what he called a "correction of purity," his expectations ringing in my ears, my father's disapproving gaze cutting through me.

This is different.

It's fear, but it's something more, something forbidden. It burns through my veins, making me feel alive in a way I never thought possible, not even in my wildest dreams.

I pick up the rest of the crackers and peanut butter,

deciding to put them away instead of taking them with me. Without something to carry them in, I'm sure I'd lose them and never see them again. At least this way, I'll know exactly where they are.

I brace myself against the sink and put my mouth under the tap, drinking my fill of cold water before standing up and gazing out the window. The sun inches closer to the horizon, dusk no more than an hour away. That gives me little time to prepare before the next game begins. Anticipation thrums through me at the thought of seeing them again.

The darkness within me smiles.

9

The last rays of sunlight filter through the glass beside me, casting a golden glow over the room. The sky clears long enough for the sun to make a brief appearance, painting the surrounding clouds with deep tones of red and orange—along with every shade in between. Its slow descent into the horizon a dramatic countdown, each fading hue like the ticking of a clock.

I'm proud of myself. My white-knuckled grip on the arms of this surprisingly comfortable antique chair is the only outward show of my building anxiety. I dragged it over to sit beside the window a little over a half-hour ago, snuggled into the comforter, and haven't moved since. The goal is to appear unaffected, as if the show in the sky is more interesting than their arrival—no matter when they come for me.

I learned to use this trick years ago to needle Josiah. It was most effective in public when all eyes were on us. He'd call my name or stand beside me, and I'd pretend not to notice, as if he were the least interesting thing in the room. I tested the limits of defiance, then greeted him with the barest amount of enthusiasm. Nothing embarrassed him more. It was my way of fighting back—though my small rebellions always came at a price.

I never let it stop me.

Chasing the vibrant display of color, twilight holds its breath, just as true dusk arrives. I resist the urge to glance over my shoulder, I know they're watching me—I can feel it. I force myself to breathe normally and maintain my aloofness.

Any minute now...

I keep my gaze trained on the dying embers of daylight, the night sky on full display, while clouds allow glimpses of stars shimmering in greeting. I pretend not to feel the weight of their attention pressing against my skin. The silence stretches—uncomfortably so, wrapping around me in ribbons of anticipation.

A floorboard creaks behind me, but I don't react. The only movements are my twitching fingers that still grip the arms of the chair. A whisper of movement and the almost imperceptible brush of fabric are the only sounds they make. The air shifts once more—I know they're right behind me now. I can feel the heat radiating from them.

I part my lips, intending to greet them with a cool, unaffected tone. Before I can speak, a hand ghosts along the curve of my shoulder and grips me firmly by the throat.

A sharp breath escapes as I tilt my chin up to see three masked figures looming over me. "Wait," I say, my voice steady despite the rapid hammering of my pulse, which I know Red Mask can feel. "Before we play our game, I need to talk to you."

They remain silent, their presence loud enough. Orange

Mask tilts his head to the side—I take it as permission to continue. I force down a swallow as the hand still wrapped around my throat squeezes a little tighter before releasing me.

"I want my purse," I say, forcing my voice to remain even, "and everything in it. It's interesting that you call me the thief when you're the ones stealing things."

"We're not thieves—unlike some people," Orange Mask drawls. "Nope, all we did was pick up something we found lying around our home. How's that theft?"

"Because it's not yours!" I snarl, my façade cracking.

Blue Mask steps around my chair and leans against the window, shaking his head as he tsks several times, considering me. "Isn't it?"

"N—no," I choke, knowing the entire plan is about to crumble around me.

I yelp when the electric-blue glow of his mask suddenly appears mere inches from my face as he grips the arms of the chair, leaning into my space. "It belongs to us, because everything—and I do mean everything—" the tips of his fingers trail down the side of my face, "in this house belongs to us. The chair you sit in, the comforter you so diligently wrap around yourself, the slip of silk that skims your curves in the most delicious way..."

"But you took my clothes," I whisper as he fingers the thin strap.

"No one's forcing you to wear it. Consider it our charitable contribution." He pushes off the arms and goes back to lean against the window.

"I'd be..." my breaths come in gasps.

Oh, God. What if they take everything?

"Not that it matters." Orange Mask laughs, tossing that

insufferable knife in his hand. Not a second later I scream. There are only a handful of inches between his blade, buried in the chair, and my head. He leans in, wrapping his fingers around the handle as his voice turns low and dark. "We might not own you yet, but you will be ours." He yanks his blade free and steps back, tossing it again in his hand like he didn't just throw it at me.

"N—no, I can't." Tears stream down my face as my body reels from the very real fear of his knife.

"A bit too comfortable, don't you think, Celest?" My head jerks over to Red Mask, the sound of my name on his tongue is terrifying, yet somehow feels right.

I swallow hard, but before I can answer, he sighs, as if he regrets whatever he's going to say next."Guess it's our turn to get a bit more comfortable with you."

"What does that mean?" my voice so soft it's nearly impossible to hear.

"Run, Celest—run fast. We won't be giving you any warnings tonight." I stagger to my feet and fumble with the comforter, before I bolt through the doorway. Their laughter follows me, dark and terrifying, yet also—

What is wrong with me?

One of them threw a knife at me, for heaven's sake. My body flinched, I screamed in horror—these are all normal reactions. The same cannot be said about the darkness within me. Tilting its head to the side, curiosity piqued. Like a cat it stretches, the movements slow and languid, ready to come out and play.

I contemplate letting it take over, but fear holds me back. What if I can't get myself back? What if I fall too far into sin —unknowingly offering my soul to be devoured?

Letting go feels as terrifying as holding on.

What's the right thing to do?

I can't think about it right now—the game has begun.

I don't worry about what hallway I turn down, or what stairs I take—I'll never take the same path twice. The way the manor shifts no longer unsettles me; it's become an expectation over the last two nights. Even knowing the dangers, the consistency is somehow comforting.

I jump through a moving doorway as the wall slides past me and end up in the same library where I found myself that first night. Just like the first time, it takes my breath away, but still, there's no time to enjoy it. Confident footsteps echo down the hall—a sound I know is intentional, meant to heighten my fear.

It's working.

There's no time to hide, so I slip into the maze of towering shelves, crouching low, hidden from view. The sound of movement—methodical, slow—catches my attention from the far end of the library. I peek around the corner, catching a hint of crimson glow before jerking back, forcing myself to slow my breathing.

Looking once more, I clamp my lips together when I see how much closer he is. Keeping low, I inch toward the opposite end, ready to dart into the next aisle as soon as his red glow reaches the shelves. My bare feet make no sound as I slip into the next row, pressing my back against the worn wood, careful of creaking floorboards.

Thud.

A book falls to the ground in the row I just fled. I snap my head toward the sound, chest rising and falling in quick, shallow breaths. Then, like a predator toying with its prey, another book thuds—closer this time. I slink behind the next row, disappearing around the corner just in time.

Thud.

Thud.

Thud.

Books fall faster as his pace increases, forcing me to do the same. My legs start to shake—I won't be able to maintain this crouch for much longer. I slide between two more shelves just as the books stop. My heart is in my throat as I force myself to peek around the edge of the previous aisle.

He's not there.

Blood roars in my ears, and my breaths come in shallow bursts. I know, with a sick certainty, that when I peek around the next corner, he'll be waiting for me, a predator eager for the kill. The darkness inside me—quiet, hungry—purrs at the promise of being caught, as if craving the moment of no escape. I take a shaky breath, my mind screaming at me to resist, yet I can't help but look.

He's not there.

For some reason, that's even worse. I'm so on edge that every little sound makes me feel like I could jump out of my own skin. There's no way he's given up and left. No. He's here somewhere, and I can't stay in the same place for long. I turn toward the aisle I just checked—

A hard chest.

Strong hands.

The glow of red light floods my vision.

I barely have time to suck in a breath before fingers tangle in my hair, yanking me violently against him and letting the comforter fall. The scent of leather, mixed with something rich and intoxicating, invades my senses as his grip tightens, forcing my chin up.

"Game over, Celest." His voice, deep and laced with amusement, caresses my ear, sending a shudder through me.

"Time to claim my prize," he says as a hand travels down my back to grip my rear—hard. He lifts my leg against his hip at the same moment my back hits the shelves. I feel the fabric of his pants grind against my bare core, the friction ripping a shocked moan from me.

Oh, my God.

"Are you dripping for me, thief?" he growls out as he presses into me harder. "Your greedy little cunt's soaking— making a mess all over my pants."

My cheeks burn with embarrassment and I desperately try to look away, but he only grips my hair tighter.

"Ah, ah, ah... don't try to hide from me. Look at you— pupils blown wide, skin flushed red, and pretty little breathy moans—you're a work of art like this."

There's something rising inside me, unfamiliar and over-whelming, slipping beyond my control.

"Fuck, you're close aren't you? Well, we can't have that can we?" Abruptly, he pulls away and just before he fades into the shadows, he says, "It won't be long now, Celest." Leaving me panting against the bookshelf.

Oh God.

What just happened?

Why do I wish he'd come back?

Something inside me must be broken—that's the only explanation. I shouldn't want their hands on me.

I shouldn't. And yet—

No—Get it together, Celest. You still have two other masked demons to survive.

I could claim I was dreading the next two encounters. I could say their touch reminded me of Josiah's. I could say a lot of things.

They'd all be lies.

THE MANOR IS EERILY QUIET, THE USUAL CREAKS AND groans of its ever-shifting structure have been absent for the past half hour. The silence tells me everything I need to know:

Someone is hunting me.

I've been searching for a place to hide, but my nerves are frayed, and the idea of waiting for one of them to find me is too much. I've been quietly moving from room to room hoping to walk off some of this...whatever it is.

I thought the music room would win the award for creepiest place in the manor, but this one is worse. From the chair rail to ceiling, the room is filled with hundreds of portrait paintings.

That alone would make this room the winner, but that's not why I want to run screaming out of here.

It's their eyes.

They follow me.

For the first time since my... *stay* began, I wish the moon were hidden behind clouds. At least then, I'd be spared the sight of the portraits and their shifting eyes.

I don't mean they *appear* to move—no, they *literally* move. I watch as one portrait locks eyes with another before shifting its gaze back to me, communicating in some unspoken language. It's unsettling—unnatural, even—yet somehow, not unexpected.

Several of the portraits glance toward the oversized antique mirror hanging on the wall. It's the only other thing in the room, and I wouldn't be surprised if it's larger than the manor's front door. I know I shouldn't inspect the mirror, especially with how the ghostly portraits seem to be urging me toward it, but now I'm curious.

A trait—one of many—that Father hates.

The mirror is—

I whip my head around, my breath catching. I could have sworn I saw Blue Mask standing several feet behind me. It must be this room and its impossible portraits playing tricks on me. I glance back at the mirror, and my heart stops—Blue Mask is there again, only closer.

Only... he's not.

I inhale deeply and close my eyes. I should leave this room and never glance in that mirror again. Unfortunately, I've always been a curious girl. I turn back but keep my eyes down as I step closer.

Maybe there's a trick to it, and I just need to look closer. I lift my eyes, heart pounding, and try to scramble backward. Blue Mask hasn't moved any closer behind me—but now he's on the other side of the mirror.

I barely have time to scream before cold fingers close around my wrist, yanking me forward—through what should be solid glass.

Endless reflections stretch around me, distorting my sense of direction. Everything is bathed in a soft blue glow, yet he's nowhere in sight. I spin around, seeing my image thrown back at me from a thousand angles.

"Oh, no," I murmur, followed by a pained cry.

Distracted by the chaos of the mirrors, I didn't notice what was missing. When he grabbed my wrist and pulled, I must have dropped it.

"My comforter."

It's silly—I know it is—but tears threaten to fall anyway. I blink several times, inhaling deeply through my nose. It's not lost forever—I'll just find the room of portraits again. Of all the things to cry over, I never thought a blanket would be one of them.

My reflection shifts with every hesitant step I take. The disjointed walls create sharp turns and dead ends, causing me to collide with them more than once. I swallow hard and wrap my arms around myself, moving cautiously forward. My mirrored movements follow—

Smack.

I step back, my heart pounding faster with each wrong turn. I try to control my breathing, but panic twists in my chest, making it harder to calm myself. What if I never find my way out? What if the last thing I see is my own reflection dying?

I move faster, then turn a corner—

Smack.

I collide with another mirror, my nose nearly smashing against my reflection—when something catches my attention.

It's him.

He watches me from a distance, never moving. His electric-blue mask glows brightly in the corner of every mirror. I jerk away, spin in the opposite direction, and slam my hands against the glass as I hit another dead end. I glance at the corner of the mirror, where I know I'll find him—he's moved.

Closer.

My breath catches in my throat. I dart down another path, ignoring how each wrong turn brings him closer to me. My vision blurs with my frantic movements.

Smack.

I slam into another mirror.

He's there—

Closer.

I backpedal until my spine presses against cold glass, my pulse thrumming wildly in my throat. I let out a shaky exhale, pressing a hand to my forehead.

I have to calm down.

I have to—

I scream.

Arms wrap around me from behind as a firm body pins me against the mirror. A hand slides up my throat, forcing my head back against his shoulder. The other snakes around my waist, locking me against him.

"Finders, keepers." His voice is a breath against my ear, low and smooth. "Keep your eyes on our reflection."

His hand slides across my body, the other gliding down my sternum, palming my breast. I inhale sharply as he catches my nipple over the silky fabric, his fingers teasing. A jolt of heat shoots between my legs. I press my thighs together, searching for relief but find none.

His hands drag in opposite directions, switching places to give my other breast the same treatment. He slides the straps from my shoulders, baring my chest to the cool air. I don't have time for embarrassment; the moment his hand grazes my nipples I cry out in surprised pleasure.

I never knew touch could feel like this.

"I can't wait to have my mouth all over these." I'm too lost in the sensation to process his words. My head tips against his shoulder, eyes fluttering shut—until a sharp pinch snaps them open. "Eyes open, Celest."

I don't look away again.

"Oh, princess," he murmurs, ghosting a hand over my core, causing me to whimper in frustration. "What sweet sounds you make. I can't wait to hear the way you scream impaled on my cock." One hand glides up my neck, the other slides down between my thighs, so close to where I need it most.

"Fuck," he groans, pulling his hand away and holding it up, moisture glistens in the neon glow. "Look how your pussy begs to be fucked. Don't worry, princess, I'll own that cunt soon enough." He drops his hands and vanishes into the shadows. The only light left is the illuminated doorway to my left.

With shaking hands, I fix my straps. When his hands were on me, it was like being sucked into a bubble where nothing else existed. Now that the bubble has popped, the intensity of his touch overwhelms me.

I need my comforter and a small, enclosed space to decompress. I just need a moment—preferably one without Orange Mask finding me.

Stepping into a sitting room, I groan. Finding the portrait room again will be a night—

I freeze. Draped over the back of a chair is my comforter. This doesn't make sense. How did it get here? Did one of them leave it for me?

Don't be silly, Celest.

But what if—

Shaking off my thoughts, I wrap the comforter around me like a warm hug, the relief immediate. I feel ridiculous— being so attached to a blanket—but right now, I don't care. I clutch it tightly and move toward the hallway.

My steps are silent; the only sound is the faint whisper of the comforter brushing against the floor. I move quickly, searching for a small, enclosed space. Somewhere dark that offers a moment of reprieve from the overwhelming sensation still coursing through my veins.

I search every shadow, expecting them to be there watching and waiting. My already frayed nerves prepare to be taken at any moment. Each safe turn only feeds the feeling that I'm running straight toward my impending doom.

I'm stranded in my own skin, burning with a need I don't understand, while memories of rough hands, teasing touches, and vulgar words leave me breathless. It's too much. I need to disappear, to fold myself away before I unravel completely.

The first narrow door I try leads to a linen closet, but the shelves leave no room to squeeze in. A few doors later, I find exactly what I need—a small coat closet, just big enough to sit in.

I slip inside, drawn to its promise of solitude. Pressing my back against the cool wood, I pull the comforter over my legs. My breath comes in shallow bursts, but the tightness in my chest begins to fade. This is the only darkness I feel I can trust. There's only one door, and no way to sneak it open without me noticing. I take my first deep breath of the night, and feel safe enough to sort through the riot of emotions bombarding me.

They're unraveling me, piece by broken piece, pushing and pulling, keeping me teetering on the edge of a steep cliff —the unknown waiting at the bottom.

I hate it.

Lie.

There are two things I know for certain: my peaceful moment is running out of time, and he's coming for me.

Orange Mask.

I lean my head back against the wall and close my eyes with a sigh. Out of the three, he frightens me the most. His actions seem more impulsive, more wild, and I don't know if I can handle playing his game right now. I feel fragile, and I don't trust him not to break me.

"I'm surprised you picked something as obvious as a closet, Celest." It's as if I've conjured him out of thin air.

"How did you get in here?" I ask, my voice thin, betraying just how breakable I am right now. It takes me a second to realize there's no orange glow filling what was once my dark sanctuary. "And where's your mask?"

"I left it behind. It didn't seem necessary. It's not like you can see me." He sounds... different. Relaxed instead of the chaotic energy I've come to expect.

"Oh."

"Come now Celest. Up you go," he says cheerfully. I feel him moving before his touch. His hands feel around until they find mine, hidden beneath the comforter. I don't resist when he pulls me to my feet; I'm too stunned by his gentleness.

His fingers trace the contours of my face, and I ache to do the same. As if sensing the need, he brings my hands to his bare skin.

My fingers drift over his brow, tracing the slope of his nose. His lips are full—and smirking. Of course they are. As I run my fingers down his sharp jaw, the roughness of his stubble tells me he must shave every day.

I'm not sure if I'm allowed to touch his neck, but I do it anyway. He grabs my wrists, and for a brief moment, I think I've pushed too far—until he places my arms over his shoulders. He cups my face, his touch soft, as if he's about to—

His lips press to mine, slow and deliberate. It takes far too long for my brain to catch up. When it does, my lips part as I gasp in surprise. His tongue invades my mouth the moment the opportunity presents itself.

I've never been kissed like this. It's as though he's consuming me as quickly as he's giving himself. All I can do is hold on and let him take the lead.

His hands slide from my face, trailing down to the back of my thighs before lifting me. Wrapping my legs around him feels natural as he presses me against the wall, the position bringing my core firmly against him.

It's instinctual—I think—to roll my hips against him. We groan against each other's mouths, the sound swallowed between us.

I do it again.

"Oh, sweetheart, you're killin' me," he groans, his voice thick and rough. He dives back into my mouth, his hands gripping my rear to support my weight. The moniker he gives me is unexpected, clashing with the image I'd constructed of him. He feels like two people sharing one body.

A hard body.

I roll against him several more times, tension coiling

inside me, rising with each movement. I pant against his mouth, while he devours the sounds of my pleasure.

Just as I'm close to finding out what happens when I finally tip over the edge, he gently lowers me to the ground while I whimper my complaints.

He presses his forehead to mine and breathes, giving us a moment to catch our breaths. "I'm sorry, sweetheart. Not just yet." I feel him step away, and I know he's gone.

Except—the door never opened.

He vanished.

I touch my lips, slightly swollen, still tingling from his kiss.

I wish he had stayed.

Oh, God.

Something is seriously wrong with me. There must be. Maybe the first thing I'll do once I get out of here is go to the hospital.

Yes. That's what I'll do.

Inside me, the once shapeless darkness begins to take form, morphing into the silhouette of a woman. She watches me, tilting her head the same way Orange Mask does. It feels like she knows something I don't—which is unsettling. She throws her head back, laughing manically, the sound a chilling, terrifying promise.

But of what?

10

Wrapped in my comforter at the kitchen counter, I scoop another bite of peanut butter onto a stale cracker from the nearly empty jar. It's a poor excuse for a meal, but it's better than nothing. The rough texture clings to the roof of my mouth, forcing me to scrape my tongue against it before I can swallow.

I clutch the comforter tighter. I hate how much I need it, but after the last couple of nights, I can't let it go. It's pathetic—how I panicked when I thought I'd lost it.

I know I dropped it in the room portraits.

I *know* I did.

And yet, somehow, it ended up on that chair, right outside the exit of the hall of mirrors. One of them must have put it there. It has to be. Right?

But why?

I force another bite, my teeth grinding against the stale cracker. The dryness sticks to my tongue, but I barely notice.

My skin prickles, as though I'm still being watched. The game is over. So why do I feel like it's not?

Because it's not—not really.

It feels like it's only paused till dusk.

Not long after Orange Mask disappeared from the closet, I slid back to the floor, exhaustion dragging at my limbs. Sleep should've come easily.

It didn't.

My body remained on edge, hyper-aware of every shift in the dark. Of the air against my skin. Of sensations I told myself weren't real.

After waking in the cramped space, I wandered for what felt like an eternity before stumbling upon a bathroom. The hallways blurred together, each turn leading me nowhere. Every door I opened mocked me—empty rooms, locked spaces—anything but what I needed.

By the time I found what I was looking for, frustration gnawed at my patience, and my bladder threatened to burst. I could swear someone—or something—had been toying with me.

With my stomach barely full, I twist the lid back on and stare at the nearly empty jar. Two days—maybe less—if I ration. If I stretch it. But I know better. Hunger doesn't listen to reason. And soon, I'll have nothing left.

With a deep sigh, my body still thrumming from last night's game, another realization settles over me.

I've been wandering this house day and night, searching every room, yet—there's no sign of them actually living here. The kitchen is practically abandoned. The fridge holds nothing edible; the pantry, just forgotten remnants. No dishes in the sink. No lingering scent of food. The hallways are eerily pristine—no clutter, no shoes by the door, no clothes draped over furniture.

Nothing.

Even their presence feels transient, as if they exist only in the shadows, emerging solely to play their games. I've seen them, touched them, felt them against me—but nothing in this house proves they truly live here. It's as if they live outside the house.

Or beneath it.

The thought chills me. What if there's some kind of crypt under this twisted house?

They only come out at night.

They leave no trace of themselves during the day.

The house shifts—bending around them like something alive.

There have been too many unexplainable moments, too many ghostly touches that have me questioning my sanity. It unsettles me in a way I can't explain, like they materialize only when they want to be seen, dissolving just as easily.

They aren't human.

They can't be.

At least—not normal ones.

The idea makes my heart stutter, a sudden, uneasy flutter in my chest. I've had the thought before, but I've never allowed myself to truly consider it. I mean, that's crazy, right?

As soon as the thought begins to solidify, a darker one creeps in.

What if I'm crazy?

What if none of this is real?

What if I never actually left?

What if I'm still trapped in Josiah's grip, rotting away in

some locked room, my mind desperately clawing for an escape that doesn't exist?

My breathing grows erratic, matching the frantic surge of panic. I grip the counter, fighting to hold myself together.

It would make sense, wouldn't it? None of this should be possible—the shifting hallways, the way they move unseen, the way my body responds to their touch—as if it belongs to them.

Maybe I made all of this up. Maybe I fractured somewhere along the way, and this is just an elaborate hallucination—a final, desperate attempt to stay sane.

I squeeze my eyes shut and inhale slowly, forcing my body to obey.

No.

That can't be right.

How could my mind conjure something like this?

I've never seen men or masks like them, and I've certainly never been touched this way. I've never lived in a house like this—I've never even heard of a house that moves like this one.

I don't think I've ever seen anything like it, not even in the few stolen moments I spent watching television.

If this were a delusion, wouldn't I imagine something familiar? Something safe?

As impossible as it seems, this place—and the men who apparently reside here—must be real. That leaves me with only one logical conclusion:

I don't know what they are, but there's no way they're human.

Even so, the thought of seeing them again tonight, at

dusk, sends a thrill of anticipation through me. Human or not, my body doesn't seem to take issue with it.

Which isn't particularly comforting.

I set the jar down with a soft clatter, my pulse steadying as determination takes hold. They *have* to be here somewhere.

And I'm going to find them.

With my hunger barely satiated, I move through the halls, determined to find something—*anything*—that could explain all of this. I push open doors at random, peering inside darkened rooms with heavy drapes and dust-covered furniture.

No signs of life.

No sign of them.

Then, I find it.

The library.

The one room with the potential to completely derail my plans.

I was never allowed to read anything that wasn't pre-approved by my father or Josiah, but even with my limited options, I've always loved to read. Books were a safe place. I could lose myself in another world, escape for a few hours— live someone else's life, even if only temporarily.

This is the first time I've found the library during the day. The two other times I've been here, I was too focused on running to notice much more than the basics. I could still make out the towering shelves, the heavy stillness in the air, and—of course—the scent of books filling the room. But now, bathed in the soft afternoon light, it's breathtaking.

The ceiling stretches impossibly high, lined with the intricate molding seen throughout the manor. Rows upon rows of bookshelves dominate the space, filled with a mix of new and ancient volumes. A massive fireplace, cold and lifeless, stands at the far end. Above it, a large oil painting stares down at me.

It's a man, frozen in time from another era entirely, his sharp gaze assessing all those that dare stand beneath him. I stare at his eyes for a few minutes as I move around, then sigh in relief when they remain lifeless. After last night's discovery, I never want to see another painted portrait again.

I shake the thought away, letting my eyes roam until they land on a bookstand near the center of the room. It's grander than the others, almost as if begging to be noticed. I'm surprised I never ran into it while rushing out of here in the dark. My fingers brush the cracked leather of the old book, and my pulse quickens as I read the faded title.

The Blackthorn Estate: A History

I scan the pages, my breath catching as I take in the handwritten words and sit on the couch facing the fireplace. The manor was built by a man named Ambrose Blackthorn. I glance above the mantle at the painting and wonder if that's him. He looks aristocratic enough.

His earliest entries seem fairly normal—if not slightly boring. He mentions the progress of the manor and some issues with the land. It's not until several entries later that things begin to take a darker turn. There's mention of workers going missing on days they stayed past dusk—many refused to remain once the sun began to set after that.

After several more entries, he notes the deaths of multiple men after a wall caved in, crushing them all. No one had ever built a house like this before, with so many moving pieces. He even writes that sacrifices must be made to achieve greatness. I look back up at the man above the fireplace, his unblinking gaze seeming to linger on me.

"I think you might've gotten along with Josiah," I say with obvious disdain as I squint at him judgmentally. I glance out the window. The sun is still high in the sky—plenty of time.

As I read on, his writing takes a darker turn. His paranoia deepens, and his egotism grows with each passing entry. He reports strange occurrences—flickering lights in places they shouldn't be. He even mentions having dreams that aren't his, dreams that seem to belong to someone else.

Several entries later, his tone shifts again. He boasts about entertaining esteemed men—those like him, who don't fear the unseen. Instead, they wish to control it, using ancient rites from forgotten times. Blood rituals that promise immortality —if one is willing to give up the sun.

Well that doesn't sound very safe—or sane.

Although...

Something like that might make you not quite human anymore.

Oh, God.

What if the men are Ambrose and his friends? That's impossible—right? I exhale sharply, my heart hammering against my ribs.

It's absurd—ridiculous.

And yet...

I think of the silent way they move—how they appear and disappear at will. I've never seen them in daylight, and the house seems to answer to them, silent at night only at their behest.

I flip ahead until something catches my eye—the handwriting has changed. Someone named Elias Blackthorn took possession of the manor after his grandfather, Ambrose, disappeared. He claims the official story is that Ambrose got lost somewhere in the woods and perished while trying to find his way back. But Elias doesn't seem to find that plausible.

Much like his grandfather, Elias's interests are far from ordinary. He's a historian, captivated by forbidden knowledge—whatever that means. Apparently there was a rumor of a room where his grandfather hid manuscripts and artifacts so powerful that even Ambrose feared them. It was during his search for this hidden room that the handwriting changed again.

Victor Blackthorn feared the manor. He writes about sealing off entire wings and never hosting guests. His staff left before nightfall every day. Several pages are covered with old newspaper clippings about the estate—some of which age has made it difficult to read.

1867 – Whispers in the Walls

BLACKTHORN ESTATE: A HOME... OR A PRISON?
Boston Daily Journal

Rumors are beginning to spread that the grand Blackthorn estate, once the pride of its eccentric owner, has turned into something of a fortress. Local villagers report that no one has entered or left the manor in months, with deliveries being left at the gates and taken only under the cover of night. Some claim to hear voices and music drifting from the empty halls, though no guests have been seen arriving.

1879 – The Vanishing Servants

WHERE HAVE THEY GONE? STAFF CONTINUES TO DISAPPEAR FROM BLACKTHORN ESTATE.

New England Chronicle

At least six domestic servants employed at Blackthorn Manor have seemingly vanished in the past two years, their disappearances unexplained. Families of the missing claim their loved ones mentioned 'strange happenings' in the house before they were never seen again. Elias Blackthorn, current master of the estate, refuses to address the claims, stating only that 'the house is not for the weak-hearted.'

1902 – A House Abandoned, a Mystery Deepens

BLACKTHORN MANOR LEFT TO ROT – CURSED OR SIMPLY FORGOTTEN?

New York Herald

Victor Blackthorn, the reluctant new owner of Blackthorn Manor, has declared the estate uninhabitable and shut its doors indefinitely. He has refused to set foot inside, instead managing the property from a distant city. The house, once a marvel of gothic architecture, now stands as an eerie monument to a family consumed by secrecy. Some claim shadows move within when no one is inside, and that on quiet nights, a soft whispering can be heard from the windows.

I turn the page, my breath catching as I scan the final lines of Victor's last entry:

Some say they are monsters. Some say they are the damned. But one thing remains constant—when the sun falls beyond the horizon, the house no longer belongs to the living.

VOICES DRIFT THROUGH MY SUBCONSCIOUS—LOW AND velvety—a half-heard melody that tugs me toward consciousness. I'm warm, cocooned in my comforter—reluctant to wake. Until the uncomfortable press of my cheek against the book's worn pages pulls me from sleep.

"Do we let her sleep a little longer?"

"Or maybe we wake her with a story of our own—something like Goldilocks and the Three Bears," another voice suggests, amusement ringing in every word.

Before the third can weigh in, there's a slight shift in the air, and I feel a presence leaning in closer. "She's awake," he murmurs.

My lashes flutter open.

For a moment, I forget where I am. The towering shelves of the library stretch into darkness; the sun must've gone down a while ago. Their glowing masks are the only source of light. Not that I need it; I can feel them—three figures standing just beyond the periphery of my vision, waiting.

I should feel fear.

Their presence should freeze my veins, send my pulse thrumming in my ears.

Instead, the sight of the masked men surrounding me

feels almost normal. I stretch, arms lifting above my head, spine arching as I let out a small sigh. I carefully close the book and rise to place it back on its pedestal, the cold air making me instantly regret leaving my comforter on the couch.

"Have any of you read this?" I ask as I turn toward them. I sigh when they don't answer, wondering why I expected them to. A long silence stretches before, as if reaching an unspoken agreement, they step closer.

"It's past dusk," Orange Mask says, his voice low, the hint of his constant smirk creeping through. "You know what that means."

I take a page from their book and stay silent. Instead, I observe them. They don't move, and I can barely see the rise and fall of their breaths. It's unnatural. The silence stretches beyond comfort. I tilt my head, considering my next words.

"I've been thinking," I say, walking back to the couch and sinking into it, wrapping myself in my warm comforter. "It's not entirely fair that y'all know my name, and I don't get to know yours."

Orange Mask chuckles, slow and mocking. "Fair?" he echoes. "Do you need to be reminded where you are, little thief?"

Blue Mask joins in. "You think you get to make requests?"

I square my shoulders, emboldened by the fact that they haven't shut me down completely. "Just a small one. A game. I thought you liked those."

That gets their attention.

A pause stretches between us, thick with something like consideration. Then Red Mask says, "Go on."

I turn to face them fully. "Tonight, don't turn on your masks. If I can guess who's who, you'll tell me your name."

"And if you guess wrong?"

I hesitate for only a second. Of course, they'd want something in return. "Then you get to..." I pause before blurting the first thing that comes to mind. "Make a request—something I have to obey."

"You're confident," Blue Mask muses after a beat of silence, interest evident in his tone.

I shrug. "I know you better than you think."

"Is that so?" Orange Mask's words, as usual, drip with amusement. I nod, careful not to reveal how I tell them apart. They exchange glances before Red Mask delivers the verdict.

"We accept."

A thrill rushes through me. This is the first time we've started a game where I feel like I have the upper hand. Even this small control is intoxicating.

I push to my feet and reach for my comforter, shaking it out to wrap it around myself more easily. I'm almost ready to head out to the hall, but something flutters to the ground.

A single sheet of aged newspaper.

I frown, kneeling to pick it up. It must have slipped from the book, likely when I used it as a pillow. I move to tuck it back where it belongs, but my eyes catch on the bold headline.

951 – The End of the Blackthorn Line?

MALCOLM BLACKTHORN FOUND DEAD IN
GREAT HALL
— New York Times

Malcolm Blackthorn was discovered lifeless at the foot of the grand staircase in Blackthorn Manor. His body was found in a state of distress, his nails bloodied as though he had tried to claw at the very walls around him. Officials list the cause as cardiac arrest, though local whispers tell another story—of shadows that move when no one is looking and whispers that beckon from the dark.

I stare at the words, my stomach twisting as I stare up at them.

Shadows that move.

Whispers that beckon.

A chill slides down my spine, as if something unseen trails icy fingers along my skin. I'd been thinking they were something... other, but it's at this moment I actually believe it. They emerge only at night, slipping through shadows, whispering things I never imagined I'd want to hear.

The things I've seen—the things I've felt—should be enough to convince me. I guess there's something about knowing others have seen the same things I have that makes me trust my mind a bit more. I swallow hard, my mouth suddenly dry.

I draw a slow breath that does nothing to steady me and raise my gaze, finding them watching me.

Waiting.

"Run," Red Mask commands, his voice smooth and deliberate, just before they turn off the lights of their masks, plunging me into darkness. I blink rapidly, my eyes struggling to adjust to the sudden blackness. Panic surges, swallowing the thrill I'd felt earlier, replacing it with something cold and sharp.

Something deadly.

My mind conjures Malcolm Blackthorn's lifeless body sprawled in the great hall, twisted in terror. That image warps, and suddenly, it's my own body lying there instead.

My mind screams at me to move.

So I do.

I run.

11

I sit on the edge of the bed, the comforter—as always—wrapped tightly around me, staring at the dark opening in the wall. It hadn't been there when I disappeared into the bathroom not more than thirty minutes ago. The wall slid away to reveal the opening the moment the sun began its slow descent—silent and waiting.

They're offering me a choice. Or at least, that's what they want me to think.

When I finally woke a couple of hours ago, the sun had already begun its descent toward the horizon. I stretched, and the moment I realized where I was, I jumped out of bed, desperate to brush my teeth and shower. I'd been making do the best I could with whatever I could find since leaving this room three nights ago.

The thought of taking a long, hot shower and scrubbing my body after thoroughly brushing my teeth—multiple times —made me giddy. While I wished for real clothes, I couldn't deny the relief of finding a new negligee draped over the end of the bed. My lips pursed as I took in the black, nearly sheer fabric. As if being half-naked wasn't bad enough, this one almost seemed pointless to wear. Yet, I wore it. It was better to feel clothed than not at all.

It wasn't until I was drying my hair with a towel that I happened to glance toward the dresser. There, on top, sat something unexpected—my purse.

I dropped the towel and rushed to clutch it with trembling fingers, my heart pounding as I yanked open the zipper. Everything was there—my phone, my wallet, my charger, and the envelope that held all the documents for my new life. I opened it and shuffled through each of the papers, checking to make sure it was all as it should be. Which it was.

They'd returned it all.

Just as I'd asked.

Dusk came and went without any sign of them—only the opening in the wall. They hadn't given me any specific instructions. I'd thought for sure they would show when I made no move to enter the secret entrance.

They didn't.

That was at least an hour ago. I stare at the hidden doorway, thinking. It feels as though they are giving me a choice. I can take my things and leave, or I can step into the dark and continue our game. The darkness within me throws her hands up in annoyance. She's known all along. The moment the opening appeared, she was waiting—impatient, eager. Whispering for me to go.

It doesn't feel like a decision I should make lightly, even if it should be an easy one. Not that I'm certain I *could* leave—

I'm not. This is an illusion of control. We all know it. But I let myself believe the lie anyway.

I bite at my bottom lip and twist a corner of the comforter over and over as the decision settles over me. If I'm being honest, it's the choice I knew I was going to make the entire time. The darkness rolls her eyes, as if to say, *I told you so.*

Letting the comforter fall from my shoulders, I cross the room with slow, measured steps. I hesitate. If I walked away now, would they stop me? Something tells me they wouldn't, but the truth is...

I don't want to leave.

The moment I cross the threshold, the entrance behind me vanishes with a quiet click. I whirl around, pressing my hands against the wall, searching for the seam where the open passage had just been. There's nothing—no edges, no latch, no way back.

I step forward, peering into the narrow passage hidden between the walls. Dim light offers barely enough visibility, while the walls close in, swallowing the space around me. I can't stretch my arms without touching the sides. The air is thick—stale, as if undisturbed for decades. It feels like I'm being buried alive, the weight of dust and time pressing in from all sides.

Maybe decades.

My bare feet move silently over the rough wooden floor, each step an exercise in caution. I refuse to think about what might be crawling in a space like this. I exhale sharply, forcing myself to keep walking—my pulse gradually steadying as I take slow, deliberate steps through the dark corridor.

The walls are rough and unyielding beneath my fingertips as I trail them lightly over the uneven surface. There are no doors or windows, only left and right turns that wind me further into its depths.

It's a maze.

And I am well and truly lost.

I've already doubled back more times than I can count, each turn leading to another dead end. Every time I retrace my steps, I only become more disoriented. The lights flicker weakly above, from naked bulbs hanging in irregular intervals, as if they, too, struggle to find their way through this labyrinth.

I pause at an intersection, trying to ignore the slow creep of unease curling up my spine.

Which way? Left again? Or had I gone right last time?

I bite my lip, forcing myself to focus on the problem at hand, as moments from last night invade my mind. The blindfold had been tight—stealing my sight but heightening everything else. I gave them my trust as their hands, rough and teasing, mapped the shape of my body. Their touches were possessive, claiming every inch of me.

Soft lips caressed my skin, sending warmth pooling deep in my belly as sharp teeth nipped at the tender flesh of my thighs. Tension coiled inside me, winding tighter and tighter —only to be abandoned, untouched. The frustration was maddening—the tension built with no release, leaving nothing but the ghost of their lingering touches beneath my skin.

Just as I'd been on the verge of breaking, they stopped— covering me in my comforter, whispering low, indecipherable words before leaving me.

Alone.

Lost in these hidden halls, that memory feels like it

belongs to someone else. I press forward, sighing as I take another turn—only to be met with yet another solid wall.

Dead end. Again.

My heart pounds in my ears as I turn back. I need to keep track of where I've been, but everything looks the same: the rough wood, the dim lighting, the thick, musty air. Every corridor stretches endlessly ahead—until, abruptly, it doesn't.

A sharp exhale slips from my lips, hot with irritation. I press my forehead against the cool wall for a moment, grounding myself. This isn't like the punishments in Josiah's cellar. There's no chain around my ankle, no locked door sealing me in. I'm not seventeen anymore—starving, afraid, waiting for footsteps on the stairs.

I have control now.

I push away from the wall and pivot, retracing my steps and committing each turn to memory. If there's a way in, there's a way out. I just have to find it. There's always a way forward.

Always.

A flicker of light ahead snaps me back to the present. A faint red glow emanates from around the next turn. My stomach clenches, and I push forward—following it. Following him.

Beckett.

Last night, the moment I was shoved against the wall, I knew. His hand wrapped around my throat—firm, but not enough to choke. "Red," I whispered, without hesitation.

His fingers tightened slightly, as he swore under his breath. Then he leaned in, warm against my ear.

"Beckett." Then he was gone, slipping into the dark as if he'd never been there at all.

The hallway is empty. But I'm not alone. The sound of construction echoes through the space—the rhythmic pounding of a hammer against stone.

At first, I think it's part of their game. That they're leading me somewhere—or just trying to frighten me, as usual. That is, until I see him.

A figure lingers at the edge of the dim light, hammering at the wall with slow, mechanical precision. His head turns slowly, his gaze locking onto mine—I suck in a sharp breath.

Oh, God.

The left side of his body is crushed inward—bone and flesh collapsed like rotting fruit. He lifts the hammer again, but this time, it's aimed directly at me. I scream and stumble backward, my feet catching on the uneven floor.

I land hard on my rear, the cold air pressing against my skin, and scramble away on desperate hands and feet. My pulse races, a frantic rhythm in my ears as I push myself up and bolt, fear gnawing at my heels.

I don't know how long I stumble blindly through the maze before I see another flicker of light—orange this time. Relief rushes through me as I follow it—follow him, last night's final guess.

"I know this one will be particularly difficult for you," he'd said, arms crossed in amusement as he leaned against a table.

I smiled. "Orange."

"Quinton," he murmured. "But no one calls me that."

Tilting my head, I asked, "Oh? What do they call you, then?"

"The greatest, perfect, gorgeous... the list goes on—oh, you mean my name?" He chuckled softly before stepping behind me, his voice low against my ear.

"Quinn."

Then the blindfold slipped over my eyes, his voice soft but firm. "Don't take it off, Celest, or you'll make Beckett cranky."

I turn another corner, expecting him to be there, but—yet again—nothing. The orange glow is gone, and I'm starting to wonder if it was ever there to begin with.

Instead, there's only the sound of footsteps. My pulse spikes. It could be one of them—but something tells me it isn't. I hesitate, lick my lips, then whisper, "Quinn?"

No answer.

Just the footsteps—their rhythm unchanging, growing closer with every beat. My breath catches in my throat as I inch forward, heart hammering violently against my ribs. I try to convince myself it's one of them, my mind screaming for it to be, desperate for the familiarity. But deep down, I know...

It's not them.

Another ghostly figure—twisted and grotesque, its form hunched and unnatural—lurches toward me. My breath stalls in my throat, panic squeezing my lungs as my mind races, flashing to the article I read earlier.

No.

Impossible.

It can't be.

Malcolm Blackthorn.

They'd found his body at the foot of the grand staircase, his nails bloodied and broken, as though he'd tried to claw his way out of something with his bare hands.

The figure's bloodied fingers twitch—reaching for me.

I freeze, paralyzed by fear, as it inches closer, its presence a cold suffocating weight. Just as its fingers graze my arm, I snap back to myself and scream, heart pounding as I tear off in the opposite direction.

I have no idea where I'm going.

I don't care.

As long as it's away from *that*.

I can't breathe.

My legs move, but they don't feel like my own.

I stumble.

Trip.

I can't…

Each step a scramble.

…breathe.

My chest burns.

Shallow gasps, too fast, too ragged.

The walls close in.

Then, finally—finally—I see it.

Blue.

He'd been the first one to find me last night. His arms wrapped around me from behind and said, "Well, little thief, who am I then?" I didn't need to think about it, I'd known the second I heard his voice.

"Blue."

"I guess you do know us better than we thought," he said laughing.

"Are you going to give me my prize?"

"Greedy little thing, aren't you?" He laughed again, the sound making me smile. "Whitmore, but anyone who matters calls me Whit." It was a relief to learn all of their names and know for certain that none of them were Ambrose. The moment I turned around to speak to him, he was gone.

His faint, electric glow appears in the distance. I run

toward it, drawn to him like a lifeline, desperate to see the face of his neon mask.

"Whit!" My voice cracks. "Please… h—he's following me!" Just as I reach the end of the hall, the blue light vanishes.

Nothing.

There's no one there.

I spin in circles—disoriented, frantic. I wonder if it hadn't been the guys who opened the secret passage in my room after all. Perhaps the ghosts of this house used it to lure me to my death.

Would they search for me, or would they forget about me? Maybe they'd think I took my things and left.

More footsteps, growing closer. More running in a directionless path, and more wrong turns.

There! An opening—a doorway into the unknown, into darkness.

I throw myself through it, desperate for escape. Hoping and praying that another ghostly figure isn't waiting for me beyond it.

The second I'm through, I yelp as something slams shut behind me, and I plunge into pitch black. There's no light, no sound—nothing but my own frantic breathing.

My skin grows damp with cold sweat as I press my shaking hands against the walls, frantically searching for a way to open the door again.

A way out.

I need a way out.

There must be…

Oh, God.

I can't breathe.

… a way out.

There's nothing.

I'm trapped.

The darkness within me jumps, clapping with excitement while terror grips me. I find it impossible to trust her. She clearly knows something I don't. What still remains to be seen.

But I think she's been waiting for this moment all along.

12

Fear—it wraps around my throat, feeding the panic clawing at my ribs. Every gasp of breath, uneven and shallow, is a desperate plea for air. And the silence…it feels eternal.

I'm alone.

Or I thought I was.

Until the first glow flickers to life.

Red.

Then blue.

Then, finally, orange.

Their presence ignites the space, halos of neon light carving out the shapes that form their exaggerated expressions. They sit sprawled in ornate chairs—thrones, really—without a care in the world. The sight of them makes it easier to breathe, which can't possibly be the appropriate response.

They look like kings, lording over the subjects of their court. A lethal grace radiates from the edges of their posture. Their presence hums with restrained violence, a coiled energy just beneath the surface—predators who know exactly when to strike.

I lean against the wall in relief and close my eyes, trying to slow my breathing. I need to tell them about the ghosts. Have they seen them? They must've seen—

"Well, look who finally decided to join us. You've kept us waiting, Celest." Beckett's sharp voice slices through my thoughts. He leans forward, forearms resting on his thighs, eyes locked on me. "Now, get on your hands and knees—and crawl to me."

I freeze.

My mouth opens, but nothing more than a squeak escapes. At first, I think I must've misheard him.

Crawl?

The command slithers through me, a strange and unwelcome heat curling in my belly before I shove it down with indignation. He can't be serious.

"I—wait—but there's—" I stammer, my voice shaking under the weight of everything I just saw. "You don't understand—I—there are ghosts out there." The words tumble from my lips, frantic and raw, faster than I can filter them. "I saw them. They—they were following me. One even raised a hammer at me!"

Whit tips his head, the blue glow of his mask catching the light from the others. I can't see his expression—but I don't need to. I can hear the smirk in his voice. "Oh, princess, does it look like we give a fuck about some ghosts you think you saw?"

Do they think I'm making this up? Frustration flares, burning through my fear. "I did see them! They chased me through—"

Thunk.

A blade buries itself in the wooden wall beside me. I jerk, a yelp escaping before I can choke it back. My heart slams against my ribs as my gaze snaps to the knife lodged just inches from my head. I cross my arms and hug myself, regretting leaving my comforter behind. I thought after last night I wouldn't need it anymore.

Apparently I was wrong.

Quinn hums, the sound light and playful, mocking my fear. "Beckett gave you an order. Why aren't you crawling?" He tosses another knife in the air, catching it as he watches me, the blade glinting as it spins.

My breath shakes out. "I—I just—" I swallow, trying to make sense of the moment, trying to bridge the surreal horror of the ghosts with the threat humming in the air around them. My mind can't decide what the bigger danger is—them or the ghosts. Not that I can go back into the hall either way.

Thunk.

This one grazes so close that I feel it move my hair—the violent thud of it burying into the wall echoes in my skull.

I cry out, my arms snapping up in surrender. "Okay! Okay!" I watch as Quinn pulls out another knife, casually tossing this one as well. "Please, Quinn—please, don't," I plead.

Silence stretches a second too long before Beckett exhales slowly, like he's already weary of my defiance. "Then, crawl."

I hesitate for only a breath longer before lowering myself to my hands and knees, my palms pressing against the cold floor. Humiliation burns my skin as I start forward, moving stiffly, mechanically—the space between us shrinking with each inch I close.

"Slower," Beckett growls.

I whimper, forcing myself to obey, each movement making my pulse thunder in my ears. By the time I reach him, my body is trembling, but I don't know if it's from fear, exhaustion, or something else I refuse to name.

Beckett leans forward, reaching out, and his fingers slip into my hair. He strokes gently, almost affectionately, before gripping my strands and tilting my head back to look at him. "Good girl."

The darkness inside me preens from his praise. She wants to do whatever it takes to hear it again.

"You see, Celest, we think we've made you wait long enough. However, to get what you so desperately want from us, you're going to have to earn it. Do you understand?" Beckett's other hand skims the side of my face before gripping my throat. I can't find my voice to respond, so I shake my head.

He stands up, pulling my hair to get me to sit up on my knees before he unbuckles his belt and undoes his pants. "Reach in and pull my cock out." I hesitate, glancing up at his glowing red face.

"Do as you're told, Celest." With trembling hands, I obey, and the darkness purrs with satisfaction as he praises me again. "Good girl, now open your mouth and stick out your tongue—that's it."

I gag the moment he hits the back of my throat. He uses the grip in my hair to hold me in place as he thrusts in and out of my mouth. I gasp for air each time he pulls completely out.

"Now, swallow my cock down like the good little slut you are." His words should make me cringe and pull away, but it's not indignation I feel coursing through me. Nor is it my good sensibilities causing me to grow wet between my legs.

He pulls away, and my face is pulled toward someone else. I look up to see a blue mask staring down at me just as Whit's thick member forces my lips wide. I choke and gag around him, coughing up saliva each time he gives me a chance to breathe.

A new hand grabs my hair, dragging me across the floor on my bruised knees before shoving himself all the way down my throat in one seamless motion. The force makes my eyes water, and I feel warm tears tracking down my face.

"Fuck, sweetheart, you're so beautiful when you cry," Quinn says as his thumbs brush away my tears. "You're going to take what I give you until I've decided you've had enough. Now, take a deep breath." I moan around him, his words making me clench, wishing there were something there for me to squeeze around.

I choke and gag with each bruising thrust, trying to focus on my breathing. The moment I'm pulled off of him, I cough as I try to choke down each breath. They pass me around so quickly that by the time I realize they've switched off again, I'm already being shoved onto the next one.

"Whit, how wet is our little slut?" Beckett asks.

I feel fingers slide up the inside of my thighs and brush across my damp folds, making me whimper.

"She's fucking soaked," Whit groans.

Hands grip my waist, pulling me to my feet while my head is held firmly in place. Fingers brush against me again and groan when the pad of one finger circles around the sensitive bundle of nerves. I've been dying for one of them to touch me like this for the past couple of nights, and I think I might instantly combust with only a few swipes. Just before it happens, the fingers are pulled away, and I whine in protest.

"I'm going to come," Beckett says. "You better swallow every drop, Celest." He picks up speed, and just as I feel like I'm about to pass out, I feel something warm and salty shoot into the back of my throat. "That's a good girl."

Whit and Quinn stand side by side as they take turns pushing into my mouth. Quinn reaches down, grabs my hand, and wraps it around him just as Whit does the same. They use my hands to pump along the lengths of their shafts when they aren't choking me with them.

"Open your mouth, princess, and stick out your tongue," Whit says as he and Quinn place their tips on my tongue. I move my hands as they instructed, without their guidance, each motion making them take turns sliding across my tongue.

"You're going to hold our come on your tongue until we tell you to swallow. Do you understand, Celest?" Quinn says, groaning.

"Fuck, I'm close," Whit grunts. Not even three pumps of my hands later, I feel their releases coat my tongue at the same time. I have to stop myself from instinctively spitting. When they tell me to swallow, I have to choke it down; the texture is not my favorite.

"Well, would you look at that? Looks like she's earned it. Since there's three of us, we'll make her come three times?" Beckett asks. They seem to have come to an unspoken agreement because then he leans down, picks me up, and sits back in his chair.

Beckett turns me so that my back rests against his chest, then reaches down, grabs under my knees with both hands, pulls my legs up and wide, exposing me to the rest of the room.

"For fucks sake, she's made a mess out of herself. And that's just from taking cock down her throat. Think we can get her to make a puddle?" Quinn asks with his usual amusement. I feel my face heat and try to close my legs.

"Uh-uh, don't you try to fucking hide this cunt away from us," Whit says as he slaps the insides of both thighs before his fingers slowly sweep through my folds. I scream when he pinches my sensitive nub and an electric jolt shoots through me. "She's so responsive."

Quinn slaps my core a few times, hitting the pulsing nerves in quick succession. I cry and try to scoot away from him, but Beckett's hold keeps me in place. Quinn's fingers blur as he rapidly swipes across my still stinging center, and before I can even process it, I'm climbing too quickly to the very peak of the cliff's edge. He smacks me once more, and I explode.

All I can hear is the ringing in my ears. I know my mouth is open in a scream, but I can't tell if any sound is escaping. Before I can even process why, I'm begging for it to stop while Quinn continues, viciously sliding his fingers across me, refusing to let me come down.

"There's one!" Quinn laughs, and for a moment, a trickle of doubt weaves its way in—Is he laughing at me?

Then Whit's finger slides easily into my slick entrance. "How about another?" he asks, sliding a second one in beside the first. He curls his fingers, tapping them against my front wall, and I moan something incoherent that makes him laugh.

His fingers pump in and out of me hard and fast. The

sound of his hand slapping against my wet center is embarrassing, but I'm too far gone to react. Tension coils tight inside me, and I know it's about to snap and send me soaring any second.

"Hear how drenched you are?" Beckett growls into my ear. "Your pussy loves every sloppy second of this. You're going to come again, and then we'll make you do it once more." I shake my head. I don't think I can handle twice more.

"Yes, Celest. Your pleasure belongs to us, and you'll take whatever we decide to give you." I cry out and feel my eyes roll back. "Come now."

I do.

I swear my heart might've stopped beating. My senses are slow to return, but when they do, I'm immediately overwhelmed.

"No—no more. Please," I beg.

"What did I tell you, Celest? You don't get to tell us no. We'll make you come as many times as we want, and there's nothing you can do about it."

"Shit, I think we can get her to squirt," Quinn says. He brings his fingers back to my beyond sensitive core, sliding his fingers across me while Whit never stops pumping his fingers in and out.

"Add a third, Whit," Beckett demands. The third finger slides in, and the stretch is almost painful. Neither of them slows their pace as they work together to bring me to one last dive into oblivion.

"Are you going to squirt for us, little thief?" Beckett asks, his voice low and thick with desire. I'm not sure what he means, but there's something new building inside me—something that makes me feel like I can't let it go. "Don't fight it. I see you trying to hold back from us. Let it go, Celest."

"No, I can't," I beg them. "Please, I-I—oh, God!" I scream, feeling my whole body shake as that pressure builds even more. It's like a dam is about to burst, and there's nothing I can do to stop it.

"Yes, Celest. You can and you will. There's no God here to save you. Come—Now!" Beckett's growled demand sends me over the edge, and I lose the battle against whatever I was trying to hold back. A rush of warmth spreads between my legs.

"Told you she could squirt," Quinn says, sounding pleased with himself. I'm aware they're talking, but only peripherally.

I think they broke me.

I can't move a single muscle, and thought is beyond my capabilities. I feel myself being lifted and carried, but I have no way of knowing or asking where. I know everything about this night should feel wrong, yet it doesn't. The last thing I recall before everything goes black is the darkness within, giving me a wicked grin—looking very pleased with herself.

And I think I might agree.

13

I'm being ridiculous.

I know I am, but that doesn't stop the frustration bubbling inside me—clawing and twisting into something sharp and ugly. The first night they didn't show, I barely let myself acknowledge it. Just a night off to relax, I told myself. They're trying to throw me off balance, keep me guessing so they can terrify me tomorrow.

That's all.

But when they didn't show the second night, something inside me cracked.

I'd waited.

Like a fool.

I sat in my room at dusk, my heart pounding with anticipation—only to be met with... nothing. No flicker of red, blue, or orange. No cryptic words or hidden passages. No teasing touches or cruel games. Just silence.

I sat there all night.

Waiting.

Which is what I'm still doing now. The sun is starting to rise, and I take a deep breath as a decision solidifies within me. I slowly stand and wrap my comforter around me before approaching the dresser. I stare at my purse for a few moments before grabbing it with shaking hands. I check that all of my things are still inside, then march toward the door.

Fine.

If they don't want to play their own games, then neither do I. I'm not going to sit around like some obedient little pet waiting for their attention.

No.

I'm leaving.

I find my way to the foyer and descend the curved stairs, pausing at the front door. I take a couple of breaths, wondering if they will appear out of nowhere and force me to stay. When nothing happens, I reach for the knob and turn it.

Or at least, I try to.

The door doesn't open. I try again—perhaps it's only stuck. Again, the knob doesn't turn. It's sealed shut. I huff in annoyance and decide to try every door and window I come across.

None of them open.

Every possible exit is locked up tight. The only thing I've managed to do is waste my time and feed the burning resentment curling inside me. It's not that I'd truly expected to just walk away.

Not really.

However, a small part of me believed they were giving me a choice. They returned my purse and didn't show up for two nights, as if giving me space to make my own choice. Now, standing in a house that suddenly feels more like a prison, I realize I misunderstood.

They left me.

Without a thought.

They could have at least written a note.

Now, I prowl through the manor, rage simmering beneath my skin like a fever while the silk of this ridiculous nightgown clings to the tops of my thighs. The cold floor bites at my bare feet as I clutch the comforter tighter around my shoulders. I've been wandering this freezing, lifeless manor with nothing to do and nothing to eat for days.

The clock on the wall ticks toward dusk, and I wonder if they'll bother to show up. If they do, they'll demand I play their game as if nothing happened. I doubt they'll even give me an explanation as to why they left me here.

Alone.

I hate that I'm lonely enough to want them to show up—to settle for scraps of attention.

My jaw tightens in anger—at them and myself—as I stomp through the halls, past grand chandeliers, flickering sconces, locked doors, and abandoned rooms filled with sheet-draped furniture. Just because I haven't seen them in days doesn't mean they aren't here.

Watching.

Waiting.

Probably laughing.

I know I won't find them, but that doesn't stop me from yelling. "Cowards!" My voice echoes, swallowed by the vast, empty halls.

Nothing.

I move deeper into the house, my anger mounting. "You

think you can just disappear? Just—just abandon me after—"
My throat tightens, and I swallow the rest of my words with a
sharp breath.

This is what infuriates me the most—that I feel abandoned at all.

By my masked kidnappers.

What the hell is wrong with me? I can't help it, though.
They made me care in their strange, twisted way.

I dig my nails into my palms and keep moving. Past the
library, the grand hall, and the winding corridors that feel like
they shift under my feet. I throw open doors one after
another, slamming them shut when I find nothing but dust
and emptiness. I press a hand to my chest, hating the erratic
beat of my heart, hating the gnawing ache in my stomach that
has nothing to do with hunger.

"I know you're watching!" I spin in place, my breath
uneven, my pulse hammering against my ribs. "I know you
can hear me, so why don't you stop being cowards and come
out?"

Silence.

The only reply is the low creak of the floorboards beneath
my feet. I wasn't truly expecting a response, but it would have
been nice to get one, all the same. My eyes burn, and I take
several deep breaths through my nose to keep the tears at bay.

I should be relieved they're gone.

I should be planning—searching for some way out,
preparing for what comes next.

Instead, I feel hollow.

I hate them for making me feel like this.

I squeeze my eyes shut and grit my teeth.

"Fine," I whisper to the nothingness surrounding me. "Play your little game."

I won't be the one who loses.

I didn't escape one prison to be locked in another.

By the time the first sliver of moonlight spills through the windows, I'm fuming. I've torn through the manor, yelling at empty rooms—my anger growing hotter with every unanswered shout. It feels like every time I've had to bury my rage before is now bubbling to the surface. I won't be told to control my emotions this time.

My chest heaves as I pace the parlor, my eyes darting to the window and the growing darkness outside. If they don't show tonight, I'm going to start throwing things.

The faint creak of a floorboard sounds from behind me.

I whirl around to see them standing in the doorway, their masks glowing in the dim light of the hall behind them.

My anger boils over. "Where the hell have you been?" I snap, the words flying out before I can stop them. Father would be horrified by my choice of vocabulary.

They don't respond, and it drives me absolutely insane. I stomp up to them, reach for Quinn's mask first, and yank it off his head. He could've stopped me if he wanted to. Of course, he wears an insufferable grin on his stupidly handsome face, leaning casually against the doorframe like he doesn't have a care in the world.

He probably doesn't.

"Do you think this is some kind of game?"

Quinn raises an eyebrow, his grin widening. "Isn't it?"

"That does it." I spit, ripping the masks off the other two. It would help if they looked horrid, but of course, there's not a flaw to be found on any of them. Beckett's gray eyes pierce me, while Whit's hazel, softer ones study me closely.

My voice shakes, but not with fear. No, it's full of everything I've been holding in for days—years. "It's not. I'm starving. I'm freezing. I don't have any clothes, or shoes, or anything! Do you think crackers and peanut butter are enough to live on?" I hear my voice echo down the hall as the silence stretches.

Beckett's expression doesn't waver, but I see the faintest flicker of something in his eyes—whatever it is, I don't care. Just like he doesn't care about me.

Quinn shrugs, his tone as infuriatingly casual as ever. "You're still alive, aren't you?"

The words hit like a slap to the face, and I snap. "You think that's good enough? You think that's okay? You've taken everything from me—my clothes, my freedom, my life—and left me to rot here while you go wherever it is you went!"

The silence is worse than any taunt, and it makes my rage burn hotter as traitorous tears roll down my face. "Do you even care?" I shout, my voice cracking. "Do you even realize how miserable you've made me?"

Of course, they don't. Even if they did, it's not like they would do anything about it.

Finally, Beckett steps forward, his tone calm but firm. "It's time."

"What?" I blink at him, my anger momentarily giving way to confusion.

"The game," he says simply, motioning toward the door. "It's past dusk."

I stare at him, my chest heaving, my blood roaring in my

ears. Of course—of course, this is all they care about—not me, not what I'm feeling—just their ridiculous game.

The anger flares again, and I tighten the comforter around me, glaring at them as I step toward the door. "Fine," I snap, feeling my lower lip wobbling. "Let's play your stupid game. Maybe I'll be lucky tonight, and one of you will put me out of my misery and kill me already. At least then, I would be free —for once in my life!"

There are a few beats of silence, and then Quinn laughs. He actually laughs at me. My rage finally snaps, like a rubber band stretched too tight. I don't even realize I'm yelling until my voice echoes off the walls.

"You think this is funny?" I scream, my hands clenched so tightly at my sides that my nails bite into my palms. "Do you think I would ever choose this? That I want to be here, with you, playing your twisted little games?"

Quinn leans casually against the wall—does he ever stand straight?—barely reacting. That stupid smirk—so smug and antagonistic—stays plastered on his face. I have the urge to reach out and brush back the dark hair falling into his eyes with my fingers. "You're still here, aren't you?" he says, his voice infuriatingly calm, like I'm not worth taking seriously.

I'm probably not.

"Maybe you like it more than you think."

The words are a spark to a powder keg. "You—" My voice breaks, and my vision blurs with hot, angry tears. "You have no idea what I've been through. None of you do! And you just stand there, grinning like this is all some fun little hobby for you and not my life!"

"Relax," he says, his tone light, dismissive. "No need to get your panties in a knot—or lack thereof." He lets his eyes drop slowly down my body. "It's not the end of the world."

"Relax," I repeat, my voice escalating into a shriek. "How dare you tell me to relax!"

Before I even know what I'm doing, my hand flies up, and the crack of my palm against his cheek rings out, loud and sharp in the room. The sting travels up my arm, and I know I've made a grave mistake, but I can't seem to find it in me to care.

Quinn's head snaps to the side, his smirk finally gone. For a moment, there's nothing but the sound of my ragged breathing and the faint hiss of blood rushing in my ears.

And then the weight of their scrutiny sets in. The silence feels like a living thing, pressing down on me, smothering the fire that had fueled me only moments ago. My hand still stings, but it's nothing compared to the sinking weight in my stomach.

Quinn stands there, his head turning back slowly to look at me. Gone is his grin, replaced by something darker—dangerous—as he clenches his jaw.

Maybe I really will die tonight.

"You're brave for such a tiny thing. I'll give you that," he says finally, his voice low, the edge of amusement making my chest tighten. "But bad girls get punished."

Punished.

"N—no, please," I gasp, the words barely audible, and I feel my body trembling. My body goes cold, my blood freezing in my veins as the other two step forward, their expressions hard and unreadable. "Not t-that."

Memories flash through my mind of the punishments I received at Josiah's hand.

"You'd better run," Beckett says, his voice calm and devoid of emotion. I've feared them, but this is the first time since the woods that I've thought they would truly hurt me. It's almost worse being able to see their faces. "And you'd better hide, but even that won't prevent your punishment."

My heart pounds, and I can barely hear anything over the rushing of blood in my head.

Run.

Hide.

Punishment.

The words echo in my head alongside the memory of the last time Josiah took his belt to me and the dark stone room where he left me bloodied and chained to the wall for days. I stagger back, clutching the comforter around me as if it could protect me.

"Go," Whit says, his voice low and firm. "Now."

I don't wait for them to tell me twice. I turn and run, abandoning the weight of my comforter as I dart down the hallway. My breath comes in sharp, shallow gasps—panic slicing through me. My father's voice fills my head, loud and condemning: *You brought this on yourself, Celestina. Bad behavior must be corrected.*

Tears blur my vision as I stumble into a room, slamming the door behind me. I press my back against it, chest heaving, mind racing. They're going to kill me. I was stupid—so, so stupid—to strike him.

My father would have locked me in the reflecting room for days for something like that—left me alone in the dark until I begged for forgiveness. I don't want to think about what Josiah would have done. I choke back a sob, shaking my head.

No. No, I won't let them do this to me. I should have just stayed in Alabama.

I dart across the room, looking for somewhere to hide—but there's no time. I hear them coming, their footsteps heavy and deliberate. My heart races, my hands shake as I search for something—anything—to barricade the door. My breaths come in gasps, and I fear I might faint.

It happens faster than I expect. The door bursts open, and before I can scream, strong arms wrap around me, pinning mine to my sides. I thrash against the hold, my mind convinced that Josiah is the one who grabbed me.

There are many ways to hurt you, Celestina, without leaving a permanent mark. Let us begin.

"Please, no!" I scream, my voice breaking as they drag me from the room. "Not again! Please!"

My pleas echo through the hallway, but they don't slow. If anything, it seems to amuse them. Quinn's laugh cuts through the haze of panic—sharp and mocking.

"Again?" he says, his breath warm against my ear as he leans in. "I promise we've never truly punished you before, and I doubt anyone has punished a sweet little thief like you the way we will."

The others chuckle, their voices low and dark—my fear spikes again. I struggle as hard as I can, tears streaming down my face. "Please!" I sob, my voice cracking. "I—I'll be g-good! I'll be good, I p-promise!"

They don't respond, their laughter fading as we near my room—my sobs the only sound left. The door creaks open, and I'm thrown onto the bed—the impact knocking the breath from my lungs.

My chest aches from the effort of my sobs. I curl into

myself, reaching for that place in my mind where nothing can touch me—preparing for the pain I know is coming.

"You really thought we'd hurt you?" Quinn asks, his tone dripping with mockery. The question pulls me out of my mind just enough to look over at him—leaning against the doorframe, holding my comforter. His signature smirk returns, though there's still a sharpness to his gaze that sends a shiver down my spine.

Beckett steps closer, his piercing gaze locking onto mine. "You shouldn't throw fits based on assumptions," he says, his voice calm—yet I see him seething. His thoughts seem far away.

Whit doesn't say anything—just keeps his steady gaze fixed on me, studying my every reaction. Something he sees makes his jaw clench.

My body trembles, my breath coming in short, shallow gasps. I don't trust them—or the way they're looking at me.

"You should rest," Beckett finally says, his tone unreadable. "You'll need your strength for tomorrow."

His words leave me confused, and I can't bring myself to respond. Quinn drops my comforter over me before they turn and leave, the door clicking shut behind them. My mind races, fear refusing to subside as it churns over what kind of torture they might have planned. What could possibly take them an entire day to come up with?

Do I really want to know?

14

They left me to anticipate my punishment all day. I sit on my bed with my comforter wrapped as tightly as I can around me, and stare out the window watching the sun fall lower as the sky becomes an explosion of color.

I considered hiding from them, but I've barely moved all day. I haven't even felt the gnawing hunger that has been my companion for the last... how long has it been?

Seven—no, six days.

I think.

Any minute now, they'll emerge from—wherever it is they spend the hours while the sun is up. Every creak this old manor makes causes me to flinch. I swear I've been hearing footsteps coming from down the hall for the last few hours. However, the ones echoing outside my door right this minute are clearly real. Any second now, they'll walk through my door.

There it is—the groan of my door opening, followed by the soft click of the latch as it shuts.

It's time.

Silence stretches before Beckett speaks. "Come, little thief."

I keep my head down, neither crying nor begging this time, but each step feels like I'm walking to my death, while the soft whisper of the comforter drags behind me.

I stop when I see the tips of their shoes, and hesitate to look up. When I finally do, I'm greeted by Quinn's mischievous grin. The lack of anger in his expression gives me hope that I might survive this after all.

"Evening, sweetheart," he says, his voice almost cheerful. "Hope you're well rested."

Well, I suppose it was foolish to hope.

I meet Beckett's calm, calculating gaze. I expect him to taunt me with their plans, yet somehow, his silence is worse.

Whit lingers a few steps behind them, his expression unreadable, but there's a tension in his shoulders that makes me uneasy. It's almost as if he doesn't want to be here—or as if something about this is unsettling him.

Whatever's about to happen to me must be truly horrific.

My anticipation grows as the silence stretches. Unable to stand it another second, I swallow hard, my voice barely above a whisper. "What do you want?"

"What do we want?" Quinn repeats, tilting his head, amusement flickering in his eyes. He steps closer, and I instinctively shrink back, tightening my grip on the comforter. "We told you, bad girls get punished."

I take another step back—only to collide with a hard body.

I'm immediately enveloped in something rich and woodsy—sandalwood with a hint of worn leather.

Beckett.

His voice vibrates behind me. "You hit Quinn," he says, his tone leaving no room for argument. "And actions have consequences."

"I—I didn't mean to," I stammer, my voice trembling, hoping they'd see reason. "I was angry, I—"

"Save it," Whit says, finally speaking. His voice is low but firm, sending a shiver down my spine. "You've got two choices: take your punishment like a good girl, or make this harder on yourself. Personally, I'm hoping you'll go for option two."

The words make my stomach twist, and I can feel the heat rising in my cheeks. "Okay," I whisper. "W-what are you going to d-do to me?" They circle me, crowding me between them, causing my fear to skyrocket and my teeth to chatter.

Quinn snaps his hand out, grabbing me by the jaw and bringing his face close to mine. "I love how fear makes the blue of your eyes impossibly bright," he says, ignoring my question. "Now, drop the blanket."

I do as I'm told.

"Good girl. Now, take this off." He brushes one of the thin straps off my shoulder. His firm grip never leaves my jaw as he kisses me hard before pushing me away.

I feel my face burn with embarrassment. I know they've seen every inch of me, but I'd been blindfolded. This is crossing the line into sin—welcoming shame—that I can no longer rationalize.

I don't know if I can do it.

Beckett's lips brush my ear. "Do as you're told, little thief, or I'll rip the damn thing off of you. Then I'll bend you over my knee and spank your sweet little ass until your cunt is dripping with need."

I'm too stunned to move as I try to unravel the meaning of his words. I must take too long, because his arms snake around me, his hands dragging along my body. He grips the top of my little silk nightie—my last line of defense—and tears it down the center. Cool air brushes against my naked body.

"I'll be honest," he says, ghosting his lips down my neck. "I was hoping I'd get to do that." He buries one hand into my dark hair, gripping tightly at the scalp before pulling my head back and exposing my neck to them. "Are you going to be a good girl for us, little thief?"

All I manage is a squeak.

Whit drags a chair to the center of the room, and Beckett takes a seat, pulling me across his lap by my hair. He positions me with my naked rear in the air, and my face grows impossibly hotter being so exposed, as his callused hand makes soft circles across my naked skin.

"Here's what's going to happen, princess," Whit says, crouching to look me in the eyes. "Beck here is going to set that ass on fire, and each time his palm cracks against your cheeks, you're going to count for us."

"How many, Quinn?" Beckett asks, his circles never ceasing. The gentle movements make me squirm as my core begins to ache for... I don't know what.

"How old are you, sweetheart?" Quinn asks, stepping in front of me as Whit moves aside.

"Twenty-five," I say, my voice breathy and unfamiliar.

"Twenty-five it is," he says, bringing his hand up to caress the side of my face. I instinctively lean into his touch. "Be a good girl for us and don't forget to count. I'd hate for Beck to have to start all over." His tone suggests that he would, in fact, not hate that at all.

Quinn keeps staring into my eyes as the first smack sends fire across my skin. "One," I gasp, as Quinn's smile grows into something wicked.

The next two land in quick succession. "Two, three!" I shout. Between Quinn's icy blue unwavering stare and Beckett's unpredictable timing with each strike, electric anticipation pulses through me.

Moans sneak out as inferno grows across my skin. At least there's no room left for embarrassment, and for once, my racing mind is silent. Right now, the feeling is freeing. Later, I'll feel differently, but at the moment, I can't seem to care.

"You know," Quinn says, "I thought I loved the way fear brightened your eyes best, but it turns out I was wrong. The way they are right now is my favorite—pupils blown wide and desperate for release." A sharp crack sounds, and the heat building in my rear intensifies.

"Eleven," I cry out, feeling the sting of tears trying to escape. After two more smacks, I lose the battle, and feel them streak down my cheeks.

"Fuck, sweetheart," Quinn groans. "Just when I thought you couldn't get any more beautiful, you go and cry." He leans in and kisses the salty tracks.

After I finally reach twenty, I hear Beckett ask, "Whit, her cunt's dripping isn't it?" His voice is deep and gravelly.

"She's such a mess," Whit groans. "It's running down her legs." A quiet voice in the back of my mind whispers how shameful it is for my body to respond like this. I barely hear it before the next strike has the darkness within me smothering the tiny voice entirely.

"Twenty-one," I gasp between sobs.

"Good girl," Quinn murmurs as Beckett rubs the sting away. "You're doing so well." I barely register the final cracks, though I manage to count them out.

As the final strike lands, I sob uncontrollably, not even sure why. It's nothing compared to Josiah's belt, but the desperation inside me mingles with their praise, making me feel... adored.

I don't understand what's happening to me.

"Need to come?" Beckett asks. That must be what I'm so desperate for. My rear is on fire and yet I can feel my core clenching, aching to be filled. I manage a nod.

"Oh, sweetheart, you can do better than that," Quinn says with a laugh. "Say, 'Please, Mr. Beckett, sir, let me come.'"

I moan, the words slipping out in a whisper so low that even I can't make sense of them. Another smack lands across my bare bottom, the heat in my skin nearing unbearable.

"Speak up, little thief," Beckett says. "You were more than happy to raise your voice last night."

"Please, Mr. Beckett, sir, let me come!" I manage between sobs.

"That's better, but the only way you're coming tonight, is around our cocks. Understand?" Beckett asks.

"Oh, God," I whimper. "I—I don't... that is..." Words stumble from my mouth, none forming a complete thought or even coming close to conveying my feelings. I'd convinced myself that everything until now wasn't really bad—even if I had to squint to see it that way.

This, though?

There's no denying I'm going to hell once all three take me. Josiah always said this is something only a husband—or a future husband—is supposed to have intimate knowledge of.

Is this how a soul gets devoured?

"We've told you, there's no God here. If you want to come, all you have to do is beg for our cocks," Beckett says as two of his fingers enter my sopping center. "Fuck, baby, you're soaked for us." He thrusts in and out a few times, but the second I moan he pulls out. I flinch when I feel one of his fingers, wet with my arousal, rub the tight ring that I know—for a fact—is not meant for this.

But apparently I'm wrong.

"Relax," he commands, just as I feel his finger push past the resistance, and slowly slide into me.

It's a strange feeling. I'm not sure I hate it, but I don't think I love it either. All of these sensations confuse me. My hips move on their own—my center desperate for something to fill it. The motion makes Beckett's finger slide in and out. It's not unpleasant—it even sends a wave of pleasure through me. I release a desperate whine, the sound so wanton I barely recognize it as my own.

"Her cunt's so greedy. Look at it, searching for a cock to fuck," Quinn says. I whimper, knowing I'm about to willingly cross yet another line—the final line—one my purity will not survive.

"Please," I whisper, embarrassment and shame finding cracks and weaving their way into my mind.

"Please, what?" Whit asks. I gasp as Beckett's finger slowly pushes deeper.

I nearly forgot it was there.

"Please, I—I want your c-cocks," even I can hear how pathetically desperate I sound.

"What do you want our cocks to do?" Quinn asks as he grabs me by the jaw and lifts my face to look at him. He brushes his thumb over my bottom lip, his eyes heating into liquid silver when my lips part, and he pushes his thumb into my mouth. My tongue swipes across the tip without thought.

"Fuuuck," he swears under his breath.

"Fu-fuck me... please?" The plea is a muffled question—one I'm too embarrassed to demand, even if it's exactly what I want.

"Go ahead, Whit," Beck says.

I hear a belt unbuckle, fabric shifting, before something firm nudges at my entrance. He's large. I panic. He'll never fit—it's impossible. Quinn removes his thumb, the movement distracting, and Whit presses forward—burying himself inside me. Quinn takes advantage of my scream, and shoves himself down my throat.

I gag.

And gag again.

Yet I feel myself release something warm and wet around Whit as he slowly slides in and out, giving me a moment to adjust to him.

"Fuck, princess" Whit groans. "She just soaked my cock after she gagged on Quinn's."

"Does the little thief love having all of her holes stuffed?" Beckett asks with a laugh. He brushes my hair from my face, his grip firm as he lifts my head slightly. Not a moment later Whit pulls out and slams into me, making Quinn push deeper, forcing me to swallow around him.

"Fuck, sweetheart, your mouth is too good," Quinn

groans. There's something about their praise that makes warmth coil deep inside me, leaving me craving more. "Maybe you wanted this. Maybe you slapped me because you knew we'd make you pay for it."

"Her pussy is so fucking tight and wet. She's being such a good little slut for us," Whit says, his voice sounds strained.

Beckett's laughter rumbles through him. "She tightens around my finger every time someone praises her. You like being our good girl, don't you, love?" Beckett asks. I can't respond, so I just hum around Quinn in agreement.

"Oh, fuck," Quinn groans as he pulls out of my mouth with an audible pop, leaving my chin damp. "I almost blew my load down her perfect throat." He leans down to look me in the eyes as he wipes my face clean. "That's not where I coming tonight. We're going to fill your cunt, so you know exactly who it belongs to."

Beckett removes his finger, and I'm shocked when I whimper at its sudden absence. Without pulling out of me, Whit wraps his arms around my waist and carries me to the edge of the bed. He drapes me over it, positioning me on my stomach with my feet dangling. Gripping my arms behind me, he uses them to set a punishing pace. All I hear is the wet slapping of our bodies each time they meet. The force of his thrusts is the only thing holding me in place.

"P-Please..." I beg him over and over, yet I couldn't tell you what I'm begging for. I feel something pull tight—too tight—within me, and scream when it snaps. I feel myself clamp down around Whit, as he finishes inside me not a moment later. I'm certain there's not a single bone left in my body.

I whimper as he slowly pulls out of me and then slaps my

already abused rear. Sound is all I can manage; I'm too far gone, consumed by the fog of pleasure. While I'm aware of what's happening around me, it's as though I'm somewhere else at the same time.

"I think you broke her," one of them—Quinn, I think—says with a laugh. I feel hands grip me, and I know I'm being moved, yet my body is like a rag doll—too limp to help. They move me further onto the bed, shoving my knees under my hips, and lay my head at the edge.

Beckett stands naked in front of me, having shed his clothing at some point—probably while Whit was stealing all of my bones.

And they call me the thief.

"Look at you, such a beautiful mess," Beckett murmurs, caressing my face and sweeping my hair back so he can see me clearly. If I were in my right mind, I'd think he was lying —there's no way I'm anything close to beautiful right now. From somewhere beside me, Whit gathers my hair in his grip and lifts my head just enough to align my mouth with Beckett's hard length.

It's so thick. I don't remember it being this thick— maybe it's the angle? Whit must sense my trepidation because he brings his lips to my ear and says, "Don't worry, princess. Trust me—it'll fit." Then Beckett's tip brushes my lips, and my mouth opens instinctively, stretching my jaw impossibly wide. Just as he pushes at the entrance of my bruised throat, Quinn fills me from behind in one hard thrust.

I hear their words of praise, and I feel them stretching me to my limits, but it's not until I feel a tightening pull throughout my body again that some of the haze clears. I don't know if I can handle another one, and this one feels like it's going to shatter me completely.

"That's it princess, be a good girl and come all over Quinn's cock," Whit says, as Beckett pulls out of my mouth.

"Now Celest—come now!" With Beckett's words, I plummet over the edge, and fall hard into pleasure.

I was right—I'm completely shattered.

Quinn thrusts into me twice more before finishing, his release mixing with Whit's. When he pulls out, I sigh and collapse on the bed, ready to sleep for an eternity.

"Not yet, good girl," Beckett says. "Once more, and then you can sleep." He pulls me away from the edge and then rolls me onto my back. He handles me with a gentle tenderness, as if I'm something precious. An emotion I buried long ago surfaces, and a tear tracks down my cheek.

He climbs on top of me, holds my gaze for a moment, then steals my mouth in a searing kiss. "Alright, Celest?" he asks when his lips leave mine. His voice is soft and caring—I'm certain no man has ever spoken to me like this before. I've never felt so cherished.

"Yes," I respond, the word puffs out on a breath, barely audible.

"That's my good girl," he says with a wolfish smile before he pulls one of my legs over his shoulder and surges into me. "You're so fucking perfect." Each word is punctuated by the sound of our bodies colliding. I fight against the exhaustion threatening to pull me under. I don't think I can handle shattering all over again—it might be the end of me.

"I—I can't. Oh, god. Please Beckett, I can't," I say as an exhausted moan, filled with pleasure, rips from me. Laughter ripples through the room.

"Yes, you can," he says. Beckett's relentless in his pursuit of my pleasure and I feel myself starting to clench around him. "You're almost there, my good girl. Come for me."

I do.

My vision flares white, and the world drowns in a muted hum as wave after wave of pleasure crashes through me. My mind is blissfully empty, my body weightless.

Maybe I'll just float away.

I hear someone calling my name—once I remember I even have one—but exhaustion wins out, and sleep beckons. I'm almost positive I mumble something about sleep and barely register the cool drag of a damp cloth against my over-heated skin. It's possible I even sigh before succumbing to the depths of sleep.

On some level of consciousness, I know that when I wake, I'll have to face the guilt and shame lurking beneath the surface. However, right now, my mind is too blank to care—and I love the way that feels.

The darkness within me sighs—a satisfied, lingering presence.

15

The manor's heavy silence presses in around me as I sit on the windowsill, staring out at the storm-darkened woods stretching endlessly beyond the glass. Weak sunlight filters through the trees, its warm glow battling the rain-filled clouds drifting lazily overhead. The air feels thick and oppressive, reminding me of Magnolia Hollow, where the humidity threatened to suffocate with every breath.

My fingers clutch at my neck, searching for the small silver locket that had always hung there until recently. It would be cool to the touch—smooth and familiar. It would provide a small comfort in a house that feels like it's waiting to devour me—and the three men inside it.

They might have already.

Instead, all I find is the lace trim of yet another negligee they've provided. How considerate—it's not like I'm starving or anything.

The locket's absence feels like missing a limb. My fingers hover over the empty spot at my neck, and the faint echo of its weight is enough to pull me back to those moments—when I would trace the edges, the familiar and repetitive action comforting. The memories are overwhelming—heavy—as if my past will never let me go.

I'm fourteen.

Powerless.

The Sacred Hall is cold—not just chilly, but freezing, like the stone walls are sucking the warmth from the air—and from me. It's impressive, considering the merciless heat outside.

I feel so small standing here with everyone watching. My hands shake as I clutch the flowers they gave me with no explanation when I arrived. They told me lilies symbolize purity, but all I can think about is how they decorated Old Mother Prior's casket at her funeral. The bouquet feels heavy in my hands, and somehow, the weight of death seems fitting.

The candles flicker along the walls, their light casting long shadows that appear to move, giving me something to focus on. The room reeks of incense, sharp and sweet, making my stomach churn. I have the desperate urge to turn and run as far as I can.

My dress is beautiful—everyone says so. It reminds me of the dress I wore for the Purity Ritual. The lace is soft, and the little pearls sewn along the bodice catch the light when I move.

Mother made it, spending hours at her sewing machine in the quiet of our house. She smiled when I tried it on, but her eyes held no joy when they briefly met mine. I didn't know why then, but I'm beginning to think I do now.

Josiah stands in front of me, tall and overbearing, like he's made of stone. His eyes never leave mine, and they make me feel... powerless. Like a mouse caught in a trap. I drop my gaze, unable to face Josiah any longer. My eyes search out my father, his chest puffed out with pride. His gaze is heavy with expectations, but I don't understand what he wants from me —what he desires his daughter to be.

I want to go home.

Josiah lifts his arms, silencing the soft hum of conversations before his voice consumes the room—commanding attention. "Today, we witness the hand of God uniting two chosen souls," he proclaims. Everyone leans forward hanging on his every word, desperate to hear what he'll say next.

I wish he'd never speak again.

"Celestina Abernathy, pure of heart and spirit, has been promised to me—by divine decree. Together, we will fulfill the Covenant's sacred mission."

What?

My stomach twists, my grip tightening on the bouquet.

Promised?

To him?

He's nearly as old as Father.

My heart pounds so loudly I'm sure everyone can hear it. I glance at my mother, seated on the wooden bench in the front row—like always. Two empty spots beside her beckon with a false promise of safety. Her hands are clenched in her lap, gripping her skirt like it's the only thing holding her together. When our eyes meet, she looks away quickly, as if ashamed.

Or scared.

I'm scared.

Josiah keeps talking, but his words blur together, only registering in the back of my mind. "...devoted to the Covenant's cause... twenty-fifth birthday... my bride." Each phrase is another stone upon my chest. Each one heavier than the last, making it impossible to breathe.

Bride.

The word makes my skin crawl. I'm only fourteen. How can I be anyone's bride? The congregation murmurs their approval, a low chorus that reverberates off the walls. My stomach churns. Why is everyone fine with this?

I'm just a child.

I turn to my father, whispering so only he can hear, "Why is this happening? I'm too young, Father. This must be a mistake, right? It can't be true."

His hand clamps down on my shoulder, hard enough that I wince. There will be bruises there by morning. "Celestina," he bites out, his voice low and cutting through clenched teeth. "This is an honor. Do. Not. Embarrass us."

Honor.

That's what everyone keeps calling it, but it doesn't feel like an honor. It feels like a nightmare. I glance at Josiah again—he's looking at me with that smile. It's not kind or warm; it's greedy. It's as if he's already claimed me, like I'm something he owns.

No longer a girl.

An object.

Josiah steps closer, holding out his hand. His voice softens, but it still fills the room. "Celestina," he says, his tone carrying a false warmth, like he's talking to a child too naive to understand what's best for her. "Do you vow to dedicate your youth to the Covenant's divine mission and fulfill your destiny as my bride on the day ordained by God?"

I freeze.

Oh, God.

I can't move.

I take a breath—nothing.

I can't.

I can't breathe.

I can't speak.

I can't.

No.

Please.

The room falls silent, but I can't hear anything over the rushing of my blood—loud and frantic in my ears. I'm both hot and cold at the same time and feel my head growing dangerously light as my vision darkens around the edges. My father leans down, his voice sharp—full of the promise of pain later. "Answer him, Celestina."

I glance at my mother again, silently begging her to do something—to help me, to tell me this is all a mistake. She shifts in her seat, her knuckles white as she grips her skirt.

She doesn't move.

She doesn't say anything.

She doesn't even look at me.

She won't save me.

No one is.

I'm alone in a room full of people.

The weight of everyone's gazes crushes me. Josiah's hand is still there, waiting. I know I can't say no. My voice is barely a whisper as I force the words out in one breath.

"I vow."

The room erupts into prayers, their voices rising alongside their hands.

I can't hear them.

I only hear Josiah.

He takes my hand—his touch cold and possessive. "Well done, Celestina," he says, his smile widening—an uncanny resemblance to a wolf. "You are a true servant of the Light."

Everyone moves into the dining hall to celebrate. It's loud —filled with laughter and clinking glasses—but it all feels distant. I sit at the head table, Josiah beside me, unable to eat. I push the food around my plate, pretending. The smell of roasted chicken, fresh bread, and golden potatoes makes my stomach twist. I can't bring myself to swallow a single bite.

Josiah talks to me the whole time, his voice smooth, almost patronizing. "You'll grow into this role," he says, as though it's inevitable—his words carrying an underlying threat. "It may seem daunting now, but in time, you'll understand the depth of your calling. I will help prepare you until our wedding day, so you know exactly what is expected of you —and how to... meet my expectations."

I fight the desire to run from him. I might not fully understand his words, but something in the way he says them—and the look he gives me—makes me feel unsafe. I nod, not knowing what else to do. The dress feels too tight, the noise too loud, and I want nothing more than to wake up—to realize this was all just a bad dream.

I pinch my arm to wake myself up.

It's not a dream.

Later that night, long after I should have fallen asleep, my mother sneaks into my room. She sits at the edge of my bed, combing her fingers through my hair—like she did when I was little and woke from a bad dream. Her hands tremble, and I wonder if she sees this for the nightmare it is, too.

"I'm sorry," she whispers, her voice breaking. "I couldn't stop it."

I sit up, the words tumbling out in a hushed, urgent whisper before I can stop them. "Why didn't you try? Why didn't you say something? Why didn't you save me? You wouldn't even look at me!" My voice cracks as hot tears roll down my cheeks.

Her face crumples as she takes my hands in hers. "Because if I had, they would have punished not just me, but you—or worse. They might have taken you away from me forever." Her words falter, tears welling in her eyes. "I'll find a way, Celestina. I promise. Just… stay strong for now."

She presses a silver locket into my palm, the cool metal grounding me. "Keep this with you—always," she says, her voice trembling. "And remember—no matter what they say, no matter what they do—you are more than this. They can't take everything from you."

I clutch the locket tightly, but her words feel hollow, repetitive, and—more importantly—too late. The vow has already been made. The promise has already been sealed. And there's nothing anyone—besides God himself—can do to undo it.

I wish there were.

The memory fades, but its weight lingers, pressing against my chest like a hand shoving me back into the past. My gaze stays fixed on the dark woods beyond the manor, but the trees blur from view.

I see the Sacred Hall, the flicker of candles, Josiah's cold smile, and the crushing weight of a future I never chose. My mother's face, my father's pride, Josiah's domineering presence—it all swirls together, a toxic reminder of the life I left behind.

Tears sting my eyes as I whisper into the silence, "I should have run that night. So much pain would have been avoided. If I'd fought harder..."

But I didn't.

Now here I am—trapped in another prison, haunted by the same ghosts. The difference is, this time, I'm determined to break free. No matter how enjoyable this prison may be.

The absence of the locket feels heavier now that my hand is empty—its once comforting presence replaced by a sharp edge of guilt and anger. I unclench my fingers, staring at my empty palm, imagining the delicate silver surface, worn smooth by years of holding it in moments like this. My mother's words echo in my mind: *You're more than this.*

I want to believe her. I want to believe I've become someone stronger, someone braver. But right now, all I feel is...

Small.

Broken.

Weak.

I press my empty hand to my chest, my thoughts spiraling with self-reproach, sharp and unrelenting. I was just a child, I remind myself, but the excuse feels hollow. I spoke the vow. I let Josiah take my hand. I sat at that table, nodding like a puppet while my life was stolen—

Piece by piece.

Year by year.

My stomach twists, a sick mix of shame and regret bubbling to the surface. I'd been so terrified of disappointing my father, of angering Josiah, of defying a room full of people who saw me as nothing more than a tool for their "divine mission."

I'd thought staying silent was survival—but now I know it was surrender.

Shame gives way to something hotter. Something angrier —volatile.

Anger at Josiah for taking everything from me.

Anger at my father for forcing me into it.

Anger at my mother for her whispered promises and weak excuses. She'd said she couldn't stop it, but wasn't that her job?

To protect me?

To fight for me, no matter the cost?

It's unfair to question such things—I know now why she couldn't—yet knowing doesn't change what happened to me over the last decade.

More than anyone, I'm angry at myself—angry at the girl I was, too scared to scream, to run, to fight back. Angry at the woman I've become—still haunted by their echoes, still doubting that I can ever truly be free of them. Angry that I'm still afraid to make demands—to advocate for myself.

The missing locket feels like a brand in my hand, the memory of its shape imprinted into my skin. I wish I had it so I could throw it across the room and watch it shatter against the wall—but I can't. I don't have it any more.

It's just another thing I lost to him.

Like my childhood.

My innocence.

Hope.

Now, all I have are memories and they are a heavier burden than the ghost of the locket. No matter how much anger I feel, it doesn't erase the love I know my mother bore for me. Or the sacrifices she made—even if I wound up in another prison, lorded over by men again.

I close my eyes, taking a deep breath—as the storm inside me threatens to spill over and join the one rioting outside my window. I can't let myself drown.

Not here.

Not now.

Not ever.

Never again.

The shadows outside the window shift, and for a moment, it looks like Josiah's disciples are watching—waiting—ready to drag me back if I falter. I close my eyes, willing the hallucination away.

"I'm not her. Not anymore," I whisper, my voice shaking but determined. "I'm not that scared little girl."

Even as I say the words, part of me wonders if they're true. Am I really free? Or am I still that scared little girl—running from a cage I don't know how to escape?

The thought claws at me, sharp and insistent, but I push it down, burying it in the back of my mind. I have to. If I don't, the thoughts win. And if they win, Josiah does too.

I glance toward the door, half expecting one of them to reappear—the glow of their masks, their unhurried footsteps hunting me, their gazes piercing, full of fire and ice.

They won't return until dusk, I know that, but the mere thought of them brings a fresh wave of conflict—and guilt.

I don't trust them.

Well... I shouldn't trust them.

They're dangerous. Unpredictable. Far too good at pulling on my loose threads, unraveling parts of me I don't even understand—or want to face.

It's getting harder.

When they're around, I don't feel small. I don't feel like a pawn. Or a victim. I feel... alive. Empowered, even. They manipulate, hunt, and control me, and yet I feel freer than ever.

And that terrifies me.

I know it's wrong—to feel this way about them. To let them slip under my skin when I've spent my whole life trying to escape men like Josiah. Still, I know they're not like him— not exactly.

They don't lie about their intentions. They don't preach purity while stealing my agency. They might not give me a real choice, but they're honest about the game they're playing.

Even wearing masks, they're more honest than Josiah's ever been.

I shake my head, shoving the thoughts aside. It doesn't matter how they make me feel. What matters is staying strong —staying free—and not breaking. That starts with figuring out what I want and who I want to be.

I clutch my empty hand, my resolve hardening. "I won't be controlled again," I whisper, the words a promise and a challenge all at once. "Not by Josiah. Not by my past. Not by anyone."

Not even by them.

16

After last night, the air is thick with anticipation as the last streaks of daylight disappear, leaving the manor bathed in twilight. I stand in the grand hall, clutching the comforter around my shoulders. It's starting to feel less like armor and more like something to keep me warm—exactly the way a blanket should.

I sense them before they emerge from the shadows, circling me like wolves. Their eyes glint in the dim light, their presence feels heavier, more purposeful than usual.

"Our sweet little Celest," Whit drawls, his tone dripping with mock affection, while his eyes scan me hungrily.

"By the end of the night, you'll belong to us," Beckett says, his tone calm—matter-of-fact—as if it's a foregone conclusion.

I feel my chest tighten, but I push back the rising fear. I clench my fists around the comforter and stand up straight, my voice shaking but strong enough to carry. "I don't belong to anyone. I didn't escape my past just to become someone else's property."

Never again.

For a moment, all three of them go still. The tension stretches taut, their eyes boring into me. Then Quinn grins—wicked and amused. "Is that so?"

"Yes," I snap, my voice sharper this time. "I won't. I refuse." I'll never let anyone claim me as property ever again.

"Why's that?" Beckett asks, his tone placating as they step closer, crowding me, their movements slow and deliberate.

It's enough to crack the flimsy walls I've built around my composure. The words spill out of me before I can stop them, tumbling over each other in a panic-fueled rush.

"I—I'm afraid of you, okay?"

"As you should be, princess. But what makes you fear belonging to us?" Whit asks.

"Past experiences, and…" I trail off, afraid to say what I really think of them.

"Aaand?" Quinn teases.

"And you're—well, that is—I have a theory." Oh, God. What happens when they find out I know?

Beckett raises an eyebrow, tilting his head slightly. "A theory?"

I nod quickly, my throat dry, my voice a couple of octaves higher than normal. "Yes. I've noticed some—uh—peculiar things. Unnatural even."

Quinn's grin widens as he steps closer, eyes gleaming. "Go on."

Oh god, this is it.

I really don't want to say it.

"Well, I've never seen you during the day. Not once. You

only ever show up at night. And y'all have this… air of danger about you. And—and you travel through shadows."

"So, your theory?" Beckett asks again.

I swallow hard, my heart racing—I'm certain they can hear it.

I wonder if that makes them hungry?

Not the time, Celest!

I never thought these words would come out of my mouth, and I'm terrified to speak them. I really don't want to know what they'll do once they find out I know their secret.

I've thought long and hard about it. There really hasn't been much else to do. I even found books in the library that, for all intents and purposes, confirmed my theory—as much as they could, anyway.

The silence stretches as my eyes flick from one to the other. I swallow hard, taking a breath before I finally say, "You—you're…" I clear my throat, wishing I could crawl under my comforter. Beckett waves me on.

"V-vampires," I whisper, staring at the floor, my voice barely audible. "Right?"

There's a beat of silence.

And another.

And then Quinn bursts out laughing, doubling over and clutching his stomach. "This is the skin of a killer!" he declares, holding his arms out dramatically, grinning like an idiot. He's laughing so hard that his voice cracks. I stare at him, bewildered. I really don't see what's so funny about this.

"Quinn, shut up," Beckett mutters with a deep sigh, pinching the bridge of his nose. A faint twitch of a smile tugs at the corner of his lips. Whit rolls his eyes and smacks him on the back of the head while Quinn's doubled over, trying to catch his breath.

Quinn straightens, still chuckling, and shakes his head. "You're killing me, sweetheart." He laughs again, muttering under his breath, "Vampires."

Before I can protest, Beckett steps forward, his gray gaze locking onto mine. Without warning, he throws me over his shoulder—again—like I weigh nothing. I gasp, flailing for a moment, but freeze when he slaps my rear hard enough to sting.

"Put me down!" I screech, kicking my legs and pound my fists against his back, but he doesn't so much as flinch—only tightens his arms around my legs, pinning them to his chest.

"No can do," he says dryly. "We've got somewhere to be."

They move with purpose, their strides steady and silent as Beckett carries me down the maze-like halls. I twist, trying to see where we're going, but the angle makes it impossible.

They haul me through several turns before stopping in front of a wall covered in framed paintings. I do *not* trust the paintings in this place. Beckett shifts me slightly, allowing me to see over his shoulder. Whit steps forward and swings open a small frame in the wall. He lines his eye up with what looks like a scanner, and with a low hum, the entire wall slides away, revealing a dark staircase leading into the unknown. I'm stunned into silence by the discovery.

My stomach drops as they step toward the stairs. "No," I whisper, my voice trembling. "No, no, no—I don't want to go down there."

It's their crypt.

It must be.

What are they planning to do to me once they have me down there?

I don't think I want to know.

"Oh well," Beckett says, tightening his grip. He starts down the stairs, the others following close behind.

"I'm serious!" I cry, panic bubbling over. "I—I don't… please don't eat me! I swear, I won't tell anyone!"

Quinn snickers, his voice dripping with mischief. "Oh, we're going to eat you, sweetheart—just not in the way you're thinking."

Beckett shakes his head, the vibrations from his movement reaching me before I hear the quiet chuckle slipping through his otherwise stoic demeanor. Whit barks out a laugh and claps Quinn on the shoulder. "Nice one."

I expected torches, dripping stalactites, and the stench of death and decay on the way down—not this. It's massive and more like an underground military base than a basement—or a crypt. High ceilings and sleek black walls gleam faintly under the motion-sensor lights. It's both awe-inspiring and eerily organized, as if chaos and control met somewhere in the middle to create this place.

Beckett sets me down, and I wobble slightly, my legs still shaky from the stairs—and everything else. I clutch the edge of a nearby table to steady myself, my eyes darting around the room. It's overwhelming: a mix of high-tech equipment and carefully arranged weapons, all neatly contained in their designated sections around the expansive space.

Who are they?

"This," Whit says, sweeping his arms out dramatically, "is the Batcave."

I blink, brow furrowing as I take a step forward, rubbing

my arms against my chill-pricked skin. I realize my comforter must have been dropped somewhere along the way. "Why do you call it that?" I ask cautiously, half-expecting an ominous response.

"Why do you think?" Whit grins, clearly expecting me to get it.

Whatever *it* is.

"Are there... bats?" My voice wavers as I glance around nervously, scanning the high corners of the room for any sign of fluttering wings.

"No bats," Beckett says dryly, crossing his arms over his chest. His tone is flat, yet there's a glint of amusement in his eyes.

Quinn groans dramatically, throwing his hands in the air. "Don't tell me you've never seen Batman!"

I shift uncomfortably, a flush creeping up my neck. "I haven't," I admit quietly, my voice barely above a whisper.

Quinn looks like he's been physically wounded. "Unbelievable. Absolutely unacceptable." He points a finger at Whit. "We're fixing this—tonight."

Whit chuckles, throwing an arm around my shoulders. "Don't worry, Celest. We'll just have to show you. There are several movies, but *Batman Returns* is clearly the best."

"He's lying to you," Quinn interrupts, his voice dripping with mock seriousness. "*Batman Forever* is the masterpiece."

"He's the only person in the world who thinks that," Beckett mutters, his lips twitching into a smirk.

Whit snorts, and I can't help but smile, the tension in my chest easing just a little.

But only a little. It's like they're totally different men, and I don't trust it.

Whit leads me toward one side of the room, where an entire wall is covered in weapons. Knives, guns, small metal things in the shape of stars, and even more things I can't begin to identify are arranged with almost obsessive precision. Each piece gleams under the faint light, proving how meticulously each has been cared for.

That's... terrifying.

"Impressive, huh?" Whit asks, his tone light but proud.

I nod, swallowing hard. One word for it, I suppose. "Do you... actually use all of them?"

"Every single one," Beckett says from behind me, his arms crossed and his voice more casual than I've ever heard it. "Each has its purpose."

Oh, so they plan to use all of these on me? Is that the point of showing me this?

Quinn leans against the wall, twirling a knife between his fingers. "And some are just for fun," he adds with a grin.

I give him a wary look, and he laughs. "Relax, sweetheart. We don't bite—unless you ask nicely."

We move toward a bank of computers, their screens glowing brightly. Sleek and modern, they display complex graphs, maps, and what appears to be surveillance footage. I stare at them, my mind racing to make sense of what I see.

Again, I ask myself—who are they?

"What's all this?" I ask, my voice barely above a whisper. This is so far beyond the scope of what I thought I'd find down here.

"Our work," Beckett replies, stepping forward to tap a few keys on one of the keyboards. Work? The screen shifts, revealing a detailed map with dozens of blinking red dots. "This is how we track our targets."

I glance at him, a growing sense of unease building. "Targets?" I repeat.

Whit leans against the desk, his expression softening slightly. "We're contract killers. This is how we plan, how we move. Everything starts here."

"Assassins!" Quinn yells, and the others groan. I'm getting the sense this is a regular debate for them.

"That sounds far cooler than 'contract killers,'" he adds, altering his voice to mimic Whit's in a ridiculous way.

Contract killers? Assassins?

I knew they were dangerous—but this? They stand around me, acting as if announcing they're killers is akin to announcing they're architects, which, to them, it might very well be.

They're not just killers; they're professionals—trained, organized, and incredibly lethal. I swallow hard, my mind scrambling for something—anything—to distract me from the fact that I'll likely never leave this place alive. I'm not sure what's more frightening—vampires or assassins?

I shove that thought down, tucking it away for later.

The farther we go, the more this place feels like something out of a movie—dark, sprawling, almost too incredible to be real. Yet, the reality of it is unmistakable. Everything has a purpose, a function, and every corner tells me this is more than just where they work—it's where they live.

I knew they lived under the manor—I knew it.

As we pass through another heavy steel door—this one opening with the simple push of a button—I step into a hallway that feels... warmer. Not in temperature, but in atmosphere. The ceiling is lined with recessed lights, casting a softer glow than the cold fluorescents that lit the rest of the space. The air carries a faint scent of leather and cedar. It's less a cave, more a home.

"This is where we live when we aren't working—that's why you've never seen us in the big house," Whit says.

The first door opens, and I immediately know it belongs to Beckett. The room is stark—clean and precise, just like him. The walls are deep charcoal gray, the only splash of color coming from a single piece of abstract art hanging above a low, modern bed, which is neatly made, the dark sheets pulled tight without a single wrinkle. Almost militaristic.

A desk sits against one wall, its surface meticulously organized. A leather-bound notebook lies closed beside a set of perfectly aligned pens and a small, sleek laptop. A shelf holds a handful of books—history, strategy, philosophy—all lined up like soldiers in formation.

I step inside hesitantly, running my fingers over the edge of the desk. "It's so... neat," I murmur.

"Control freak," Quinn says under his breath.

Beckett stands in the doorway, arms crossed. "Clutter is a distraction," he says simply, his sharp gaze watching me carefully.

"It's very... you," I say before I can stop myself. His lips twitch into the faintest hint of a smile, but he doesn't respond.

The next room couldn't be more different. Whit's space feels warm and inviting, like stepping into a cozy cabin. The walls are paneled in rich wood, and the furniture is sturdy yet comfortable, with a large leather armchair positioned near a tall bookshelf crammed with novels—everything from classics to thrillers. A soft, well-worn throw blanket drapes over the arm of the chair, and a small table beside it holds a mug and a stack of what looks like journals.

The bed is large and unmade, the thick plaid comforter rumpled as if he's just climbed out of it. A faint scent of coffee and something earthy—like pine—lingers in the air.

"You're messy," I blurt out, my cheeks heating as Whit laughs. I really need to get better control of my mouth.

"It's called lived-in, princess," he says, throwing an arm around my shoulders. "Not all of us have control issues like Beck."

"I heard that," Beckett calls from the hallway.

When we step into the following room, I can't help but laugh. It's... chaos. The walls are covered in posters—some framed, others tacked up haphazardly—of bands, movies, and random quotes that make no sense to me but clearly mean something to him. The bed is a mess of mismatched pillows and blankets, while the floor is littered with a strange mix of workout gear, clothes, books, and what appears to be a half-assembled gadget.

A vintage record player sits in one corner, surrounded by stacks of vinyl records. The air hums faintly with the scent of something spicy—maybe cologne or aftershave. On a small table near the bed, an open notebook filled with doodles and scribbles catches my eye.

"Don't judge me," Quinn says, grinning as he steps around me and flops onto the bed. "Creative genius looks a lot like chaos to the untrained eye."

I raise an eyebrow and fold my arms. "Is that what you're calling this?"

"Hey, it works for me," he says, kicking his feet up and tossing a pillow at Whit, who catches it with ease.

"It's... interesting," I say diplomatically, earning a bark of laughter from Whit and a mock-wounded expression from Quinn, which makes me smile.

They're so... normal. Which version of them is real?

At the end of the hall is a shared lounge area. It's a mix of all their personalities—a massive sectional sofa piled with mismatched pillows, a coffee table covered in files and empty coffee mugs, and a flat-screen TV mounted on the wall. A stack of board games leans precariously atop a shelf, while the other shelves are filled with books, movies, and a few odd knickknacks.

"This is where we unwind," Whit says, gesturing to the space. "Well, some of us. Beck only sits here if he's forced to. The guy is allergic to relaxing."

Beckett rolls his eyes. "I'm more than capable of relaxing —I'm here more than you think."

"Sure, sure," Quinn says, flopping onto the couch. "But only if a documentary's involved."

I glance around, taking it all in. The space is chaotic, cozy, and somehow... normal. For all their sharp edges and dangerous games, this feels like a glimpse of something softer.

Something real... but can I trust it?

Off to the side, a cozy kitchen area is tucked into one corner of the space. It's smaller than the massive, outdated kitchen upstairs, but it feels warmer and more inviting. The cabinets are dark wood, and the countertops are smooth, polished granite. A stainless steel fridge hums quietly in the corner, a wide island with barstools tucked under it, and an open shelf filled with mugs, plates, and jars of what appear to be spices and... *snacks*.

They have snacks? My gaze snaps in to the fridge, and before I can stop myself, I imagine it filled with food.

Real food.

My stomach growls loudly, breaking the silence. All three men turn to look at me.

"Something on your mind, sweetheart?" Quinn asks, a grin tugging at his lips.

I can't help it, and I don't care to try—the words spit out, sharp and angry. "You've had all of this down here the whole time while I've been starving for nearly a week?"

Whit's brow furrows, and Beckett straightens from his lean against the counter. For once, Quinn doesn't have a smart comment.

"You've been starving?" Whit asks, his voice quieter, as if he didn't quite hear me.

"Yes!" I snap, my frustration boiling over. "The kitchen upstairs is practically empty! I've been eating crackers and peanut butter like some stray dog while you've had this whole... feast hiding down here?"

Quinn blinks, startled by the outburst, then lets out a nervous laugh. "Well... that's on us, I guess."

"You think?" I say, throwing my hands up and heading toward the fridge.

I yank open the door, my jaw dropping. It's stocked—overflowing, really—with fresh fruits, vegetables, cheeses, deli meats, cartons of eggs, and even a couple of pies. There's milk, juice, soda, and energy drinks. My stomach twists painfully, a sharp reminder of how little I've eaten since arriving here.

I turn back to them, my expression a mix of disbelief and

anger. "You mean to tell me I could've been eating real food this whole time?"

Quinn scratches the back of his neck, looking sheepish for once. "Uh, yeah. Guess we should've thought about it."

Whit steps forward, holding his hands up as if he's trying to calm me down. Fool. You can't calm a hungry woman. "We didn't think you'd go hungry. There's food upstairs—"

"Barely!" I snap, cutting him off. "Did you not hear me? I've been living off crackers and a half-empty jar of peanut butter. That's it."

Beckett lets out a long breath, his jaw tightening. "That's... fuck, I'm sorry. It's unacceptable," he says, his tone firm, leaving no room for argument. "We should have made sure you had enough to eat."

"Really? You don't say." My voice drips with sarcasm. My stomach growls again—louder this time—and I glare at them. "Move. I'm eating everything."

Quinn grins and steps aside with a dramatic bow. "All yours, sweetheart. Knock yourself out."

I grab an apple from the fridge and bite into it so hard that juice runs down my chin. I don't care. It's the best thing I've tasted in days.

Whit leans against the counter, watching me with a small frown. "We'll make it up to you," he says, his voice softer. "We didn't realize."

I swallow a mouthful of apple and give him a hard look. "You didn't ask. And you should've."

Beckett nods, his expression serious. "You're right. It won't happen again."

Quinn nudges Whit with his elbow. "Better make her a

real meal, big guy. She's not going to forgive us for crackers and peanut butter."

"No, I'm not. But later. I'm too hungry to wait," I mutter, reaching for another apple.

I eat, but I don't let my guard down—not completely. Their apologies comes too quickly, too easily, like flipping a switch. They've spent days making me feel helpless, and now I'm supposed to believe they just... forgot? My fingers tighten around my sandwich. No—I won't be that easy to win over.

The apples are just the beginning. By the time I've raided the fridge and cabinets, I've assembled a mismatched feast: a turkey sandwich, grapes, a handful of chips, and a slice of pie that looks too good to ignore.

"You can have more," Whit says, rubbing the back of his neck sheepishly.

"I don't want to get sick. You have to reintroduce food to an empty stomach carefully." He looks at me with his far-too-observant eyes.

"How do you know that?" he asks. I don't want to tell them about Josiah. I'm not sure they wouldn't hand me over to him.

"Experience." His eyes squint as if he's considering more questions, but he doesn't push, and I relax—just a little more.

Tucked into a corner of the couch in the lounge, I balance my plate on my lap as the guys move around the room, their energy noticeably lighter than before.

It puts me on edge.

"All right," Quinn says, clapping his hands together as he drops onto the opposite end of the couch. "Time to fix your tragic lack of cultural knowledge. Beck, hit the lights."

Beckett, already standing near the wall, flips a switch. The room dims as a massive screen slides down from the ceiling, covering the mounted television. I stare at it, my sandwich halfway to my mouth. "That's a bit excessive. You have a perfectly large flat-screen television."

"It's awesome," Quinn corrects, grinning. "And it's perfect for what we're about to do. The TV can't compete."

Whit settles into the armchair next to me, throws a blanket over his lap, and gets cozy. I'm having a hard time reconciling this Whit with Blue Mask. "We're starting with *Batman Returns*," he says, shooting Quinn a warning look before he can object. "You can get your weird *Batman Forever* agenda out of the way later."

Quinn groans but doesn't argue. Beckett takes the seat closest to the remote, his movements calm and deliberate as he navigates the menu. The opening credits roll, the eerie orchestral music filling the room, and I can't help but feel a small thrill of excitement about watching a movie I know I'm not supposed to.

I take a bite of my sandwich, my eyes glued to the screen as the first scenes play out. It's darker than I expected—both literally and figuratively—and I find myself drawn in almost immediately. The shadows, the music, the characters—it's captivating.

"Michelle Pfeiffer's Catwoman," Whit whispers, nodding toward the screen. "Best portrayal, hands down." I nod, like I have any idea what he's talking about, as I chew.

"Debatable," Quinn mutters, shoving a handful of popcorn into his mouth.

"Not debatable," Beckett says not looking up, his tone flat but resolute.

I glance at them, a smile tugging at my lips despite my

wariness. They're nothing like I thought they were—assuming they're being genuine. Each is so different, yet they fit together in a way I don't quite understand. For the first time since I arrived, I feel a little less like an outsider and a little more like... I belong.

Which is insane. It's too soon for that—too soon to think about what this is or what it could be. They're still the same men who have been holding me against my will for a week. This is still a prison—just a much larger, nicer one than I thought.

I shake off the thoughts quickly, focusing on my food and the movie. For now, it's enough to sit here, eat my sandwich, and lose myself in Gotham's dark and twisted streets.

I can worry later—much later.

17

The faint smell of something delicious wafts through the air, waking me—eggs, syrup, and... bacon? My eyes flutter open, my mind sluggish as I try to recall where I am. The couch beneath me is far too comfortable, and the blanket I've snuggled into smells like... them. The events of last night catch up—movie, food, and... oh right, assassins with multiple personalities who are most definitely not vampires.

I sit up, stretching as the smell of breakfast grows stronger. My stomach growls loudly, a clear reminder of how hungry I still am, even after last night's feast. Across the room, Whit stands—shirtless, mind you—at the stove, a spatula in one hand and a frying pan in the other. His broad shoulders shift as he flips something, the sizzle filling the quiet space.

"Morning," Whit says without turning around. "You slept like a rock, so I figured I'd better get a head start on making up for the lack of meals."

Before I can respond, Quinn hops over the couch, landing in an easy sprawl at my feet. He yawns through a full-body stretch, lazy and unbothered, but the movement pulls his muscles taut, making the ink shift over his skin. Dark lines coil around his arms—serpents weaving through jagged symbols, their meanings unknown to me. Across his chest, a black dagger plunges downward, its blade fractured by old scars, the hilt curling across his chest in ornate filigree—elegant but unforgiving.

"Must not have thought much of the movie if you conked out before it ended," he says, his voice rough with sleep.

I turn toward him, narrowing my eyes as he smirks and lifts my feet into his lap—casual, comfortable. Like he wasn't the same man who threw knives at me.

"I didn't fall asleep because of the movie," I shoot back. "I was just tired and finally had a full belly."

"Sure," Quinn says, his grin widening. "That's what they all say."

Whit glances over his shoulder, giving Quinn a pointed look. "Leave her alone, Quinn. Not everyone wants to sit through hours of explosions and brooding in tights."

"Or," Quinn starts, "it's clearly a subpar Batman. I don't make the rules." He looks at me and winks.

The Quinn who dragged the tip of a knife across my skin is not the same Quinn holding my feet in his lap. I think my mind finally broke. Maybe this is all a hallucination.

Beckett steps into the room, his sharp eyes scanning me before flicking toward the stove. "Ignore him," he says simply. "He's been insufferable about this ever since *Batman Forever* came out when we were kids."

"Because it's a masterpiece!" Quinn protests, throwing up his hands. "The world just wasn't ready for it."

I can't help but laugh—loud, unguarded, shockingly carefree.

"For the record," I say, glancing at Whit, "I liked what I saw of the movie. I've never been allowed to watch anything like it before, and I'd love to finish it soon."

Whit smiles, a warm, genuine expression that lights up his face. "Good answer. And we'll *definitely* be revisiting that whole strict upbringing thing." He nods toward the counter. "Sit. Breakfast is almost ready."

For a moment—a brief, fleeting moment—I forget.

Forget that they've kept me captive, terrorized me through the night, left me shivering in nothing but scraps of fabric. Forget that they feasted while I starved.

Forget their hands on my skin.

Until I remember.

The small smile I'd been wearing slowly melts away.

I pull my feet from Quinn's lap and move toward the kitchen, tightening the blanket around me as I take a seat at the island. It's not my comforter, but it's a barrier—thin, but enough. A reminder not to let my guard down.

The smell of eggs and bacon is stronger now, my stomach growling louder this time. Quinn snickers, and I shoot him a glare as he slides onto the stool beside me.

"Don't start," I warn, brandishing a butter knife at him. "This is your fault, after all."

Quinn leans in, letting the tip of the knife press into his throat, his heated gaze locking with mine. "Oh, sweetheart, if you wanted to play with knives, you should have just said so."

I swallow hard, lowering the blunted utensil as he laughs.

That's a flash of the Quinn I thought I knew. Maybe both versions of him are real. Without his mask, it's easy to forget how terrifying he can be.

Beckett leans against the counter, arms crossed, shaking his head at Quinn's antics. He's the only one who looks like he's been up for hours already—probably picking out their next person to murder. Or "target," as they call it.

"I hope you like pancakes," Whit says, sliding a plate stacked high onto the counter. "Figured even if you didn't, they had to be better than crackers and peanut butter."

Right on cue, my stomach growls again.

"I love them, and I think I could eat everything in this kitchen," I admit, eyeing the stack hungrily—yet again struggling to reconcile who they are.

Pancakes. Murder.

"Good. You're going to need the energy," Quinn says, stealing a piece of bacon from the plate.

"For what?" I ask, cursing myself for getting too comfortable. Letting my guard slip.

Whit sets a plate in front of me, his expression serious but kind. Hard to believe he's the same man who hunted me through the hall of mirrors.

"We've still got a lot to show you, and we"—he gestures to the three of them—"have a lot of work to get done today."

Work.

Right. Murder.

I glance between them, certain they're hiding something. A strange mix of curiosity and apprehension knots in my chest. It shouldn't be this easy—sitting here with them, doing something as normal as eating breakfast. It's dangerous.

I'm just waiting for the other shoe to drop. But as I take

the first bite of pancakes, I decide I don't care. If this is the only bit of peace I'm going to get, I'm taking full advantage of it.

Every.

Delicious.

Bite.

Once full and with the dishes cleared, I'm more confused than ever. They're planning something, yet they make it impossible to stay ready for whatever they might throw at me.

Maybe that's the whole point.

Maybe they get a thrill out of tricking me. Wouldn't surprise me.

I trade the blanket for a discarded sweatshirt draped over the back of the couch and slide it over my head. It's huge, hanging lower than the scraps of nothing I've been wearing. I sigh, my bare feet padding across the cold floor as I follow the men back into the *Batcave*.

Now, if only I could get some socks.

The massive space is just as overwhelming the second time as it was the first. At least now, I don't think they're planning to eat me for dinner.

Whether or not I'll get to keep my life? Still up for debate.

"We didn't get to give you the grand tour last night," Whit says, striding ahead with easy confidence. "Now, we'll show you the true heart of the place."

I nod, rolling up the too-long sleeves of my borrowed sweatshirt. It smells faintly of cedar and leather. If Whit's smug grin is any indication, it's his.

It's warm. He'll be lucky to get it back.

Honestly, he deserves far worse—never mind that he could take it from me anytime he wanted.

Our first stop is a wide-open space lined with padded mats and an assortment of equipment. Heavy punching bags hang from chains, and a rack of sparring gear sits in one corner.

"This is where we keep ourselves sharp," Whit says, gesturing to the room. He almost sounds excited for me to see it.

I glance around, fairly certain I know exactly what *sharp* entails. The thought of how many people he's killed with his bare hands sends a chill down my spine—especially when I recall the feel of those same rough hands on my skin.

Is it a chill? Or is it a thrill?

What is wrong with me?

The mats are worn, scuffed from countless fights. The punching bags look rock hard, like they'd hurt even with the padded gloves Quinn now holds in his hands.

"You ever thrown a punch, sweetheart?" he asks.

I've noticed they like to use monikers for me, as if I'm something special to them—which is impossible. Crazy to even contemplate.

Quinn tosses the gloves into the air, catching them with a grin. I swear I've never seen the man without some form of amusement on his face.

Now that I think about it, the expression on his mask suits him.

I shake my head, taking an involuntary step back as my father's words echo through my mind. *Fighting is for men, and men protect women.* At least, according to him. The same men meant to protect me were the ones I needed protecting from.

"No. It's not something I was ever allowed to consider."

"Well, maybe you should now," Beckett says from behind me. He sounds genuine. "It's a skill worth having."

They're the first men to suggest I learn to defend myself. Yet again, I find myself struggling to reconcile the masked men with the ones standing in front of me.

What does it mean that I like both versions of them?

Probably that I'm broken. That something is *severely* wrong with me.

The darkness inside me grins, nodding in agreement. *Well, that's nice.* I roll my proverbial eyes at her.

I don't respond, my gaze darting between the gloves and the bags. They're right, of course. I *should* learn to protect myself. And the thought of punching Josiah in the nose if I ever see him again? That fills me with joy.

Yes. I'd like that very much.

The darkness inside me grins wider, her smile turning sharp as a blade. Apparently, she wants to see him hurt as much as I do. Wait—*do* I? It's not something I've ever let myself consider. Now that I have? Yes. I want to see him suffer.

Immensely.

Shaking the vindictive thoughts from my mind, I follow them into a tucked-away, soundproofed corner—a shooting range. The air smells faintly of gunpowder—or at least, I assume that's what the acrid scent is. A dizzying array of firearms lines the walls, while targets hang at varying distances, some already riddled with holes.

"This is Beck's domain," Quinn says with his signature smirk, nudging me toward the room. "He's got a bit of a thing for precision."

"I hadn't noticed," I say, my voice dripping with sarcasm, causing even Beckett to quirk a smile.

"You shoot?" Whit asks, his tone curious.

I shake my head again, my brows scrunching. I'm not sure what makes him think I wouldn't be able to fight, but shooting a gun would be fine. "No, I've never even touched a gun."

Quinn whistles low, leaning against the wall—never standing straight. "Let me guess," he drawls, eyes gleaming. "Another thing you weren't *allowed* to consider?" He stretches out the word, like the very idea offends him.

"Exactly," I say, nodding.

"Well, that'll change soon enough," Whit declares.

"Not today," Beckett says as he disassembles a gun, then starts cleaning it. "She's not ready. Maybe after a few good meals, when the recoil won't knock her on her ass."

He's not wrong. I was already too thin when I arrived—stress gnawing at me for weeks before my escape—and after nearly a week of barely eating, I've lost even more weight.

Not that it's my fault.

I glance at the wall of guns and shiver. What if I shoot my foot off or something?

"Don't worry," Beckett says like he can read my mind. "First, you'll learn to handle, disassemble, reassemble, and clean this guy." He holds up a small handgun, almost comical in his large hands.

I *suppose* I could manage that.

The darkness inside me makes moon eyes at the gun, practically bouncing at the thought of firing one. She grows more terrifying by the day.

Quinn grabs my hand, practically vibrating as he tugs me toward a side chamber. "Now *this*," he says, grin widening, "is where the real fun happens."

The space opens into a massive warehouse garage. Sleek

cars gleam under bright lights, motorcycles line one wall, and in the far corner...

A helicopter.

My mouth falls open.

"You have a *helicopter*?" My voice squeaks slightly. Who just *has* a helicopter lying around?

Apparently, they do.

Quinn beams. "Technically, we have two, but one's in the shop."

"Of course it is," I mutter. Correction—how silly of me. *Two.* Because one isn't enough.

Whit laughs, patting my shoulder at the disbelief I'm sure is written all over my face. "Quinn likes to push the limits. Let's just say it doesn't always end well."

"It was *one* time!" Quinn protests, flipping him off with both hands. "And the building wasn't even *that* damaged."

I huff a laugh, shaking my head as my gaze drifts over the vehicles. "You guys have... twenty-three cars?" I do a quick count. "What could you possibly need that many for?"

"Options," Beckett replies with a shrug.

Whit chuckles. "And maybe just a little indulgence. This one goes particularly fast." He pats the hood of a sleek, low-slung car. I know nothing about cars, but most of them look like they're meant to go *much* faster than necessary.

Quinn slings an arm around my shoulders—he seems to have an *urge* to touch me as often as possible. "You know what they say—boys and their toys."

"Right," I murmur, looking around again, unable to help but wonder how much all of this costs. More than I can fathom, I'm sure. Killing people must be lucrative.

My stomach twists at the thought of taking money in exchange for someone's life.

The final space they take me to must be their hub of operations. I caught a glimpse of it last night—a large table dominates the center, covered in maps, blueprints, and photographs. Screens glow faintly along the walls, streaming surveillance footage and data.

Beckett takes his place at the head of the table, his sharp gaze scanning the materials in front of him. Whit moves to one of the screens, brow furrowed in concentration, while Quinn pulls up a chair and starts fiddling with... something. Wires, metal, bits of tech—assuming that's what it is. To me, it just looks like a mess of scraps.

They all seem to have their roles.

Now that I'm not panicking, I pay closer attention to the monitors.

Oh.

My.

God.

They've been watching me this whole time.

Multiple cameras monitor the front lawn, the main entrance, the library, several hallways—*and my room.*

When I felt eyes on me, *this* isn't what I imagined.

Then I see a panel with several buttons labeled: East Wing Halls, Projectors, Great Hall, etc.

"What's all this?" I ask, gesturing toward the monitors and panel.

"Controls for the house," Beckett says, his tone distracted.

"Controls?" I repeat, my heart racing. It can't be.

"Yeah, all the shifting. The guy who built the place was a bit loony and had all these levers that could spin rooms to face new halls or slide halls to access different doors. We just automated everything," Quinn says with a shrug, smirking as I frown in confusion.

"But the ghosts... and that creepy portrait room!" I protest. They had to be real.

"Digital projections—even that mirror I pulled you through," Whit says, never taking his eyes off the screen he's studying.

"So none of it's real?" I ask, disbelief thick in my voice.

"Nope." Beckett pops the p, not bothering to look up from the papers in front of him. "The house is our first line of defense if anyone tries to come for us."

"Is that why you were so convinced I was trying to steal something?" I ask, my brain struggling to process everything.

"Yeah, but after that first night, we knew you weren't." Quinn looks up, flashing me one of his grins before laughing at my growing fury. "We checked you out based on the information in your little bag. Funny thing—you, Celest Monroe, don't actually exist. Didn't take us long to guess it was some kind of WITSEC."

"So you used all of that to terrorize me? For what—fun?" My voice shakes with rage. I choose to skip over that last part.

"Well, yeah," Quinn says, rolling his eyes like it's the most obvious thing in the world. As if their behavior is as mundane as a stroll downtown.

Whit and Beckett nod along without really paying attention, too focused on whatever they're doing.

"Let me get this straight—you thought terrorizing a stranded woman, starving her, and making her believe the house she's trapped in is haunted was just a good time?" My voice rises, sharp enough to make them flinch. A small flicker of satisfaction sparks in my chest.

"Yes? Well, not the starving part—obviously, we fucked up there—but you can't pretend you didn't enjoy our little game." Quinn flashes me a wicked smile, full of dark promises.

My face heats. I look away.

Because he's right.

On some level, I *did* enjoy it.

But I won't tell them that.

"If you're finished, we've got work to do," Beckett says, tone curt, completely disregarding my concerns. "Try not to touch anything."

Like I'm a child. Like I'm going to wreak havoc.

I stare at him in disbelief. **Two sentences.** That's all it takes to shove me right back into that comforter upstairs, small and powerless.

It hurts.

Which is *incredibly* annoying.

I hover awkwardly at the edge of the room, watching as they fall into a practiced rhythm, feeling out of place. They know each other well enough that they have more silent conversations than spoken ones. The way they work together is almost mesmerizing, but the chaos on the table makes my hands itch.

It's beyond disorganized—the kind of mess that would have driven the Covenant's planners insane. And it's something I'm extremely well-versed in handling. I'm surprised Beckett can stand it after seeing his room.

Before I can talk myself out of it, I step closer to the table. My fingers hover over a stack of files, hesitating for only a moment. "I can help," I say, my voice quiet but confident.

Beckett looks up, his eyes narrowing slightly, as if the thought of me being capable of helping is beyond belief. The doubt in his expression fuels my irritation, sharpening my resolve. I'll show him exactly how capable I am.

"How?"

I take a deep breath. "I went to the Covenant's college and earned a degree in... well, that's not important. What matters is that I was trained to organize—mostly events, but it's more than that. I can look at all this—" I gesture toward the table, where maps and files lay scattered in disarray. "—and make sense of it. I can spot patterns, identify connections, and find the most efficient way to structure anything."

Whit turns away from the screen, curiosity flickering in his expression. "What other secret skills are you hiding?"

"Well, for the role I was meant to fulfill, I had to master the art of reading people," I continue, my words tumbling out now. "I learned how to blend in, how to ask the right questions to gather information without anyone noticing—especially in social settings."

Quinn lets out a low whistle. "Well, damn. What exactly was this role you were meant to fulfill?"

"I—um... I don't really want to talk about it right now," I whisper, lowering my gaze.

Beckett studies me for a long moment before I lift my gaze and meet his. He nods once. "Show us."

I dive in, grateful they don't push, and begin sorting the files into logical piles while flagging inconsistencies in their notes. Then, turning to the maps, I align points with the corresponding data streaming across the screens. My training takes over instinctively, and for the first time since arriving, I feel on solid ground, letting the work consume me. I relish the distraction.

By the time I finish, the table is orderly, the gaps in their plans filled, and the tension in the room subtly altered. Whit regards me with something like respect, and even Beckett's usual stoicism softens. I'm accustomed to being underestimated, but there's a particular satisfaction in proving people wrong.

"You've got a good eye," Beckett says simply, and I can't help but smile.

"Welcome to the team," Quinn adds with a wink.

And then I realize—I just became an accessory to murder.

18

"Celest," Beckett says, his tone unreadable. "Don't think we've forgotten." I pause, plates in hand, a flicker of confusion knotting my brow. The whole day had been oddly domestic.

"Forgotten what?" My gaze shifts to Whit and Quinn, expecting their usual teasing or at least some level of shared confusion. Instead, they wear the same smug expressions as Beckett.

"You still haven't admitted you belong to us, sweetheart," Quinn murmurs as he comes up behind me, his fingers brushing my hair aside. His lips trail soft, deliberate kisses along the curve of my neck, sending shivers down my spine.

"I told you," I manage, my voice already breathy. "I belong to no one but myself."

"No need for lies," Whit interjects smoothly, borrowing one of Quinn's signature smirks. They all seem to think quite highly of themselves right now.

"I'm not." I twist, trying to shake myself free of Quinn's distracting kisses, only to yelp when he sweeps me into his arms, carrying me effortlessly down the hall.

"Guess we'll just have to persuade you," he teases, his laughter rich as I squirm against his hold.

"I think you're right," Whit agrees, pushing open his bedroom door and stepping aside as Quinn strides in, depositing me onto the bed with ease.

Beckett is the last to enter. He strips off his shirt as he crosses the threshold, making quick work of his pants before shaking his head and tsking at me. "Being a bit of a brat aren't you, little thief."

I'm so distracted by Beckett's bare skin and the hard planes of his body, I don't notice Whit tugging the sweatshirt along with my barely-there nightgown off in one swift motion —until the chill in the air prickles my skin.

"Hey, wait!" I cry out, scrambling to cover myself with my hands. "I'm not being a brat!"

Quinn grabs my wrists and pins them above my head. "No hiding. Well, at least not tonight," he says, laughing at his own joke.

When did everyone get naked?

Beckett moves up from the foot of the bed, spreading my knees before lowering his mouth to capture a nipple. A moan slips from me; I'd be embarrassed if I were able to think clearly.

"You won't get what you want until you're a good girl and give us what we need," he murmurs.

"W-what is it I w-want?" I stutter, my voice breathy.

"Guess you'll know when you start begging," Whit says, leaning over from the side of the bed to kiss me. His tongue teases the seam of my lips, and I part for him, letting him claim my mouth, steal my breath, take what he wants.

I break the kiss with a cry as Beckett's tongue drags a slow, deliberate lick up my center, followed by several more. The pressure—it's not enough. Not nearly enough, and I whimper in protest. Quinn chuckles before lifting and flipping me over in one smooth motion.

Beckett slaps my rear and commands, "Up you go, hands and knees." The moment I obey, I squeal as he slides beneath me, gripping my hips, pulling me down to sit on his face. I try to lift, afraid I'll hurt him, but he doesn't let me move.

Quinn kneels in front of me, his fist gathering my hair at the nape of my neck. "Go on then, sweetheart, show me what you've learned." I lower my mouth to his tip, tracing a hesitant lick before wrapping my lips around him, sucking just the head into my mouth. "Fuck," he groans, voice rough. "You're a quick study."

Beckett keeps his slow, deliberate pace, and when I shift, seeking the pressure and speed I need, he tightens his grip on my cheeks, spreading them apart and holding my hips in place with unyielding strength. I let out another frustrated whimper, only for Quinn to hiss and drive deeper into my throat.

Something cold and slick glides against my tight ring before a finger follows, massaging the slippery substance around before pressing inside.

"I'm taking this tonight, princess," Whit murmurs, pumping his finger in and out, gradually increasing his pace. I whimper, a plea forming on my lips. "Don't worry, I promise you can take it."

I'm not convinced, but when he eases in a second finger,

the low groan that emanates from me suggests he might be right.

Finally, the string inside me pulls tighter, coiling to the breaking point I've been desperate for—only to have Beckett and Whit still their movements, letting the tension unravel. When I let out another muffled, frustrated sound, they just laugh. Which infuriates me further.

"All you have to do is give us what we want," Quinn grunts before driving into my throat, forcing a gag from me. Suddenly, it clicks—they're going to keep me teetering, denying my release until I surrender to their demands.

My body betrays me, trembling with need, but my mind refuses to yield. They want me to say it—to surrender, to let them claim me. And maybe... maybe I crave it too. But I won't break so easily.

Beckett and Whit resume their movements, making me gargle a whimper. Pleasure twists with the ache of Whit's fingers stretching me open. Before long, he and Beckett find a rhythm, driving into me in perfect opposition. I fight to conceal how close I am to unraveling, but they know—somehow, they always know. And just when I'm ready to shatter, they all pull away.

"No!" I try to cry out, but Quinn smothers the sound.

"She's ready," Whit declares. I'm lifted again, but just as I'm about to be lowered, Beckett shifts, bringing me face-to-face with him.

"You belong to us. Say it and you'll be rewarded," he commands before positioning himself at my entrance. He yanks my hips down, filling me in one swift thrust—I forget to breathe.

Quinn kneels beside me again. He fists my hair, tilting my head to align perfectly with his hard length—still glistening from moments ago. I part my lips without hesitation before he drives deep, hitting the back of my throat and making me gag again.

"Good girl," Beckett praises from below, guiding my hips to rock against him. More of that slick substance is worked around my now stretched rim, and this time, Whit's fingers slip in with ease. The sensation shifts with Beckett inside me —I feel impossibly full. Whit thrusts his fingers a few more times, twisting them before withdrawing.

I gasp as something much larger presses against me. Beckett stills, and I cry out as the stretch pushes beyond what I thought possible.

"Fuck, princess, you look so good stretching around me like this," Whit groans.

The burn is relentless—oh God, it's unbearable. If not for the tears already streaking my face from choking on Quinn, they'd be falling now. I cry out, but Whit doesn't stop pushing in until he's buried to the hilt.

"So fucking tight, she's strangling my cock," Beckett grits out. They give me a moment to adjust—as if that were possible. I'm so full I can barely breathe. Their shallow movements begin, the sensation overwhelming, stealing what little air I have left. Slowly, the burn fades into something like pleasure edged in pain, and I'm hurtling toward the edge faster than ever before.

No. No. No. No—

Not again.

They still, and slowly withdraw, laughing as I let out a

raw, frustrated scream. "Please, I can't take it," I rasp, my voice raw from Quinn's ruthless thrusts down my throat.

"Say it. You're ours," Quinn commands, tilting my chin until our eyes meet. "Such a beautiful mess. You know how much I love your tears."

I need to fight this.

I should fight it.

But Beckett grips me like I'm his, Whit stretches me—marking his claim, and Quinn—damn him—tilts my chin, forcing me to meet the hunger in his eyes. My breath hitches.

Their hands, their mouths, their control—it drowns me.

I don't want to break free.

My body has already surrendered.

And when Quinn whispers, "Say it, sweetheart," my mind follows.

"Okay," It's breathe.

That's all they need. Whit and Beckett don't bother with gentleness this time, driving into me without hesitation—not that they need to, not when I now take them so easily.

"Not going to last," Quinn admits, his voice strained and his grip tightening. "Be a doll and swallow every drop."

He holds me firmly in place, as I gag around every inch of him, shuddering when he finally spills down my throat before easing out. He tilts my chin, his thumb tracing my swollen lips.

"Look at you," he breathes, voice thick with satisfaction. "Our perfect little mess. So full of cock, just like you should be."

"S—s-so f-full." I manage to agree. He laughs, gently releases my chin, allowing me to collapse onto Beckett.

Beckett and Whit quicken their pace, though Whit

remains measured while Beckett takes me hard and fast. Whit anchors my hips as Beckett thrusts up, slamming into me again and again.

Beckett's arms wrap around me, one hand tangling in my hair as he holds me tight, his breath hot against my ear. "Are you going to come all over our cocks like a good girl?" he growls.

"Y-yes, I'm... I'm come—" I scream, tumbling over the edge, shattering into a million pieces. I'm certain I'll never be able to reassemble myself in the same way again.

Somewhere on the fringes of my mind, I hear Whit groan about how tightly I'm gripping him, before he follows me into bliss—Beckett right behind him, each giving into their releases.

When I finally surface from the haze, time feels irrelevant. I don't bother opening my eyes.

I'm in the bath, though I have no memory of getting here. The hot water is bliss, easing the ache deep in my muscles. Fingers work shampoo into my hair, another set smoothing body wash over my skin. The sensation lulls me, warm and weightless, and I could drift off completely.

Before I know it, I'm lifted from the water, wrapped in a towel, and—faintly, barely there—I swear I feel fingers braiding my hair.

I'm carried from the bathroom and laid gently on the bed. Two soft kisses graze my forehead, followed by murmured goodnights. I mumble a response, already drifting, rolling onto my side as footsteps fade and the door clicks shut.

There's a body. Whit—I think, wrapped in his scent— slides in behind me, tugging the covers over us. One arm slips beneath my head, the other cinching around my waist, holding me flush against him.

Just as sleep claims me, his lips brush my hair, but slumber steals me away before I catch the words he whispers.

THE SOUNDS OF COOKING DRIFT FROM THE KITCHEN—I assume that's where he's gone. He seems to handle every meal, and I'm certainly not complaining.

I was never taught to cook. Growing up, I was told hiring a chef was a mark of status. But now, I suspect Josiah simply wanted to ensure I couldn't fend for myself.

I stretch, wincing as a dull ache settles low in my body—a lingering reminder of last night. My mind should be screaming at me to run.

It's not.

Instead, all I can think about is the way they cared for me afterward, how cherished I felt between them. The realization is nothing short of terrifying.

The soreness isn't as bad as I expected—the bath must have helped. Walking, however, is another story.

I move gingerly to his closet, pulling a button-up from a hanger. It's long enough to pass as a dress, and after rolling the sleeves to my forearms, I follow the scent of cinnamon rolls down the hall.

My mouth waters in anticipation.

"Oh good, you're up," Whit says, pressing a kiss to my cheek. "Nice shirt."

"Quinn was about to wake you. I wouldn't wish that on

anyone," Beckett remarks, sliding a cup of coffee along with the cream and sugar across the counter.

"Please, as if I'd wake Celest the same way I wake you fuckers," Quinn scoffs, feigning offense. "How you feeling, sweetheart?"

"Oh, um," I stammer, suddenly self-conscious. "A bit sore."

Heat blooms in my cheeks, and I can only imagine how red my fair skin has turned. Somehow, I flush even deeper as I glance at the barstool, debating whether to stand instead of sit.

"Not surprising. The fact you're walking makes me question whether those two did a thorough enough job." Quinn smirks, lifting a brow suggestively.

"Oh God, I don't think I could've survived anything more." The words slip out before I can stop them. They all laugh as I bury my face in my hands.

"Don't be embarrassed, not with us," Whit soothes, though the smug look on his face stays firmly in place.

Quinn helps me onto the barstool. It's not the most comfortable, but it's hardly worse than walking.

I splash in some cream, add a touch of sugar, then cradle the warm mug in my perpetually cold hands, sighing after the first sip.

When I open my eyes, all three of them are watching me.

"What?"

"Remember what you agreed to last night?" Beckett asks.

I know exactly what he's talking about.

Their words still echo in my ears: *You belong to us now.*

They'd surrounded me, their presence relentless, until resistance became impossible—until I couldn't deny that I wanted it too. I should feel regret. I should be ashamed. But as I sip my coffee, swallowed in Whit's shirt, their eyes heavy on me... I don't.

It's not that I've given up.

No, I'll never belong to anyone the way Josiah wanted me to.

This... this is different.

It's not control, or power, or obligation.

It's *connection*.

Yes, they're killers. Yes, they held me against my will in a house they let me believe was haunted. And yes, they starved me—albeit unintentionally.

Allegedly.

Yet, they make me feel safe. They push me to grow, to learn—not to hold me back.

As masked men, they made me feel alive. As men, they've unraveled me, shown me things I never knew my body could feel.

I know it's too soon to trust them. I know I never should.

But I want them.

And I'm so tired of fighting it.

I draw a deep breath, meeting Beckett's gaze, then Whit's, before finally landing on Quinn—who's already grinning.

"Fine," I concede, folding my arms. "I'm yours. But you need to understand something."

Quinn leans in dramatically, eyes gleaming. "And what might that be, sweetheart?"

I jab a finger into his chest. "If I'm yours, then you're mine. All three of you. No more pushing your will on me. If I'm in this, it's because *I choose to be*."

Beckett nods, his expression firm, approving. "Fair enough. But I can't promise I won't be controlling."

Not that I'd want to give up his particular brand of control anyway.

Whit smiles, his voice as steady and warm as he is. "We wouldn't have it any other way."

Quinn, of course, can't resist the drama. He clutches his chest like he's suffered a mortal wound. "She's so bossy! I think I love her even more!"

"Shut up, Quinn," Beckett mutters, though the faint twitch of his lips betrays him. I've noticed he says that at least once a day.

I tighten my arms across my chest, fixing them each with a sharp glare. "But—and this is non-negotiable—I need clothes. Actual clothes. And shoes. I refuse to keep wandering around half-naked like some... some kept pet."

Quinn gasps, flinging his hands in the air. "How dare you insult the negligees! They're luxurious, made in France, and hand-selected—"

"They're scraps," I cut in, sharp and final. "I want real clothes. That's not too much to ask."

Whit chuckles, shaking his head. "She's got a point, Quinn. The least we can do is let her choose her own wardrobe."

Beckett slips a hand into his pocket, pulls out his wallet, and without hesitation, passes me a sleek black credit card. "Get whatever you want."

I stare at the card, blinking. "That's it? No limits, no rules?"

"None," Beckett replies smoothly. "We trust you."

They trust me.

Quinn groans, throwing himself onto the couch like he's mourning a great loss. "This is it. The end of the negligee era. However will we survive?"

"You'll manage," I say dryly, taking the card from Beckett's hand. The weight of it feels strange in my palm—like a key to a freedom I hadn't realized I needed.

Whit grabs a piece of paper from the counter, jotting something down. "Here's the PO Box. Have everything sent there. It's secure."

I glance at the address, then back at the three of them, eyes narrowing. "This feels... too easy."

Whit grins, tone teasing. "It's called trust, Celest. You're ours now, remember? That means we take care of you."

"And you take care of us," Beckett adds, and I nearly topple over when he winks at me. "It goes both ways."

I swallow hard, warmth tightening in my chest—foreign but undeniable.

They mean it. They want to take care of me.

I don't know how or why this has happened, but they do, and I'm certain I've made the right choice.

"Okay," I whisper, nodding. "Thank you."

Quinn sits up suddenly, grinning wide and mischievous. "Just promise us one thing."

"What?"

"Don't get granny panties or muumuus," he teases, winking. "I'm holding out hope for at least one scandalous dress."

I roll my eyes, but the smile tugging at my lips refuses to be contained. "You'll just have to wait and see. I guess you better make sure to be a good boy, then, huh?"

Quinn groans, throwing a hand against his forehead in mock swoon. "Did I mention I think I'm in love?"

I laugh, shaking my head. "You're ridiculous."

"I know. Isn't it great?"

The other two groan in exasperation as I laugh again.

And then it hits me—I'm happy.

It's not conventional. Most would probably find it horrific. But I'm done caring what other people think.

I'm happy. That's all that matters.

The rest is just noise.

19

The days blur into weeks, time slipping by unnoticed. It didn't take long for me to fall into their rhythm. Every morning, Whit makes breakfast before we get to work.

They follow their training schedule religiously, and today is hand-to-hand combat—my favorite. That has absolutely nothing to do with their sweat-slicked, half-naked bodies as they throw each other around.

Nope.

Not at all.

The rest of the time, when they're not training, they're preparing for the upcoming mission—one I'm thrilled to be a part of. Especially after learning they only eliminate the worst of the worst. I feel charged, alive with purpose. Like I finally belong.

Not trapped.

Not forced. Just... part of it.

I doubt this is what Josiah envisioned when he sent me to

the Covenant's college—which only makes it more satisfying. Who knew those skills would find their purpose here, woven seamlessly into the art of killing?

Over the next couple days, we'll fine-tune every detail. Beckett insists on running through each possible scenario multiple times—which I truly appreciate. Quinn handles the last-minute adjustments to their gear, checking for defects, while Whit ensures they have every tool and weapon necessary for any situation that might arise.

The target is a man named Jonah Richter—a name that meant nothing to me a few days ago but now sends a shiver through me. He's a weapons dealer with no scruples about who he sells to, as long as they pay. Many of his customers leave a trail of innocent bodies in their wake. The images from one of his clients' most recent attacks made me want to vomit. Children's bodies were strewn about, broken and bloodied, left to rot. It's something now forever burned into my memory.

Richter is known for keeping a low profile, running his operations from a heavily guarded compound deep in the mountains. No lavish mansions, no public appearances—just cold, calculated business in the shadows. It made him difficult to track, but once we did, the planning began.

For days, we've been piecing together a way into his fortress. It's isolated, surrounded by dense forest, making it difficult to get clear imaging. The security system is high-tech, and he has enough guards to fend off an army. As Beckett said earlier, "It's the kind of place you don't get out of unless you're invisible—or very good."

His words made my stomach churn with nerves.

I sit at the large table in the center of the hub, surrounded by blueprints, surveillance images, and maps marked with guard rotations and blind spots. My job is to oversee it all—spotting gaps in security, identifying weaknesses to exploit, and coordinating with them once the mission begins. They've had me practice relaying information through simulations until I felt confident, for which I'm grateful. I'm still nervous, but not like before.

"We'll enter here," Beckett says, pointing to a narrow gap in the compound's perimeter. "There's a blind spot in the cameras, but we've only got a fifteen-second window."

"You know how fast we'll have to move to make that work?" Quinn asks, raising an eyebrow.

Beckett shows no concern. "That's what training is for."

Whit, standing near the table, glances at me, his presence a calming counterbalance to Beckett's intensity. "What do you think?"

I hesitate, scanning the layout again. "It's tight," I admit, "but if you wait and move the moment the guard's shift changes"—I point to one near the blind spot—"it'll be completely unmonitored. Might only give you five extra seconds, but that could help."

Beckett nods, approving. "Five seconds can make all the difference. We'll need you watching their movements, telling us when to go. But this should be just enough—long enough to get in or out unnoticed."

"We'll need a backup plan," Whit says, tracing a route with his finger. "If something goes wrong, this is our only other way out."

"I'll make a note," I reply, jotting it down.

As the plan takes shape, my stomach churns. It's one thing to sit here, looking at maps and blueprints, creating a plan when everything feels hypothetical. But the thought of them actually going into that compound, facing armed men and security so lethal it screams kill first, ask questions later, makes it hard to breathe.

What if they don't make it back?

"You okay?" Whit asks, his voice soft as he leans in toward me.

I quickly nod and force a smile. "Yeah. Just... nervous."

"Don't be," Quinn says, flashing his usual grin. "We've done jobs like this a hundred times, and now we've got you keeping track of what we can't see. It's going to be a blast."

I want to believe him—both that it will be fun and that my role will make a difference. Yet, the fear lingers just beneath the surface. I know I'll be a nervous wreck the entire time they're gone.

Quinn sprawls in his chair, a knife gliding over his knuckles—a habit as natural as breathing—while Whit and Beckett go over what they'll need to bring. As always, Quinn knows exactly how to pull me from my spiraling thoughts.

"You're getting scary good at this," he says, grin teasing but sincere. "Almost makes me wonder if we should be worried."

"Worried about what?" I ask, arching an eyebrow. Shouldn't improving my skills be a good thing?

"That you'll get so good at planning, some other team of assassins will offer you better benefits—health care, retirement options—and snatch you away from us." I roll my eyes, but smile at him.

"Don't worry. I'm not going anywhere, but now that you mention it—what kind of benefits do y'all offer?"

"The naked kind," he replies, grinning even wider.

"Hmm, I don't know. A retirement plan does seem pretty great," I say, forcing myself to keep a straight face.

"Oh, I'll show you retirement options." He jumps up, lunging for me. I yelp, dodging his grasp.

"Oh, come on, sweetheart, I just want to go over the different types of naked benefits I can offer." He chases me as I run around the Batcave. I can only avoid him for so long before he tosses me over his shoulder, spinning us around while I squeal.

"Put me down!" I yell, gasping for air as little bubbles of laughter escape. "I'm going to be sick!"

He swats my rear a few times, sighing dramatically. "Fine, I guess we can't have that." When he sets me down, he pulls me into a hug, and I return it without a thought, looking up into his ice-blue eyes—and that smile.

"I suppose this is a nice benefit." There's a beat of silence before he throws his head back and laughs.

"I suppose so," he says, draping one arm over my shoulders as he walks us back to the table. That brief moment of fun lightens the mood, making everything feel a little less heavy.

A few hours later, Beckett sets me up in my own section. I'll have everything I could possibly need at my fingertips. One large monitor dominates the space, surrounded by several smaller ones.

"You can set up the screens however makes sense to you," Beckett says, then shows me how to display the map with their markers on one side of the large monitor, and their individual camera feeds stacked on top of each other on the opposite side. Things like the aerial feed, communications from the fortress, and other random data will fill the remaining screens.

"Let me know if you think of anything else you might need. Make sure you're comfortable here for as long as the mission might take." He holds my gaze and adds, "You're a key part of this plan. We won't be able to do it without you. So anything you need, don't hesitate to ask."

"I just hope I don't mess anything up," I say, my earlier calm slipping away.

Whit's fingers trail along my jaw before settling at my chin, tilting my face toward him. "We trust you."

The words linger long after they leave me to organize my setup to my specifications. Their trust in me makes me start to think that maybe—just maybe—I can trust myself too. I'm confident in my skills, so there's no reason not to.

The routine extends into the evenings, though those hours are softer, quieter. Well, maybe not Quinn—he doesn't seem to know the meaning of quiet. Dinner is usually a chaotic affair, with Quinn cracking jokes, Whit telling stories, and Beckett steering the conversation. I've started contributing more, letting myself laugh and enjoy their company. Sometimes, I'll reference something from my past, and I can see the questions in their eyes, but I'm not ready to share that part of me yet, and they don't push.

I love how we spend our days, but the nights—those have become my favorite.

At first, I didn't know where to go when it was time to sleep. There wasn't a spare bedroom to give me a room of my own. When I asked where I should sleep, they just shrugged, as if the question didn't make sense. "Wherever you feel like," Whit said with a smile. "We don't mind sharing."

I'd been hesitant at first, but over time, it became second nature. One night, I'd curl up in Whit's bed, his arms warm and comforting around me, his presence a balm for my restless mind. The next, it might be Quinn, whose laughter would lift me, his teasing words giving way to quiet, unexpected tenderness. Then there was Beckett, whose bed was a sanctuary of silence and stability, his touch grounding me in ways I hadn't realized I needed.

Safety—that's what they've become for me.

I know it's terrible to admit, but I'm so glad they never gave me the option to leave. Like they knew I needed them from the moment Beckett found me in the study. They've given me the space to finally figure out who I am—and who I want to be.

And I'm starting to like the person I'm becoming.

Each night, I feel a little less like an outsider and a little more like... theirs. Not in the way Josiah meant when he claimed me, but in a way that feels freeing. I'm not a possession or a pawn. I'm part of them, and they're part of me.

There's power in this—in owning and being owned, not by force, but by choice. A self freely given in exchange for another's—an even trade.

Any man can take from a woman, but a real man doesn't need to. He doesn't see her as a burden or a possession. He treats her as his equal, knowing that given the chance, a woman will bloom—and his life will be all the better for it.

Men like my father and Josiah will never understand that. They fear a capable woman.

And I hope they fear me one day.

They will.

I'll make sure of it.

The darkness within me grins, nodding her head enthusiastically. She's been quieter lately, almost as if she's settling.

After everything they did to break me down, I never thought I'd trust anyone again—let alone three men who, quite literally, dragged me into their chaotic, dangerous world.

Yet here I am, settling into something easy with them, creating a life I never expected to want.

I'm still figuring things out, still untangling the pieces of myself they tried to break.

But I'm no longer running.

I'm home.

20

The sound of fists hitting pads echoes through the training area, a steady rhythm matching the beat of my pounding heart. Whit stands across from me, holding the pads, his gaze assessing as he tracks my movements, ready to correct me at a moment's notice.

"Again," he says, his voice measured, guiding rather than demanding.

I throw another punch, my knuckles connecting with the pad. It stings, but I don't stop. A small nod of approval from Whit pushes me to keep going.

"You're stronger than you think," he says, lowering the pads for a moment. "But strength isn't enough. You need control. Precision." He grabs my hips, turning them a specific way. "When you throw each punch, make sure your hips rotate like this to generate power."

"Easier said than done," I mutter, shaking out my hands.

He chuckles, stepping closer. "It takes practice. And patience. You'll get there."

I still don't know how I let Whit talk me into this.

Yesterday, I wandered into the training area, curious about the way they moved—so fluid, so controlled, like every step and strike was part of a dance only they could hear the beat of.

Okay, it might have had more to do with the way their muscles rippled and sweat dripped down their bodies.

I hadn't meant to get caught watching, but Whit spotted me anyway.

"You should learn," he said casually, like it wasn't a big deal. "Unless that's not why you were watching." His grin let me know, he knew exactly what I was doing.

And now here I am, sweating and exhausted, trying to land punches while he teaches me the basics of self-defense. All because I refused to admit I was drooling over them. Josiah and my father would be appalled.

"Good," he says with a nod. "You're getting better."

"Feels like I'm hitting a brick wall," I mutter, shaking out my hands.

He laughs lightly, lowering the pad. "That's what training is for. Build strength, get the form right, and one day, the wall shatters."

Assuming my hand doesn't break first.

I groan, wiping the sweat from my forehead with the sleeve of my shirt—it's so nice to have clothes that fit and cover me again. "You make it sound so simple."

Whit doesn't reply immediately. Instead, he grabs a bottle of water from the edge of the mat and tosses it to me. I catch it a bit awkwardly, unscrew the cap, and drink deeply as the silence stretches between us.

And then, the question that's been gnawing at me since I

learned what they do slips out before I can catch it. "How did you guys even get into this? The whole… assassin thing?"

Whit freezes, a flicker of surprise crossing his face. It's gone in an instant, replaced by that same unshakable ease he always carries. He takes a long sip of his water, as if buying time to decide how to answer.

They had to know I'd ask at some point, right?

Not that I'm ready to tell them anything about my past.

"You really want to know?" he asks finally, his voice quiet yet serious.

I nod, my curiosity is begging for the information, but I try to play it cool. "Yeah. I mean… it's not exactly what you would call a normal career path."

Whit chuckles, setting his bottle down and motioning for me to sit. "Fair enough. But you might not like what you're about to hear."

He leans forward, resting his arms on his knees as he begins. "It started at Caldwell Academy. A fancy boarding school for the elite. Beckett, Quinn, and I were sixteen, stuck in this place full of rules and expectations. We hated it."

"Hated it?" I echo, bursting to ask several other questions. What's a boarding school? What does he mean when he says it's for the elite? Somehow, I manage to keep them to myself.

"Hated it," he repeats with a grimace, his voice firm. "The pressure, the constant reminders of what we were supposed to become. Beckett's family wanted him to be the perfect heir to their business empire. Quinn's parents didn't care what he did, as long as he didn't embarrass them. And me… I was just trying to figure out where I fit."

"So you decided to… what? Run away and start killing people?" I ask, half-joking.

Whit shakes his head, a faint smile tugging at his lips. "Not exactly. It was Quinn who first brought it up."

"Why does that not surprise me?" We both laugh.

"We had this teacher, Mr. Ambrose. Charismatic, enigmatic. He approached Beckett first, and—just like now—if you take one, you take all.

Don't I know it.

That's how he pulled us into what he called 'leadership training.' Except the training was less academic than physical. He taught us how to prepare for any situation, master survival techniques, strategize for battle, and turn anything—even our own bodies—into a weapon."

"Well, that's a bit more than your average history or mathematics." I can't help but feel that this Mr. Ambrose wasn't much different from the adults I had around me growing up. They molded us to become what they wanted.

"You could definitely say that," Whit says with a laugh. "We made this old greenhouse on the school grounds our little getaway. It was falling apart—cracked glass, vines everywhere—it was clearly long forgotten, but we didn't care, it was ours," he says, his voice thick with nostalgia. "We'd go there to escape. Talk. Plan."

"What kind of plans?" I ask.

"At first? Nothing serious. Just dreams about getting out, doing something different. We were painfully bored, but then Quinn got it into his head that we could turn everything we were learning—strategy, combat, manipulation—into something real."

I blink. "He just... suggested it like he was suggesting pizza for dinner? Like it was nothing?"

Whit laughs. "Quinn's good at making wild ideas sound

reasonable. Said we could use our skills to take out bad people —arms dealers, human traffickers, you name it. Said it'd be better than wasting our lives pretending to care about stock portfolios and charity galas."

"And Beckett?" I ask, fairly certain I already know the answer.

"He was the first to take it seriously," Whit admits. "He said we'd been groomed for something our whole lives, and if this was it, at least it would be on our terms."

"What about you?" I press. "Did you think it was a good idea?"

Whit hesitates, his gaze dropping to the floor. "Not at first. The idea of killing people didn't sit right with me. But the way Beckett talked about it made it sound like... control. Like we were taking back our lives while making the world a better place. And you know how Quinn is—makes everything seem like an adventure."

"And you couldn't say no," I murmur.

"No," he agrees softly. "They were my family, even then. I didn't want to lose them."

"We made a pact in that greenhouse," Whit continues. "Beckett said if we were going to do it, we had to be all in—no second-guessing, no turning back."

"And obviously, each of you agreed."

He nods. "We approached Ambrose, somehow knowing that he would point us in the right direction. Turns out, he'd been conditioning us for something like this all along. He got us started, and... the rest is history."

I sit back, trying to process what he's told me. "So... you became assassins because you were bored and angry at your parents?"

"Sounds ridiculous when you say it like that," Whit says, his lips twitching into a faint smile. "But yeah. That's how it started."

I hesitate, then ask, "And what does it mean to you now?"

"Now, it's about getting paid to take out the scum of the earth. It's given us purpose." He holds my gaze, his expression unreadable. "And now, you're part of it."

My smile lingers as I glance down, heat warming my cheeks. "Okay." I meet his eyes again, softer this time. "Let's keep going."

Whit smiles, standing and holding out a hand to pull me up. "Good. Let's see if you can actually land a punch with passable form this time."

The tension breaks, and I roll my eyes as I take his hand. "Don't hold your breath."

Now, lying in the quiet shadows of his room, the day's tension begins to melt away. His arm is draped loosely over my waist, his warmth grounding me as my mind drifts—not toward sleep, but to tomorrow. The mission lingers at the edge of my thoughts, a quiet weight settling in my chest.

Before I can get too lost in it, he speaks.

"You know," he begins, his words carrying something heavier, something personal, "when I was a kid, I always wanted a family—a real family."

I tilt my head toward him, caught off guard by the vulnerability in his tone. "Didn't you have one?"

He sighs, his chest rising and falling beneath my cheek. "Not really. I had parents, sure, but they were... distant. Cold. They cared more about appearances than anything else. To them, I was just another thing to polish and display. It wasn't a family—it was more of a performance than anything."

That ache in his voice tugs at something deep inside me. I know what it's like to be seen as an object rather than a person, to have your worth measured by how well you play a role.

I grab his hand, weaving our fingers together and giving him a little squeeze. "How old were you when you went to boarding school?"

"They shipped me off to Caldwell Academy right after elementary school," he confirms, a faint smile tugging at his lips. "I was eleven and missed the familiarity of home, even if it wasn't the warmest. I hated it at first. It was just more of the same—rules, expectations, no room to breathe. But that's where I met Beckett and Quinn."

"How did you all meet?" I ask, glad to be getting to happier moments of his life.

He shifts slightly, his voice softening. "Beckett was the first. He was sitting in the library, surrounded by books and looking like he'd rather burn the place down than read another page. I think that's what caught my attention—he looked as miserable as I felt."

I smile faintly, picturing a younger, brooding Beckett. "And Quinn?"

Whit chuckles, warmth in his voice. "Quinn was vibrant and impossible to miss—always talking, always moving, always getting into trouble. The first time I met him, he was sweet-talking a cafeteria worker into giving him extra dessert."

"Did it work?" I ask, failing to hide my amusement.

"Of course it worked," Whit says with a grin. "Quinn could charm the horns off a bull, while dressed head to toe in red, if he tried hard enough."

The warmth in his tone shifts, turning reflective. "The three of us didn't fit in with the rest of the kids at Caldwell. We didn't care about the things they cared about—inheritances, power, following in their parents' footsteps. We just... found each other. And that was it. They became my family."

My chest tightens as I imagine what it would have been like to grow up with a friend or two. "Beckett and Quinn," I whisper. "They're everything to you."

"They were," he says, meeting my gaze. "But now... now it's different."

"How so?" I ask.

He brushes a strand of hair from my face, his touch gentle. "Because of you. Beckett and Quinn are my family, but with you... it feels complete. Like this is what I've been searching for my whole life."

My breath catches. Instinct tells me to pull away—not because I don't want this, but because I do. Because wanting means hoping, and hoping means breaking.

But Whit doesn't let go. His grip stays firm, his gaze locked onto mine.

"Do you really mean that?" I whisper.

Whit nods, his lips brushing lightly against my forehead. "Every word."

I don't know how to say exactly what I'm feeling, so I show him. I trail kisses down his bare chest, nipping along the way, drawing a hiss from him each time. I don't have to say anything—when I get to the band on his boxers and tug, he lifts his hips for me.

He's already hard when I wrap my hand around him and kiss the tip. I lick him from base to head before slowly wrapping my lips around him. His hand brushes my hair from my face, and I look into his eyes as I feel him hit the back of my throat.

"Fuck, your mouth feels like heaven," he groans. I bob up and down his shaft several times before he snaps. "I need to be inside you."

He picks me up and tosses me onto my back, quickly yanking off my tank and shorts. Draping a leg over each arm, lines himself up, his heated gaze fixating on my own, before he pushes slowly into me. We both groan once he's fully seated inside me. His movements are slow at first, his strokes languid and gentle, but it doesn't take long before he's pounding into me at a punishing pace.

"Touch yourself, princess," he demands.

I hesitate before my hand slowly slides between my legs. I'm awkward at first, but I quickly find the motion and pressure I prefer. There's something freeing about touching myself when I'd been made to fear it—one more thing I'm taking back.

The sound of the headboard hitting the wall and our bodies colliding almost drowns out the gibberish spilling from my mouth. I feel that string within me pull taut, and I know I'm close.

"Whose cock are you about to come all over?"

"Yours."

"That's right, princess, mine. I want to hear you scream my name while your cunt clamps down around me."

"Whit!" I cry as the dam bursts within me and my body floods with pleasure.

"Fuck, Celest," he growls as he finds his release. "I love hearing my name on your lips when you come."

He releases my legs and leans down to press his lips to mine. We kiss slowly, unhurried and tender.

When we finally part, he rolls onto his back and pulls me on top of him. We fall into sleep almost instantly. In that in-between space, where waking and dreaming blur, a sense of belonging washes over me.

Maybe I've found the family I've always needed—something real.

Something... like love.

21

I watch with quiet unease as gear is loaded into the back of a sleek black SUV. Guns, tech, medical supplies—all packed with precision. A stark reminder of how dangerous this mission really is.

Whit tosses the last bag into the vehicle after Beckett double-checks it against their checklist, scanning for anything they might have missed. Meanwhile, as usual, Quinn is leaning against something—this time, the vehicle. He effortlessly twirls the key around his finger and whistles, always finding something to lean on, as if it's second nature.

"Alright," Beckett says, closing the back of the SUV with a firm click. "We're loaded. Time to go."

Whit pulls me into a gentle hug, his hand warm against my back. "We'll check in as soon as we set up base," he says. "Don't stay up worrying."

"Easier said than done," I mutter, pulling back to meet his gaze before he presses a quick kiss on the top of my head.

Quinn grins as he grabs my hand and twirls me out of

Whit's arms. "Don't worry, sweetheart," he says, dipping me dramatically, making me laugh and lightening the mood. "I'll bring you back a souvenir. Maybe a keychain. Or an elephant. You know, nothing major."

"You're ridiculous. An elephant or a keychain—those are my options?" I laugh, shaking my head at the absurdity.

"Hey, you never know," he says, rubbing his chin as if deep in thought. "I'm sure they have some kind of cat-like creature I can smuggle back."

"Quinn, shut up," Beckett mutters, though he never seems to mean it. A faint smirk tugs at his lips as he steps forward. His eyes meet mine, always so perceptive, like he sees right through the anxiety I'm trying to hide. "We'll be fine," he says before pulling me into a quick embrace. "You'll hear from us soon."

"Be careful," I manage, pressing a chaste kiss to his cheek.

Beckett gives me a reassuring nod before glancing at his watch. "Gotta go if we're going to catch the jet. Celest—get some sleep. Once we're set up, it'll be a long couple of days."

"Try to switch to their time," Whit adds with a small smile. "You'll thank us later."

Quinn leans closer, lowering his voice as if sharing a secret. "Or don't—and let Beckett lecture you about efficiency. It's a real treat."

"Quinn," Beckett barks, looking up at the ceiling as if asking God for patience.

I manage a soft laugh, though the weight of what's to come sits heavy on my mind. "Good luck," I whisper, my arms wrapping around my middle as they pile into the SUV.

The engine roars to life, and I wave goodbye, my eyes fixed on them as they disappear down the long tunnel, into the outside world. The sound of the engine fades, leaving only silence as I stand there alone.

My fingers dig into my arms, grounding me against the creeping unease. They're professionals. They've done this a hundred times. Yet the thought of them out there, walking into danger in a faraway place like the Congo, makes my stomach churn.

With a sigh, I turn back toward the hub, the hum of the equipment oddly comforting in their absence. Beckett was right—I should try to sleep. I glance at the monitors, tempted to stay up and wait for their call, but I think better of it. I need to be well-rested, so I'm on my A game for tomorrow.

I curl up on the oversized couch—it doesn't feel right sleeping in their beds without them—and pull my favorite fleece blanket over myself, staring at the dark TV screen. It's strange being here alone, and I doubt I'll be able to sleep at all. I close my eyes, focus on my breathing, and drift into a fitful rest.

I'VE BEEN SITTING AT MY DESK FOR OVER AN HOUR, waiting for their call. My fingers fidget with a pen, tapping it against the console in a nervous staccato. When the comm unit finally crackles to life, I exhale deeply, finally able to breathe again.

"Celest, you there?" Whit's calm voice comes through, easing my anxiety. Something about his voice immediately relaxes me.

"I'm here," I answer, adjusting my headset. "Been waiting a while. I was afraid I'd miss the call or something."

"Did you get any sleep?" Beckett asks.

"Some," I admit, though it was anything but restful.

Quinn's chuckle filters through. "Sure you did. Bet she's been pacing the entire time. But more importantly—what are you wearing?"

"Quinn," Beckett says, tone laced with warning.

"Alright, alright! Don't act like you didn't want to know," Quinn relents, his grin practically audible. Wisely, he hurries on before Beckett can admonish him again. "How's it look on your end?"

I shift my focus to the satellite feed, already keyed into their location. The map updates, three blinking dots marking each of their positions. "You're right where you said you'd be," I reply, zooming in on the thick jungle surrounding their temporary base camp. "The fortress is five miles northeast. Terrain looks rough—dense forest, steep inclines."

"Perfect," Beckett replies. "We'll stay under the radar that way."

"You ready to go for a hike?" I ask, fingers brushing over the keyboard as I double-check the route I mapped out for them earlier.

"Ready as we'll ever be," Whit answers. "We'll keep you updated once we're in position."

As I monitor their progress, the hours crawl by. Their body cameras show a seemingly endless expanse of jungle—dark and impenetrable even with the night setting engaged. I listen for the rare crunch of leaves or snap of a twig beneath their boots as they trek silently through the dense underbrush.

It's impressive.

I would sound like a herd of elephants.

Their voices come through sporadically over the comms,

Beckett giving brief updates. "Two miles in. Terrain's as expected—thick vegetation, minimal visibility."

Quinn chimes in with his usual levity. "Minimal visibility? Speak for yourself, Beck. I see just fine—though I guess not everyone's used to working with something this thick."

"Quinn," Beckett sighs. How those two polar opposites became best friends is a mystery.

Whit cuts in. "Focus, guys. We're on a schedule." Mystery solved. Without Whit, Beckett and Quinn might drive each other mad—well, Quinn definitely would.

By the time they reach the perimeter of the fortress, the sky begins to lighten with the barest hint of dawn. From what I see on the satellite feed, the compound looks exactly like our intel indicated. It's massive—a central building surrounded by high walls, with smaller outbuildings and a heavily guarded gate. Security patrols move in predictable patterns; the place is heavily fortified.

"We're in position," Beckett says over the comms. "Security's heavier than expected."

"Yeah," Quinn agrees, his voice quieter. "More guards on the south side than we planned for."

Whit's voice follows, steady and composed. "Let's focus on getting in and out as efficiently as possible. Celest, keep tracking their patrols. Let us know if the increased numbers shifts anything."

"Got it," I reply, watching as their positions move on the map—tiny red dots weaving through the trees as they maneuver around the compound. I take the time to review the blueprints of the fortress they somehow got their hands on. I want to make sure there's no obvious places where extra guards could be a potential issue—such as blind spots and rooms that would likely be heavily fortified.

"We're good. Let's head back," Whit finally says, his voice carrying a note of relief. "Got what we came for."

"You're sure?" Beckett asks, his tone demanding perfection.

"Positive," Whit replies. "We'll go over everything at camp and make adjustments."

"All right, let's go," Becket orders.

After what feels like an eternity—but couldn't have been more than two hours—they begin their trek back to their temporary base. The early morning light is brighter now, cutting through the dense jungle. My shoulders ache with anxiety, and I can only imagine how much worse tonight will feel.

Back at the camp, they take a few hours to rest and regroup before diving into the intel. We analyze everything— new guard rotations, blind spots, weak points in the fortress's defenses.

Occasionally, I ask one of them to clarify something or make a suggestion, but for the most part, the plan remains the same. By the time all minor adjustments are made, the sun sets again.

Beckett's voice cuts through the comms. "We set out at midnight. That'll give us a few minutes to get situated, then we strike at two a.m. Security's thinnest then."

We have a few hours before they need to break down camp, so we eat and rest. Well, they do, at least. My body hums with nerves, sharpening as the minutes tick by. Soon, they're loading everything into the vehicle, and the second midnight hits, my mind snapping into razor-sharp focus.

"Celest, you ready to be our eyes?" Whit asks, his tone encouraging.

"Of course," I reply, trying to sound sure of myself. "Just... be careful."

"We always are," Quinn says, though the mirth in his voice doesn't inspire reassurance. "Don't worry, sweetheart. This'll be a walk in the park. I didn't even bring the big explosives."

"Quinn," Beckett says, a faint edge of exasperation in his tone.

"Everything's set," Beckett says, focused and efficient as always. "We'll be at the perimeter in forty minutes, then it's another thirty on foot through the jungle to the fortress."

"Don't forget to enjoy the scenic route," Quinn quips, his grin audible. "Nothing like a romantic midnight jungle drive to soothe the nerves."

Whit chuckles, but his voice is all business. "All right, Quinn, keep the chatter down. Celest, you've got the feed?"

"Sure do," I reply, keeping my eyes on the screen as I track their vehicle. "Everything looks clear so far.

They reach the perimeter as planned, parking the vehicle in a concealed location before proceeding on foot. I monitor the feed from their body cams—just shadows merging with the dense trees as they close in on the fortress. My pulse hammers, but I force myself to stay focused.

"Perimeter's clear," Beckett says. "Moving to the east side."

The satellite feed shows them approach the fortress's weakest point—a blind spot in the cameras they use to their advantage when the guards change shifts. They slip through the fence without a sound, disappearing into the shadows of the compound.

"We're in," Whit reports. "No sign of movement."

"Celest, you should be able to tap into their cameras now," Quinn says, just as the multiple feeds filter onto my screens.

"Got it. Their cameras should be looping while I maintain live footage," I say, surprised by how confident my voice sounds.

"Stick to the plan. Quinn, take point," Beckett orders.

They move deeper into the fortress, precise and silent. Everything is going perfectly—until something catches my eye.

I lean in closer to the monitor, my heart skipping a beat. "Wait," I say, my voice sharper than I intended. "There's movement near the north corridor. Several guards just changed positions, and a group is heading right for you."

"Copy that," Beckett replies instantly. "Adjust course."

I quickly map a new route, and they follow it without hesitation, seamlessly adapting to avoid detection. My heart pounds with adrenaline as I track their progress on the screen, watching them weave through the fortress like ghosts in the dark.

They near the target's location—a lavish bedroom on the top floor, guarded by four men: two stationed at the door, and one at either end of the hall. The comms are silent, except for the faint sounds of movement as they prepare to strike. Beckett and Whit wait at one end of the hall, while Quinn takes an alternate route, positioning himself at the other.

"Guards are half asleep," I whisper, my eyes glued to the feed. "You're good to go." A few moments later, Quinn and Beckett strike, taking out the two solo guards with swift, silent precision.

Without hesitation, Beckett and Whit move in on the last

two. Their takedown is surgical—fast and so quiet, the men don't have time to react.

Quinn's voice comes through next, hushed and steady. "Moving in."

The door creaks open, and they slip inside. The target is exactly where we thought he'd be—sound asleep in a massive bed, oblivious to the danger creeping toward him. I hold my breath as Quinn moves to the bedside, his knife flashing in the faint light.

"It's done," Quinn murmurs, voice thick with something between amusement and disappointment. "I was hoping for more... entertainment. He didn't even scream. What a waste."

I can practically hear Beckett roll his eyes as I try to hold back laughter. It's probably not an appropriate response, but I've given up on trying to be appropriate.

They slip out as smoothly as they came, moving with the same swift precision—every step silent. Two more guards cross their path, and they dispatch them quickly and quietly. The fortress remains unaware of the intrusion as I keep my eyes locked on the satellite feed, making sure it stays that way.

Within minutes, they're back at the blind spot, but this time, fresh guards stand watch, facing outward as they scan the perimeter. They don't sense the danger creeping up behind them until it's too late. Taken out in silence, they drop, and the team slips through the gap they used to enter. Relief washes over me, followed by exhaustion, but I don't let it take hold.

Not yet.

"We're out," Whit says, his voice a little lighter now that the hard part's over. "Heading back now—home stretch."

The hike to their vehicle is uneventful, though I hear the

exhaustion in their voices as they check in periodically. When they arrive, they quickly remove their excess gear and pack it away.

Quinn's laugh cuts through the tension—light and easy as he starts the ignition. "Told you it'd be a walk in the park."

Whit sighs, but there's a smile in his voice. "Just get us home, and try not to take any buildings out this time."

"It was one time!" Quinn bemoans as the rest of us laugh.

By the time they're on their way to the jet, dawn begins to creep over the horizon.

I track their progress to the airstrip through the satellite, and it's not until the jet is airborne, on its way home, that I see it—the fortress explodes with activity. Guards swarm the compound, vehicles moving in and out at a frantic pace. I guess they found Richter and the dead guards. I hope they're panicking. Anyone working for—well, worked for—that evil man can't be a good person.

I lean back in my chair, the tension ebbing away as the jet soars higher. They did it. They're safe and on their way home.

I try to get some sleep, but it quickly becomes obvious that won't happen until they're home. I make myself some tea and return to my computer, staring at the Google search bar. I've been going back and forth on whether this is a good idea. Ultimately, my curiosity wins, and I type *Celestina Abernathy* into the search.

The first thing I see is a *Magnolia Hallow* article. My breath hitches at the still image they used as the cover—it's Josiah. I click on the article but don't bother reading it, choosing instead to go straight to the video.

I stare at the screen, unable to look away as Josiah's face fills the frame. His familiar features—chiseled, charismatic, and deceptively kind—send a slow wave of dread curling through me.

He's a walking contradiction. How someone can look that benevolent and be that evil is beyond me.

He stands at a podium, flanked by my father—unsurprising—and another of his disciples. Behind him, the Covenant's symbol looms large on a pristine banner. The sight of it sets my nerves on edge, but it's his voice—calm, measured, and manipulative—that makes my skin crawl.

"I come before you today with a heavy heart," Josiah begins, his tone thick with feigned sorrow. *"It has been weeks since my beloved Celestina disappeared, leaving a void not only in my life but in the lives of all who know and love her."*

I scoff at "beloved Celestina." Hearing my name from his mouth threatens to revive old memories better left forgotten. I'll give him credit though—he knows how to put on a show. The way he hides his rage and dons the persona of a grieving fiancé is truly impressive.

Josiah pauses, bowing his head slightly—a perfect mime of a devastated fiancé overcome with emotion. When he looks back at the camera, his blue eyes glisten with unshed tears. The ridiculousness of his charade makes me want to laugh and vomit at the same time.

"Her car was found abandoned in rural Vermont," he says, his voice catching just enough to sell the performance, like the fraud he is. *"And while we remain hopeful, we must face the possibility that she may be in danger."*

I suck in a breath. How stupid am I? I should've had the guys take care of my car weeks ago. Because of my mistake, he knows my general location, and I hate how terrified it makes me.

"She was unwell in the days leading up to her disappearance," he continues, gripping the podium as if it's all that keeps him standing. *"I encouraged her to seek help, to talk to someone, to understand that there is no shame in addressing her struggles. But Celestina... she's always been so strong-willed, so independent."*

My nails bite into my palms as I clench my fists in anger. I shouldn't be surprised, this is standard Josiah behavior. By twisting the truth, he's turned me into a fragile, broken thing and weaponized his concern so no one will question him in the future.

Josiah lowers his voice, leaning slightly toward the microphone. His performance would warrant a reward if it weren't so malicious. *"Every night, I lie in bed terrified that she might do something rash. That she might,"* he pauses, taking a shuddering breath, *"take her own life."*

My breath catches, momentarily stuck in my throat. He's painting me as unstable and vulnerable while making himself the martyr. It's a calculated move, and it'll work if they want to make me disappear—just like he always does. He manipulates the picture until it shows what he wants you to see.

"Please," he says, his eyes locking directly with the camera as if he's speaking straight to me. *"Join me in praying for Celestina's safe return."*

I shake my head, fury bubbling beneath the fear. The audacity to use prayer—something good in nature—and twist it into a weapon. I shouldn't be surprised, he's been doing it for years to the entire covenant.

Then he says the words that chill me to my core, as his gaze sharpens and his expression becomes a perfect mask of tenderness.

"I will find you, Celestina."

My hands shake as I exit out of the screen.

It's time.

I have to tell them about my past—about Josiah. I've delayed long enough.

I swear to myself I'll tell them everything when they get home.

Josiah's words echo in my mind, and I try not to think about what will happen if he finds me—the violent warning he left.

No matter how far I run, Josiah is never far enough away.

22

Moonlight streams faintly through my bedroom window, providing just enough light to see. My heart pounds as I clutch the thick envelope my mother just shoved into my clammy hands. It feels lighter than something this significant should—the weight of a life I've never lived—a new name, a new identity. All of the details that make a person—stuffed into a single envelope, giving me a chance at freedom.

"You don't have much time," she whispers urgently. I watch as she rushes around my bed, arranging the bedclothes with trembling fingers, making it look as though I'd been dragged from it against my will. "They'll be here early in the morning to prepare you. You have to go now."

She pulls back, her face pale but her eyes determined, holding out her hand. "Give me your locket."

My chest tightens. "But—" I've never taken it off since she gave it to me, all those years ago.

"Celestina," she stops me, her voice firm despite the tears

pooling in her eyes. "I need it. I'll plant it somewhere they'll find it. I want to make them think they're searching for your body. It might distract them long enough for you to slip beyond their reach. Please."

My hands shake as I unclasp the chain, fingers brushing over the smooth silver surface one last time before I place it in her palm. She closes her hand around it, her expression faltering for a moment before she pulls out a small knife.

"Give me your hand," she demands, resolute. I place my hand in hers without question. She makes a small cut and smears my blood across the locket before dropping it into a small plastic bag. She steps back and nods. "Go. The car is hidden in the brush behind the welcome sign. Once you get past the general store, keep to the edge of the woods until you get outside the town limits. Stay off the roads and out of sight. Everything you'll need is packed and the keys are in the cup holder."

"Come with me," I plead. Mother looks at me with pain-filled eyes and shakes her head.

"No, my sweet girl, I will stay here and do everything I can to make sure they don't find you."

"But we can—"

"There's no time for this, Celestina. I promised when you were born I would find a way to get you out. I'm only sorry it's taken this long."

"I don't want to be alone," I say softly.

"You won't be alone forever, and remember the mirror. They can't take everything from you, and you will not break." She gives me a tight hug that ends far too quickly before shoving me toward the door. Just as I'm about to step into the hall, she whispers her last words to me: "Live a happy life, my love. Don't settle for less."

I nod, looking back at her once more, before making my way down the stairs—skipping the one that creaks. I almost slip on my shoes by the door, but then stop and think. I wouldn't have time to put shoes on if I were being dragged from the house.

The moisture-thick air suffocates me the moment I slip out the back door, wearing only my sleep shorts and an over-sized t-shirt. Sticking to the shadows, I cut through multiple neighbors' backyards, careful not to trigger any of the flood-lights. My pulse thrums in my ears, every sound in the still night makes me feel certain I've been caught. Once I reach the end of my row, I duck behind a line of hedges, peering out to make sure the street is clear before darting across the open space.

My feet ache, but I don't stop, and I don't let the pain cloud my mind. I have to stay alert. The night watch is always patrolling, and the moment I'm spotted, it will be over. All my mother's planning would be wasted in the blink of an eye.

I crouch behind a parked car as footsteps echo down the street. My breath catches, and I press myself against the metal —hoping there's no alarm. Thankfully, there isn't. The foot-steps grow louder, then pass, fading into the distance. I exhale shakily and move again, darting from one shadow to the next until I cut into the woods behind the general store.

By the time I reach the car, my legs tremble, my feet throb, and my lungs burn. The vehicle sits exactly where my mother said it would, tucked behind a cluster of trees just beyond the town welcome sign. I fling the door open and collapse into the driver's seat, grabbing a bottle of water from the passenger side and chugging it down in desperate gulps.

The interior smells faintly of leather and my mother's perfume, while the backseat is crammed with clothing, supplies, and more water bottles. She thought of everything.

I grip the steering wheel tightly and fight the urge to turn around and drag her with me. She deserves a happy life too. She shouldn't have to stay behind and face whatever wrath Josiah and my father will unleash.

It's not fair, and I'm equal parts grateful and angry at her. We could've at least tried to get out together. I promise myself that once I'm settled into my new life, I'll come back for her.

The road stretches out before me, dark and empty. I start the car, the low rumble of the engine breaking the silence. My hands shake as I shift into drive, terrified of the unknown. Beneath the fear, though, a thrill of adventure crackles within me.

I look down at the dash as I pull onto the narrow road, a note in my mother's handwriting catching my eye: *Don't look back.*

I don't.

With tears blurring my vision, I press the gas and drive into the night, toward my new life, leaving everything I've ever known behind.

THERE'S A STRANGE ENERGY TONIGHT, THOUGH I can't tell if it's the aftermath of the mission or the weight of what I need to tell them. They're back, safe and unharmed, and I've waited long enough.

I'll tell them after dinner.

The words stick in my throat as I watch them settle in. Whit's already in the kitchen, cooking something that smells delicious but does nothing to spark my appetite. Beckett sits at the table, typing a debrief on his laptop, while Quinn lounges on the couch, flipping through channels on the massive TV. I know they can tell something's on my mind, but none of them push.

I push the food around my plate, nerves making it impossible to eat. What if they think my past is too much to deal with and send me away? It's strange that this is my concern, considering I spent the first few days here trying to escape. Throughout dinner, they've exchanged worried glances. They know something's on my mind, but they respect my request not to push.

"Guys," I say softly once most of their dinners are finished. Three pairs of eyes snap to me, reserved yet curious. I swallow hard, forcing myself to meet Beckett's piercing gaze. "I need to talk to you."

They set their forks down, the rest of their food forgotten, and turn their full attention to me. The comfort of their presence—the patience in the way they wait without rushing—gives me the courage to start.

"I haven't really told you anything about my past," I begin, my voice trembling slightly. "A past I was running from when my car broke down and I ended up here. There are... things I couldn't bear to talk about, but feel as though I need to tell you now."

Whit leans forward, placing his hand on mine—ending the massacre of the paper napkin I've shredded without thought—his expression soft yet serious. "Take your time," he says gently giving my hand a little squeeze.

Quinn tilts his head, his usual grin replaced by something more solemn. "We're not going anywhere, sweetheart."

Beckett doesn't have to say a word. His stare strips me bare, sees too much, offers no escape. But there's something safe in that too—like stepping too close to the fire and finding warmth instead of ruin. So I keep talking, grounded by the heat.

The moment I speak, everything spills out.

I tell them about the Covenant of Divine Light—the cult I grew up in. About my father, Charles Abernathy, and his obsession with control and unattainable standards of perfection. I tell them about the ceremonies and punishments. How my life was dictated by their warped beliefs, and finally, I tell them about Josiah Wainwright. My voice shakes when I talk about the engagement Josiah announced when I was just fourteen, and how his possessiveness grew darker with every passing year.

I drop my gaze to the table, unwilling to see the disgust in their eyes. Instead, I speak—of the liberties he took once I was promised to him, how he wielded our engagement like a leash, yanking me closer every time I tried to pull away. How he whispered that my resistance only made it more exciting, that fear would make me a better wife, that love was obedience and pain was proof of devotion. And no matter how much I cried, begged, or bled, he only smiled, pressing his lips to my ear and promising I'd learn to thank him for it.

I don't stop. I couldn't, even if I wanted to. Not until I tell them about the night before the wedding—how my mother gave me the keys to freedom, sacrificing everything to get me out. I tell them about my barefoot escape and how I never looked back.

By the time I finish, the room is silent, hot tears staining my cheeks. I feel raw and exposed, my hands trembling as I twist them in my lap. I can't bear to look at them, too afraid of what I might see in their eyes.

It's Whit who moves first. He gets up, walks over to my chair, pulls me out of it, and wraps his arms around me, warm and safe.

"Celest," he says softly. "You're not there anymore. You're here with us. You're safe."

Quinn comes to stand beside us, his hand lightly brushing the tears from my cheek. "Safe, and not going anywhere. I'm sorry to be the one to break it to you, but you're stuck with us. Got it?" I choke out a surprised laugh and nod.

Beckett's voice cuts through, rough and seething with barely contained rage. There's a finality in his tone that feels like a promise. "No more running, Celest. Not anymore. Not from anyone. And definitely not from him."

I look up to see him leaning against the table right next to me, my chest tight with emotion while my body feels wrung out. "You don't understand. Josiah... he's not like other people, and you shouldn't underestimate him. He'll keep searching and won't stop until he finds me."

"Let him try," Beckett says, his tone laced with malice. "We'll be ready."

Whit leads me to sit on the couch, gaze soft as he adds, "But we're not just going to protect you, Celest. We're going to make sure you can protect yourself. Whatever it takes."

Quinn drops into the seat next to me, tossing his arms across the back. "What made you finally tell us? Not that I'm complaining, but I can't believe you'd just randomly decide to spill everything if something hadn't happened."

I hesitate, my fingers picking at the edge of my sleeve. "There was a press release," I admit, my voice barely above a whisper. "I Googled myself once your flight was on its way back, curious to see what happened after I left. Josiah... he lied, twisted everything to make himself look like the victim. But when he looked into the camera and said, 'I will find you,' I realized... y'all deserve to know what you're getting into. I... I understand if it's too much—if I'm too much."

They exchange looks, something unspoken passing between them. Beckett nods, his gaze locking onto mine. "Then we'll make sure you're ready. Whatever comes, we'll face it—together."

Whit squeezes my hand with a gentle smile. "You're not alone anymore."

Quinn's grin returns, though it's wolfish this time. "Sweetheart, if I'm not too much, then you clearly aren't. Besides, if Josiah does show up, he's going to regret it. I'd love five minutes in a room alone with him."

"Quinn, shut up," Beckett sighs. "Five minutes wouldn't come close to long enough." There's a pause before we all laugh in disbelief.

"Did you just... Beckett Harlow, did you just make a joke?" Quinn asks with a fake gasp, breaking the tension.

The knot in my chest loosens as I listen to them fake-argue over who gets first dibs on Josiah. I feel foolish now for not telling them sooner. My mother wanted me to live a happy life, and I wish I could tell her that I've found it.

For a moment, after watching the press release, I considered leaving a note and running away to continue the life she envisioned for me. But in the end, I chose to be brave and stay. I knew it was the right choice—and I wasn't wrong.

I'm done running.

23

Arms wrap around me from behind, followed by a spicy citrus scent—Quinn. I was worried they'd treat me differently after I told them about my life in the Covenant. They haven't. If anything, over the past couple of weeks, we've grown closer, falling into an easy intimacy. The more we learn about each other, the tighter-knit we become.

"Want to get out of here and go for a ride?" Quinn asks. "Maybe in more ways than one?" He laughs when I swat at him.

"Where are we going?"

He smirks and tosses me over his shoulder with far too much ease. "You'll just have to wait and see," he says, punctuating it with a sharp slap to my ass. I yelp, but the sound only makes him laugh harder.

It's like they can't help themselves. I've lost count of how many times one of them has tossed me around like this—flipped, manhandled, dominated. And nearly every time, a spank follows, like instinct. Like they can't resist reminding me where I belong—and who I belong to.

Men.

He sets me down and hands me a helmet before grabbing one for himself. Choosing a sleek black and green bike, he swings a leg over to straddle it. I adjust the helmet, and he checks to make sure it's secure before I climb on behind him. I've never ridden one of these before, but I swallow my anxiety and grip tight, determined not to show it.

The rumble of the motorcycle echoes through the garage, vibrating through me as Quinn revs the engine. He glances over his shoulder, and I imagine his grin is as wide as ever.

"Ready for some fresh air, sweetheart?" His voice crackles through the speaker system in our helmets.

"As ready as I'll ever be," I respond, trying to muster as much confidence as I can.

"Hold on tight," he says, his voice dripping with mischief.

I wrap my arms around his waist as he kicks the bike into gear. The moment we leave the tunnel, the rush of wind hits me—cool and sharp against my skin. The bike roars down the winding road, the trees blurring into a swirl of reds and oranges on either side. My heart races, not with fear as I expected, but with exhilaration. It's freeing, and I wonder if this is what a bird feels like when it's flying.

After what feels like no time at all, Quinn slows the bike, veering onto a narrow dirt path that cuts through the autumn-hued woods. He parks in a small clearing surrounded by towering trees. Scattered around us are targets —some made of straw, others simple painted wood—their surfaces scarred by regular use

"I come here when I need to clear my head," Quinn says,

cutting the engine and swinging off the bike. He holds out a hand to help me dismount. "And, you know, to throw sharp objects at things."

I laugh, shaking my head as I take his hand. "Of course it is."

With our helmets off—he has to help me with mine, and yes, it's embarrassing—he pulls a set of throwing knives from a leather pouch strapped to the bike. Twirling one between his fingers with practiced ease, he asks, "You ever thrown a knife before?"

"Not unless you count butter knives, and even then, it was more of a drop than a throw," I admit, my cheeks heating.

I'd been young—maybe ten or eleven—and had somehow managed to fumble the knife while slicing a tab of butter from the dish. Father punished me for my clumsiness, reminding me what a disappointment I was.

He chuckles, handing me one of the blades. "Well, you're in luck. I'm an excellent teacher. Plus, there are perks for good students," he says, winking.

"Oh, I know all about your perks," I reply sarcastically.

"That's what you think." He wiggles his brows suggestively, making me laugh.

Quinn walks me through the basics—grip, stance, and the proper way to release the knife. I mimic his movements, the weight of the blade unfamiliar in my hand. My first throw doesn't even reach the target.

"Try again, and put some of that rage simmering underneath all that sweetness into it."

I do, and the knife strikes the target with a thud, the handle hitting first. The third throw finally hits and sticks, wobbling awkwardly before falling to the ground.

"I did it!" I yell, throwing my hands up in celebration before clapping with excitement. All I had to do was imagine the target was Josiah's face.

Imagine that.

"Not bad for a beginner," Quinn says, his grin easy. "Try again."

I do, making a few adjustments to my grip and stance like he suggested. The knife lands with a solid thunk, just outside the painted circle, but it doesn't fall. A rush of pride warms my chest.

"There you go!" Quinn picks me up and spins me around, sounding just as excited as I am, sending me into a fit of giggles. "See? You've got it."

I keep practicing, throw after throw, while Quinn leans against a nearby tree, watching me with a thoughtful expression. "Sometimes it feels like it wasn't that long ago I was learning all of this, excited for our first mission. But other times, it feels like it's been a lifetime," he says suddenly, his tone light but tinged with nostalgia.

I glance over at him, curious. "What was your first one like?"

"Horrible," he says, laughing.

"How so?"

"We almost blew it," he admits, his signature smirk on full display. "We were so cocky—thought we were invincible. It was supposed to be simple: infiltrate, take out the target, get out. But we underestimated how many guards there'd be."

"What went wrong?" I ask, stepping aside as he picks up a knife to demonstrate a throw.

"Everything," he says, the knife striking dead center with a satisfying thunk. "Beck got clipped by a stray bullet, Whit got grazed, and I dislocated my shoulder trying to climb a fence I had no business climbing—not to mention all the knife wounds we took." He pulls up his shirt and points to a rough scar on his abdomen. "This one wound up being a real pain."

I wince. "That sounds... awful."

"Oh, it was," he says, his grin widening. "We managed to complete the mission, but by the time we got out, we were a mess. That's when we learned how to do more than basic first aid. Whit had to pop my shoulder back into place, and we spent the next day stitching each other up."

"By each other, you mean stitching you up?" I ask, grinning.

"Listen to that cheek!" he cries, miming being stabbed in the heart.

I throw another knife, and it lands closer to the center this time—like an inch closer, but whatever. Quinn nods approvingly.

"As bad as it was, that mission taught us a lot," he says. "Like not letting overconfidence cloud our judgment."

"And maybe plan a little better?" I tease, making us both smile.

He's quiet for a moment and then says, "Mostly, it taught us that we could rely on each other, no matter how bad things got."

"You've been through a lot together," I say softly. "It's made you into a family."

"Yeah," he agrees, his grin softening as he wraps his arms around me from behind. "And now we've got you, too. You're part of this family, Celest. We might've had to literally drag you into it kicking and screaming—I also believe there was something about vampires as well—but we're not us without you."

"Hey!" I cry spinning in his arms—they'll never let me live that down. Quinn finally made me watch Twilight so that I could understand his "skin of a killer" reference. The whole watching-her-while-she-slept thing was creepy, but then again, my guys hunted me in a terrifying game of hide-and-seek.

I probably shouldn't be one to judge.

"There's no getting away from us now. We'll just drag you right back. I think Beck might've gotten off on the whole 'kicking and screaming' thing."

"Do you promise?" I ask, smiling up at him.

He grabs me gently by the chin and holds me in place. "You're ours, Celest, and we take very good care of what belongs to us." His mouth crashes into mine. His kiss is frenzied, much like the man himself, and I let myself get lost in his lips. One hand grips my hair while the other finds its way under my shirt, working its way up my back to pull me flush against him.

With a growl, he slides both hands down my body, grabs the hem of my shirt, and yanks it off. My jeans and underwear follow, joining the shirt in a pile on the ground in record time. In just a few minutes, he has me completely naked while he's still fully dressed. Before I can say anything, he lifts me, carrying me to the bike and placing me on the seat.

He takes a step back and looks at me. "Fuck, sweetheart, lean back and spread your legs a little for me." I feel heat in my cheeks as I do what he asks, bracing one hand behind me. "Just as I thought, already dripping. Touch yourself. I want to watch you make yourself come."

It's still something I haven't explored that often—then again, when you belong to three men, you're never left wanting.

Tentatively, I drop my hand to my center, finding my clit. I force myself to think, getting more comfortable with my new vocabulary every day. I apply pressure, circling it slowly, and gasp at the sharp jolt of pleasure.

"Slide a finger in," he commands, squatting until he's eye level with my center—or... well, whatever I'm supposed to call it. He groans as he watches my finger glide in and out. "Add another one, and tell me how it feels."

"It feels," I start as I add the second finger. "Tight. It feels tight and wet... and..." a moan rips out of me, stealing my thoughts for a moment. "Good, God, it feels so good."

"Are you going to make yourself come for me?" I nod, alternating between circling my clit and sliding my fingers in and out as the tension builds inside me. "That's it, sweetheart, show me how fuckin sexy you are when you come. God, I can't wait to bury my cock in that sopping wet pussy." His words send me over the edge, and I feel myself clamp down around my fingers.

Quinn stands in front of me, belt already undone. He quickly unbuttons his pants and then grabs my hand, still coated in the evidence of my pleasure, and sucks my fingers into his mouth. He slowly pulls them out with a pop, grinning wildly at me.

"You taste too good to let it go to waste," he says as he grabs me and yanks me forward. His grip on my hips and my forearms on the seat are the only things keeping me from falling as he drives into me, thrusting hard and fast.

"You feel so fucking good. Do you hear how wet you are

for me?" he asks as the sound of our bodies collide together in a wet slap, sounding even louder in the middle of this quiet forest.

"Y-yes. Oh, god. Please—" I fly even higher, edging closer to another decadent plunge.

"Fuck, Celest," he groans. "I feel your cunt fluttering around me. Let me have it, sweetheart. Come for me."

A few more thrusts and I shatter, crying out his name. He follows not long after, and I feel the warmth of his release inside me. Bringing his forehead against mine, neither one of us moves while we catch our breaths.

"I fucking love that, the entire drive back, I'll be leaking out of you while you're pressed up against me." He flashes one of those wicked grins as he puts himself away and grabs my clothes. I reach for them, but he pulls them just out of reach.

"Quinn!"

"It's my night to have you in my bed. I just want to let you know I plan on filling you with my come multiple times tonight." He gives me my clothes and then leans in so that his mouth is next to my ear, his voice low when he says, "And the last time I do, I'm going to fall asleep while still inside you and stay there the rest of the night. Then, when morning comes, I can wake up fucking you."

His words leave me speechless with anticipation. I stand there, holding my clothes, still naked, my jaw practically on the floor. He kisses my cheek, then walks around me, whistling like he didn't just say the filthiest thing. He picks up the helmets that had fallen to the ground, puts his on, and once I'm dressed, helps me into mine. Then he waits for me to climb on behind him before starting the engine.

I hold on tight, and without another word, he takes off down the path, getting us back onto the main road. Just like he said, I feel him leaking out of me the whole way back, and I can't wait for him to keep his promise tonight. My core clenches at the thought. He must have some idea of what I'm thinking, because he reaches back with one hand and squeezes my thigh, his laugh filtering through the speakers.

His laugh makes everything feel a little lighter—even if it sounds a bit feral at times. I'm not sure what this feeling is that's growing between all of us, but I have a pretty good idea. Every day, I fall harder for them—harder than I thought possible.

Maybe I've already fallen.

24

The SUV idles quietly on the side of a residential street near the edge of Princeton's campus. The sky is dark, moonlight hidden behind a veil of clouds, and the faint glow of fluorescent lights can be seen in the distance. I sit in the backseat, my eyes fixed on the live feeds of the interior cameras inside the lab displayed on my laptop.

Around me, the guys prepare to head out. Whit adjusts the strap on his vest a few times until he has it just right, his calm demeanor the complete opposite of the adrenaline thrumming beneath the surface. Beckett checks the route I've highlighted for them on the map again, while Quinn sits beside me, radiating restless energy, drumming his fingers against the armrest of the door.

"This guy better be worth it," Quinn mutters. "Don't get me wrong—I live for a challenge. But a favor for a favor?" He exhales, shaking his head. "Feels like a lot when it means cracking Princeton's security. This isn't some back-alley smash and grab."

"Trust me," Beckett says, without looking up. "When we need him, he'll be worth it."

I take a deep breath and focus on the feeds. Their unnamed friend—the one who called in the favor weeks ago—wasn't kidding about the lab's interior cameras.

They're everywhere.

"Most of the guards are moving toward the parking lot," I say, watching the skeletal crew dwindle on the screens. "Dr. Voss just left. They'll be gone in five minutes."

Whit turns and gives me a reassuring smile. "Deep breath, princess. There's no rush—it's better for this to take longer and not be seen than leave a trail of bodies."

Quinn grins. "Except, you know, the part where we're sitting in a car on a quiet street, and it's only a matter of time before someone notices us. Oh, and leaving a trail of bodies is way more fun."

I shoot him a mock glare. "Gee, thanks, no pressure." He leans across the seat and gives me a kiss on the cheek.

"Nah, you got this, easy-peasy," he says before he pulls away from me.

I was surprised when they invited me to go with them. They said it was a straightforward job—just an eight-hour drive—and that I'd be out of harm's way, working from the SUV. At first, I didn't understand. How could I do my job without the equipment and programs I rely on to track them and get them home safely?

I shouldn't have been surprised that the SUV was loaded with nearly all the tech I'm used to. Now, I'm already wondering how many more missions I can worm my way into. I like not being left behind.

Our moment comes a second later. The remaining guards

are stretched thin and the last of Dr. Voss' security detail pulls out of the parking lot, I nod. "You're clear. Go now."

Without a word they move, slipping from the SUV and disappearing into the shadows.

"Celest, you with us?" Beckett's voice crackles through my earpiece.

"I'm here," I reply, trying to keep my voice steady.

"Moving in," Beckett says, his tone all business.

I track their movements on the screen, watching as three dots creep toward the edge of the lab. No one would notice unless they were looking right at them. Now, I understand how they moved seamlessly through the shadows of the manor.

The moment they reach the perimeter, I disable the lock on the first door.

"You're clear," I say, setting the hallway feed on a loop. "Go now."

Quinn's voice crackles through the comms, low and full of mischief. "Damn, sweetheart, you're so fucking hot. I can't wait till we get back so I can bury—"

"Quinn, shut up," Beckett and Whit say simultaneously. I stifle a small laugh and then clear my throat, my focus staying firmly on the mission at hand.

They slip through the now-unlocked door, efficient and silent. They move as one, fluid and practiced as they make their way toward the specified lab. I keep my eyes glued to the feeds, tracking the few guards patrolling and making sure their paths don't cross, setting off the interior security protocols.

Their body cam feeds fill one of the monitors, showing the cold, clinical halls of the lab. Every inch is polished to perfection, from the shiny tiled floors to the sterile white walls, all under the harsh glow of fluorescent lights. Glass panels line some corridors, revealing rows of state-of-the-art equipment and workstations—likely filled with research students during the day.

I wonder if any of them know who they're actually working for.

"Everything's clear," Beckett murmurs through the comms, his voice low.

They move silently through the shadows of the dormant lab, their dark clothing slightly less inconspicuous against the clinical, white surroundings. Long, stainless steel tables stretch across the vast room, covered in microscopes, vials, and neatly organized instruments. Screens on the walls display data streams and blueprints of complex machinery I can't begin to decipher. Shelves of labeled samples line one side, each glowing faintly under UV lights.

"Celest, how we looking?" Whit asks.

"Everything's still quiet," I reply, double-checking the feed. "No signs of you being spotted."

When they reach the door to Dr. Voss's office, I unlock it remotely. The faint beep of the access panel clicks through the comms as the door swings open. My chest tightens as the body cams reveal the room beyond.

The office is an unsettling blend of precision and chaos. The desk is meticulously arranged: a stack of neatly labeled research files, a sleek laptop, and a set of gold-plated pens arranged in perfectly spaced alignment. The walls, though, they tell a different story.

Scattered across the walls are haphazardly pinned sketches and diagrams, some faded and curling at the edges.

Equations are scrawled on a whiteboard that stretches across an entire wall, symbols looping in a manic frenzy. A corkboard is covered in photos—blurry shots of test sites, explosions, and grainy images of weapon prototypes in various stages of construction.

Behind the desk, a shelf holds an odd collection of items: an antique compass, a globe marked with points, and a pristine model of a weapon prototype encased in glass. Altogether, it looks as if the room had exploded with chaos, while the interior remains untouched.

Quinn lets out a low whistle. "Hot damn. Beck, this guy's desk is somehow more meticulous than yours. Didn't think it was possible to out 'neat' the control freak."

"Fuck off, Quinn," Beckett snaps.

"Love you too, Becky." There's a scuffle, followed by Quinn's quiet chuckle. "Alright, alright, I'm done. Promise."

"Can we focus?" Whit asks, though he's clearly trying to hold back his laughter.

"What do you make of this guy?" Beckett asks the group, pulling everyone back on track.

"I'll tell you one thing, this guy definitely has dead bodies in his freezer," Quinn says, far too casually. I make a mental note to avoid any deep freezers around here.

"No kidding," Whit mutters. "How does he come across as stable to anyone?"

"I'm not sure," I add thoughtfully. "He's not just methodical—he's obsessed. I don't think it's just work for him; it's his entire life."

Not bothering to make any observations on the doctor's mental state, Beckett moves to the filing cabinet on the far wall. When he opens it, a faint beep sounds. I freeze.

"Celest," Beckett says sharply. "We've got a problem."

My pulse spikes as I stare at the screen. RF trackers. Shit. If we trigger this, everything goes to hell.

I force myself to breathe, to calm down and think. I just read about this. What was it? I sift through my mental files, searching for the information I know is there. Seconds stretch, but then—I remember.

I exhale slowly, my gaze flicking between the feeds. "The tracker is tied to the files, and it looks like if you try to open the case, it will trigger an alarm. Don't move them yet."

I quickly pull up the schematics of the lab's security system that their nameless friend provided, scanning for a workaround. My heart races, but I shove the panic aside. I've read about RF tracking systems before, and suddenly the solution comes to me in a rush of adrenaline.

"Okay," I say, my voice steady. "You need to scan the tracker first. Use the portable scanner in your pack."

"On it," Whit says.

While they prepare the scanner, I access the lab's central system and start isolating the RF signal. "Once you scan the tracker, I'll duplicate the signal and loop it before terminating the original. The system won't know the files are gone, and the alarm on the case will be disabled."

A few tense seconds pass before Whit's voice comes through again. "Scan complete."

I key in the duplicate signal, my fingers flying over the keyboard. "Done. It's looping. The files are good to go, and the alarm is no longer a problem."

"Not a particularly strong bit of security, is it?" Quinn asks, amusement curling in his voice.

"Not on its own, but the building itself is locked down

tight. Without the information your friend provided, we would never have been able to get this far." It's true—I'm gaining more knowledge every day, but I am nowhere near that guy's level. This job would've been impossible without the backdoor into their systems he gave us.

"Fair point," Quinn says.

They retrieve the research and grab anything else that looks remotely related to it, then make their way back out. I guide them through the camera blind spots, adjusting as necessary when a group of researchers comes out of nowhere.

"Cameras are clear," I say, my voice steady. "You're almost out." The body cams show the same cold, clinical corridors as they move back toward the exit.

I can't shake the weight of what I saw in that office; it lingers in the back of my mind. Dr. Gideon Voss isn't just a scientist—he's a man obsessed with power, destruction, and control. And now, thanks to the guys, his work won't go any further.

At least, not this time.

"Exit's clear and unlocked," I say as they approach the last door and trigger the release. "Go now."

"Too easy," Quinn jokes as they slip outside.

"Don't jinx it," Beckett mutters.

"Since when are you superstitious?" Whit asks, to which Beckett mumbles something about never being too careful under his breath, barely audible through the comms.

Minutes later, they're back. I let out a shaky breath and sink into my seat as the SUV roars to life. Within moments, we're speeding down the highway, Princeton fading behind us.

"Nice work, Celest," Beckett says from the driver's seat. "That was smooth."

"Flawless," Whit adds, glancing back at me with a warm smile.

Quinn leans over the small space between us, brushing my hair behind my shoulder. "You were brilliant, sweetheart. That whole tracker thing? Genius."

I feel a warm flush spread across my chest as a shiver runs through me. "It's not just me; we made the plan together," I say softly.

Quinn smirks. "Don't sell yourself short. Well, I guess not shorter than you already are—my little fun-sized genius."

Laughing, I swat at him. "Hey! I'm not that short!"

"You are pretty small, Short Stack," Whit adds.

"No! I'm average. I looked it up."

"Nothing about you is average," Beckett says, before ruining the compliment. "Polly Pocket."

"Oh, my god," I huff, fighting the smile creeping onto my face as they laugh.

Driving down the dark highway, everyone falls into a comfortable silence. Beckett's focused on the road, Whit's leaned back, relaxing in the passenger seat, arms crossed. I wouldn't be surprised if he's asleep. I sit in the back, laptop in hand, still monitoring the lab's communications, waiting for the alarm to be raised.

Next to me, Quinn flips through the stolen research files. It's easy to underestimate his brilliance, especially since he never seems to take anything seriously. But Quinn is a genius. He's reading through the files, clearly comprehending their contents, but his normally easygoing demeanor has shifted into something darker. He's been quiet for the past twenty minutes; it's worrisome.

Finally, he lets out a low whistle, shaking his head. "This guy... he's not just brilliant—he's sick. And you know it's bad if it makes even my stomach churn."

Beckett glances at him in the rearview mirror. "I assumed that much, but what did you find?"

Quinn doesn't look up, flipping to another page. "I mean, this weapon isn't just designed to destroy—it's designed to make people suffer slow, agonizing deaths. There's no efficiency or strategy here, just widespread destruction. It's fucking sadistic."

Whit shifts in his seat, his jaw tightening. "I'm afraid to even ask, but what does it do?"

Quinn pauses, reading a line aloud. "'The compound triggers a chain reaction at the cellular level, causing widespread organ failure over several days. Death is inevitable and excruciating.'" He snaps the file shut and tosses it onto the empty space between us. "He wants people to beg for death—even women and children."

"That kind of weapon," Beckett says, his tone even but grim, "isn't meant for war. That kind of suffering is about sending a message—he's a fucking terrorist in the making."

Whit nods, his voice low. "You can control an entire country with something like that. If you make people too terrified to fight back, you've won before the fight's even begun."

Quinn leans back, draping his arm across the back of my seat. "And Voss? He wasn't just creating one weapon. These notes..." He gestures toward the pile of files. "They're prototypes for something bigger. He wasn't just working on a bomb

—he was building a system. Something scalable. I bet those pins in his globe have something to do with it."

A chill runs down my spine, and I glance back at Quinn. "How does someone even think like that?"

"He's not thinking like a human being," Quinn says, his voice quieter now. "He's thinking like a megalomaniac playing God."

The weight of his words settles over the car, and I can't help but picture what that kind of hell would look like. It's horrifying—yet that kind of cruelty is familiar. Too familiar.

I never imagined it was possible for someone to be worse than Josiah. If he ever got his hands on something like this, he'd use it and call it an act of God. The thought is horrifying. Beckett breaks the silence, pulling us from our spiraling thoughts. "Good thing our contact requested everything be destroyed."

"What about the digital files?" Whit asks.

"He said he was taking care of them. That's why he asked us to go in and extract the physicals. He said something about planting a virus that will 'eat' everything and then infect the cloud," Beckett says, and I breathe a little easier.

"Who is this guy?" I ask.

"I only know his code name—Wraith. I met him in an online forum a couple of years ago. He's a vigilante hacker. Remember when that senator from Florida had his search history released, causing him to resign a few weeks later?"

Quinn barks out a laugh. "Ha! Yeah—wasn't there something about furries?"

"Yeah—that was him."

"That was absolutely brilliant," Quinn says, sounding like he might have a new idol.

As the car falls quiet again, I glance at the files—something's been nagging in the back of my mind. "Do you think Voss was working for or with someone? Or was this all his own twisted genius?"

"Hard to say," Beckett replies. "But someone had to fund him. A project this big doesn't happen without serious backing."

Whit frowns. "If there's a client or a group, they won't stop just because the research is gone. They'll either find someone else or start over with what they remember."

"If they do, we'll just have to find them first," Quinn says, his grin sharp and dangerous now. "But that's a problem for another day."

When we get back, I watch as they throw all the files into the industrial incinerator—the reason they have one is not something I want to think about—the flames consuming everything. The smell of burning paper fills the air, sharp and acrid.

"Good riddance," Whit mutters, his jaw tight.

Quinn claps his hands together once, making me jump. "Well, I don't know about you all, but I suddenly find myself in the mood for pizza."

Beckett sighs. "Quinn..."

"Shut up?" Quinn asks. Beckett just looks at him for a minute. I can see the corners of his mouth twitching as he fights to maintain his stoic demeanor.

"Pizza is the greatest thing in the world. If you disagree, I'm gonna need to see some ID," Quinn says, changing his tone to something over-the-top and cartoonish, making us all burst into laughter.

I'm barely paying attention to their chatter—Whit and

Beckett discuss the logistics of pizza delivery while Quinn sings something about... *turtle ninjas*? All I can think about is how bright my life has become with them in it.

I watch them, their voices filling the space with warmth. Whit, watching Quinn, arms crossed, shaking his head with a quiet smile. Beckett, ever the leader, keeping them from getting too off track. And Quinn—unapologetically chaotic, making us all laugh when the night should be too heavy for humor.

It should terrify me—how much I need this, how much I crave it. The chaos, the certainty, the way their voices stir something deep inside me

It doesn't.

It feels—right.

25

The shooting range echoes with the steady crack of gunfire as I adjust my grip on the small pistol Beckett gave me a couple of months ago. The air is thick with the acrid scent of gunpowder, a smell I've come to know well during our training. Beckett stands beside me, his gaze constantly assessing my posture and technique.

"Good," he says as I line up another shot. "Keep your elbow firm. You're handling the recoil better."

I nod, steadying my breathing before firing. The shot lands squarely on the bullseye, and I allow myself a small smile. I'm getting pretty good at this, and knowing I can be lethal with a gun sends a thrill racing through me.

Beckett steps closer, his eyes widening as he tracks my progress, almost like he's impressed. "You're picking it up fast. Most people flinch for weeks before they even settle in— let alone hit anything."

As I reload, Beckett watches me, a flicker of amusement in his gaze. "If we'd had you backing us up years ago, maybe this one mission would've gone better. The view definitely would've improved."

I glance at him, arching a brow. "Oh yeah? What happened?"

His expression shifts, the humor in his eyes giving way to something more serious. "Let's just say it involved a hell of a lot of gunfire—and Quinn deciding to turn himself into a human shield."

I lower the pistol, a knot forming in my chest. "Wait, what? You need to back up and start from the beginning."

He exhales slowly, his gaze distant. "It was years ago, shortly after we first got started. We were tracking a target in Eastern Europe. The guy had security like you wouldn't believe—mercenaries with military training, fortified compound, the works. We were deep in hostile territory, and everything was going according to plan... until it wasn't."

"What happened?"

"It was my fault," Beckett says, voice even—but there's something hollow beneath it. Something that still hasn't left him. "I got distracted for a minute—long enough for one of their guys to take aim. Quinn saw it. Instead of letting me take the hit, the fucker stepped in."

My grip tightens around the pistol. A second of hesitation —that's all it took. "Is that..." My throat tightens. "Is that what those scars on his back are from?"

Beckett nods, his jaw tightening. "Two bullets. One grazed him, the other went clean through. We thought..." He pauses, his voice catching. "We thought we were going to lose him."

"What did you do?" I ask, taking aim at a fresh target.

"Got him out," Beckett says, his voice controlled, but guilt lingers beneath it. "He finally collapsed, so Whit and I carried him—the idiot wouldn't let us fucking help him—through what felt like hell and back. Got him to a private hospital. But not before the asshole nearly got himself killed refusing to leave."

I blink, lower the pistol slightly, and glance at him. "What do you mean he refused to leave?" The words leave me cold. Quinn's lack of self-preservation is... worrisome.

Beckett exhales, shaking his head. "The stubborn bastard wouldn't let us pull him out until the target was neutralized. Two bullets in him, barely able to stand, and he's telling us to finish the job before thinking about him. Said it'd all be for nothing if we didn't."

"Did you?"

"Of course we did," Beckett says with a sharp laugh. "Didn't give us a choice—reasoning with him was impossible. The second it was done, we dragged him to a private hospital. One of those places that won't ask questions as long as you pay upfront. He pulled through—somehow. But ever since then..." He pauses, his gaze locking with mine. "I don't let myself lose focus. Not for a second. That night, Quinn nearly died because I let my attention slip. Never again."

The weight of the story settles heavily in my chest, and I wonder if that's where some of Beckett's control issues come from. Their dynamic makes more sense now—Beckett's control balances Quinn's theatrics. Yet, when it matters, Beckett knows Quinn won't hesitate.

"Quinn's always testing the limits, isn't he?" I ask softly.

"He sure fucking does," Beckett replies, frustration clear in his voice. "Any way possible. But, at least out there, he does it to make sure we all come out alive. That's just who he is. But sometimes..." He trails off, his jaw ticking. "Sometimes, it's more than that. Quinn's got this never-ending need for adrenaline, always chasing the next high. When things get dangerous, he pushes it as far as he can—every fucking time."

I glance at him, brow creasing as I try to read the flicker of frustration and concern in his eyes. "You think he's reckless?"

Beckett lets out a low breath, leaning against the partition. "Reckless isn't the right word. Calculated, sure, but… like he's got something to prove, like he doesn't care if it's the last thing he does. Sometimes, I wonder if he's got a death wish."

I can't help but picture a future without Quinn, and my throat tightens. "Do you think it has something to do with his family? What if he—?"

Beckett cuts me off gently before I can spiral further into what ifs. "It doesn't matter why. What does is making sure he doesn't take it too far. That's my job—keeping us all alive, even if Quinn's hellbent on throwing himself in the fire to get it done."

I turn back to the target, raising the pistol again. My next shot lands just shy of the bullseye. I grit my teeth and adjust my stance without Beckett having to correct me. The next two shots are near perfect.

"Good," Beckett says, giving me one of his rare smiles. "Soon you'll be graduating to something bigger."

Thinking we're done for the day, I lower the gun and pull off my ear protection—until Beckett steps in behind me. His hands settle on my hips, firm, possessive. The range is silent, but my pulse pounds. "Don't stop now."

I freeze as his fingers brush the waistband of my leggings, sliding them down just enough to expose me to the cool air of the range. My pulse quickens, but I don't dare turn around.

"Eyes on the target."

"Beckett," I start, voice unsteady.

A soft click echoes as he hits a button on the wall, setting up a fresh target—lower than the rest. Before I can protest, he bends me over the partition, one hand firm between my shoulder blades, the other gripping my hip hard enough to bruise.

He leans in, breath warm against my ear. "Don't lose focus, Celest. Now, be a good girl and line up your shot." He releases my hip long enough for me to hear the sound of his belt unfastening.

"Show me how good you can be," he murmurs, sending a shiver down my spine. His body drapes over mine before he whispers into my ear. "Now, Celest, when my cock slides between your folds, how soaked are you going to be for me?" Before I can think of a response, he places my ear protection back in place.

I grip the pistol tightly, my breath uneven as he slowly presses into me, filling and stretching every inch of my core until his body is flush against mine. My hands tremble, my head dips for a moment, my mind drowning in him—but his voice cuts through the haze, low and gravelly.

"Focus," he says. "You can take it. I know you can."

I raise the gun, taking aim as his hips snap behind me, each of his motions just as deliberate and unrelenting as the man. My body fights to split its attention—the fast, rhythmic pace of his movements threatening to pull me under.

The force of him driving into me pushes my arms across the partition, making the target seem as if it's moving. I lock my elbows, tighten my shoulders, and pull the trigger. The shot rings out, landing just shy of the bullseye.

"You can do better," Beckett says, voice rough, and I cry out when I feel his hand smack against my rear. "Again."

My breaths come in short pants, and I try not to focus on the way he feels moving inside me. I fire again, and this time, the bullet lands dead center.

"Good girl. Now do it again." A thrill runs through me, mingling with the heat building quickly as he continues to push me. He tests the limits of my focus, and when his hand reaches around, rubbing gentle circles on my clit, I gasp before crying out his name.

I line up the gun with the target again, steadying my breath. His free hand slides up my back, fist in my hair, and tugs my view upward. The shift forces me to lift my arms, readjusting my aim.

I pull the trigger just as he pinches my clit, and I scream my release. I don't bother checking the target as my body turns into liquid. His hand covers mine, easing the gun from my grip. I watch his fingers move quickly to unload the weapon, rendering it harmless, never slowing his relentless pace. The ear protection is removed, and the sound of our bodies smacking together fills the room.

"You're incredible," he murmurs against my skin as he pulls me up to stand, sliding out of me long enough to spin me around, remove my shoes and pants, and then pick me up. My legs wrap around his waist on instinct as he moves. Seconds later, I feel the cool wall behind me.

He fills me in one thrust, then wraps his hand around my throat, forcing me to meet his eyes. He drives into me like a man possessed, and the cries spilling from my lips are nothing but a chorus of his name on repeat.

"Beckett... please," I beg, as the tension builds within me

again. I feel myself on the precipice, preparing to dive head-first into pleasure.

"Fuck, you're such a good girl, aren't you? So tight and wet for me. I'll never tire of fucking you, do you understand? We'll never let you go." His words are a mix of praise and possession. "You're ours till the end of time."

"Yes... yours... Oh God, Beckett. I'm going to..." If you asked me later, I'd swear I was speaking in full sentences. But right now? My brain isn't capable.

"That's it, Celest, I want to feel your cunt strangle my cock. Come for me," he says, his eyes never once leaving mine. "Now."

I explode.

All I can hear is the static in my ears, my mouth open in a silent scream, and I think my eyes have rolled to the back of my head. Beckett thrusts into me a few more times before filling me with his release.

Our breaths are labored as he drops his head into the crook of my shoulder. We stay like that for a few more minutes, my legs still wrapped around his waist, his body pinning me against the wall as he begins to soften inside me.

When he lifts his head, his lips touch mine and kisses me —unhurried and languid. It's both sweet and domineering. Slowly, he lowers me to the ground, does his pants back up, and then helps me step into mine. Once we're both fully dressed, he puts my gun and our ear protection away before coming to stand in front of me.

"You're stronger than you think, Celest," he says softly, hands gently holding my head between his callused palms. "Don't ever forget you're the badass who hit two perfect bullseyes while be fucked from behind."

I laugh as he drops his hands, flashing me a smug grin I've never seen him wear before. Then, I look over to the target and see two holes nearly on top of each other. I stare at it, two perfect bullseyes staring back at me. Then, I meet Beckett's gaze.

"Not a chance."

26

The tension in the room is suffocating. The command center's table is buried in blueprints of the Waldorf Astoria, with security feeds flickering across the monitors. Beckett stands stiff, arms crossed. Whit leans against the wall, his expression unreadable, but his clenched jaw gives him away. Quinn paces. No grin. No joke. Just a restless energy that sets my nerves even more on edge.

"This is insanity," Beckett says finally, breaking the silence. "He might as well be the president with how well he's protected. Every step we take will be a risk, and if this goes sideways, there's no coming back."

Quinn stops pacing and throws his hands up in frustration. "So what's the alternative? Let him keep funneling money into people like Voss?"

I sit quietly, listening to them go back and forth. My heart pounds, knowing what I'm about to say. It's not that I disagree with their concerns—it's that I see the solution, and I know it's not one they're going to like.

Alaric Hawthorn isn't just a financial powerhouse—he's a predator in every sense of the word. A man who's built his empire on manipulation and exploitation and who views people as nothing more than tools to be used and discarded. His reputation precedes him. I know he lives for the thrill— taking whatever or whoever he wants, simply because he can.

"He's a known womanizer, right?" I cut in, breaking up their argument.

All three heads snap toward me. Whit's eyes narrow. "What are you getting at?"

I take a steady breath, knowing this won't go over well, and meet their gazes head-on. "We use that to our advantage."

"How do you suggest we do that?" Quinn asks, suspicion lacing his tone.

"Simple. I'll be the bait."

"Not a fucking chance," Beckett snaps, his voice like stone.

"It's the only way," I argue. "You've been going in circles trying to figure out how to get him alone. He's not going to meet you in some dark alley without his guards. But if I can get him to take me to his room, you guys can handle the rest."

Whit shakes his head. "No. Out of the question." Now they're just making me mad. They've spent all this time training me and telling me how strong I am, yet they don't believe it?

Quinn's jaw tightens, and for once, he seems to be taking something seriously. "Celest, you don't know what kind of man—"

"I know exactly what kind of man he is." My voice cuts through his. I stand, locking eyes with him. "And I know what I'm capable of. I thought y'all did too." My words make them flinch. "Look, he likes a challenge, right? If one of you shows up flaunting me on your arm as a possession—an accessory—he'll want to steal me away from you. I'll play along, get him to his room, and y'all take it from there."

"You don't understand," Beckett says, his voice quieter but no less firm. "He's going to touch you. He's going to—"

"I do understand." I glare at him. "This isn't about me—it's about stopping him. If it means putting up with his hands for a few minutes, then so be it. And I'm telling you, I can handle it."

Whit's expression hardens, fists clenched at his sides. "There has to be another way."

"There's not," I say firmly. "This is the best shot we have, and you know it. Look, I know you hate this. I hate it too. But if we don't take this chance, more people are going to get hurt. And I'm getting really tired of the three of you telling me what I do and don't understand."

Beckett exhales, pinching the bridge of his nose. "Fine. But it has to be airtight."

"Would we ever do anything less than perfect?" I ask, breaking the tension, and give them a moment of silence to let the idea sink in.

"Promise me that if we say it's time to abort—you'll listen," Beckett demands.

"I will." But none of them look convinced. "I promise!"

"We'll arrive as guests," Quinn sighs, finally sinking into his seat. "I should be able to use my family's name to get us an invitation." His tone is still tense, but he's more focused now. "Celest will go by a different name. I'll introduce her as someone I met recently—someone I just couldn't resist showing off. Hawthorn won't be able to help himself. He'll take the bait."

"Meanwhile, Beckett and I will act as Quinn's personal guards," Whit adds reluctantly.

"Yeah—but disguised in case any of our parents are there," Quinn says, all three of them flinching at the word *parents*.

"What about the cause of death?" I ask, thinking it over. "It has to look natural."

"Poison," Beckett replies. "A delayed neurotoxin—something that mimics a heart attack but leaves no trace after a few hours."

"Subtle," Quinn says, nodding. "We'll slip it into his drink before they head upstairs." He grimaces, as if those last words left a foul taste in his mouth.

For the next few hours, we go back and forth on the plan until Beckett lays out the final details. "We'll take the helicopter into the city. Quinn and Celest will arrive at the gala as high-profile hotel guests. Whit and I will stay in the background as security, keeping an eye on the room."

"Once I get him upstairs, y'all need to be there waiting. That means you'll have to get into position before we arrive. We'll need a signal." I finish, my voice steady despite the knot tightening in my stomach.

"When you hand him my drink—dosed with the neurotoxin—that's our cue to move," Quinn says, his voice edged with reluctance.

None of them look happy, but they nod—we're all in agreement. Whit's gaze lingers on me, eyes full of unspoken worry. "We'll be close the entire time," he says quietly. "The second you need us, we're there."

"I know," I reply, forcing a small smile. "I'll be fine. Trust me."

"It's not you we don't trust," Beckett grumbles.

"It's going to be all right, you'll see," I say, my tone brighter than I feel.

As the discussion winds down, everyone scatters to finalize their preparations. I call the Waldorf, slipping into the role of Quinn's personal assistant. Within minutes, they've booked us a penthouse. Then, I request a gown befitting Mr. Delaney's guest for the Christmas Eve Gala. I give my measurements and coloring, and the woman assures me that several options will be waiting in the master closet. It's amazing what money—and a name—can do.

I take a slow breath, holding it for a moment before exhaling. This is the riskiest mission we've ever attempted. I'd be lying if I said I wasn't scared, but fear's nothing new—and this cause is far worthier. If letting Hawthorn put his hands on me means stopping him, then so be it.

I watch them work, never tiring of the quiet precision in their movements—there's something undeniably attractive about the way they operate, all skill and certainty. For all their grumbling, they trust me—and I trust them. Whatever happens tomorrow night, we'll face it together.

THE HUM OF THE MONITORS AND THE FAINT RUSTLE OF papers are the only sounds as we finalize the plan—again. I know the repetition comes from fear, and I don't blame them. My body is just as tense. I pace the Batcave, running through every step I'll take tomorrow night—on repeat. It's the kind of focus that leaves no room for anything else.

Finally, feeling like I've exhausted my mind, I glance up

and find them watching me. Their expressions are unreadable, but there's something simmering beneath the surface—a heat in their eyes that makes my pulse quicken.

Beckett's the first to move, stepping away from the table and crossing the room to stand in front of me. His usual hard-edged demeanor eases—just enough to make my chest ache.

"You're ready," he says, his words quiet but confident. "You've proven that over and over, and we should've remembered from the moment the idea left your lips. But I need you to remember something tomorrow night."

"What's that?" I ask, the words barely more than a breath.

His hand cups my jaw, his thumb brushing over my cheek. "That you're ours. Not his. Not anyone else's. Ours. Only ours."

Whit steps behind me, his broad chest pressing against my back. His hands settle on my shoulders, his touch warm as he kneads the tension away. "You're not in this alone, princess," he murmurs, voice rough, and my eyes close as I lean into his touch. "We're with you every step of the way. And when you're out there playing your role, when his hands are on you, just remember who you really belong to."

Quinn clears his throat. When I glance over, he's leaning casually against the table—but his usual grin is still missing. It hasn't made a reappearance since before we started planning this mission. His gaze flicks over me, dark and intense, making my skin erupt with chill bumps.

"We know you can handle him," he says. "Hell, you'll probably have the fucker wrapped around your finger before the first drink is gone. But we're not letting you walk into this without a reminder—without making damn sure that every time he touches you, it's us you feel."

My breath catches, their words igniting an inferno inside me. "You don't have to remind me," I say softly. "I could never forget."

"Good," Beckett says, his hand coming to rest against my neck, fingers curling just enough to cause shivers. "But we're going to make sure anyway." Then his lips are on mine, commanding my submission—that I willingly give.

Whit's hands slide beneath my shirt, skimming up my body before dragging my thin bra with them. His palms cup my breasts, fingers kneading, teasing. My nipples are already stiff, and he rolls them between his fingers—pinching, pulling—sending a sharp gasp from my lips. Beckett steps back as Whit tugs my shirt over my head and tosses it aside.

Quinn—never one to be left out—drops to his knees, hands gripping my thighs. When he looks up, that cocky smirk I've been missing is back, full of promise. His lips graze my stomach as he unbuttons my jeans, his mouth following every inch as he eases them down my legs.

"You've got no fucking idea what you do to us," Quinn murmurs, his voice low. "Watching you take charge, and putting us in our place when we underestimate you... It's the sexiest damn thing in the world."

Whit's hands glide down my arms, pulling me tighter against him. "We want you to feel that power. To know exactly what you do to us. Tomorrow, he might have your attention. But it'll be our touch burned into your skin."

Beckett's hand slides back to my throat, his grip possessive. "He can look, and the bastard might touch, but that's all he'll ever get—and he'll fucking die for it," he says with a growl. My eyes flash open, trailing down his naked body—all hard lines and raw strength, like a sculpture carved by the gods themselves.

"Who do you belong to, Celest?" he demands, as his grip tightens.

"You—the three of you." My voice is breathy, caught between his grip on my throat and the heat searing through me.

"And we belong to you," Whit responds, his voice rough. "Don't forget that."

Quinn's lips brush over my knee, and I can feel his grin against my flesh. "Not that we'd let you."

My heart pounds as their touches and words consume me, the heat of their presence chasing away the nerves twisting my stomach. I'm drowning in them—so lost in sensation that I barely notice Quinn lifting my leg over his shoulder. But I sure as hell notice when his mouth finds me, licking, sucking —devouring—until I'm nothing but a trembling mess, pleading for more.

"Fuck princess, you're making a mess all over me," Quinn says, giving one last, long lick before standing. Whit picks me up and carries me to his room.

"You're going to be such a good fucking girl for us, aren't you, Celest?" Beckett growls the moment my back hits the bed. Before I can answer, he grabs my ankles and drags me to the edge. His grip shifts to the back of my neck, forcing me sit up and rise to my knees—his face so close, I feel the heat of his breath.

"What do you think, Celest? Can you fit two of us in that tight, dripping cunt of yours?" His words should terrify me—but instead, heat floods my core, slick and undeniable.

"Fuck yeah, she can," Quinn drawls. "Don't worry, sweetheart, we won't break you—much."

Whit smirks, reaching into a drawer for the lube. "And if we do? We'll just put you back together."

Beckett releases his grip, hooks his arms around me, and lifts me effortlessly—tossing me onto my back. Before I can catch my breath, he yanks me to the edge again, throws my legs over his shoulders, and drives into me—one brutal thrust, bottoming out. No warning. No mercy. Just raw, relentless force as he pounds into me, over and over, until all I can do is grip the sheets and scream.

"Whose name is all over this pussy?" Beckett demands.

"Yours," I whimper.

"Say it."

"Yours, Beckett!"

His groan is pure satisfaction. "Good. Fucking. Girl." He pulls out, tossing my legs aside before delivering a sharp slap to my rear. Then he steps back, making room for Quinn.

Still on my side, Quinn lifts my top leg, draping it over his chest, the bend of his elbow locking it in place. Then he thrusts into me—deep, so deep I swear I see stars. I grip his arm as he uses my leg for leverage, pulling me to him with every sharp snap of his hips.

"Tell me, sweetheart, whose cock is buried so fucking deep inside you, you'll never forget the way it feels?"

"Your's, Quinn. Oh, God... Quinn... I can't."

"You can. And you'll take every fucking inch I give you." He slams into me, hard and unforgiving, each thrust pushing me closer to the edge—until, just as the cord inside me is about to snap, he pulls out.

I cry out, wrecked, denied.

Before I can beg, strong hands lift me, shifting my body until I'm lowered onto Whit—impaled, my back flush against his chest. His arms wrap around my center, locking me in place as he thrusts up, deep and deliberate. I grip his forearms, my nails sinking into his skin, but he doesn't stop. A guttural moan rips from my throat as my head falls back against his shoulder.

One of his hands slides between my legs, fingers pressing hard and fast against my clit, sending me hurtling back to the razor's edge. "That's it, princess, you're so close—I can feel your walls clenching around me. Now tell me... whose name are you going to scream when you come?"

"Y—" I start, and then shatter, screaming, "Oh, God, Whit!"

"Mmm, I love hearing my name screamed from your lips." His pace slows, teasing, drawing out my torment. Beckett steps in front of me, his gaze dark with intent. He slicks himself with lube, then lifts my legs, propping my feet on Whit's thighs—positioning me exactly how he wants.

"I'm going to go slow at first," he murmurs, his gaze locked onto mine. "But I'm not stopping. Do you under-stand?" His eyes bore into me, unwavering. I know—if I told him to stop right now, he would. No hesitation. But I don't. I nod, trusting them to take care of me. His lips curve, approval dark in his eyes. "That's my good girl."

I feel his slick tip press into me—slow, deliberate. It's tight, almost too much, but he doesn't stop. Just like he said he wouldn't. A whimper slips from my lips as my head falls back onto Whit's shoulder. He's there instantly, his mouth trailing along my neck, kissing, nipping—claiming.

"Look at you, princess," Whit rasps, his voice rough with

hunger. He grips the back of my neck, tilting my head forward—forcing me to watch as he and Beckett stretch me wider than I thought possible. The sight alone wrecks me, my body tightening, pleasure surging. I don't know why it pushes me closer to the edge—but it does.

"Fuck, that's hot," Quinn groans, stroking himself as he watches. Beckett starts slow, pushing in with shallow thrusts until my body gives way, stretching around him. Then he's driving into me—hard, possessive—while Whit holds me still, keeping me locked between them, taking everything they give.

"Goddamn, I'm not gonna last much longer," Whit grits out, his voice tight with restraint. "So fucking tight." A few moments later, pleasure crashes over me—I clench hard around them, free-falling into bliss, shattering at the bottom. Whit curses, his grip bruising as he thrusts deep one final time, spilling inside me. Beckett doesn't slow—he just keeps driving into me, relentless.

I feel them both slide out before Beckett lifts me, effortlessly passing me into waiting hands. For only a moment, I'm suspended—before I'm placed back where they want me. Beckett grips my hips, lines me up, and drives me down onto him—filling me in one sudden, overwhelming thrust. A deep groan rips from my throat at the intrusion.

"Not done yet, princess," Quinn says, pushing me down onto Beckett's chest. I barely have time to catch my breath before I feel him nudge my entrance—before he forces his way in alongside Beckett. A cry rips from my throat, a sharp mix of pleasure and pain. He doesn't wait. Doesn't give me a second to adjust. "Fuck, I can't go slow."

"Oh God," I moan, my body already spiraling, flying higher at breakneck speed.

"Fuck, she's taking you both so well," Whit murmurs, awe thick in his voice. He lies beside us, eyes locked on where his best friends are buried inside me.

Beckett's breath shudders. "I'm close." His voice is tight, strained.

"Just a few more minutes," Quinn grits out, his thrusts unrelenting. "I'm almost there."

"Come on, good girl," Beckett whispers against my ear, brushing my hair from my face. "Give us one more."

I want to tell him I can't—that I won't survive another—but my brain refuses to form words. Yet, even as I think it's impossible, my clit rubs against Beckett's pubic bone, unraveling me, the tension inside snapping like a live wire.

This time, when I scream, Beckett and Quinn fall with me—dragged under by the same oblivion. We lie there, bodies tangled, breathless. I don't know how it's possible, but every time I take all of them, I end up like this—spent, nearly comatose. My eyes flutter shut as Quinn pulls out, only to collapse beside Beckett.

"Don't ever forget who you belong to," Beckett whispers against my ear, his voice the last thing I hear as exhaustion drags me under. I sink into their embrace, knowing that no matter what happens tomorrow night, forgetting them is impossible.

Because I'm theirs.

And they're mine.

27

The rhythmic thrum of the helicopter blades hums through my chest as we descend onto the Waldorf Astoria's rooftop helipad. Sunlight bounces off the skyscrapers, gilding the city in a sharp, golden glow. Inside the cabin, tension coils beneath a forced calm. Beckett watches me too closely, searching for cracks in my resolve, while Whit's stare all but confirms that if he had his way, I'd never step foot off this aircraft. The only one who looks remotely entertained is Quinn, effortlessly guiding us to a smooth landing like it's just another casual afternoon flight.

"Well, at least you didn't crash us into a building this time," Whit says dryly.

"For fuck's sake, it was once! And there was no getting around it." Quinn turns to me, unfazed. "They're just jealous because I've got the big stick," he adds with a wink, one hand stroking the helicopter control between his legs. I can't help but laugh as Beckett and Whit groan.

The hotel staff greets us with flawless efficiency, escorting us off the helipad, through the lobby, and straight to our penthouse suite without so much as a pause. The space is absurdly opulent—soaring ceilings, crystal chandeliers dripping light, and furniture plush enough to swallow a person whole. It feels almost insulting to give it nothing more than a passing glance before Beckett pulls out a tablet, swipes across the screen, and projects a detailed map of the hotel onto the wall.

"Let's go over this again," Beckett says, voice carrying that unmistakable command he slips into when he's in work mode. "Celest, you know the ballroom layout. Hawthorn will surround himself with the who's who of society—he always does. He's predictable. As long as Quinn makes a spectacle of showing you off, he'll already be watching before you're even introduced. He'll stay in the ballroom until he finds someone to entertain him. That's where you come in."

Whit's jaw tightens. "Stay close so we can keep things under control. Do not let him take things too far. If you need an out, you signal. Got it?"

I nod, even though we all know there's an entire elevator ride where I'll be alone with Hawthorn. "Got it."

We don't have much time to review the plan before I need to get ready. It'll take me longer, so I leave them to go over the exit strategy again. It's been a while since I've had a chance to get dolled up, and I'm curious to see how they'll react when they see me next.

I take a final look in the mirror, adjusting the delicate strap of my gown. The deep red velvet clings to my body, soft and rich, molding to every curve as it drapes down my figure. The backless design plunges daringly low, exposing my bare skin to the cool air. Behind me, the train flows, a cascade of luxurious fabric that sweeps with each step.

My hair is loosely pinned to one side, soft waves tumbling over my shoulder. My lips match the exact crimson shade of my dress, and a smoky winged liner accentuates my eyes, giving them an air of mystery and allure. Honestly, it's the best my makeup has ever looked.

I exhale, steadying myself. It's not nerves—this is all part of the plan. But as I turn to leave the room, a flicker of anticipation curls inside me. I open the door and step into the main suite, where the guys are already scattered, dressed in their tuxes, focused on the final details of the mission. The sound of my heels clicking against the marble floor draws their attention.

I stop just shy of the center of the room, turning slightly so that the train of my gown sweeps dramatically behind me. I hold my hands loosely clasped in front of me, lifting them slightly to ensure my arms bend just right, giving my figure the perfect lines. Glancing over my shoulder, I catch the way their gazes snap to me in unison—it's almost comical.

The air freezes. Quinn's jaw drops first, his expression pure, unabashed disbelief. Whit leans forward slightly, arms crossed, but his fingers dig into his biceps as if grounding himself. Beckett remains ever composed, not moving, but his eyes darken, tracing every detail of the gown—and what it reveals.

"Well?" I ask, letting a hint of a smile tug at my lips. "Do I pass inspection?"

Quinn throws his hands in the air, shattering the silence. "Nope. Absolutely not. Turn around, go back in there, and put on a potato sack. No way am I letting you leave this room looking like... like that."

"Like what?" I ask, feigning innocence as I arch a brow.

"Like a goddamn wet dream," Quinn snaps, his voice laced with both frustration and desire. "No other man is touching you when you look like that."

I laugh softly, shaking my head. "Too bad. You're just going to have to deal with it. And besides…" My voice drops as I turn fully to face them. "You get to stare at me in it all night—and work together to figure out the most interesting way to peel it off later."

The tension in the room spikes. Whit clears his throat, but his eyes remain locked on me. Beckett's jaw tightens, just enough to notice, as he rakes his fingers roughly through his short hair. Quinn, though, is still muttering about potato sacks and murder, giving me the perfect opportunity to push them a little further.

"Want to know a secret?" I ask, my voice teasing as I perch on the arm of the couch, the slit in my gown falling open, offering them a glimpse as I glance between them.

Their eyes narrow, interest piqued. "What secret?" Beckett asks, his voice low, just a hint of curiosity threading through the calm exterior.

I lean back, crossing one leg over the other, exposing my naked hip. My voice drops, almost a whisper, but it's louder than the weight of the silence between us. "I'm not wearing any underwear," I murmur, letting the words hang in the air. "The lines showed."

Quinn groans, a dramatic sound that fills the room as he drags a hand down his face, like speaking has physically pained him. "You're actually trying to kill us."

Whit's lips curl into a playful, mischievous grin—that could rival Quinn's—his eyes dark with something far more intense. "Good thing we'll be keeping a close eye on you all night," he murmurs, stepping into my space, his hand trailing up the length of my exposed leg. "I'll be taking note of anyone who dares to touch you."

Beckett's voice stays even, but the subtle steel behind it makes it clear he means every word. "Let's hope for their sake, hands don't wander. They'll end up joining their buddy Hawthorn by the end of the night if they do."

When the elevator doors open, we step into the grand hallway leading to the ballroom, and it feels like entering a different world. Dozens of chandeliers sparkle overhead, their light casting an ethereal glow, while the soft murmur of the elite fills the air. The grandeur around us—gleaming marble floors, towering columns, and guests draped in their finest—makes everything feel surreal.

As we stroll down the black-and-white checkered corridor, Quinn adjusts his cufflinks and leans in, his voice playful yet underneath lies something seductive that sends a ripple of heat through me.

"You know, Celest, you're about to cause an absolute scandal tonight," he murmurs, the words curling around me like a challenge.

Suddenly, I can't wait for the night to end.

I let my gaze linger, trailing up the length of his body, savoring every inch of the perfectly tailored tuxedo that clings to him so damn well. A teasing smile tugs at my lips as my eyes finally meet his. "You're one to talk. You in that tux?" I pause, allowing my gaze to drop lower before locking back onto his. "It's really doing it for me."

He grins, his shoulders relaxing slightly. "Careful, Celest. Flattery will get you everywhere." Then, his voice drops lower, and he leans in, adding, "At least, it'll get me everywhere inside you."

A flush heats my cheeks, and I briefly wonder if they're the same shade as my dress.

Behind us, Beckett clears his throat, his voice steady but edged with concern. "We won't let you out of our sight."

Whit's voice follows, still wrapped in that same intense focus. "If you need to bail, signal. It doesn't matter if it blows the mission—we'll get you out."

Before the ballroom doors swing open, Quinn inhales deeply, straightening his bowtie, then takes my hand, pressing a kiss to my palm before tucking it into the crook of his elbow. "It's showtime."

The room hums with energy, filled with glittering elites, champagne flutes in hand, their laughter ringing out in soft waves. Quinn moves through the crowd with ease, effortlessly charming everyone. His grin is wide, posture relaxed, the epitome of confidence. It's not long before someone spots him.

"Quinton! Haven't seen you at one of these in ages." An older gentleman in an ostentatious tux greets him from a small group, raising his glass in the air to catch Quinn's attention.

Quinn smirks, raising his glass in acknowledgment. "Just happened to be in the neighborhood. Thought I'd show my face—especially after meeting the most gorgeous arm candy and needing to take out my new accessory." He gestures toward me with a charming grin, smoothly adding, "This is Evelyn Ashford."

I step forward, offering a polite smile as I slip into the role we rehearsed. "It's lovely to meet you all," I say, my voice warm yet poised, striking the perfect balance between elegance and approachability. As I extend my hand, the older man takes it, pressing his lips to my knuckles, his smile too wide, too practiced. What is it about ridiculously wealthy old men? It's rare to meet one who doesn't immediately make my skin crawl.

Quinn's hand rests lightly on the small of my back, casual yet purposeful—significantly lower than what's proper. "Evelyn's been kind enough to let me drag her to one of these stuffy gatherings," he says with a wink, earning a chuckle from the group. "I couldn't resist showing off something so beautiful... something that's mine."

I let my gaze sweep over the small crowd, keeping my expression composed. "Oh, stop, he insisted," I tease, swatting at Quinn lightly. "But I have to admit, the company makes it worthwhile."

Finally, we reach a circle of guests that includes Alaric Hawthorn. He's everything I expected—charismatic, charming, with a sharp undercurrent of arrogance that immediately puts me on edge. Quinn's playful jabs quickly escalate into competitive banter, and I catch the exact moment when Hawthorn's gaze shifts—he's decided to make his move, if only to one-up Quinn.

He asks me to dance, and I glance at Quinn with a coy smile before accepting. On the dance floor, it doesn't take long for Hawthorn to lean in, his lips grazing my ear as his voice drops low. "A girl like you doesn't belong with a little boy like Quinton. You deserve a real man."

I laugh softly, my fingers lightly trailing along his arm, just enough to tease. "A real man, huh? And who might that be?"

"I could show you." I stifle the shiver of disgust, twisting it into something that feels more like intrigue as I catch the way his gaze shamelessly roams over my body.

The dance ends, and as Hawthorn guides me off the floor, his hand lingering just a beat too long on my lower back, I spot Quinn waiting off to the side. His eyes meet mine, and there's an edge to his gaze—like he's holding something back, fighting to keep his anger contained beneath the surface.

As we approach, Quinn's grin spreads, easy and confident, but his posture is stiff, his movements deliberate. He steps between Hawthorn and me with a little more force than necessary, his arm wrapping around my waist and pulling me tightly to his side, his touch firm and possessive. "There you are," he says, his tone smooth, but it holds a warning beneath it. "I was starting to miss you."

Hawthorn raises an eyebrow, clearly amused. "Didn't take you for the clingy type, Quinton."

Quinn laughs, the sound dismissive, and light—too light. "Oh, I'm not," he replies with a flicker of something dangerous in his grin. "But Evelyn here?" He glances down at me, his smile widening just a little too much. "She's worth keeping close."

Before I can respond, Quinn presses his drink into my hand, not waiting for a reply. "Hold this for me, sweetheart," he says, his voice casual, but there's something darker beneath it—a command disguised as a favor. "I'll be right back." He glances at Hawthorn, his grin sharp and almost mocking, then grabs my free hand, pressing a kiss to the inside of my palm. I know it's his way of telling me to stay safe. "Try not to steal her while I'm gone." His gaze locks with mine, and for a brief moment, a flicker of unease flashes across it, disappearing as quickly as it came. He slaps

Hawthorn on the back—just a little too hard—and laughs, making it seem friendly before walking away, calling out to someone across the room.

Hawthorn's glare morphs into a smirk, his eyes glinting with something dark as he watches Quinn disappear into the crowd. "Tempting offer," he says, turning back to me. His gaze sharpens, unnervingly intense, sweeping over me like a predator sizing up its prey, lingering just a touch too long. I force a smile, pushing back the chill creeping up my spine, doing my best to keep my composure. "I hope you're worth it."

"So," he murmurs, stepping far too close, his hand reaching out to twirl one of my loose curls around his finger. His voice is low, and this close, I can smell the whisky on his breath. "What do you say we get out of here? I'd hate for you to waste your evening with a boy when I could show you what it's like to be with a real man."

I hesitate just long enough to make him think it's a difficult choice, letting the moment linger, making him think he's won. "Alright," I finally say, as if coming to some reluctant decision, passing him Quinn's drink. "Looks like you've successfully taken both Quinn's date and his drink."

Hawthorn laughs, knocking back the glass with a smug grin. He's a ticking time bomb now, the drug working its way through his system.

As we step into the elevator, the doors close with a soft hiss, and I'm alone with him. For the first time tonight, unease creeps in. Hawthorn glances at me, a predatory smile curling on his lips. "You know, I made a new friend this evening—a southern guy. Said he lost something important to him."

I blink, genuinely confused, but I keep my smile in place, playing the part. "Oh really? I'm not sure I follow," I say lightly, tilting my head just enough to mask my unease. "What did he lose?"

Hawthorn's smile widens, the look on his face predatory and cruel. "Why, you, Celestina. I hope you know how to beg."

No.

It can't be.

My ears are ringing.

I'm going to be sick.

I can't breathe.

Oh God, no.

I need to get out of—

The elevator dings, and the doors slide open, revealing a figure I never thought I'd see again. Perhaps if I'd paid closer attention to whose eyes were on me tonight, or if the guys had noticed the man lurking in the distance, watching my every move, I wouldn't have been so surprised to see him now.

"Josiah," I whisper, my blood running cold, the name slipping from my lips like a death sentence.

Before I can react, Hawthorn shoves me into Josiah's waiting arms. A sharp sting at my neck—cold, cruel—sends a jolt through my system, and within seconds, my vision blurs. My legs betray me, and I lean heavily into Josiah for support.

His scent, familiar and sickening, fills my nose—a reminder that this is no dream. It's a nightmare come to life. The last thing I see clearly is Josiah handing Hawthorn an envelope, his voice as quietly sinister as I remember.

"Everything you need's in there."

As my consciousness fades, all I can think of is my guys—

how they've promised to never let me go. They'll come for me. I know it. But what if they can't find me? The thought twists my stomach, but I push it away. They're my anchor, my strength. They won't break their promise.

I hold onto that belief as everything fades to black. Wherever they are, I know they're coming for me—no matter what it takes. I know they are.

But what if they're too late?

The darkness within me screams.

28

The sharp bite of metal around my wrists and the damp chill seeping into my bones drag me from unconsciousness. The drug Josiah used leaves a brutal headache, and my vision swims, but even through the haze, I recognize my surroundings. The flickering bulb overhead casts just enough light to reveal the cold stone walls—haunting reminders of a place I thought I'd escaped.

I gasp in pain as I try to sit up, my head pounding harder with the effort. The familiar ache only amplifies the dread coiling in my chest.

When I'm finally able to open my eyes without the world spinning, I glance down at my gown—once perfectly elegant, now a shadow of what it was. Torn and soiled, its rich velvet stained with grime. A swell of emotion rises in my throat, but I force it down. The gown is the least of my concerns, though it's easier to focus on than what's really happening.

The sound of slow, deliberate footsteps descending the stairs breaks the silence, each echoing step a jagged beat that intensifies the throbbing in my skull. I don't need to look to know who it is. I can feel his presence already.

Josiah steps into view, hands casually tucked into his pockets, but the rage radiating off of him is unmistakable. His eyes burn with fury, each glance like a lash against my skin. The air around him seems to grow heavier, suffocating, and I can feel the weight of his presence pressing down on me.

"Welcome home, Celestina," he sneers, his voice dripping with venom, the mockery in his tone making it clear how little he values me. "And a merry Christmas to you."

I don't answer. I won't give him the satisfaction.

He crouches down, bringing himself closer, his gaze piercing mine as he lingers over me like a predator eyeing its prey. His lips curl into a sneer that twists my insides. "I've prayed for you every day, you know. Prayed that you'd find your way back to the Light. But instead, you've let the devil consume your soul."

When I don't respond, Josiah's eyes flash with irritation, the tightness in his jaw betraying his control. "Don't think I don't know about the man you were with at the gala. I can practically feel the darkness he left on your skin. I know you let him touch you."

My lip twitches, but I force my voice to stay steady, the words slipping out like silk. "Well, if that's what you think, Josiah, you're in for a rude awakening."

He studies me for a long moment, trying to gauge my response, his gaze sharp, searching for cracks. "How so?" he finally asks, his patience wearing thin.

I lean forward just a fraction, a slow, sinful smile spreading across my lips. "It wasn't just the one devil," I drawl. The smile that curves my mouth is pure sin itself, and I know without a doubt that it's enough to stoke the fire and brimstone in him.

His sneer falters, just for a moment, as he processes my words. "What are you talking about?" he asks, his voice low and dangerous, jaw ticking, fists clenching.

I lean back against the wall, a faint laugh slipping free despite the dull ache in my head, despite the dizziness threatening to take me down. "I've been living with three men, Josiah. I love them. Each of them. Just as they love me. And they've all more than touched me."

The reaction is instantaneous. Before I can blink, his arm swings out, a backhand that snaps my head to the side with a sickening crack. Pain explodes across my cheek, the throbbing in my skull intensifying to a degree that makes my stomach churn. I fight the wave of nausea that crashes over me, but I don't let the pain show.

"You disgusting, ungrateful whore," he hisses, standing tall enough to loom over me, his presence suffocating. "Our wedding is set for New Year's Eve, one week from today. And I will spend the rest of your life using every means necessary to purify your soul. You'll beg, Celestina. And I'll enjoy every second of it."

I turn my head, glaring up at him with as much defiance as I can muster. "You can try, Josiah. But when they come for me—and they will come—you'll wish you'd never touched me."

His laugh shatters the silence that had begun to stretch between us, like shards of glass splintering inside my skull—dark, humorless. "Oh, I'm counting on it," he says, his smile widening. "They'll come, and you'll watch as I slowly destroy them, piece by piece. I was expecting just one, but three? Now that's a real treat. Consider it a wedding gift." He leans closer, his voice a venomous whisper. "I'll make sure the last thing they see is my hands, leaving marks all over you."

He goes into grotesque detail, each word more twisted than the last, savoring every cruel scenario. His voice is painfully sharp, like claws scraping across my aching skull, as he describes how he'll destroy them. He claims it will bring him pleasure to be the architect of their misery. He promises to make them witness every depraved act he plans to "restore my purity," before sending them to the fiery pits of hell. Each sentence is a strike, meant to tear me apart, but I refuse to let them touch me.

Ignoring him is my only power. Every word I don't respond to is a silent blow to his ego. I force my gaze down, focusing on my broken nails as if they're more important than the horrific agenda spilling from his lips. I tut, as if irritated by something trivial—like he's not even worth the iota of my attention. In that moment, I decide: He isn't. His words don't exist in my world. The only thing that matters is the distance I create between us with every second I don't react.

He can talk, but with silence, I'll win.

His composure fractures, and with a swift kick to my gut, he knocks the breath from my lungs. I try to retaliate, but the chains yank me back, and I glare at him, my vision blurring from the pain. The defiance in my eyes seems to unnerve him, making his nostrils flare.

"What's wrong, Josiah?" I force the words out, my voice shaking but laced with defiance. "Afraid of a little thing like me? Is that why you need to chain me up?"

He doesn't answer, but the tension in his jaw tightens,

betraying his irritation. Instead, he straightens his jacket, eyes scanning me with a look of disgust.

"You're going to rot down here in that filthy dress, and think about what you've done," he spits, his voice colder than ice. "By the time our wedding day comes, you'll be begging me to save you."

The darkness within me rages as she snarls at the sorry excuse of a man. I laugh, the sound thin and weak, yet it carries a manic rage that echoes through the empty cellar. It's like a dozen versions of me are laughing at him in unison, and that thought fuels me, giving me the strength to look him dead in the eye and say, "Fuck you, Josiah. Behold, your harbinger of death."

It's a promise—one that rings with finality.

His eyes widen for the briefest moment, trying to mask his shock. I see the realization dawn on him—he was expecting me to crumble, to beg for mercy. Instead, I stand firm.

The silence that follows is thick, before he storms up the stairs, his fury palpable. He slams the door behind him, the force of it making me flinch, but my resolve never wavers.

I press my head to the wall, the adrenaline bleeding out, leaving room for every ache and pain to crash in. My chest heaves, tears clawing at the back of my eyes, but I bite them back, knowing they'll only make things worse. Beckett's grounding presence, Whit's quiet strength, and Quinn's wicked mouth—these thoughts are my anchor. They'll come for me. I know it.

And if they can't—for some impossible reason—I'll fight my way out and back into their arms, just like they taught me.

This isn't the end of my story.

TIME BLURS AS MY MIND DRIFTS IN AND OUT OF SLEEP. The veil between memories and reality thins, making it impossible to keep them at bay. I'm sixteen again, dragged to this same cellar by my father for some minor infraction. Josiah waits, cold and smug, as he chains me to the wall. My terror seems to fuel him, his satisfaction in my fear unmistakable.

"You'll learn obedience," he says, his voice unnervingly calm. An eager gleam flickers in his eyes, as though punishing me is not just his right, but his divine purpose—and he will savor every agonizing second of it. He strips me of my clothes, leaving me exposed, shivering in the cold, vulnerable in a way that makes me want crawl out of my skin and leave it behind. I beg him to stop, telling him it's not right, but he doesn't listen. He tells me to be quiet, saying it's fine because we're betrothed.

That it's his right, that I can't tell him no.

The first time he forces himself on me, I scream, I sob, but he only laughs. My fear amuses him. He calls me ridiculous, insists it's for my own good. When my cries don't stop on command, his slap cracks across my face. His breath scorches my skin as he roars about how grateful I should be.

Grateful?

For what?

I can't understand.

After that, the punishments come more frequently. My father searches for reasons to hand me over to Josiah. A bed left improperly made. Stepping outside my room without permission—even just to use the restroom.

My father doesn't care how much Josiah hurts me because it elevates him in the covenant—and there is no greater honor.

He once told me to stop complaining—that this was the only value I had, the only way I'd ever mean anything to him. For a long time, I believed that if I could be perfect, I'd be enough, he'd love me. But now, I realize he's never been capable of love.

At least, not toward me.

Each day I spend chained in his cellar, Josiah takes another piece of me, hollowing me out, leaving only what he wants to remain. I learn, out of necessity, to hide the best parts of myself —tucking them deep, locking them away where he can't reach.

My mother told me not to let them break me. I don't have the heart to tell her they already have.

Once, when the Covenant's doctor visited, I told him what was happening to me, trusting him to help. That's what doctors do, right?

I couldn't have been more wrong.

He said defying Josiah was like slapping God in the face— then pressed a syringe into my arm, injecting something he claimed would prevent pregnancy.

Not thirty minutes after the doctor left, Josiah arrived. He never knocks. He simply barges in. I heard his footsteps pounding up the stairs, fear locking me in place. My body started shaking the moment he stepped into my room. He grabbed me by the arm, his grip bruising, and yanked me down the stairs, out the door. I didn't go home for days.

When I turned eighteen, I moved into the Covenant's college dorms. I thought I might be free of him, at least for a few years.

That was just a naive girl's wishful thinking.

He still found ways to get to me. Not that he even had to try. Nowhere was safe. He made sure I never forgot—I was his.

Countless times, he barged into my dorm in the dead of night—no warning, no discretion. I'd wake, screaming, as he yanked me from bed by my hair. The girls I shared a dorm with could do nothing but watch in terrified silence, too afraid to move, too afraid to help.

After the first night Josiah dragged me out, the other girls began to warm up—lukewarm, at best. I think, before that, they had a fairytale vision of my life. A twisted romance, gilded in devotion.

Until they saw the truth.

Until they saw *him*.

Drifting back into consciousness is a mercy, the memory fading as the cold, damp air pulls me into the present. The cellar walls come into view, a harsh reminder of where I am. My body aches, my wrists raw from the chains, but the throbbing in my head is bearable. I force myself upright, relieved when the motion no longer makes me dizzy.

More painful memories threaten to pull me under, dragging me back to the mindset of the Celest I used to be, before I escaped. I inhale deeply, closing my eyes, and let the past few months push the horrors of before into the darkness.

Celestina no longer exists.

That part of my life is over.

She's dead.

Buried in the past, along with the memories she carried.

"I'm not that girl anymore," I whisper.

My past does not define me. It is not my future.

My future is coming for me. And this time, I'm not leaving my mother behind. She deserves happiness just as much as I do.

"Hold on," I whisper, gripping the chains. "Just a little longer."

I stretch out my legs, forcing the blood to flow, then push myself upright. It's a struggle, but once I'm standing, movement comes easier. I have to keep my strength. I will walk out of here when the time comes.

They're coming.

I can almost hear them now.

I haven't forgotten who I belong to.

And they haven't forgotten me.

29

They've fed me seven times... or maybe eight. Meager meals—bread and water, mostly—delivered at random intervals, making it impossible to track the days. I know it's been at least a few.

Sometimes, they surprise me with a bowl of hot oatmeal. Comforting and cruel all at once. The heat soaks into my hands, spreads through my belly—but it never lasts. Just a fleeting reminder of how cold I am, shivering in my ruined dress.

At least the slit in the skirt lets me wrap it around my arms and legs, curling into the smallest shape possible to conserve warmth. It helps, but my bones still feel carved from ice.

I'd kill for one of Whit's oversized sweatshirts right now— the ones that always smell like him. Cedar and soap.

The cough came out of nowhere, and it came on fast.

At first, it was just a scratch in the back of my throat— something I could blame on the limited water they give me.

But lately, it's worsened. Grown deeper. A harsh rattle in my chest that stabs with every breath.

I haven't had it long—maybe a day or two—but it's persistent, growing worse with each hour I spend in this damp, freezing cellar.

I think the cold triggered it, the stone walls leeching away whatever heat I have left. The air, thick with moisture, only makes it worse. Now, every inhale feels weighted, every breath dragged through my lungs like wet cement. My throat, raw as sandpaper, burns with each scraping cough.

My body protests with every movement as I stand, shaking the numbness from my limbs, fighting to stay upright. Even with regular attempts to move, my muscles throb from days spent curled on the freezing floor, desperately trying to find warmth. Dizziness comes in waves now, spiraling through my skull with every rise.

Pins and needles stab at my legs, but I force myself to ignore the weakness tearing through me.

I will stand.

I will straighten.

They're coming for me. They have to be.

Even the best need time to plan—I know this.

I do.

But the waiting gnaws at me, whispering doubts into the cracks forming in my resolve. I won't let it break me.

Not yet.

Not when I know they're out there, somewhere, figuring out a way to bring me home.

Not after I've just put myself back together.

Yet that hope—the fragile thread I've been clinging to—is fraying.

Silence is my oppressor, stretching endlessly as the days blur into a haze of hunger, cold, and despair. I wrap the tattered skirt of my dress tighter around my legs, knowing it will do nothing to warm my frozen limbs. The ache in my chest sharpens as my mind drifts—to the comfort of their arms, to the safety I once felt, to the promise of a life worth living.

A muffled thud jolts me like an electric shock.

I freeze, pulse hammering.

Chaos erupts above—bodies slamming, the clang of metal, then a crash so loud the floor trembles beneath me. My breath catches as I stare at the stairs, straining to listen.

They're here.

I know it.

A beat of silence. Then, a voice rings out, clear as a bell.

"Suck my dick, you sick pedo!"

It's so absurdly Quinn that a relieved giggle slips out of me, even as fear tightens in my gut. My heart races, hope flickering to life.

They've come for me.

Just like I knew they would.

But as fast as that hope rises, it plummets.

Josiah's cruel laughter spills down the stairwell—a sound I've learned to loathe. The crash of the door swinging open cuts through the chaos, silencing the fight. A sickening scrape follows, bodies being dragged.

My fingers dig into the chains as footsteps descend—slow, deliberate.

The air rips from my lungs as Josiah's hired guards—mercenaries, if I had to guess—drag the three men who make up my entire heart into the room.

My stomach twists into a cold, hard knot.

They barely move. What little they do is slow, sluggish—like they're trying to wade through molasses.

"Make sure to give them a warm welcome!" Josiah calls down, not even bothering to make an appearance.

The guards laugh as they toss them to the ground. Then, one by one, they take turns beating them.

I have to fight to keep from vomiting.

"Please," I beg, voice shaking. "Please stop. Don't hurt them."

The guards glance over, and if I'd expected surprise to flicker across their gazes at seeing a woman chained down here, I'd be disappointed.

Two of them leer, their gazes crawling over me like a second layer of filth. But at least they stop.

Whit's head lolls to the side, his face pale, streaked with blood that drips sluggishly from a gash above his temple. His broad shoulders—usually so strong, so proud—sag, as if the fight has been beaten out of him.

"Princess," I barely hear the word leave his lips. The sound so small for such a large man. I choke on a sob.

I want to call out, tell him to lift his head, to look at me.

But I already know.

It's too late.

He's unconscious.

Beckett stirs, his eyes fluttering open for a fleeting moment—but they're dull, unfocused. The sharp precision, the calculating awareness that defines him, is gone.

Whatever they drugged him with is winning.

His body jerks weakly as one of the mercenaries shoves

him forward. He stumbles, only staying upright because they're dragging him along like a broken doll.

But it's Quinn who shatters me.

He's still fighting to stay conscious, his lips pulled into a bloody grin—God, that maddening, reckless grin—as his swollen eyes flicker toward me.

His voice is weak, thick, the words spilling like molasses, but that unshakable, infuriating confidence is still there. "D'n't cry, sweetheart," he slurs, teeth stained red. "Ev'rythin's goin' perf'ly t'plan."

I didn't even realize I was crying until he said it.

The tears burn as they fall, streaking down my face as I whisper hoarsely, "I think your plan might be shit."

He doesn't hear me. His head tilts forward, the fight slipping from his body as he finally goes under.

I can't stop shaking. My hands tremble against the chains as the guards lock them up—securing the shackles around their wrists before disappearing up the stairs, leaving me alone in the silence.

THE SOUND OF HEAVY FOOTFALLS DESCENDING THE cellar stairs sends a violent shiver through me. I've spent days dreading Josiah and his disciples coming through that door. But I never thought *he* would come.

Somehow, that makes it worse.

The room seems to shrink, damp stone walls pressing in, threatening to swallow me whole.

"You're more of a disappointment than I always thought you

to be," he says, his voice devoid of emotion. No fire, no brimstone. None of the theatrics Josiah wields so effortlessly. My father never needed the spectacle—only cold, unwavering certainty.

"I should have drowned you when you were born. It would have spared us all the trouble." The words hit harder than I expect, stealing my breath like a fist to the gut.

But I won't let him see.

I bite down on the raw ache in my chest and meet his gaze, my glare unwavering. "You've thought about that a lot, haven't you?" My voice is hoarse, throat raw from coughing, but I force it to sound unaffected. "How many times have you wished I never existed?"

His mouth tightens, his gaze darkening.

"Every single time you defied me. Every time you questioned your place in this world and thought yourself deserving of more."

He shakes his head, disappointment so absolute it makes my eyes burn with tears I refuse to let fall.

"You had one duty, Celestina. One purpose. And instead, you threw yourself to those... *animals*."

Across the room, Quinn lets out a low, bitter laugh. His head wobbles unsteadily, dried blood caking his chin. But there's venom in his voice when he speaks.

"That's rich. You sold her off to a monster and called it devotion." He lifts his head just enough to sneer, his swollen face twisted with fury. "You're the failure here, daddy dearest."

My father barely spares him a glance, his contempt razor-sharp.

"And what are you? Some gutter trash who thinks playing hero will change the fact that you're nothing?"

Whit growls low in his throat, his arms straining against the restraints. "You failed her. You let a child predator groom your daughter—then had the audacity to blame her for saving herself."

Beckett's voice is colder than I've ever heard it, slicing through the room like a blade of ice. "You don't deserve the title of father, let alone the honor of being hers."

My father stands firm, completely unmoved, unbothered. Their words don't touch him. His gaze stays locked on mine, as if they don't exist. Which, to him, they don't.

They're nothing but background noise.

Flies buzzing in his ear.

"Tomorrow, you *will* marry Josiah, Celestina," he says, as if it's already decided—as if no other reality exists. "You will restore this family's name and bring us back into good standing. Or—" he tilts his head, eyes flashing with the cruelty I know he's capable of, "—you will spend the rest of your miserable life wishing for death."

A cold, bitter laugh escapes before I can stop it.

"Is that what you think is going to happen?" I shoot back, my voice sharp with exhaustion, raw with rage. "Because I promise you—you'll be rotting before I ever kneel to that sorry excuse for a man."

His expression doesn't shift. No anger, no frustration. Just that same impenetrable wall of certainty—unyielding and emotionless. "You think you have a choice?"

He exhales slowly, like I'm being difficult on purpose. "This union is bigger than you. Your life is not your own, Celestina. It never has been. You are, and have never been, more than currency for me to spend. And I intend to get a return on my investment."

The weight of his words crushes me. I wish it didn't. I've always known he sees me as nothing more than a possession. That he truly believes I belong to them.

To him.

He's wrong. Neither he nor Josiah can claim that privilege.

Slowly, I rise to my feet, lifting my chin. The defiance in my veins burns hotter than my fear. "Where's my mother?" I demand, my voice raw but firm. "I want to see her."

His sneer deepens. "You won't be seeing her."

Something in the way he says it chills me.

"Why not?" I step forward, as far as the chains allow. "What did you do to her?"

My father watches me, the shadow of something like twisted glee curling at the corner of his mouth.

He wants me to ask.

He wants me to beg.

Then he says the two words I unknowingly feared most.

"She's dead."

My world shifts. The walls tilt. My breath catches in my throat, solid and painful.

"No," I whisper, the word barely forming on my lips. "You're lying."

He takes a slow step toward me, eyes gleaming darkly. "It was my right as her husband to punish her for her betrayal."

A slow, horrible smile stretches across his wrinkled face.

"And I did."

I shake my head, vision blurring as I try to make sense of a world where someone like him can snuff out the light of someone as good as my mother.

No.

No, she can't be gone.

She can't be—

The chains rattle as my body sags, my knees slamming into the cold stone floor with a crack. The pain doesn't register. I promised I would come back for her.

What if I'd come back sooner?

I can't breathe. The room is too small. The air too thick.

I feel myself breaking apart, piece by piece, my mother's face flashing through my mind—her sad smiles, her trembling hands as she sewed my engagement dress, the last whispered words she gave me before I ran.

She gave up everything for me.

And now she's dead.

Oh, God.

She made the ultimate sacrifice—and I failed her.

Even with all her efforts, I'm right back here, preparing to marry the Devil himself.

My father looks down at me, calm, satisfied. He's said what he came to say.

He's broken me.

And now, he's done.

Without another word, he turns on his heel and ascends the stairs, leaving me drowning in the darkness.

In the guilt.

The door creaks open at the top.

It slams shut.

I barely register it.

My sobs break free—guttural, desolate.

The room is silent, save for my ragged breathing, each inhale interrupted by harsh fits of coughing.

My thoughts spiral, dragging me down into a pit of guilt

and self-loathing. If I hadn't left, if I'd just done what Josiah wanted, maybe she'd still be alive.

Maybe she wouldn't have had to suffer because of me.

Across the room, the guys are shouting—words of comfort, of fury, of vengeance—but I can't focus.

Their voices are muffled, distant.

Like they're calling to me from underwater.

I shake my head, squeezing my eyes shut against the tears.

My voice cracks as I whisper, "I can't... I can't talk right now."

A thick silence falls between us. I can feel them watching me, waiting. But I can't face them.

Not now.

Not like this.

Tears spill freely down my cheeks, my body trembling as I curl into myself. I clutch my knees to my chest, the chains rattling as I squeeze my eyes shut and try to block it all out.

She's gone.

I didn't come back in time.

She's dead because of me.

This is my fault.

30

When I wake, my face is puffy, my throat thick from crying. The heaviness in my chest is unbearable, pressing down like a weight I can't shake. I clutch the chains around my wrists as if they could anchor me to something solid—something real. The cellar is quiet, save for the occasional shifting from the guys across the room. I keep my eyes shut, clinging to the silence, trying to delay the moment I have to face them.

I should know better than to think they would give me a choice.

"That's enough," Beckett says, his voice low but firm—the tone familiar, steady, grounding. When I open my eyes, I find him staring at me, his face battered yet resolute. "We're not letting you sit here and blame yourself any longer."

Whit watches me like I'm something unbreakable, like he refuses to see me as anything less. His voice is softer than Beckett's but no less certain. "What your father did? What

Josiah's done? None of that is on you. Their insanity is their own—you don't carry it."

Despite the mottled bruises across his face, Quinn's grin is pure defiance, "You're a goddamn force, sweetheart. Most people wouldn't have lasted a day in your shoes, and look at you now." His swollen lip quirks, even through the pain. "You crashed into our world, learned to fight, and somehow made yourself the piece we didn't even know was missing."

Their words weave into my guilt-ridden mind, little by little, until the haze begins to lift. Beckett's voice cuts through it. "Remember who you belong to, Celest."

"And who we belong to," Whit adds, his eyes locked on mine.

There's a pause, their gazes heavy, waiting. Finally, Quinn asks, his tone deceptively casual, "Who do you belong to?"

I swallow hard, my voice barely above a whisper. "You. I belong to all of you."

The tension breaks, their grim expressions softening. "Fuck yes, you do," Quinn says with a wink. How they all seem unfazed by our current predicament is baffling.

"And who do we belong to?" Whit asks, his gaze intense in a way I don't often see.

"Me," I say, my hoarse voice crackling.

"Exactly." Beckett's tone is final, leaving no room for discussion. Not that any of us would.

"What time is it?" Whit asks, after a long stretch of silence. "It should be getting close."

I frown. "What are you talking about?"

Quinn smirks, all smug confidence. "I told you we had a plan."

Beckett leans against the wall, shaking off the last traces

of drowsiness. His voice is calm, confident, despite the circumstances. "The first step was finding you. After sneaking in a few times and not finding the cellar door—"

"Who hides their damn cellar door?" Quinn interrupts.

"You have an entire house that moves," I deadpan.

"Touché."

Beckett nudges Quinn in the ribs before continuing. "Anyway. When we couldn't find you, we had to go with Plan B. We knew Josiah would set a trap, so we prepared for the worst. Getting caught was always part of the plan."

Whit nods, a faint smile tugging at his lips, his eyes sharper now, more alert. "The drugs were a surprise. Didn't see that coming. Oh well. Minor inconvenience," he says with a shrug.

My jaw drops.

A minor inconvenience. Minor?

I shake my head in disbelief. Sometimes I forget just how insane they actually are.

Before I can ask what exactly they mean by "minor inconvenience," a distant explosion rips through the manor, shaking the walls. Dust and debris rain from the ceiling.

"What the hell was that?" I half shriek. Not a full shriek—just half.

"It's about damn time," Beckett mutters, rolling his shoulders like he's readying for a fight.

The cellar door creaks open, and a moment later, a figure steps out of the shadows—a man dressed head to toe in black, his face obscured by a sleek mask. He moves silently, almost unnaturally so, his presence more shadow than man.

Without a word, he kneels in front of Beckett's lock, shoving a device into it.

A click.

The chain falls away.

As he passes the device to Beckett, he murmurs, "We're square."

Beckett's lips curl into a faint smile. "Don't hesitate to reach out in the future. Seems like we have similar goals." The masked man gives a curt nod before slipping into the darkness as silently as he arrived. I don't even hear his footsteps on the stairs.

Come to think of it, I never heard him come down them either.

Once Beckett frees himself, he quickly moves to unlock the others. Quinn staggers over with the device, and the weight of the chains falls from my wrists. It's both a physical and emotional relief.

"Well, this is cozy," he drawls, his smirk intact despite the bruises. "Family reunion in a dungeon. Can't say I've had one of those before."

I glare at him, equal parts exasperated and grateful. "You really can't take anything seriously, can you?"

"Not if I can help it." His grin widens. "Besides, it's nice knowing I still look this good after a beating. Honestly, I'm not surprised."

"Quinn," Whit says, cutting in as he pulls a couple of syringes from a hidden compartment inside his tactical vest.

"What's that?" I ask.

"Just a little something to give us a kick in the pants," Quinn replies with a grimace—right before Whit sticks the needle into the side of his neck. Not even a few seconds later, he's hopping around with possibly even more energy than usual.

Beckett pulls me to my feet, his hand steadying as I stumble—then I dive into his arms. "I knew you would come," I mumble into his chest before moving to Whit, then Quinn, pulling them close, wrapping myself in their warmth.

"We'll have a proper reunion once we get the fuck out of here—no time now," Beckett says firmly, his gaze flicking toward the stairs. "We have to move." Before the last word leaves his lips, the unmistakable sound of boots thundering above us grows louder with each passing moment.

The moment we start up the stairs, the door swings open. There's a brief moment where no one moves—just before chaos explodes.

They say fighting an uphill battle is difficult, but I think fighting your way up a narrow staircase is worse. I'm just thankful no guns are fired.

Whit is the first to meet them, his broad shoulders slamming into the nearest mercenary. The impact sends the man flying back into two others, their bodies tangling as they stumble. Whit doesn't hesitate, using his momentum to drive a punch into the gut of the next man, then throwing him down the stairs with a grunt.

Behind him, Beckett's movements are lethal and precise. He ducks under a wild swing from one mercenary, grabbing the man's wrist and twisting it sharply until the knife drops into his own hand. With a swift, brutal motion, Beckett drives the hilt of the knife into the man's temple, dropping him instantly.

Quinn follows close behind, his usual grin plastered across his face as he slips past Beckett to take on two mercenaries at once. He moves like liquid—his body twisting and turning with an agility that's almost impossible to track. One man swings a baton at him, but Quinn ducks, grabs the weapon mid-swing, and yanks it free. With a flourish, he spins it in his hand and cracks it across the man's jaw. "Thanks for donating to the QFA and helping a Quinn in need," he quips, twirling the baton in his hand before planting a solid kick into another mercenary's chest.

"What's the QFA?" I wonder aloud.

Whit groans before answering. "Quinn's Funtime Association. He made that one up a few years ago, and no matter how dumb we tell him it is, he keeps using it."

"At this point, it's out of spite," Quinn says with a maniacal laugh, bringing his new toy down on another man's temple.

I don't think I'll ever get used to his ridiculousness.

I follow behind them cautiously, knowing my strength is only half there.

One of the mercenaries lunges at me, his face twisted in determination as he tries to grab me around the waist, but I sidestep the attack and drive my knee into his stomach. He doubles over, and I bring my elbow down hard on the back of his neck, sending him sprawling and tumbling down the rest of the steps.

My breath comes fast and sharp, triggering a fit of coughs, but the adrenaline keeps me steady.

"You don't sound so good, princess," Whit says, worry clear in his voice.

"Well, I guess you better hurry up and get me out of here so y'all can nurse me back to health." I laugh, which only makes me cough again.

Beckett's gaze cuts to me for a second, assessing me with a furrow between his brows.

"Yes, ma'am," Quinn says, taking a moment to salute me.

It's amazing how he can still joke and carry on with his usual antics, even though he was beaten half to death less than a day ago.

Another guard moves to block my path, raising a baton to strike, and I don't think—I just react. I grab his wrist, twisting it as hard as I can, the baton clattering to the ground. He shouts in pain, but before he can recover, I bring my foot down hard on his knee. The sickening crunch echoes in the confined space, and he crumples, howling in agony.

Quinn glances back at me, his eyes wide with surprise and approval. "That's my girl!" he calls out, before ducking under another attack and slamming his fist into the side of his opponent's head.

The narrow staircase is both a hindrance and an advantage. The tight space forces bodies to collide, punches and kicks landing in rapid succession. A knife slices across Whit's shoulder, but he doesn't seem to notice it, grabbing the offending mercenary by the collar and slamming him into the wall with enough force to crack the plaster.

"Duck," Whit roars, using the momentum of the man's fall to toss him over his back and down the stairs—right over where we're crouched.

Beckett uses the close quarters to his advantage, trapping one man against the wall and driving his knee into his ribs before shoving him into the steps of the guards coming down the stairs, tripping them. They tumble on top of each other, effectively blocking the remaining mercenaries as they struggle to get up.

One manages to break through the mess of limbs and charges toward me, his knife gleaming in the dim light. My heart pounds, and time seems to slow as I raise my fists, preparing to defend myself—even though I know I won't win.

Before he's close enough to reach me, Whit grabs the man by his jacket, yanking him away from me. "Stay away from her," he growls, before delivering a brutal kick to his back, sending the man tumbling down the stairs, landing with his neck at an odd angle.

We fight our way up, step by grueling step. I'm almost certain the staircase has doubled in length. My arms ache, my legs burn, but I refuse to stop, even as my vision goes in and out of focus and coughs continue to wrack my body.

One mercenary lunges at Beckett, but I shove him off balance with my shoulder, giving Beckett the opening to knock him out with a single strike.

Quinn spins around, grinning, once again bleeding from his mouth. "You're stealing my kills, sweetheart."

"Stop counting and keep moving!" I shout back, panting.

Whit glances over his shoulder, his face set in grim determination. "Stay close, Celest. Don't let them separate you from us."

By the time we reach the top of the stairs, the number of mercenaries has dwindled significantly. The last couple seem desperate, their movements sloppy as they throw themselves at us. Whit grabs one by the collar and hurls him down the stairs, while Beckett drives his boot into another's chest, sending him crashing into the wall.

Quinn pauses just long enough to look back at the carnage, his grin widening at the sheer volume of bodies piled at the bottom of the stairs. "Nice warm-up," he says, breathing heavily.

Then he glances at Beckett and Whit, a mischievous glint in his eyes. "What's the bet this time? Highest kill count?"

Whit snorts, shaking his head. "Nah, I'd like to just get the fuck out of here as soon as possible."

"Suit yourselves," Quinn says with a shrug, turning to me. "What about you, Celest? You in?"

I roll my eyes, a small smile tugging at my lips despite the chaos. "Just keep moving, Quinn."

He winks at me, whistling as we press on, ready for whatever comes next.

"Is that... Sk8r Boi?" Whit asks incredulously.

Quinn stops whistling long enough to say, "Maaaybe."

Beckett sighs as Quinn continues to whistle. I don't know the song, but it seems catchy. I wonder what's so exasperating about it.

"Quinn," Beckett says, "shut up."

I look at the three of them and smile. I almost lost this. I almost lost them.

My boys.

The air is thick with tension the moment we step into the great hall. The pounding in my chest is almost deafening as my heart races. Realization crashes over me—the fight on the stairs is nothing compared to what we're about to face.

Josiah stands in the center of the room, flanked by my sneering father and at least a dozen more mercenaries, while his sycophant disciples encircle him. His eyes gleam with malice, and the cruel smile he wears is locked directly on me.

"Well, well," he sneers, spreading his arms in mock welcome. "If it isn't my lovely bride-to-be, and her little knights in tarnished armor." He laughs as his attention shifts to them. "You've come all this way for what? Something that was never yours to take? She's been mine for eleven years, and no matter how far she runs, she'll always belong to me. You can't save her. You'll never take her from me. You can't claim what's already mine."

His gaze returns to me, something terrifying glinting in

his eyes. "Now, Celestina, it's time for your little game to end. You've condemned them to die for daring to touch what's mine. Painfully. I promise you that. And when they're gone, you'll accept your place by my side—or not. It matters little to me how willing you are. You know how much I enjoy hearing your screams, and there's nothing they can do to stop me."

"Does this guy ever stop blowing smoke up his own ass?" Quinn murmurs to us.

Whit shifts protectively in front of me, Beckett and Quinn move into position on either side, forming a wall between me and Josiah, who throws his head back, laughing manically at the display.

I can tell they're exhausted, their injuries catching up to them. Whatever they took in the cellar has got to be wearing off by now. Despite all that, they stand tall and resolute.

I stay behind them, knowing they need to focus and not waste energy worrying about me. Being unarmed and weak from my time in the cellar makes me more of a liability than a help. But still, my fists clench at my sides, ready to act if the chance arises. The least I can do is watch their backs.

"Bring them to me," Josiah orders, his voice flat, as though the idea of anything being a challenge bores him. "Don't damage her too much—I still need her to look like a bride later. But if they resist... well, I've always found pain to be a good motivator. They'll learn quickly enough what happens when they get in my way."

The hall erupts into chaos. The mercenaries charge, their weapons gleaming in the soft light of the chandeliers as they close in on us. The air is thick with tension, the sound of boots on stone echoing through the room.

Whit ducks under a brutal slash from a mercenary's large

serrated knife, the blade cutting the air just above his head. Without hesitation, he reaches up, grabbing the mercenary's arm with both hands, and in one smooth motion, he dislocates the elbow. The knife slips from the now-useless hand, falling straight into Whit's grip. In a heartbeat, the blade moves from his side to his opponent's throat, and with deadly precision, Whit ends the fight, the man crumpling silently to the floor.

The second mercenary doesn't even see it coming. In one fluid motion, Whit steps forward, slashing upward. The man's body jerks, and just like that, he joins the first in a bloody heap at Whit's feet—both throats slashed cleanly, the floor darkening beneath them.

Beckett fights with cold precision. The knife he took from one of the guards on the stairs flies from his hand, its trajectory sharp and sure as it embeds itself into the eye socket of a man lifting a gun.

The guard stands for a moment longer, his gun slipping from his hand, clattering to the floor and disappearing into the chaos of the fight. Then, with a muted thud, he crashes to the ground.

Beckett doesn't bother to watch.

It doesn't surprise me when I hear Quinn's taunting voice cut through the fray. "My God, man, who taught you how to fight? Guess we'll never know," he says, glancing down at the now-motionless body at his feet.

He dances effortlessly through the chaos, weaving between bodies and blades as if the world around him is a blur of movement. He shifts, spins, and ducks—his movements fluid and unpredictable. The fight rages on around him, but Quinn moves in his own rhythm, as if there's music only he can hear. And, apparently, there is, because he starts to hum, then sing, his voice sharp and clear.

The tune cuts through the chaos, his voice strangely upbeat while his eyes burn with a cold, steely rage. "In my dreams I have a plan..." One of his knives leaves his hand, burying itself in the gut of one of the guards. "If I got me a wealthy man..." Then, without missing a beat, he drives another blade down hard into the base of the guard's neck while he's doubled over. "I wouldn't have to work at all, I'd fool around and have a baaaall..."

His voice drags out the word "ball," as if he's performing for an audience. "Money, money, money..."

I blink, trying to make sense of what he's singing—it's a tune I don't recognize, but the way he spins and fights, I can't look away.

"Must be funny..."

Just when I think he can't possibly shock me more, he grabs one of the guards by the hand and twirls him into another, like a ballroom dancer, knocking them both to the ground. He continues to sing, "In the rich man's world."

"Jesus, Quinn, what's with the soundtrack," Beckett murmurs, a mix of disbelief and amusement in his voice, while Whit just laughs.

"Come on, Beck," Whit says, "you know you love ABBA."

"Money, money, money..." Quinn continues, unbothered, as he collects the knives off the bodies around him, avoiding blades slashed at him, his movements effortlessly smooth and carefree.

"Always sunny..." He throws two knives back-to-back into his next target. "In the rich man's world." One of the three guards attacking Whit crumples to the ground. Quinn takes a bow, as if the fight were nothing but an afterthought.

I drop low and kick out the knee of one of the mercenaries as he tries to stab Whit while he's dealing with someone else. He screams as he falls, clutching his ruined knee, but Whit silences him permanently with a swift motion of his knife.

"Thanks, princess," Whit says with a wink.

Finally, the mercenaries' numbers dwindle to a final few, but the guys are breathing hard, their movements becoming lethargic as their energy wanes. Just then, Josiah's disciples' fanatical eyes lock onto me. My blood runs cold as they rush forward, bypassing the guys entirely while they're still occupied with the remaining guards.

I manage to fight off several, landing punches and using their momentum against them to send them stumbling, but there are too many, and my body is already running on fumes. Their hands grab at me, pulling me away from the others.

"Celest!" Beckett's voice calls out, and it's the first time I've ever heard him sound panicked. He tries to get to me, but the remaining mercenaries are of a higher caliber than the ones scattered across the floor.

Josiah steps forward, the rest of his disciples parting for him like water. He moves with a calm, deliberate stride, rolling the sleeves of his oxford up his forearms without a glance at the chaos around him, as if he has all the time in the world. I watch in horror as he approaches Beckett, casually waving off the two guards he was fighting with, his confidence unwavering.

For all his manipulations and hiding behind others, Josiah proves to be a skilled fighter.

Beckett lands a few solid blows, but Josiah barely flinches, his focus unshaken. It doesn't help that Beckett is weighed down by his earlier injuries, his strength already depleted from the prolonged fight, while Josiah stands fresh and rested, seemingly unaffected by the battle.

"You're impressive," Josiah sneers, his voice dripping with mock admiration. "But let's see how well you fight after I make you watch your friends die. I know a few... creative ways to make death last longer." His eyes gleam with sadistic delight, a twisted smile playing at the corner of his lips. "And maybe—if you're lucky—I'll even let you watch me take Celest on our wedding night."

Rage flares in Beckett's eyes, and he surges forward with renewed strength, landing a brutal punch to Josiah's jaw. But exhaustion quickly takes its toll, and soon, Josiah overpowers him. I cry out as Beckett collapses to his knees, his arms pinned by a few disciples while Josiah looms over him, a knife gleaming in his hand.

My breath catches as Josiah lifts the blade and presses it against Beckett's throat. I glance at the others—they're beginning to falter, their movements slowing, losing the force they once had. My vision narrows, and my gaze locks onto the fallen pistol lying just a few feet away. Without thinking, I rip out of the disciples grip and dive for it, the cold metal heavy in my trembling hands.

Josiah watches with sick fascination, his cruel laugh echoing through the hall. "Oh, how sweet. Do you think you have it in you, Celestina?" he asks, forcing Beckett to stand, using him as a shield so that only Josiah's face is visible. "Go ahead. Take the shot. Let's see if you can kill me without hitting your failed hero."

My hands shake, the gun—larger than I'm used to—visibly unsteady in my grip, which only makes Josiah laugh louder. I look at Beckett, his eyes calm despite the blood dripping down his face. He gives me one of his rare smiles, and my eyes burn with emotion as a tear slides down my cheek.

Memories from the past few months with them flash behind my eyes. I spent such a small amount of time with them in the grand scheme of my life, but it left the largest impact. They've pushed me to become stronger, they've never doubted my capabilities, and they've shown me what it is to love.

"Be a good girl for me," he says, his voice confident. He gives me the slightest nod—a reassurance only he can give.

I close my eyes and take a deep breath. I focus on everything Beckett has taught me, blocking out everything else. I recall every lesson he drilled into me, every moment we spent at the shooting range, every second he spent pushing me to be better.

When I open my eyes, the world sharpens, and the edges of reality narrow to a single point. I adjust my stance and lock my arms, bracing for the recoil with my shoulders. My eyes dart to Beckett one last time to see him nod his approval.

That's all I need.

I line up the shot. "I was never yours," I seethe, my finger tightening on the trigger, and I fire just as Josiah's eyes widen in shock.

The bullet strikes true, hitting Josiah directly between the eyes. His head snaps back, and he crumples to the ground, lifeless. Beckett jerks away just in time, the blade grazing his neck but leaving only a shallow cut.

For a moment, the room is stunned into stillness. The only sound is the ringing of the shot in our ears.

Then, all at once, everyone begins to move again as the remaining disciples scatter, the unknown now their biggest nightmare. The guys don't bother chasing them. Their focus is on me.

Quinn is the first to reach me, his grin once again bloodied, but still intact. "Well, damn," he says, shaking his head in amazement. "Remind me never to piss you off, sweetheart."

Beckett cups my face, his eyes searching mine. "You okay?"

I nod, my hands trembling as I lower the pistol, the weight of it suddenly overwhelming. I hadn't even realized I was still holding it out.

I sway on my feet, my body demanding rest. Whit pulls me into his arms, his grip firm and comforting. "You did it," he murmurs, his voice thick with emotion. "You're safe."

Tears blur my vision, but a smile breaks through the shock. My voice is barely above a whisper, but there's strength in it.

"I'm finally free."

I'm free. I'm finally free. I keep replaying the words over and over in my mind, but it feels too big to hold. My chest tightens as I take in a shaky breath, the weight of the gun still heavy in my hand.

Disbelief and elation war for dominance, but neither emotion is enough to calm the storm still raging inside me. Still trembling, I force my body to move, stepping out of Whit's arms. I ignore their protests and shake off their hands as I begin searching the fallen disciples.

He must be here.

I have to find him.

It's the only way to be certain I'm truly free. My fingers shake as I shove aside the linen robe covering the face of a man, his wide eyes unseeing.

"Where is he?" I demand, my voice raw. "Where's my father?"

No one answers, not that I expected one. The guys help me search, their movements slower and heavier than usual. Finally, after checking every corner of the great hall and inspecting every empty face, my stomach sinks. He's not here. He's gone.

I sink onto a splintered chair and sigh, the weight of the moment crashing down on me. I thought I was free. How free am I if he's still out there? "He got away."

Beckett crouches in front of me, his bloodied hand brushing hair from my face. "He's nothing without Josiah," he says, his tone steady and sure. "He won't be a threat without someone pulling his strings."

I nod, though the bitter taste of disappointment lingers. "Maybe you're right." I hope he is.

Quinn gently grabs my chin, lifting it so I'm looking him in the eyes. "We'll find him, sweetheart." I nod when he releases me.

"Yeah," Whit says, reaching out to pull me to my feet. "We won't let his shadow keep you looking over your shoulder."

As soon as he says it, I know that's exactly what I fear. Not necessarily that my father would be capable of pulling off what Josiah could, but what if he does? It's the possibility of retaliation that will haunt me.

We limp out of the manor, battered, bruised, and exhausted. The cool morning air hits my face, a stark contrast to the stifling heat from the battle we just fought. The first rays of dawn streak across the sky, softening the edges of the carnage behind us. My dress is torn and filthy, hanging in tatters around my legs, and my bare feet are scraped raw. Yet, I don't care. The air smells of freedom, and despite everything, I've never felt so light.

As we step onto the gravel driveway, the sound of tires crunching on the pea gravel breaks the silence. A lone white van comes into view, its headlights muted by the morning light. As it gets closer, a florist logo becomes visible—Petals for Prayers. It stops a few feet away, and the slogan becomes clear, making me giggle.

"Flowers speak louder than gossip."

The driver's door opens, and an older woman steps out. Her expression shifts from confusion to concern as she takes us in. Her eyes sweep over me, lingering on my disheveled state before flicking to the men flanking me.

"I'm here to set up for the wedding," she says tentatively, her gaze darting between us. "Is... is everything all right?"

A laugh bubbles out of me before I can stop it, a sound somewhere between relief and hysteria. "There won't be a wedding," I say, wiping a hand across my filthy face.

Quinn, ever the opportunist, adds with a cheeky grin, "Yeah, next time, the groom should make sure the bride actually wants to be the bride."

Whit shakes his head, his tone dry but tinged with humor. "You should still make sure you get paid. I'm sure there's someone around here who can handle that for you."

The woman's jaw drops, horror dawning in her eyes. "You were going to be forced into marriage?"

I nod, and her face crumples with sympathy. She moves to

the back of the van, rummaging through the riot of colorful blooms before pulling out a bouquet—delicate white roses interwoven with soft greenery. She steps toward me, pressing the bouquet into my hands.

"Take this," she says, her voice soft and sincere. "Congratulations on your freedom."

She pauses, her eyes flicking to the three men at my side. A knowing smile plays at the corners of her lips. "Seems like you've got plenty to keep you busy celebrating—for a while anyway. Bless their hearts."

Her words draw a startled laugh from me, and this time, it's pure and light. I glance at the guys, their expressions ranging from amused to exasperated.

"She's not wrong," I say, unable to keep the smile from spreading across my face.

"Well, I'm going to go hunt someone down to take care of this bill. I'm sure the other vendors will be here shortly. Now, be dears and go clean yourselves up. Y'all are right filthy."

We watch the spunky old lady—clearly someone's favorite granny—disappear into the manor.

"Should we have warned her about the state of things in there?" Whit asks.

"Something tells me she can handle it," I say, turning back to them, clutching the bouquet tightly and lifting my chin.

"Take me home."

32

Everything feels different now.

Lighter. Warmer. Safer.

Maybe it's because Josiah is gone—a nightmare finally put to rest. Maybe it's because, for the first time, I know I'm free.

Even if my father is still out there.

The moment we boarded the jet, the weight on my chest eased. Even with the lingering cough, I could finally breathe.

Once we were in the air, Whit led me to the shower—because, of course, their jet has a shower. I nearly cried when the hot water hit my skin, thawing me from the inside out, rinsing away the filth that had clung to me like a second skin.

Dressed in a mishmash of their clothes, I was finally warm. The tight coil of cold that had lived in my bones for days had finally unraveled.

After taking the antibiotics and pain meds one of them had left out for me, I sank between Whit and Beckett on the lounge, tucked between their warmth. My body was exhausted, but my mind refused to quiet.

I needed to know.

So I asked them to tell me what happened after I disappeared.

It took effort to get them talking—each of them hating to relive the moment the elevator doors opened and I was gone. More than once, they had to stop mid-sentence, fists clenched, swallowing back the rage.

I understood why.

Because the more they talked, the more I realized just how close we had come to losing everything.

Things got messy after Alaric Hawthorn's body was found in the elevator.

Security footage placed me as the last person seen with him—a flashing red flag that no one could ignore. Within thirty minutes, Hawthorn's people were circling Quinn, demanding answers.

He had no choice but to throw up a shield of indifference, claiming I was nothing but a social climber—that I disappeared the moment he stepped away to speak with someone. The entire time, he masked panic with disgust.

But everything shifted when hotel security footage showed the handoff—me, passed straight into Josiah's grasp.

That single revelation turned the entire narrative on its head.

It still didn't stop Hawthorn's people from trying to detain Quinn and his 'security' team, desperate to untangle the mess.

The guys weren't willing to leave me in Josiah's grasp a

second longer than necessary. Waiting around—with their "thumbs up their asses," as Quinn put it—wasn't an option.

When the hotel staff hesitated to grant clearance for takeoff from their helipad, the decision was easy: fuck the clearance. Within minutes, they'd packed up, armed up, and were moving for the rooftop—expecting a fight.

And it was a good thing they were.

Josiah had mercenaries waiting, locked and loaded—ready to put Quinn in the ground before he could reach the helicopter. What they didn't know was that Quinn wasn't some fragile, trust-fund socialite.

And he wasn't alone.

They fought their way out under a hail of gunfire, barely reaching the chopper before escape became impossible.

They knew who had me. But they didn't know where. All they knew was that they needed to get home—to track me, to make a plan, to tear apart anything standing in their way.

"What was in the envelope Josiah handed Hawthorn?" I ask.

It's the last thing I remember before everything went dark, and I couldn't shake the thought—what price had Josiah paid to have me back?

"Hawthorn's people kept it very hush-hush," Beckett said, his tone edged with irritation.

"Yeah, and it wasn't our priority," Whit practically growls. "We didn't give a fuck what was in there the second we knew who had you."

Quinn clenches his jaw, staring at me, his nod slow and deliberate. The intensity in his eyes, combined with the distance, makes it seem like he's reliving the moment they discovered I was back in Josiah's clutches.

Beckett exhales, frustration tightening his features. "Whatever it was, it must've been explosive, because the moment it got out, no one gave a damn about you anymore. All the focus shifted to the contents."

"People are so fucked. How does the contents of an envelope trump a missing woman?" Quinn mutters, pushing to his feet.

He starts pacing the aisle, restless, coiled with frustration. Where he found the energy, I'll never know.

"This is why we do what we do," Whit says, gripping my hand like he needs the contact just as much as I do. "People don't become billionaires without making several horrific choices along the way."

Beckett leans back, exhaling slowly. "Think of us as knights on a chessboard. We aren't the ones playing the game. But the head of the syndicate we take jobs from? He sees the entire board—plays against multiple opponents at once."

I don't have the heart to tell him I have no idea what chess even is, so I just nod. I get the general idea of his analogy—for the most part, anyway.

"Who's the head of the syndicate? Are they the ones who recruited you?" I ask, realizing I've never really given it much thought before.

"We don't know his name. He just goes by 'S' whenever he communicates with us directly. Which isn't often." Whit hesitates, searching for the right words to answer my second question. "In a way, the syndicate is responsible. But not directly."

He shoots Beckett a glance before continuing. "Mr. Ambrose was the one who put the idea in our heads—he was the connection. He's the one who brought us to 'S.'"

"Ultimately, we chose this life, sweetheart." Quinn's voice

drops, his words heavy with guilt. "If you're looking for someone to blame, it's probably me."

His fists clench, jaw tight, as if bracing for the weight of my judgment.

"Oh, I'm not judging. I'm just trying to understand," I say, my voice soft but clear.

I stand, moving toward him, and without thinking, my arms instinctively wrap around him. "I could never think poorly of any of you. Not when I love you." The words are a whisper, fragile yet full of conviction.

I hold my breath, the fear of rejection heavy in the air. I know they must feel the same, but my heart pounds, desperate for their answer.

Quinn gently grips my chin, tilting my head back so I had no choice but to look up at him. "You love us?" His voice soft, full of wonder.

My voice seems to have fled, so all I can do is nod.

"Oh, thank fuck." His grin's possessive, his lips claiming mine with a force that steels my breath.

Hands grip my waist just before I'm being pulled back down between Whit and Beckett.

Whit cradles my head between his hands, pressing his forehead gently to mine. "We knew how we felt," he says, his voice thick with emotion. "But... we didn't think you could ever feel the same towards us."

When Whit finally releases me, Beckett pulls me onto his lap, his hands firm on my neck, gently forcing me to meet his gaze.

"The way we started wasn't the kindest, and definitely wasn't the most romantic," Beckett says.

"I don't know, I kind of liked it," I smirk, desperate to hide my anxiety. We all laugh before Becket continues.

"We were willing to accept whatever affection you were ready to give us. Your love... it's more than we ever allowed ourselves to hope for." He murmurs the words softly, his thumb dragging across my bottom lip with a tenderness that cracks something deep inside me.

Quinn's voice pulls my attention back to him. "In case you can't tell, sweetheart, we love you too." Quinn's grin turns wicked, teasing. "Even though you like the wrong Batman movie."

I couldn't help but laugh, hiding my face in Beckett's chest, the weight of their declarations of love crashing over me.

The anxiety coiling inside me drains away, leaving me utterly spent. Suddenly, it feels impossible to stay awake. There's still more to the story, I'm certain, but it can wait.

I'm safe.

I'm happy.

I'm going home.

Later, I found out that we still don't know what was in that envelope.

Beckett spoke to Wraith, who said he's handling it. That tells me it must be pretty bad if he's making it a priority. I wonder if it's tied to the research we confiscated from the mad doctor.

Beckett also reported that Wraith made it clear he wasn't pleased about the favor they called in to get me out—which Quinn found hilarious.

Apparently, explosives aren't his thing. He's more of a shadow, preferring digital warfare over anything in person.

No one's complaining though—he returned the favor he owed.

The guys have a bet going on whether or not Wraith will ever ask for another favor in the future. Personally, I think he will. Like Beckett said to him in the cellar, we have common interests.

There were some other details I found fascinating. When they were creating their plan, they knew that if Plan A failed, they'd have to let Josiah catch them on the way in.

Every other scenario they worked out put me at too great a risk—and would've likely meant at least one of them wouldn't make it out alive. Considering how close we came to the worst-case scenario, I believed them.

Knowing they'd probably take a beating, they couldn't figure out how to recover fast enough once the bombs went off. That's when 'S' got involved.

The syndicate contacted them for a hit, but when they had to turn it down, 'S' made a call.

They told him the basics of what they were up against. When he heard where their plan hit a roadblock, he gave them something to give them an edge.

An experimental drug still in the testing phases. Designed to override exhaustion, push past pain, and enhance speed, strength, and focus. A supercharged version of adrenaline.

Beckett and Whit agreed it made them feel like fucking superheroes, and it was the only reason we all made it out alive. Quinn says it made him horny and homicidal in equal measure. Which, let's be honest, totally tracks.

And now... we're home. I'm at peace. I'm where I belong. It took a few days, but my cough is gone, my body's well-rested, and my bruises are fading. More importantly, I'm surrounded by love, and my heart is full.

Life picks up right where it left off. I dive headfirst into the next assignment—tracking information, gathering intel, feeling useful.

It feels wonderful. Everything is running smoothly. Until, out of nowhere, it hits me.

I killed someone.

I took a life.

I'm a murderer.

The feeling washes over me like a wave—heavy, suffocating, disorienting.

It's not guilt. Josiah deserved it—and then some.

The thought knocks the breath from my lungs. My fingers freeze over the keyboard as I stare at nothing, caught in the grip of the memory.

It replays in my mind—his knife at Beckett's throat, his mocking words, the way I shut everything out, aimed, and fired.

Then there's the gore I haven't allowed myself to think about—the blood, the sickening spray of brain and bone that exploded out the back of his head.

I don't regret it. Not for a second.

But I feel... something. Remorse, maybe. But not over killing him. I'm not sure what it's for.

Shouldn't I feel worse about pulling the trigger? Instead of... being equal parts disgusted by the memory and empty from the action?

The guys notice—they always do—the second something's off. Within moments, they close in, a silent wall of steady hands and quiet concern.

I tell them what's gnawing at me: the hollowness, the disgust. But not for the reasons I'm supposed to feel them. Am I a horrible person for feeling the wrong thing?

They cut the thoughts off before they can take root.

"If you didn't feel something," Beckett murmurs, rubbing warmth into my arms, "then we'd be worried."

"It's not about whether he deserved it," Whit says. "Because he did. It's about what it takes from you. The first kill... it buries something inside you. Something you don't get back. And that's worth mourning."

Quinn's voice is quieter than usual, gentler, as though he's smoothing the edges of something raw. "But that doesn't mean you have to let it eat you alive. Acknowledge it. Then let it go."

They tell me they all felt it—the first time. How they know exactly what it does to you, how it settles under your skin.

It took time, but eventually, they decided the sacrifice was worth it—if it meant keeping the worst of humanity from hurting anyone else. Maybe it took something from them. But it helps to know they gained something too—the peace of knowing they're doing good.

I nod. I understand. I do.

It doesn't change the fact that I hate how numb I feel.

"Now that," Whit says, lifting my shirt over my head and tossing it aside, "we can do something about."

"It's been hell waiting for you to get all better, sweetheart. Especially after what you told us on the plane."

Quinn grins up at me from where he kneels, dragging my leggings down with deliberate care. He guides each foot free, his touch lingering just enough to make it known, before tossing the fabric somewhere near my discarded shirt.

I'm left standing in nothing but a dark-green lace bralette.

"Oh, princess," Whit murmurs from behind, his breath warm against my neck. "Have you been bare under those thin little things you call pants this whole time?" He buries his face into my hair, inhaling the soft floral notes of my shampoo like he's savoring it.

"Yes," I gasp out as Quinn lifts one of my legs over his shoulder and buries his face into my heat. His tongue glides through my folds in slow, languid strokes, and I scream out his name when he sucks hard on my clit. I can feel his grin against me along with the vibrations from his hum of approval.

Beckett pushes my bralette up just enough to bare me, his mouth latching onto a hardened peak. Teeth sink in—just enough to sting—before his tongue soothes over the ache. A groan rips from my throat.

Behind me, Whit's palm lands sharp against my rear—a quick sting before Quinn slides a finger in.

"Oh, God, please," I gasp.

"Please what?" Whit asks, his tone dripping with satisfaction as his hand fists my hair.

"I-I need... please!" The words break from me, my core clenching around his finger, desperate for more.

"Come now, sweetheart," Quinn purrs, "we want to hear you beg—with all the filthy words you've surely picked up from us by now."

Two fingers press into me, stretching, filling—but he keeps them still. Waiting. Smirking at the frustrated sound that spills from my lips.

"What do you want my fingers to do, Celest?" His voice is all dark amusement. "Let me hear you be a dirty girl for us."

"I—I want you to... to f-fuck me with them!" The words barely leave me before Quinn moves—fingers plunging deep, mouth closing over my clit.

I scream when his teeth graze the swollen nerve, his bite landing the second "fuck" spills from my lips.

Behind me, Whit grips my hip tighter, his other hand dropping, a finger teasing at the tight ring. "Come on, princess," he murmurs, "tell us exactly what you want."

The words catch in my throat, strangled by the sheer, aching need coiling deep inside me. "I want—" A sharp slap lands on my rear, Whit's patience wearing thin.

"Use your words, Celest."

Quinn hums against me, dragging his fingers slow and deep, keeping me teetering on the edge. "What do you want, sweetheart?" He presses a kiss just above where I need him most, his breath hot against my skin. "If you want to come, you have to say it."

"My... my... oh God, it's... I can't—"

"Yes, you can." Whit's voice is nothing but certainty, nothing but command. His grip tightens as he pushes in slightly, forcing a gasp from my lips. "In fact, you're going to take two of us back here tonight—just like your sweet cunt did."

I whimper, my body already betraying me, already wanting.

"Now, tell me, princess," he purrs, pulsing his finger, teasing at the impending stretch, "where are you taking two cocks tonight? And who's fucking it with me?"

I don't respond.

They pause—all of them—as if some silent agreement has settled between them. A test. A waiting game.

It doesn't take long for them to win.

"Quinn," I whisper.

Still, they don't move.

My breath shudders. "I want you and Quinn to fuck me in m-my ass."

"Good fucking girl." Beckett growls the words before his mouth crashes into mine, his kiss nothing short of possession. His teeth, his tongue—he devours me.

Quinn lowers my leg, stepping back just as Beckett moves. Sweeps me up. Instinct takes over—I lock my legs around his waist, my body yielding to the way he carries me through the hall, his grip unshakable, his intent unmistakable.

The world tilts as Beckett drops me onto his bed, flat on my back, hands already in my hair—already positioning me. His grip is firm, deliberate, dragging my head to the edge and cradling it in his palms—holding me exactly where he wants me.

Whit grips my legs, spreading them wide as he settles between my thighs.

A plastic cap clicks open.

I watch as he squeezes out a generous amount of the cool, slippery substance. A shiver rolls through me at the first slick press of his fingers—then, a few minutes later, the slow slide of two fingers inside my—

My breath stutters.

My... *ass*.

I suppose I could start saying it. Even if the word still catches in my throat. Even if it feels wrong. Even if it stumbles in my mind.

"Hold on tight, princess," Whit warns, pushing my bent legs toward my chest until I have no choice but to hook a hand around each one. His gaze locks onto mine—setting me ablaze "I'm not going easy on you tonight. You're going to feel every inch of me buried deep as I ride you hard. Gotta make sure you're stretched enough so Quinn can get in here too."

Whit pushes into me—slow for only a breath—then all at once.

He worked me open, stretching me with his fingers, but it's still not enough to dull the burn as he fills me in a single, merciless thrust. A cry rips from my throat, but Whit only smirks, watching me come apart beneath him before he pulls out and drives back in.

A few thrusts, and the pain fades, pleasure crashing over it, drowning it out. Even more so when Quinn's mouth finds my clit again—hot, consuming.

"Tell Whit thank you for making you feel," Beckett orders.

"T-thank you... oh God... f-for making me—"

"Fuck!"

The word rips from me as Whit thrusts deeper, his slick fingers joining the stretch, forcing my body to take more.

Beckett laughs, dark amusement curling in his voice. "That'll do just fine. Now, be a good girl and open wide."

His grip eases, releasing my head just enough for it to hang over the edge of the bed. The moment my lips part, he doesn't hesitate. He surges forward, filling my mouth in a single, unstoppable motion.

I gag when he hits the back of my throat, but it doesn't stop him—he forces his way deeper, claiming every inch.

"You're stretching out so beautifully, princess. Won't be long before Quinn can get up in this." Each word is punctuated by the sharp, unyielding snap of Whit's hips.

"I can't fucking wait," Quinn murmurs, dark hunger

lacing his voice. "But first, let's see how soaked we can make her."

His fingers find my clit—too fast, too hard. The pressure is overwhelming, the sensation too much, too sharp, too consuming.

I try to squirm away, legs trembling, instinct screaming for escape, but it doesn't matter.

They hold me open. Keep me still. Make me take it.

Between the lack of air and the pressure coiling deep inside me, there's nothing left to do—nowhere to run—except let go.

The moment I do, humiliation slams into me. My body betrays me, the release so intense it feels like I—

Oh God.

"Oh, fuck, she squirted," Quinn groans, his voice thick with something that's definitely not disgust. If anything, he sounds wrecked. His fingers don't stop, don't slow—they coax more out of me, more than I thought possible.

"Fuck yes, here she goes again."

More wetness spills from me, unstoppable, undeniable. Whether I wanted it to or not.

"That's so fucking hot, Celest. Look at you being such a good fucking girl for us." Beckett's thrusts grow fevered, restless, and I already know—my throat will be raw for days.

"She's ready," Whit says, and just like that, they both pull out, leaving me boneless, gasping, trembling.

I drag in a breath, but it barely registers.

Somewhere along the way, my mind slipped—untethered, floating. I'm still here, still feeling everything—but I'm also way up in the clouds, weightless and undone.

"Look at you," Quinn laughs, voice thick with amusement. "You're dicked out of your mind, aren't you, sweetheart?"

I have no idea what he means, but it sounds right—so I nod.

Beckett lifts me effortlessly, holding me against him as Quinn and Whit shift up the bed, stretching out across it.

Quinn drapes his legs over Whit, and Whit slides his under Quinn, their bodies aligning so that their lengths press together, their backsides nestled close.

Without a word, Whit flips open the lube, squeezing a thick, glistening stream into his palm. He reaches down, wrapping his fist around both of them—stroking slow at first, then firmer, slicking them up in long, deliberate pulls.

Watching him stroke both of them makes me whine with need.

"Don't worry greedy girl, just a few more minutes," Beckett whispers against my ear before shifting me in his arms, turning me effortlessly before lifting me up, my legs wrapping around him.

With controlled strength, he crawls us up the bed, positioning me above Quinn and Whit—waiting, ready.

He holds me there, suspended, before slowly, carefully, deliberately lowering me down. My body stretches to accommodate them, the burn sharp, overwhelming—perfect.

"Breathe," he murmurs against my ear, his voice steady, a grounding anchor for my scattered thoughts.

Each lift, each slow descent, is measured, controlled—his strength the only thing keeping me from unraveling completely.

"It's too much," I rasp, my voice hoarse, barely more than a breath.

Beckett tightens his grip on me, his lips brushing my ear. "You can take it. And once you've got both of them filling you, I'm going to fuck your poor, neglected cunt at the same time."

A helpless whimper escapes me, the sheer thought of it making my body tense, clench—anticipate.

Quinn and Whit groan as they finally sink in fully, stretching me to my limit, pushing past every last inch of resistance.

I'm panting, shaking—overstimulated to the point of madness.

Everything is too much.

Too deep.

Too sensitive.

And it's only just beginning.

"See? I knew you could take it."

Beckett eases me back against a pile of pillows, positioning me just how he wants. My breath hitches as he spreads me open and slides inside—stretching me, filling me like never before.

A shattered whimper escapes me.

The moment he's fully seated, we all groan—bodies locked together, breath catching in unison. For just a few seconds, we exist in it—in the unbearable pressure, in the sheer, impossible fullness.

Then, all at once, they move.

I cry out, the sound ripped from my throat as my body is forced to take it—all of it, all of them, all at once.

Quinn and Whit thrust up in perfect sync, their rhythm precise, measured, devastating.

Beckett drives into me, fucking me with raw, merciless intensity.

It's so much.

Too much.

And not just for me.

"God damn, I'm not gonna make it much longer," Whit grits out, his voice wrecked, strained.

Quinn sucks in a sharp breath as I tighten around them, my body locking down, desperate to hold on.

"She's so fucking stuffed—her ass is strangling my cock."

I sob, trembling beneath them, every nerve frayed, overloaded, burning.

"Please... I can't—"

The words break apart as a fresh wave of sensation crashes through me—too much, too deep, too consuming. I already know—when I fall this time, it won't just shatter me. It'll eviscerate me.

"You will." Beckett's voice is steady, absolute. "Every time you say you can't, you prove yourself wrong. Don't hold it in, Celest."

His hand slides down, fingers finding my overstimulated, swollen clit, pressing down with cruel precision. The contact is too much, too sharp—pleasure laced with pain.

I cry out, trembling, my body trying to escape but having nowhere to go.

"Nononono... no, I can't," I chant, shaking my head, panic curling into the pleasure.

Beckett moves without hesitation, his fingers wrapping around my throat, squeezing just enough to steal most of my breath.

"Stop saying you can't," he growls, his grip firm, inescapable. "And come for us."

Tears spill down my cheeks, my body torn between fighting it and surrendering completely. The tension pulls tighter than it ever has before—too much, too deep, too consuming.

"Stop fighting it, Celest," Beckett growls, his nose nearly touching mine. "Come. Now."

His demand overrides everything—my thoughts, my will, my ability to resist.

I shatter.

A silent scream parts my lips as my body locks up, clenches tight, pleasure detonating inside me like a star going supernova. I wouldn't be able to say if they finished with me or after—because the world ceases to exist.

Everything vanishes.

I'm floating—adrift in a haze of bliss, unmoored, weightless.

I have no idea how much time passes before awareness gently pulls me back. A blanket tugs over my skin, warmth surrounds me, strong arms wrapping tight around my center.

Lips brush my ear, and the last thing my fading consciousness picks up is a whisper, low and reverent:

"I love you, my good girl."

33

My curiosity gets the better of me a week after our escape. What started as a quiet nagging has grown too loud to ignore. I sit in front of my monitors, pull up Google, and type "Magnolia Hollow Alabama Covenant of Divine Light news" into the search bar. There are far more results than I was expecting—it's even made national news.

For a moment, I hesitate. What if they're looking for me? What if I'm a suspect? What if—

Possibilities race through my mind. I take a deep breath, then click on a video from the night we escaped. I just have to trust we'll figure it out, no matter the outcome.

A somber-faced newscaster stands before the front doors of Josiah's sprawling antebellum manor, flashing police lights behind them. Officers and investigators move in and out of the building, grim-faced, while the occasional black body bag is wheeled out on a gurney.

"Good evening, I'm Lisa Vaughn, reporting live from Magnolia Hollow, where law enforcement officials are scrambling to make sense of the horrific events that unfolded here last night.

Details remain scarce, but what we do know is that this once-isolated religious community has now become the scene of what authorities are calling a mass homicide.

According to initial reports, gunfire and explosions rang out just before dawn, drawing local authorities to the historical manor home behind me early this morning. What they found inside remains unclear, but sources close to the investigation suggest that the Covenant's leader, Josiah Wainwright, is among the deceased. The circumstances surrounding his death —and those of multiple others—remain unconfirmed.

The Covenant of Divine Light, once regarded as an evangelical retreat, has long been the subject of whispered rumors from locals. Many believed the group to be self-sustaining and devout, if a bit reclusive. But early evidence points to a much darker truth.

Authorities have yet to disclose the total number of casualties, and it remains unclear whether any members of the Covenant escaped during the chaos. What is clear, however, is that something terrible transpired here last night, and this tiny town may never be the same.

For now, Magnolia Hollow is left reeling, desperate for answers. Who orchestrated this attack? What truly went on behind the Covenant's closed doors? And most importantly— how long has this nightmare been brewing?

We'll be on the scene, bringing you live updates as they become available on this developing story—one that has left this quiet town shaken to its core."

. . .

THE BROADCAST ENDS WITH A DRONE SHOT OF THE entire estate, crawling with authorities. Even the Sacred Hall is being roped off with police tape. Feeling a bit of relief, I release my breath slowly—so far, none of our names have been mentioned.

I scroll to a more recent update and find another clip from the same reporter. She stands before the Sacred Hall, the sun setting behind her, casting fresh shadows over the scene. Her gaze is directed toward the side of the hall closest to the woods, her expression clouded with concern.

A gentle wind tugs at her shoulder-length auburn hair, and she tucks thick strands behind her ear before gripping her microphone tightly. Then, she turns to face the camera, her gaze sharp, focused.

"Tonight, we bring you chilling new details about the Covenant of Divine Light, the so-called religious sanctuary that, in reality, was a front for something far more sinister.

What was originally believed to be a tragic mass homicide has now turned into something even darker. Authorities have confirmed evidence of what appears to be a ritualistic murder and an attempted violent takeover, which led to the brutal deaths of dozens of the Covenant's men.

The remaining Covenant members—primarily women and young girls— have been taken into protective custody and are receiving treatment for severe trauma after decades of abuse and brainwashing. Their identities remain strictly confidential, as several remaining male members of the Covenant have already made attempts to reclaim them. Federal agents are actively searching for these fugitives.

But what investigators uncovered today has shaken even the most seasoned professionals to their core—a mass grave. Thirty years of secrets buried beneath the soil."

She takes a breath, then nods to the cameraman, who pans over to the tree line.

A large rectangle of exposed, reddish-brown dirt is roped off in a grid-like pattern, where excavation crews carefully work to unearth the remains of those buried and forgotten. Tears begin streaming down my face, a heaviness settling deep in my chest.

"Forensic experts have confirmed the discovery of human remains—dozens of them—at various stages of decay.

While authorities have not yet released an official count, initial estimates suggest that the death toll could be staggering. Some of these victims, mostly women, may have perished recently, while others appear to date back decades.

Law enforcement officials urge anyone who believes their loved one may be among the unidentified victims to come forward immediately. A dedicated tip line has been established for families seeking closure."

A number appears in a banner across the bottom of the video as the camera cuts back to the reporter. Her face remains stoic, but her eyes make it clear how atrocious the scene truly is.

"The true horrors of the Covenant of Divine Light are only just beginning to be discovered, and tonight, one question remains: How many more bodies are waiting to be found?

This is Lisa Vaughn, reporting live from Magnolia Hollow."

The broadcast fades out, cutting back to the studio, where the newscasters are momentarily lost for words, still processing the details their colleague just reported.

They shake themselves out of their stunned silence and say a few words about the station's thoughts and prayers being with the true victims. They assure the public that they will be with them every step of the way as more information about this tragedy unfolds.

The last thing I hear before my pulse roars in my ears is the end of the emergency hotline number.

The rest of the words don't matter. I don't need to call the hotline to get confirmation. I already know.

She's there.

My mother.

At some point, the guys came to stand behind my chair while I watched this last video. I'm not sure how much they saw, but their silence tells me they saw enough. I don't even have to say it—I'm sure they already know.

"I have to go," I whisper. "I owe it to her to at least give her peace in death."

Whit leans against the desk beside me, his hand finding mine. "We'll go with you."

I nod, swallowing hard. For a moment, I thought I'd have to do this alone—the weight of it nearly unbearable.

The tension slowly bleeds out of me as my shoulders drop in relief. I should know better by now. I'll never stand alone again. They will always hold me up when I can't, while never holding me back in the process.

I call the hotline and give them my details. The fear of being a suspect is no longer an option. The investigator on the other end asks several questions. I tell her the story of my original escape—how my mother facilitated it—and how I fear she may have been killed in retaliation.

She is silent for a moment before clearing her throat. "As a mother myself," she says softly, "I would gladly give my life for my children's safety."

Hot tears track down my cheeks again as she goes over the details of what I will need to do to identify my mother's remains and have them released to me.

At the end of our conversation, she asks if I'd be willing to give a statement to help them piece together a full picture of the cult I grew up in. I agree, knowing we have time to figure out exactly what to leave out. We set a meeting time for tomorrow morning, and she promises to personally walk me through everything.

A few hours later, we're on a plane, heading back to Magnolia Hollow.

The guys booked a hotel in a town close enough, knowing I wouldn't want to stay *there* again. They packed for a few days, just in case it takes longer than anticipated, and had the jet ready to take off as soon as possible—all without me having to ask.

The silence is comforting as I process everything. They don't speak, but they don't leave my side either. Each of them takes turns holding me, kissing the top of my head, or simply giving my hand a gentle squeeze. Each action is a reminder that I'm loved, that I'm not alone.

It took a few days to jump through all the hoops, but—just as I knew she would be—my mother was, in fact, one of the bodies recovered.

The investigator, Laura Calder, stayed true to her word and made the process as painless as possible for us.

I chose to have my mother's remains cremated. I liked the idea of being able to send her ashes to blow in the wind—finally free.

Which is exactly what I do when we get home.

They take me to the top of a nearby mountain lookout, and with one glance, I know my mother would have found the view stunning.

Snow coats the naked trees, and white blankets the land as far as I can see. The mountains in the distance kiss the clouds as dawn begins to peek out from behind them.

No one says anything as we take in the peaceful beauty.

The bag I hold should feel heavier—it shouldn't be possible for the weight of a life to be carried in one hand.

I open it as the wind whips through my hair, pulling the remnants of my mother with it, carrying her toward a freedom she never knew in life.

The January air in Vermont freezes my tears as fast as they fall, but I barely feel it.

I tip the bag, allowing the final ashes to join the others as they dance across the swirling wind.

The four of us stand as sentries, until the sun—and the world around us—finally wakes, breaking the spell.

With an arm around my shoulder, Whit guides me back to the SUV. We make the short trip home, our frozen bodies thawing in the heat blasting through the vents.

"Thank you," I whisper to them, grateful for their silent support.

"You never have to thank us for taking care of you, Celest," Beckett says from the driver's seat, his usual sharp tone uncharacteristically softened by tenderness.

Whit turns from the front passenger seat to look at me with a gentle gaze. "We'll never leave you to shoulder the burdens of life alone."

Quinn's been holding my frozen fingers from the moment we slid into the backseat. He gives me a slight squeeze before pulling me into his arms. "We love you, and there's nothing we wouldn't do for you."

I have no words, so I just nod and bury my face into his chest.

When we pull into the garage, I'm surprised when the guys lead me to one of the Gators. Quinn drives us up a winding path, finally stopping at a small cemetery.

"We wanted to make sure you had a way to visit your mom, even if she's not really here," Quinn says, rubbing the back of his neck uncertainly.

I follow Beckett and step through the gate as he holds it open for me. Whit takes my hand and leads me to a brand-new headstone, flecks of shiny minerals glinting in the early sun filtering through the trees.

I kneel beside her gravestone, pressing my palm against the freshly carved granite. The inscription makes me gasp—it's perfect.

In Loving Memory
Naomi Grace Monroe
A Mother and Hero
"A mother's strength is a force to be reckoned with,
forged through the fires of adversity."

"You gave her my last name," I whisper.

"Your father no longer has any claim on her," Beckett says, his voice firm.

Whit places his hand on my shoulder and gives it a reassuring squeeze. "And she was the one to give you the last name Monroe."

I'd never really thought about it, but they're right. My father has no place here. My new name was a gift from my mother—something untainted by my past, a reminder of her that will stay with me for the rest of my life.

"We'll be waiting by the gate. Take your time," Whit says, giving my shoulder one last reassuring squeeze.

"I'm sorry," I whisper, my voice breaking. "I should've forced you to come with me." I run my fingertips across the quote at the bottom of the stone, the words offering me strength.

"They picked the perfect quote for you. I'm not surprised. You would've loved it, even if you would've been horrified at me being with three men." I pause, laughing quietly to myself. "Or, who knows, perhaps you would've surprised us all."

"You told me to live a happy life, and I can assure you that I will—I already am."

I glance over at the gate, watching the guys in a quiet conversation. Quinn says something that makes him laugh, and Whit punches him in the shoulder, though I can tell from here that he's chuckling. Beckett rolls his eyes, even as the corners of his mouth twitch.

I shake my head and turn back to my mother's memorial.

"I love them. More than I thought possible. You gave me this life, and I will not waste it."

I take a few deep breaths of the crisp morning air, rising to my feet. Looking up at the sky, I let the sun warm my face, while resolve flows through me.

"Father will get what he deserves," I finally say to her.

"I promise."

Epilogue
2 Years Later

The guys are gathered around the table, their sharp eyes scanning the specs of the location I spent the past few weeks meticulously researching.

Blueprints, tunnel layouts, security reports—every piece of information I could dig up is spread out in front of us.

Beckett studies them with his usual meticulous perusal. Whit leans back with his arms crossed, processing the details. And Quinn—well, Quinn looks downright excited. He's highly entertained by the YouTube videos I've provided.

"You're sure you don't want to handle this at home?" Beckett finally asks, his voice level.

It's a solid question. The manor would work, and we know it well enough to walk it in our sleep—even with its never-ending shifting.

I shake my head. "No. This is our home. It's where we eat, sleep, live… Nothing about it should feel tainted."

Which it would if we were to do this here.

Whit nods, his quiet agreement settling into the room. He understands that this place is our sanctuary.

"Alright then." He glances back at the plans. "Looks like we've got some work to do in Louisville, Kentucky."

Beckett exhales, already mentally running through logistics. "We'll need to make some calls. Getting access, off the books, isn't going to be as simple as breaking into a corporate office or a private estate. An abandoned sanatorium draws attention. We don't need anyone poking around and finding more than the ghosts they're looking for."

"We can make it happen," Whit assures. "I'll reach out to Wraith, maybe he can help keep the thrill-seekers away."

"Yeah, that's a good idea," Beckett agrees.

Quinn stretches his arms over his head, grinning like this is the most fun he's had all week. "You know, while we're there, we should do some ghost hunting. Really get into the *spirit* of things."

The collective groan from the rest of us is immediate.

"For fuck's sake, Quinn," Beckett mutters, pinching the bridge of his nose.

Whit sighs. "Jesus Christ, here we go."

"Oh, come on! You don't think it would be fun to fuck with some ghost hunters?" Quinn grins, wiggling his fingers in an exaggerated spooky motion. "Make them think we're the ghosts?"

"That's literally the plan, just minus the ghost hunters," Whit says, looking at Quinn in disbelief.

"Practice." Quinn shrugs.

"It would be fun, but let's focus," I remind him, though I can't help but smirk. "How long do you think we'll need?"

Beckett studies the plans again. "A couple of days to prep. How long will you need to complete it?"

"From dusk till dawn should cover it," I respond, a vicious smile cutting across my face. Then, looking at each of them, I ask, "Y'all still have your masks?"

Their slow, wicked grins are confirmation enough.

Waverly Hills Sanatorium.

Even if you don't believe in ghosts, you've probably heard of it.

A decaying relic of history, one of the most haunted buildings in America—if you buy into that kind of thing. The long, crumbling halls once housed thousands of tuberculosis patients, many of whom died within its walls.

It's the kind of place where history seeps into the bones of the structure, where the air carries the weight of untold stories. The perfect environment for the notoriety of ghosts to thrive.

We don't believe in ghosts. Not even a little bit. Living people are far more terrifying than dead ones.

However, *he* does. If he didn't before, he sure does now.

For months, we've been feeding him breadcrumbs—sending him anonymous letters, delivering unsettling messages scrawled in what looks like old patient notes.

He's been receiving details about the histories of Waverly's most infamous deaths, the eerie tales of those who allegedly never left. We've even sent him actual patient files.

And for the final touch?

We made him a patient.

Naturally, it was Quinn's idea—and a brilliant one at that. One final file arrived on his doorstep weeks ago, detailing his admittance into Waverly Hills.

It was fabricated, of course—painstakingly recreated using era-appropriate documentation. Every grim detail, every symptom, every scheduled "treatment" meticulously noted.

We know he read it.

We know because his search history led him straight to late-night deep dives into Waverly's haunted past. Because he's been losing sleep, refreshing his security cameras, jumping at shadows.

It's been highly entertaining.

The groundwork has already been laid with months of paranoia, carefully crafted to make him believe that something—or someone—is watching him.

Which, to be fair, someone is.

Me.

He believes that Waverly Hills isn't just a story, isn't just a decaying building where history has rotted into legend, but something more. Something hungry.

And then, we pushed him off the edge.

Last night, the first part of the game began.

It was simple, really. He'd already been primed to believe in the unseen, desperate for confirmation that his growing unease wasn't just in his head. So we gave him exactly what he feared most—proof. While also satiating Quinn's unending desire to practice on unsuspecting ghost hunters.

The blackout happened at exactly 2:37 AM.

His security cameras went dark for precisely six minutes and thirty-two seconds—long enough for a skilled team to slip inside, for shadows to move unnaturally through his home, for the air to feel wrong. Exactly like we'd done for the past several nights.

When the power returned, so did the cameras. And with them, a gift we left behind.

The footage showed his house, just as he left it—almost. He would see himself standing in the living room, just as he'd been when the power went out. There, in the reflection of his glass coffee table, if he looked closely, he would see a figure standing behind him.

A blurred shape, just out of focus, watching. Waiting.

The moment he saw it, he bolted—just as expected.

He threw a duffel bag together, barely bothering to check what he packed. Keys, phone, gun. But he was too rattled, too panicked, too desperate to think clearly. The supernatural had come for him, and he needed to get as far away as possible.

He didn't think to check his car. Just hurried into the driver's seat, his keys missing the ignition several times. Perhaps if he'd looked in the rearview mirror, he would've noticed the syringe. But he didn't—not until it was too late.

Whit had been the one to do it. He slipped into the backseat and waited for the predictable coward to do exactly what we knew he would.

All it took was a single press of the needle against his neck. There was a sharp inhale of confusion, and then... silence.

He was out before he even realized what was happening. Which is almost a shame.

We took his phone, powered it off, and tossed it. His car was left where it was, door slightly ajar, the keys on the ground. A staged struggle, just enough to make it look like a theft gone wrong—just another missing man in a world full of missing people.

Not that anyone would miss him. Nor would anyone care to find him, once the authorities realized he was a fugitive with a list of crimes that would make anyone's stomach churn.

The world would be a safer place without the likes of someone like him.

We drive all the way from Pulaski, Tennessee, where he'd been hiding out. It's a long, quiet ride to Waverly Hills, the road stretching endlessly beneath the cover of night. By the time we arrive, the sanatorium looms in the darkness, its jagged silhouette cutting against the sky, as if it's waiting to swallow him whole.

We waste no time. His body is heavier than expected as we haul him inside, dragging him down the ruined halls, past broken beds, and rooms that haven't housed life in decades.

Past the remnants of ghosts we don't believe in—but he does.

When we strap him into the chair, his breathing is slow and steady, his mind still lost in a drugged unconsciousness. The outdated medical recliner creaks under his weight, the cracked leather rough against his skin.

The fun will really begin once he realizes where he is.

I lean back, watching the grainy monitor in front of me as he begins to stir. His fingers twitch, and a gasp of an inhale escapes him.

A slow smile spreads across my face at the sight.

"Have I told you lately how fucking terrifying you are?" Quinn asks.

I laugh at the look of pure adoration on his face. "It's been at least thirty minutes since the last time you did."

"Allow me to rectify that. You are fucking terrifying, and I don't think I've ever loved you more."

Beckett and Whit laugh, nodding in agreement.

My cheeks heat, as they always do when all of their attention is directed at me at once.

I glance out the window and watch as the sun begins to disappear beyond the horizon.

The man comes fully to, right on time, and begins thrashing in his chair. Which is hilarious, considering he's not restrained at all.

It took very little time to find him. However, it took a year to come up with the perfect plan. Then, a few months after that, to set everything up and bring us to this point.

It's been two years since we buried my mother, but I never forgot the promises I made. My life is exceedingly happy.

While it might not be traditional in any sense of the word, it's mine—and I wouldn't choose any other life or life partners. I've never loved anyone as much as I love the three men around me, and I've never been loved as thoroughly as they love me.

That leaves just one promise left to keep.

"Hello, Father," I say through the speaker hidden in the room. He stills instantly. "I hope you're enjoying your accommodations."

"You little bitch!" He screams into the empty room. "Where the fuck am I?"

"Language, Father."

Whit and Quinn chuckle as they each kiss me on the

cheek before pulling their neon masks on and moving to their positions throughout the building.

Before Beckett leaves, he leans in, voice a quiet snarl against my ear. "Be a good girl, and I'll bend you over the nearest surface before his blood even cools." Then he's gone. No glance. No pause. Like he didn't just wreck my focus.

I shake my head, exhaling through my nose. "Ass," I mutter under my breath—more habit than heat—then turn to my father.

"As for where you are? This is it. Your forever. I even sent over files on your new roommates."

"I should've known you were behind that evil insanity!" my father seethes, face reddening. The past two years have stripped him bare—skin slack, hair thinning. He looks like a ghost already.

"Now, now," I murmur, savoring the moment. "Let's not throw stones, especially when you live in a glass house." A thrill shoots through me, "Shall we go over the rules of our game?"

I've been waiting for this far longer than the past two years—since before I even understood what vengeance tasted like. Back to the first moment he made me feel less than. I might not remember the details exactly, but it doesn't matter.

His fate was sealed then.

And it ends by my hands.

"I'll make sure you rot in the same hole as your mother!"

His eyes are wide with fear, and satisfaction hums through me. Good. He deserves this—deserves to feel what Mother and I lived with for years. And worse. Which he will get.

"That might be difficult," I say smoothly. "Considering you no longer know where she is." I tilt my head, watching realization settle over him. "I'm surprised you didn't hear about the authorities finding the bodies. But don't worry—you won't be seeing Mother again."

His breath stutters, then, as if clinging to something sturdy, he steadies himself. "What is this, then? If you're not planning to kill me?"

I watch it happen. The hope. The desperate, reckless belief that maybe—just maybe—he still has a way out.

And I love that he let it in.

"Oh, I fully intend to kill you." I let the words settle, let him feel them. "You just won't end up anywhere near whatever heavenly plane Mother has. I have a feeling you'll burn with your dear friend Josiah for eternity."

He splutters, mouth opening to spit his twisted beliefs—

I don't let him.

"The rules are simple. Make it till dawn without getting caught, and you walk free."

For a second, nothing. Then he laughs, sharp and derisive, shaking his head. "You'll never catch me, Celestina. And when I walk out of here, I'll find you and kill you like I should have decades ago."

"Hmmm. I guess we'll see."

I slide the Momo mask over my head, adjusting the edges. The old nurse's uniform clings to me in all the wrong ways—eerily out of place, like something yanked from a nightmare.

"Run and hide, Father."

He doesn't hesitate. Good. He bolts down the dark hallway —straight toward Quinn. He'll be thrilled to have the first crack at him.

I turn to the mirror, tilting my head as I study my reflection. A walking horror story. A smear of fake blood here, a touch more there—just for fun. Hopefully, he doesn't die of a heart attack before I get my hands on him. I'd be really upset if my fun got cut short.

Outside, I watch him stumble, arms outstretched against the dark.

I press the button.

A low click echoes through the space as the rigged doors engage, the traps wake up, and the asylum turns against him.

Somewhere in the blackness, a motion sensor triggers. A baseball rolls lazily down the hall, bumping against the walls —an invitation. A little game of fetch from Timmy O'Shea himself.

I inhale, slow and deep, letting the weight of this moment settle into my bones.

The darkness within me smiles wickedly, and I smile back.

It took some time after killing Josiah for me to realize, that the darkness within me—

had been me the whole time.

A pause...

"Ready or not..."

Just long enough for the darkness to breathe.

"Here I come."

Acknowledgments? More Like Accomplices.

To the voices in my head—you were relentless. You clawed at my skull, whispering in the dark, refusing to let me sleep until I gave you life. I tried to ignore you, to drown you out, to lock you away. But you only laughed and said, *You can't hide.* So here you are. You win.

To my dark romance girlies—you get it. You know the difference between **dangerous** and *deliciously dangerous*. You see a neon red flag and think, *but what if he'd burn the world down for me?* You've never sided with the hero in your life, and you never will.

To Jess and Jamie—you **fed the monster.** You let me drag you down into the dark, only to whisper, *I love it.* You saw the worst of these characters and said, *He's my favorite.* You are **sick**, and I love you for it.

To The Distracted Inklings—the best damn writing group a chaos gremlin like me could ask for. You cheered me on, hyped my darkest ideas, and somehow managed to keep writing despite our **collective inability to focus on a single task for more than five minutes.** I couldn't have done this without your support, your laughter, and your mutual love of morally gray disasters.

To my parents—I doubt this is what you had in mind when I said, *I wrote another book.* But here we are. You raised me to be fearless, to chase what I love, and unfortunately for you... **this is what I love.**

To my friends, clients, and loved ones—you may not understand why this book exists, and that's okay. Just know that if I ever send a text that says, *don't ask questions, but if the police call, I was with you last night,* your only response should be, *got it.*

To Jessica—Happy Birthday! 🎉 I hope this book is everything you never knew you wanted. Consider this my gift to you: an unhinged, morally gray fever dream where no one is safe and red flags are the only décor. May your year be filled with obsessive love interests and just the right amount of danger.

To the creators of the Neon Masks—Thanks for giving us dark romance whores **yet another reason to lose sleep.** You didn't just make masks—you created **obsessions, fantasies, and walking red flags we'd sell our souls for.** Now we'll never know peace, and honestly? **We wouldn't have it any other way.**

And finally, to the readers—you were warned. You still came. You still opened the door. You still let the shadows claim you. **There is no way out now.**

If You're Wondering Who to Blame for the Depravity in This Book— Hi, It's Me.

Amber Thoma spends her days **writing, reading, and unapologetically rooting for the villain.** She believes red flags are **just plot devices waiting to unfold,** and if a love interest isn't **a little bit unhinged, dangerously obsessive, or morally gray,** she doesn't want him.

When she's not crafting **feral, possessive characters that leave readers questioning their morals,** she's weaving **dark fantasy romance,** where magic is as deadly as the love interests and the stakes are always life or death.

She lives somewhere between **fantasy and reality,** but mostly in the **delirious haze of too many late-night writing sessions, fueled by caffeine and increasingly questionable life choices.**

She also spends an alarming amount of time yelling at her

dog and cat to leave each other alone, all while losing hours to the fictional men who live rent-free in her head.

Follow her descent into madness at:
AuthorAmberThoma.com
Discord: https://discord.gg/YpkMsKWbXM

instagram.com/author_amber_thoma
tiktok.com/@author_amber_thoma
amazon.com/stores/author/B0BYY4BS8J

9 798987 661581